GANTASH

Book four of the Lissae Series

R. Lennard

Cantash

First published in 2022 by R. Lennard

Edited by Anna at CREATING ink.
www.CREATINGink.com

Published by Rebecca Lennard.
lissae.com

A catalogue record for this book is available from the National Library of Australia

To Jodie,
Bought some full stops. Just for you.
Thank you for being such a brilliant friend.

After years of fighting, something inside the Innarnian snapped, and Sarina could no longer encompass her magic and the Xanderri.

One day, whilst she was paying homage to the leader of her nation, the excitement was too much. The vibrations were too high, and Sarina was everywhere.

The backlash from her Innarn escaping melted the flesh off the face of a leader, but the Xanderri were not worried.

They had found a host.

Chamele.

CHAPTER ONE

Permian
Suncrest 4060
Third month of Summer

A growl rose from his throat as a flash of flames licked at Samuel, leaving a blur of pain with every sizzle and slice of his skin. Time seemed to slow as soon as the battle started and he fought beside Jonathan in the squishy form the Guardian was familiar with.

They had been on Permian for far too long now, steadily clearing out the oozing mess created by the Denfur. A race of gelatinous beings, the Denfur had entered from a neighbouring Realm intending to make the locals into a slave army who would, in turn, take over Lissae.

Everyone is becoming more desperate to take over the Mother Realm. Samuel's thoughts turned to his own race, and he shivered at what his Queen's desperation would look like. His inattention earned him another wound, a curse spilling from his lips as a blade sliced through his ridiculously thin bipedal hide.

His back to Jonathan, Samuel transformed his hand into a claw and ripped the guts out of his final foe, fangs gleaming as he grinned in triumph.

Silver glinted against the bark of the thin tree trunks as someone moved, their form flitting in front of the red moon, the glow bouncing off familiar scales.

A twang of a bowstring had his head snapping to the side.

The Guardian may have been strong, but Samuel knew the shooter, and even Jonathan's shields would crumble before it.

If the target had been anyone else, he would have let the arrow find its mark.

Sighing, he transformed, his chest against Jonathan's back. Even as scales replaced skin, the Guardian froze against him.

'*Arrow,*' Sam sent.

Jonathan relaxed as much as one could in the middle of an ectoplasmic battlefield, the Guardian's heartbeat racing as he continued to fight.

Another arrow weaved through the air. Sanithane slapped it aside with a claw. Yet another swooped in from above. His massive golden wings enveloped the Guardian, protecting the squishy human from harm.

He smiled down at Jonathan, who quirked his lips. '*With a mouth full of razor-sharp teeth, you inspire more pants-filling fear than any sort of joy.*'

The Q'Aralide shuddered.

'*Sam?*'

'*Knarec arrow,*' he grunted. '*No matter how many times I do that, it still hurts like a fempar.*'

Cautiously lifting his maw, Sanithane took a quick glance around. The battlefield had cleared.

Apparently, no one wanted to be in the presence of the Q'Aralide priest.

Releasing Jonathan from the shield he'd created with his wings, Samuel carefully tucked his tail in and pivoted.

In four long strides, he crossed to where the archer was hiding behind a boulder, claws trembling as he tried to notch another arrow. Sanithane didn't give him a chance. He reached down and bit the Knarec in half.

Blood and entrails dripping from his maw, he spat out the shooter. A swift blast of Air and Water Innarn and his maw was clean enough for him to return to the Guardian.

Jonathan was hiding his face with a hand. "Not everyone needs to be bitten in half, you know?"

'If you have it, use it.' Sanithane smirked.

'And what do you think Shari would say if she were here? Or if anyone else from Lissae had been with us?'

Sanithane blinked and shuddered as his scales withdrew, and he resumed his fleshy form once again. "Claim to be a shapeshifter?" He shrugged, trying to belie the churning of his gut. After all Shari had endured, was she ready to discover his true nature?

Not yet. The voice whispering inside his head reminded him far too much of Izarrk. Samuel shook his head. He hadn't thought of his original mentor in centuries. She needs more time. Izarrk's voice sounded again, and Samuel shuddered.

No matter how much time he gave Shari, he had a feeling it wouldn't be enough.

Ducibus' Hall

The ground under their feet heaved.

Amara glanced at the rest of the Altoriae's Guild, wide-eyed as the walls of the museum on Ronah seemed to shudder. White particles drifted from the ceiling. She turned to ask the Guardian what had happened, but the double doors had already swung closed.

They were on their own.

As she swung back to the group, the Returned look at each other and shrugged. They were expected elsewhere. As a group, they stepped through the doors and into the Ducibus' Hall, the rest of the guild following along.

"What, exactly, are we meant to be doing?" Alistair asked.

"While the attack on Wiaxatale's gateway has cleared, they've asked for help with the clean-up and relocation of the bodies of the fallen," Amara said.

The group swung into the darkest of the Light corridors, their footsteps echoing as they drew closer to the tiny, grey-cloaked figure waiting for them. A steel door with bolt heads around the border swung open. Amara bowed at their guide and stepped through.

Groaning, she covered the lower part of her face. The stench was overpowering, making her eyes water. She tried not to gag, but as the closest Returned reached around and poked at a fallen giant, the smell of death grew too much, and she rushed to the side to revisit her lunch.

And possibly last week's breakfast.

Amara wiped her mouth with the back of her sleeve and turned to survey the area.

The Returned had set up a neat system. Three wore bubbles around their heads, presumably to keep the smell out, while casting the same on the others in the group who were using Fire Innarn to burn the corpses to ash.

Trying to quell her heaving stomach, Amara moved closer, tempering her fire and adding her flames to the rest.

If the smell was any sign, they were going to be here for a while.

Tocithas

Tendrils of hair escaped Shari's plait and mingled with the blood drifting past her nose in the water.

It was her own fault, really. She should have ducked instead of twisted when the zarsuth came out of the depths. Now the ancient aquatic fish with a penchant for fresh meat had her scent.

Shari had long heard tales of how beautiful and serene Tocithas was. She'd barely had a moment to appreciate the forest of seaweed racing past below her, or the stunning coral architecture that was said to adorn Startide, the capital of the Realm and home to the Aestques.

The ancient, mammoth fish was proving to be a merciless pursuer.

The water surrounding her trembled, and Shari pushed her Innarn outwards to find a huge capsule of ice rocketing out of the depths.

Shari used Air Innarn to propel herself, narrowly missing the zarsuth's open mouth. The ice capsule ploughed right into the smooth-scaled hide, shattering on impact. A dozen warriors armed with sleek spears rolled from the wreckage.

The Aestques warriors took up positions along the flanks of the zarsuth. Fingertips touching their closest neighbour, they brought their hands down, slamming spear butts and shards of ice along the beast's hide.

The zarsuth swung around, head aiming straight at Shari as it dived. A tooth jutting out from the side of the massive maw snagged against the armour around her waist, sliding through it like butter. The warrior on the other side of the beast caught Shari's eye as she hastily stitched the tear with her Innarn.

Ze quirked zir eyebrows at her, and Shari shrugged. Zir nodded at the blood still streaming from her nose.

Groaning at her incompetence, Shari syphoned it away, creating a little Innarn pouch to store the spilt blood in. She didn't dare try to put it back in her body when she was on another Realm.

Scent lost, the zarsuth circled the warriors and Shari once more. It opened its mouth, and the surrounding water rippled.

The warriors were still. As much as she wanted to swim away from the beast with teeth larger than she was tall, Shari copied them.

Scales gleaming and tail flicking, the zarsuth dived, heading back for the inky depths of its home.

Shari sighed.

'So, Altoriae, you finally made it,' the warrior opposite her sent.

'I apologise. I've heard your call for some time, but things have been...' Difficult? Dangerous? Deadly? Dare she admit such a weakness to a being she just met? 'Busy on Lissae.'

'And off, by what the currents have flowed to our ears.'

Offering a tiny grin, Shari nodded.

'We were hoping to get word to you, Altoriae. Of the Light hiding in the deep. It seeks you, and we fear it won't rest until you are no more.' Ze's large purple eyes were wide, and Shari could feel the concern drifting through the water to her from all the warriors present.

'I am not a warrior, Altoriae. I am Prime Lakin, second in line to the Throne of Startide and the people of Tocithas.'

'Well met, Prime Lakin.' Shari bowed her head. 'I'm afraid I don't really understand your warning. How can light hide in the deep?'

Lakin slowly closed ze's eyes. The warriors around the Prime shifted uncomfortably. 'You will understand sooner than we hope. Return to Lissae, and stay on guard, Altoriae.'

Shari was mildly disappointed but bowed as best she could in the water. Lakin grinned at her efforts, and as quickly as the Aestques had arrived, they were gone again.

Alone once more, Shari leisurely took her time getting back to the gateway. The forest she'd longed to see passed by mostly unnoticed as she tried to puzzle out Prime Lakin's words.

Lissae

Samuel slumped through the gateway, intent only on his bed and making sure the shadow under it had enough food to survive after Shari ended his life.

The girl in question was waiting for him on the other side, leaning against the opposite wall. Her gaze was dark as it met his.

"Well met, Samuel," Shari purred. Her hips swayed as she stepped forward and plastered herself to his side.

He froze.

Jonathan stumbled into his back as the Guardian tried to exit the gateway.

Samuel couldn't move as Shari ran a hand over his chest, nuzzling her nose into his neck.

Did I die? Did Jonathan actually kill me, and I just didn't realise?

'*Don't be a fool. You're very much alive. But Shari—*'

White noise blanked out whatever Jonathan sent to him next, as Shari's tongue found the back of his ear. He made a suspicious squeaking noise as his knees almost buckled. *Humanoid forms will never cease to amaze me.*

Part of him noted the Guardian moving around him, the brown tuft of his hair appearing on the opposite side of Shari. Boot steps sounded as his brain was kicked back into gear by Shari biting down on his earlobe.

Of all the beings in the Realms, Samuel expected the Altoriae to know he'd had enough pain already.

Gently, he grasped her by the arms and pulled her away. She made a disappointed noise and reached for him, only to be stopped by a yellow blade appearing at her throat.

Samuel growled, eyes flicking to the side, his gaze landing on a second Shari.

The first flinched away from the blade. "Protect me from the imposter!" she cried.

Shari, begging for help? Roughly, he marched her backwards until she hit the opposite wall. "Who are you?"

The real Shari snorted behind him. "I thought you were going to eat her face before you got around to that question."

Wrinkling his nose, he stared hard at the fake. She met his gaze, chin up, but the longer he stared, the lower her chin got.

Lifting his forearm so it was in her field of view, he changed his arm enough so that scales appeared. Steeling his features, he ripped one from his skin.

Ignoring the twin gasps from identical girls, he pressed the still dripping scale onto the imposter's forehead, right where he expected her third eye to be.

She screamed and writhed as his blood dribbled down her nose. If it reached her mouth, she'd die. There was one option for survival—she had to change back to her natural form.

The pitch black line drip off the tip of her nose.

Only she didn't have a nose any more. The black line seemed to spread and lighten. If his hand hadn't been pressing against her skin, he would have lost the being among the shadows.

"Jonathan?"

Obligingly, the Guardian created a cage around the being, leaving just enough space between the bars for his hand to withdraw.

"Think I'm the only one?" fake Shari asked, icy-blue eyes standing out against her grey skin. "The Queen has eyes everywhere. And when they heard you..." She slumped to the side.

The real Shari rested a sizzling hand against the Light bars of the cage. "What in the name of Nar'eh is going on?"

CHAPTER TWO

Adonday

First day of the third week of Suncrest

Jonathan shifted the prisoner straight to the holding cells in the castle, as far away from the guild and the remaining Returned as he could get. Shari and Samuel arrived barely a second behind him.

The room could barely be called that. Ronah had sensed their need and created a rough-hewn space straight from the bare rock beneath the castle.

The heavy door creaked as Shari pushed it open with a negligent wave of her Innarn and guided the cage inside without saying a word. She created an Air bubble around the contraption, making sure no sound could get in or out.

The Guardian ran a tired hand over his face. Samuel was slipping. Showing himself on the battlefield, then again when he changed his arm to scales right in front of Shari...

"When did we first properly meet?" His Altoriae was staring at Jonathan with hard eyes. He was mildly proud that she had thought to suspect him, even if it stung a little.

"After you sustained an axe wound to the back."

She slumped, relief rolling off her in waves. "And when did we first meet Samuel?"

"*You* first met him when the Wisara came to visit. *I* first met him..."

Shari's gaze hardened again when he paused.

"On Shunar," Samuel said. Jonathan's head snapped around as he looked at his new apprentice properly. Samuel's head was down as he carefully wrapped a bandage around his still-weeping arm.

"Feels like a lifetime ago," Jonathan said, his mouth quirking up at the corners.

"Twenty years, actually. You were a scrap of a thing, but so ready to fight." Samuel tucked the end of the bandage in and lifted his head. He seemed weary, suddenly.

"Really? You met twenty years ago?" Shari's head tilted, and Jonathan tried hard not to squirm under her gaze.

"We really did. It was in the middle of a battlefield, and I'd only been training with Joshua for a few months. One night, I went to bed exhausted, and the next thing I knew, I was laying next to a dead body." Jonathan sighed. He hadn't thought about that night in so long.

"How old were you?"

"Just gone eight," he said.

"You really had just hatched," Samuel said, arching a brow.

His voice seemed to snap Shari from her odd mood, and she glared at the cage containing their guest.

"And her?" Shari's voice was harsh as she gestured to the being in the cage. "Why were you kissing her?"

Shari's scrunched expression made Samuel glanced back down at his bandage. "Technically, she kissed me. And for a moment, I thought... she was you."

"Ew. Why would I want to kiss anyone?" She shook her head, as if getting rid of an unpleasant thought. "Who is she anyway?"

"Ze is a spy from m... from the Q'Aralide Queen," Samuel said.

The Guardian held his breath at Samuel's near miss. For a moment, he'd thought his apprentice had been going to say '*my Queen*'.

"And what shall we do with ze?"

Was Shari ignoring what Samuel had almost said, or was she truly tired enough to not pay attention?

"Ensure the cage has constant Light Innarn being pumped into it." His apprentice sneered at their trapped guest. "It may take weeks for ze to break." He stepped close enough to the cage that it sizzled at him. "But I'll make sure ze does."

Their new guest snarled and snapped, lunging at the bars and shrieking again as zir skin sizzled and smoked where it came in contact with the Light Innarn.

Still smirking, Samuel turned and led the way from the room.

Shari and Jonathan followed. The trio silently made their way to the main level of the castle, each lost in their thoughts.

"If I may take my leave?" Samuel said, giving an odd, jerky movement like he'd been about to drop into a bow but thought better of it.

"Of course. I bid thee well," Jonathan said. "We'll reconvene tomorrow and see if our guest has any info for us."

"Guest." Samuel snorted and shook his head before shifting away.

Jonathan was half-smiling at the man's antics when Shari stepped into his field of view. The Altoriae was decidedly not smiling.

"I... uh..."

"Care to explain?" Shari held out her hand to him, palm up.

"Perhaps we'd best sit down for this?" Jonathan suggested. He turned to lead the way to the castle library, hoping the movement hid his paling features.

Adonday - midnight

The shadow who'd been living under Samuel's couch growled menacingly as he stepping inside his front door, causing the hair on the back of his neck to rise.

"Protective, are we?" Samuel asked, chuckling.

His shadowy friend was looking more solid every day. The creature had only been with him a short while, appearing soon after he'd become Jonathan's apprentice. Samuel found he couldn't really remember a time without the temperamental beast waiting to grump at whoever dared to come through his door.

He wouldn't want it any other way.

The growl stopped, and an odd, chirrupping noise sounded.

"You've no idea how difficult this was to track down," Samuel said, twisting his hand just so. His Innarn spilled out and allowed him to reach into his pocket Realm. Hissing slightly as the weight pulled on his still-healing flesh, he withdrew a limb he'd ripped from the Knarec he'd bitten in half. "Just for you, little shadow."

The creature chirrupped again as he laid the limb down, the bloody end closest to his pet.

Bones clacked as they were drawn over the floor. The shadow's slurping filled the silence, and Samuel grinned. Never had he been so glad to have someone to come home to.

Inthday—1am

Second day of the third week of Suncrest

"You were eight," Shari said, blankly staring at the book she'd pulled from the shelves.

"When I became the Guardian's apprentice, yes."

"Why? Did your parents nominate you?" Shari's mind flew over the recent spate of candidates. Talofa had been the youngest, and her family hadn't seemed to...

Oh.

Now she thought of it, Talofa hadn't mentioned her family at all.

"Jonathan?" Shari asked in a small voice. She turned to look at her Guardian, wrapping her arms around her waist and flinching as she brushed against her wound.

'*Anything broken?*' Jon sent to her calmly. Shari could still sense the concern buried underneath.

'*All in one piece,*' she replied, trying to ease her Guardian's worry.

"Never knew my mother. And my father had just joined the Spirit Realm." Jonathan moved closer, green light spilling from his fingertips and healing the wound from the zarsuth painlessly. "I scraped together enough coin to come to Ronah and tell the old Guardian off for letting him die. Joshua must have seen something in me he liked, and that was it."

"You never talk about it."

"It feels like forever and yesterday ago. Sometimes, there are things that are better left in the past than just casually dropping them into conversation."

"True," Shari agreed. "So, what happened on Permian? Did Samuel get injured, or does he regularly wear a glamour to cover the scales on his arm?" She was grasping at straws, and she knew it. Her grandmother's words echoed through her head 'You *must know, dear one, that one of your guild is not who they claim to be.*'

"Shari," Jonathan sighed. "Samuel doesn't wear a glamour."

"Then why..." Zana's warning of one flaunting his power to others sounded loudly. "He's a shapeshifter."

Her Guardian nodded.

Shari could think of only one race with scales that held so much power and were feared throughout the Realms. She rubbed her arms, trying to ward off the chill creeping into her bones. "I can't imagine when you meeting a Q'Aralide on your first battlefield might be an appropriate topic to bring up."

Jonathan winced. "So, ah. There's a thing I may have neglected to mention. Um, you know the being who crossed over... Ow! Shari!"

"He's been here since *before* we announced I was the Altoriae!" She hit him with the book in her hand again. Hard. "I kept *asking* what had crossed over," *whack* "and," *whack* "you," *whack* "lied," *whack* "to," *whack* "me!"

With each hit of the book, Jonathan backed away. Pressed against a bookcase, he had nowhere to go. As Shari raised her hand to hit him again, he caught her wrist.

'*How would you have taken the news then, Shari? You would have tried to hunt him down, rightly seeing a Q'Aralide as the bigger threat, and ignoring your test. You would have let Anriluka win.*' Her Guardian stared into her eyes.

Trying to contain the sobs threatening to heave from her throat, Shari ducked her head in acknowledgement.

Hastily, Jonathan let Shari's wrist go. Stepping back from her, he rubbed the bridge of his nose.

'*I thought we had no more secrets.*' Shari's send was barely a thought, it was so soft. She put the book down and crossed her arms around her stomach, hunching as if to hold her emotions in. 'I promise, that's the last one.'

As Shari searched his face, she had to decide if she dared to believe him this time.

Samuel wandered into the grounds of Ridden Hall, idly scratching at his arm. It itched fiercely where he'd ripped the scale from his hide.

Shari had seemed unbothered by his scales, his hide, or that he'd have happily killed the spy to keep her safe.

She'd do the same for him, surely? Although he doubted she had to worry about her very blood being a deadly toxin to other races.

Starting up the staircase to their office, Samuel sighed. While the Altoriae hadn't appeared bothered, she'd also not spoken to him since just after they'd secured the prisoner, and that worried him. If their positions were reversed, he'd have a deluge of questions to throw her way.

Pulling the class plan off his desk, he scowled at it, unseeing. His thoughts churned until the door to the office squeaked as the one he was thinking about arrived.

"Slept in. Sorry," Shari said, not meeting his gaze.

"Well, you had a big night, with the spy and all." Samuel tried for casual, and missed, if the tightening around Shari's eyes was anything to go by.

This was her cue to say *no bigger than any other*, as she always did.

Instead, she grabbed a heavy tome from her desk and muttered, "Uh, huh."

"Want to discuss..."

"Nope, sorry. Don't want to be late for class!" Practically shifting from the room, Shari could not have made her position clearer.

Samuel's hearts sank. *Wait. One heart—mortal body.* Maybe sank was the wrong word? Shattered. His heart had shattered.

Knew it was too good to be true.

His Innarn flared for a moment, and the paperwork in the room lifted. A few curls of smoke started in the box of scrolls closest to his hand before he ruthlessly quelled it.

If the Altoriae could pretend nothing was wrong, then surely he could act like the fragile new foundations of the world he'd begun crafting for himself weren't crumbling.

Squaring his shoulders, he marched from the room.

Shari was greeting the hatchlings as they entered the classroom. She gave each one a soft smile and a sheet of paper as they entered.

Waiting until the last one was inside, Samuel asked, "Shall I leave?"

Head snapping towards his voice, but still not quite meeting his eyes, Shari mutely shook her head. She slipped inside before he could say anything else.

That one tiny shake made his chest swell. There was still hope then.

As soon as he crossed the threshold into the room, Jonathan's send filled his mind. *'Sorry, Samuel, you'll have to take the class by yourself. I need Shari now.'*

Shari finally met his eyes. He gave her a curt nod, and she disappeared.

Morosely, he stared out the window. What had gotten Jonathan's bow string in a knot this time? Shoving back from the desk, Samuel stood. He sent Liza a quick message that he had to leave on urgent guild business and disappeared from the room in a golden mist just as the last student took their seat.

Their uninvited guest glared at them through the bars of the Light cage.

Shari glared back, unimpressed. "What are we going to do with..." She gestured to the being, unsure how to refer to zir. The malnourished figure had yet to take ze's dark eyes off Shari.

Jonathan shrugged. '*I don't know. I can't find anything in the handbook that looks close to this race, and I'm not sure if I can break zir mental shields. I think we...*' He cut off, turning to look at the opening door.

'*This being is a Datzal. Said to come from the Ninth Realm of Hell. They are ruthless and loyal only to one,*' Samuel sent as he entered the room, coming to a stop just behind Shari's left shoulder.

She refused to flinch, but the Datzal slowly grinned at her, malice made more evident by the sharp cheekbones and razor-tipped fangs. '*What else do you know about them?*' Being this close to someone who could rip her to shreds in seconds was making her skin crawl. Shari had always known Samuel was dangerous, and Lissae knew Jonathan had warned her. It was different now, knowing for sure what he was capable of. Glancing at Samuel, Shari realised one thing was certain. After everything they'd been through already, she trusted him.

'*They're hybrids. And if this is who I think it is, ze is out for vengeance. I killed their partner a few thousand years ago.*'

Snapping her gaze to Samuel, Shari frowned. '*Just how old are you?*'

'*Around four thousand? I'm not sure exactly when I hatched.*'

Four... four thousand. Or more. He was... Shari blinked. '*We are not having that conversation here.*' Hastily shoving the idea that Jonathan's new apprentice was older than Vannali into a neat little box, she pushed it into the corner of her mind to be examined when they weren't in the presence of the deadliest—second most deadly being she'd ever come across. '*Right now, we need to know more about our guest.*'

'*Ze has been spying on me for years. Although if it was this one or another, I cannot say. Ze is a hybrid, who can move in the shadows, transform into anything ze sees, and ze reports back to the Queen.*' Samuel hadn't moved his gaze from the being in the cage, but Shari could feel the heat of his hand, hovering just over the small of her back.

Did he know that was where her shielding was weakest? Had he been waiting to strike all this time? Shari shook away the thoughts. She'd trusted him this far, and he hadn't turned on her. Surely, she could afford to trust him a bit longer.

But could she?

Shari snapped her head around, glaring at the Datzal. *'Power of suggestion, hey? Good try.'* Scowling at zir, Shari doubled down on her mental shields and purposefully leaned back into Samuel's hand.

A puff of air ghosted past her ear, and she could feel the tension seeping out of the Guardian's Apprentice.

The being in the cage smiled. "Planting the seed is all I need to do."

"What other seeds are you here to plant?" Samuel asked, his voice like smoke and honey.

"Just thinking of fond memories." Zir body wavered and changed, and a stout man appeared, hefting the smoky form of an axe. "Remembering times gone by." Outline blurring and changing again, the bronze maw of a Q'Aralide grinned at them. "Lazy days spent exploring the Realms." Changing before the wings could hit the bars of Light, ze turned into a pale grey twisted form of the Datzal in the cage, a sizzling hole through the middle of zir chest. "And promises past due."

Samuel swore.

CHAPTER THREE

Kerday

Third day of the third week of Suncrest

The air in the castle's study felt heavy. Jonathan ran a hand over his face, trying to wipe away the exasperation he felt.

"Tell me again what you think the spy being here means." Shari was glaring so hard at Samuel, it was surprising he didn't combust.

"I'm being called to chair the Dark Conclave on Altum."

"What's that?" Shari asked, wrinkling her nose.

"The conclave happens once every twenty one passes. This one will decide the fate of the Realms."

"How do you know that?" Jonathan asked.

Samuel tapped a finger on the Dark book in his hands, the title, *Hekkor Mafae*, pulsing in time with his heartbeat. "This book updates as the delegates agree on the discussion topics. It helps the Chair to keep on track, despite the madness."

Shari was looking at Samuel as if she was trying to figure out which type of Innarn would bring him down the fastest. "Which Realms?"

Jonathan was impressed, and slightly terrified by her expression.

"Lissae."

"And if you don't go?" she asked.

He wasn't sure how Shari was taking the news that the Realm she swore to protect was the one at risk of destruction.

"The Queen will burn everyone on Lissae to a cinder after she tortures them into madness." His apprentice was trying to be blithe about the whole thing, but the tightness of his jaw and the way his hand had remained balled in a fist belied his attempt at a causal tone.

"And you expect us to let you go alone?" Shari glared at him from across the room.

Samuel's eyes flashed golden. "It's the safest way."

"Safest for who? You?" Shari pressed, scowling.

"For you," Samuel snarled.

"You think I give a tuzar's arse about me? There's no way I'm letting you go into that hanotqe pit alone!" Shari yelled.

"Why? Because you don't trust me?" The hurt under Samuel's bitter words was evident.

Shari slammed the book in her hand down and marched across the room, standing toe to toe with his apprentice and craning her head to meet his gaze. "No, you trusnuck. I know exactly where your loyalty lies. It's because I don't trust *them* to let you leave." She took a step back and wrapped her arms around her middle. "And I'd be lost if you didn't come back."

For a second, Samuel's face crumpled. "You can't come, Shari," he said, hesitantly reaching out to grasp her elbows. "It wouldn't be safe. Not just because, as you so eloquently put it, I'd be walking into a hanotqe pit, but because it would be too Dark for you to bear."

"Don't be ridiculous. I've travelled to the extremes of Dark and Light across the Realms during my training," she said, waving away his concerns.

Jonathan groaned, and the pair jumped. He had the distinct impression they'd forgotten he was in the room. "Ah, actually..."

Shari spun around and levelled her glare at him. "Seriously?"

"I forgot. I swear on Lissae. It was a long time ago."

"Not that long ago," Shari grumbled, rolling her eyes.

"I had the Ducibus block off the three Darkest and Lightest hallways after you struggled with the fourth so much."

"The fourth was hard, but not life-ending." Shari shook her head and turned back to Samuel. "You're still not going alone."

"Shari, I almost died when I attempted a Realm too Light for me. My hide started burning the instant I stepped through the gateway. It was a new torture, and one that the Datzal inflicted on me."

"Then how do you stand it? You grew up in a Dark Realm, and yet you walk around just fine on Lissae."

"Glad I make it look effortless," he laughed mirthlessly. "Being on Lissae, or on any Realm on this level, leaves me in a constant state of discomfort."

Jonathan snorted. "Discomfort is putting it mildly." He slumped farther into his seat. "I agree that someone should accompany you. We'd never let anyone patrol on their own, and the conclave will be far more dangerous than any patrol. And"–he held up a hand before Samuel could do any more than scowl at him–"I'm agreeing for the same reasons as Shari. I'd like you to return and continue your apprenticeship as Guardian."

It was hard to tell, but from across the room, it looked like Samuel's eyes were welling up.

"I suppose the only way to test if you'd be able to stand it is to go into a Realm on the same plane," Jonathan said.

"There is another way." They all ignored how husky Samuel's voice sounded. "We'd need to be somewhere bigger, though."

"Would the training ground be big enough?" Shari asked.

For the first time since facing the Datzal, Samuel smiled. "Eager to be proven wrong, Altoriae?"

Shari rolled her eyes and led the way from the room.

His apprentice waited until she was far enough gone before he murmured, "The last thing I want is to put Shari in danger."

Running a hand over his face, Jonathan nodded. "I know. Although, once Shari has something in her head, it's hard to stop her."

"I have noticed that," Samuel said.

His bones creaked as he stood and followed Samuel from the room. He was feeling every injury he'd sustained over the years. Shari's words about *planting the seed* echoed in his mind, and Jonathan took a moment to strengthen his mental shields. The pain in his body faded to his everyday aches. Clearly, some seeds the Datzal planted took longer to germinate than others. Making a mental note to strengthen the wards around zir cell to ensure no one else would fall to the spy's morbid attempts at gardening, Jonathan stepped into the open area.

Shari was waiting at the far end of the training ground. The rest of the guild had joined her.

"Why the audience?" Samuel asked.

"When they heard about you testing me, they decided they wanted in." Shari shrugged.

"That's not a great idea." Jonathan frowned. It was a horrible idea, actually. What would happen when they were all taken out?

"Far be it for me to dissuade those who wish to suffer." Samuel smirked at Shari as she walked backwards into the middle.

'Holli? Might want to put the Healing team on standby,' Jonathan sent.

'Where are we going?' The Head Healer asked.

'*Lissae. Training ground. Likely Innarn burns. Don't come yet. I'm sure you'll know when.*'

'*Jonathan Baun. You'd better not be subscribing to your old Guardian's training methods!*'

Hiding a chuckle behind his hand, Jonathan shook his head. '*Hardly. Shari wants to test something out.*'

There was a groan, and Holli cut off the send.

Turning his attention once more to the spectacle about to start, he noted Shari was on the other side of the grounds, arms by her sides, palms out, almost as if she was taunting Samuel.

This is going to be worse than I thought.

"Well, what are you going to throw at us?" she called.

"Better to take you by surprise," Samuel called back. "Guardian, stay behind me."

"Why?"

In a low voice, he said, "The Dark Spirit Wall is not something you wish to experience. Your Innarn is Lighter than Shari's, and it would... hurt." '*Incapacitate you beyond reason. Then Shari would kill me,*' Samuel sent.

Jonathan dipped his head. "I'll wait by the doors."

"Anyone else have a Light affinity?"

Dealon, Mu, and Raven looked at the others then scurried past Samuel to wait with Jonathan.

Jonathan regarded the remaining members of the guild. Quite a few of the Returned had shown up as well, and he would wager they'd fare better than the others, having spent so long in a pocket Realm created by a Darker being.

Rolling his shoulders, Samuel closed his eyes. '*It has been an age since I've called on this sort of Innarn, and never on a Grey Realm,*' he admitted. "Last chance," he called aloud.

Amara and a handful of Returned skittered passed him to join the Guardian.

'*Make sure no one kills me,*' Samuel sent to Jonathan. Before the other man could respond, he changed. Scales gleamed in the sun, and he lifted his maw to the sky, stretching out his wings. '*Oh, it's good to be me again!*'

Sanithane ignored the shrieks of fear and pulled on the Darkest part of his Innarn.

Shivering as Dark spirits oozed between the scales of the Q'Aralide's hide and wove themselves into a wall, Jonathan took a deep breath. Even standing behind Sanithane was intimidating. It took everything he had to stay still as the wall careened towards Shari and the others with her.

The tiny mortal beings on the other side of the training grounds screamed and yelled, some dropping to the ground as the Spirit Wall crashed into them.

Shari appeared serene amongst the wailing spirits, hair whipping around her as she seemed to gather them closer. When he looked closer, he could see her skin blistering under Sanithane's attack.

Jonathan wanted to cross the field, to fight at her side, but he stood firm. She was their best chance at having someone join Samuel at the conclave, and he wasn't about to ruin it for her now.

Centuries of practice made it easy for Sanithane to mask his expression at how much the sight of Shari injured pained him.

'*Feel the burn, little Altoriae. This is what every second would be like on Altum. You could never falter, never be able to break. Oalark would test you beyond your comprehension. If she found you lacking, she'd torture you just for fun.*' Sanithane stalked forwards.

Others scurried out of the way, but Shari stayed still, staring up at him.

Lowering his head towards her, Sanithane blinked his three golden eyes and made a conscious effort to keep his poisonous breath behind his fangs.

The Altoriae raised a hesitant hand, fingers blackened and smoking. She stroked the side of his maw, fragile digits coming awfully close to his teeth.

Then she pushed the Dark Spirit Wall directly into his face.

Sanithane stumbled backwards as the spirits wailed at him. He was dimly aware of Shari shifting the fallen bodies of her guild out of the way. The spirits swarmed his vision and shrieked loud enough to wake the dead. Opening his maw, he drew in a breath, taking in their tormented souls and locking them away safely.

Panting with the effort, he changed back to his squishy Samuel form.

"Well?" Shari said. She had soot on her face, blistered skin, and her fingertips were charred, but the Altoriae had fared surprisingly well.

Perhaps not so surprising, seeing it is Shari, after all.

"Fine. You can come."

Shari beamed at him.

"You just have to talk Jonathan into letting you go."

Her face fell.

Shari turned to look at the Guardian and caught sight of the bodies littering the training ground.

She'd never seen a Spirit Wall as effective as the one Samuel had thrown at them, and Shari had the sneaking suspicion he'd held back on what it could actually do.

"Suppose we'd best get this lot fixed up," she sighed.

Samuel smirked at her, and the Altoriae fought hard not to flinch as the image of the razor-sharp teeth from his other form superimposed over the grin.

Reaching for Amauran, who was closest to her, Shari hid a flinch for another reason. Amauran was covered in large blisters, as if she'd been burnt by the wall. Maybe that's what Samuel meant by being in pain all the time? As if the sight of Amauran's wounds were a reminder of her own, Shari's torso and hands began to ache.

She glanced out of the corner of her eye and found Samuel with a look of concentration on his face. He was clearly sending to someone he was unfamiliar with. Biting back a hiss of pain, she laid a glamour over anything that hurt. Shari dared not to use Healing Innarn on herself with Samuel so close—he would be sure to notice if she did.

"The Healers are on the way to help," he said.

Shari nodded. "I'll do what I can till they get here."

Samuel bowed his head and made across the grounds to Jonathan, who was already healing those closest to him.

Carefully leaning down, Shari let the Healing Innarn flow from her fingertips to the worst of Amauran's blisters, soothing the burn and taking the pain away.

Amauran's eyes fluttered open, and she blearily looked at Shari. "He took us all out. In one go." Raising up on an elbow, she held out a hand expectantly to the Altoriae.

Shielding her hand so the blisters hidden by her glamour wouldn't pop, Shari helped Amauran to her feet.

"Don't think I've ever been so glad to say someone was on our side before. Apart from you, of course." Amauran grinned, but missed how forced Shari's return smile was.

"Know if anyone else here is a healer?"

Amauran pointed out Lira, Kieran, Ashlen, and Elani. Nodding her thanks, Shari set about healing the named, and directing them towards the rest.

She'd been working for what felt like hours, and despite the other healers, there were still more injured to attend to. Shari swiped at her forehead and moved to the next being.

"Almost done!" Lira looked just as tired as Shari felt. She leaned over her patient and started murmuring the focus words to send her Healing Innarn out to the correct area.

Giving a weary smile, Shari bent over Amara and healed the superficial burns on the side of her face. The Daen looked so peaceful sleeping, Shari couldn't find it in her to wake the other girl. As she stood, she swayed.

"Shari?"

Of course, it was only now that I'm was feeling the effects of Samuel's test that Jonathan would check in on me. Her knees buckled, and her palms protested as her hands hit the ground.

"Shari!" The Guardian was by her side, and healers were gathering around.

"Sis' fine," she slurred. It was possible she'd overdone things just a tad. The glamour was taking up so much of her energy. If she dropped it, she'd be able to get back to her feet. There were only a few more left to heal before she could rest.

"Oh, Shari." Jonathan sighed.

Despite dropping her glamour, Shari was exhausted. Maybe she just needed to close her eyes for a while.

"Stubborn," Samuel's voice sounded like it was far away. "She might even last more than a day on Al…"

Narday—1am

Jonathan sank into his lounge with a sigh.

Shari had proven, once again, how good she was at glamours. The soot and charring she'd shown after Samuel's test had been the least of her injuries. Her torso, hands, and neck had suffered horrific blisters, and yet she still demanded to go.

To be fair, she had done far better than the rest of the guild. Shari's glamour had only cracked and faltered when she'd been healing the third-last member to undergo the test. Jonathan had made sure she was tucked up in the Hospital under Holli's care before returning home.

He couldn't figure out if he should be proud or exasperated with his charge. Unless they thought of something else, Samuel would have to go to the conclave by himself.

Clattering in the kitchen had him scrambling to his feet, Innarn reaching out to discover the intruder.

"Long day?" Zac asked, poking his head through the door.

Jonathan sighed and collapsed back into his seat.

Zac's soft smile lit up the room as he entered, two frosty glasses of quass juice in hand. With a rueful smile, he took a sip from one and passed the other to the Guardian.

"It's always a long day when I'm up for patrol," Jonathan said. Taking a long drink, he sighed.

"Is there ever a day you're not?" Zac looked at his own glass, finger tracing the rim.

"Rarely. Shari is talking about setting up patrol groups with permanent members, which, in one way, would reduce our load."

"And make yours more difficult."

Jonathan tipped his cup towards Zac. "Precisely. But only until they get up and running."

"How long do you expect that to take?"

"Three months if everything falls into place. About five if it doesn't."

"Good. It's a date then."

Jonathan choked on liquid that had gone down the wrong way. "Sorry?"

"When the patrols are ready. You, me, celebratory night in the pocket Realm of your choice. But until then," Zac slapped his knees and stood, rounding the back of the lounge and digging his fingers into a stubborn knot next to Jonathan's spine. "We are going to get to know one another again. Find out if we want that date after all."

"Are we?"

"We are."

"Best start organising those patrol groups…"

"In the morning. You've had a long day, and I need to rest." Zac leaned forward to leer at him. "In my own bed." He stopped an inch from Jonathan's nose. "Good night, Guardian." His soon-to-be-friend tossed him a grin over his shoulder and slipped out the front door.

Jonathan let out a shaky breath and ran a hand through his hair.

Friends.

He could do that.

Narday—9am

Jonathan looked around at the piles of paper scattered over every flat surface of his desk and ran his hand through his hair.

Organizing the patrol groups was a nightmare. Four times a year, each Innarnian from outside the Shifting Island came to help patrol, and trying to add them in to pre-existing groups was proving next to impossible.

The bell at the front of the shop rang, signaling another customer. Bolting to his feet, Jonathan almost slipped on the loose pieces of paper. Swearing under his breath, he righted himself and made it into the shop proper without falling.

"Well met," he called out. "Welcome to Books 'n' More. How can…"

Tania grinned at him and wriggled her fingers in his direction. "Just me."

"What are you doing out of school?"

"It's the weekend. You asked me last weekend to work this afternoon, so you'd have time to eat and do Realm-saving stuff." The tiny teenager smiled.

Jonathan ran a hand over his face. "Ah. I remember something about that."

Tania handed him a container. "Mum made too much stuffed yaqueona last night. I heard what happened at the training ground and thought that you might appreciate an easy lunch."

"Thank you, Tania." Jonathan lifted the lid, and the smell had his stomach rumbling.

"Eat," she laughed. "Fuel will help everything come more easily." Tania's white hair gleamed in the lights of the shop as she stacked the books customers had decided they didn't want onto a cart to re-shelve them.

Crookedly smiling at Ronah's Linked, Jonathan nodded. "Food sounds like a good idea." He slipped behind the counter and onto the stool. After picking up a spoon, he dug in.

"What are you working on today?"

Swallowing, he took a moment to reply. "Setting up patrol groups. It's a logistical nightmare, to be honest."

"Why?"

"There are so many Innarnians, it's hard to keep track and to fit them into pre-existing groups in a way that complements rather than strains the group."

Tania tucked another book into the right place on the shelf. "Do they come one at a time?"

"No, there's probably close on five thousand Innarnians a night. Most arrive in their own groups and go patrolling together."

"And how many gateways do we patrol?"

"There's the standard three hundred and seventy-four gateways, including Lissae, that we monitor. All the Grey Realms, and a handful of the Light and Dark ones as well. Patrol groups are usually made up of fifteen Innarnians, although it can be less if there are those with stronger Innarn involved. That leaves twenty-six to thirty groups to take on special assignments for the night."

"Wouldn't it be easier to have the set patrol groups from Ronah and the other Shifting Islands, then have the others from elsewhere set their own groups up? They would have to know their capabilities better than we would."

Taking another spoonful of the stew, Jonathan let the idea roll around in his head. That would leave only a thousand Innarnians a night from the Shifting Islands for him to organise. Around sixty-six groups. Far easier than the four hundred he'd been trying to do. "That sounds more workable than what I've been attempting. I'll have to put word out in the *Sentinel*."

"I kind of miss reading the *Sentinel*. Mum would get it, but my father didn't like having it in the house." Tania looked blankly at the book she was holding. "He shattered the crystal slab one day. Over the back of Mum's chair. A shard caught the side of her face and cut her. That's when she packed us up and left."

Jonathan bit back words of apology that were clanging against his teeth. "What happened?"

"We moved halfway around Lissae. From Kenorvia to Hulios. Mum met Jordan, and we learned not to be scared." A shadow crossed the young girl's face, making her seem older than her years. She blinked away a sheen of tears, and a bright, false smile lit her face. "Then she got the job offer for Ronah, and we moved here."

"Is here better?"

"Anywhere my father isn't is better." Tania shoved the book onto the shelf harder than necessary.

"We're glad to have you," Jonathan said. "All of us."

Tania's false smile fell into a smaller one that reached her eyes. "Go! Finish your food and patrol groups!"

"As you wish." Jonathan rose from the stool and bowed slightly. Taking another spoonful of the gourd stuffing, he entered the back room and idly created a whirlwind to gather all the loose papers together in the middle of the room.

Sixty-six groups a night was all he had to focus on.

And maybe getting a subscription for the *Sentinel* delivered to the Hollingsworth household. He was already doing it for the shop and the Freehorne Library. What was one more copy?

Sitting at his cleared desk, Jonathan set to work drafting an article for the paper. He felt better than he had all day.

By the time Tania knocked on the back-room door, the patrol groups were mostly sorted, and the article for the paper had been sent away.

Jonathan rose, stretching out the kinks in his back, and beckoned the door open.

"All finished for the day. Did you want me to lock up?"

"Yes, please. Eva is coming in for training tomorrow, and it'll be good for her to get the full experience."

"Oh, Eva from Talhan?"

"Yes." Jonathan smiled.

"That reminds me, I'm visiting Temira tomorrow. Want me to get some more femto crystals for you?"

Scowling, Jonathan flicked a tiny twister of air her way.

Tania shrieked as it tickled her ribs. "Mean! Fine. I won't ask," she laughed. "So long as you finish up for the night, too."

"I will. Thanks to you, I've accomplished quite a lot today."

Shooting him another grin, Tania slipped from the room.

After gathering the papers with his notes for the patrol groups, Jonathan flicked out the lights. He'd check on Shari before heading out tonight.

As the Guardian left the dim room, light pulsed behind him, and a pitch-black book appeared on his abandoned desk. The writing on the cover flickered into being and started to glow and throb.

CHAPTER FOUR

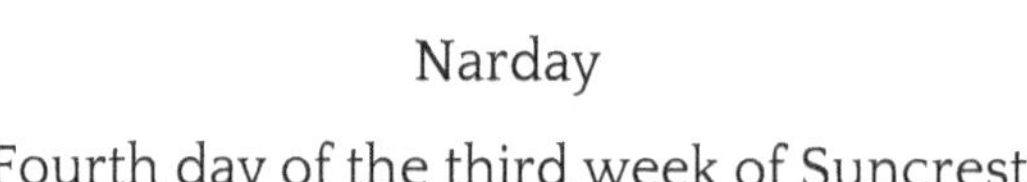

Narday

Fourth day of the third week of Suncrest

"And she still wants to go?"

Samuel growled into the cup Lizbeth had handed him earlier. "Of course she does. All hatchlings here seem to think they're invincible."

Lizbeth laughed as she sat in the seat opposite him. She had cornered him as he'd left Ridden Hall for the day, politely demanding that he accompany her for an afternoon meal. They had wandered to her house, as Samuel wasn't sure how the shadow under his bed would take to her.

"Rutenberry cookie?" she offered.

He snagged two, balancing them on the tiny plate underneath his cup. Before she could withdraw the plate, he grabbed another one.

"You and your sweet tooth," Lizbeth said fondly.

"Who else on this too-bright Realm will make cookies for me?"

"I heard tell the Altoriae might." The older lady unerringly lifted her cup to her lips and took a sip.

How long it had taken her to master the skill of eating and drinking without sight? He knew plenty of beings with their eyes intact who still regularly missed their mouths.

"The last thing on the Altoriae's mind is cookies," Samuel grumbled.

"Has she spoken to you since you transformed in front of her?" Lizbeth asked gently.

"She's barely looked at me." He viciously bit into his cookie and tried not to sigh as the rutenberry bits melted on his tongue. "I don't know how I'm going to keep her safe."

"Honestly, I don't think the Guardian knows how he's going to do that most of the time. Shari has a mind of her own, and she's not afraid to use it."

"She should be afraid. My kind are nothing to mess with," Samuel growled, taking another bite.

"Are there others who could go? Or offer her protection?"

"There's only a clawful of my kind I'd trust for a moment around Shari, and only one of whom I know the location of. But even they would be more likely to eat her than help."

Lizbeth laughed. "Perhaps she'd be better off in their bellies than standing alone on Altum. Could you set up a side-Realm or something like Anriluka did?"

"It wouldn't work. Our insides are too..." Samuel paused. Shari wouldn't be safe inside a Q'Aralide, but perhaps, just under their scales, and bound in protective runes... All attention would be on him. There'd be no way that he could sneak her onto Altum without both of them meeting their end, but maybe he could convince another to take her. Create the pretense that he was training them up to replace him. "She still wouldn't be safe," he mused aloud.

"I think you forget what it's like to believe yourself young and invincible. Our Altoriae would fight through the worst of the Realms and the fiercest of beings to ensure the safety of one of her own."

"I'm not..."

"Don't belittle yourself, Samuel," Lizbeth said. "Shari may struggle to accept this new facet you have presented her with, but she has promised to protect you as much as she has the rest of Lissae." Lizbeth reached out and took a cookie from the platter before daintily biting into it. "Give her more credit than those who would leave you to die."

"I still don't see why she should..." Samuel stopped at her look. "But you are right." His shoulders slumped. "I suppose that I'll have to see if an acquaintance of mine would help."

"That sounds like a wonderful idea," Lizbeth said and passed the platter his way again.

Shari looked down at the paper and sighed. She was taking her last exam on the Realms subject, as the elders wanted her to use the time she would have spent in this class to teach instead.

On which Realm are Minotaurs found?

Ugh. Trick question. Minotaurs could be found in every Realm—including Lissae now. Making a mental note to check on Asterion, she set her pen to paper and scribbled out the answer.

No doubt she'd be marked incorrectly, but if they were going to ask stupid questions, then she was going to put annoyingly truthful answers.

Native to Canak—Maku, minotaurs are now found all over the Realms, including Atlantis and Lissae.

Moving on to the next question, Shari tried not to roll her eyes.

Lissae's nearest neighbours are ______ and ______.

Fill in the incorrect blanks. Really, there should have been at least four spaces. Assuming the teacher wanted the two Realms on either side of Lissae, Shari penned in *Libertatia* and *Earth*, just to be annoying.

Give examples of an ice Realm:

Another sigh as she wrote *Rataeo and Vastilda.*

Give examples of a desert Realm:

Neharne and Bazaven.

When she read the last question, Shari didn't know if she should laugh or groan. *Name a Grey Sentient Realm:*

All in capitals. Really? *Lissae.*

Pen down, she looked at Ms Boyce.

"Done?"

"Yes."

"Congratulations, Shari. I look forward to seeing what you can teach our students," Ms Boyce said. She smiled and wrote a 100 without looking at her answers.

At Shari's gobsmacked look, she winked. "I think, if anything, you know too much about the Realms. We both know this was nothing more than a formality."

Squirming, Shari forced a smile and nodded. "Thank you," she said, trying not to let her gritted teeth show.

"Go on, I believe the Guardian is waiting for you. I'll lodge your results by the end of the day."

"Thank you, Ms Boyce." Shari stood and left the classroom. Pausing outside the door, she glanced back, tears suddenly stinging her eyes. As much as she had looked forward to dropping the classes she hadn't really been paying attention to, the thought that this was her last Realms lesson had her choking up.

'Shari?' Jonathan's voice sounding in her head made the Altoriae blink her eyes and swallow heavily.

'Yes, Jon?'

'*I have an idea I want to run past you. Can you meet me after...*'

Shifting before he could finish, she landed in front of the Guardian and grinned, batting away the crossbow he hefted in her direction.

'*... your last class.*' Jonathan sighed and put the crossbow down in favour of running a hand over his face. "Perhaps a warning next time?"

"Where's the fun in that? What's your idea?"

"I think it's time for me to set up an office in the castle."

Shari frowned and looked around the back room of Books 'n' More. "What do you mean?"

"Intuition is telling me it's time to move."

"But what about the store?"

"I've asked a few of those who were affected by the femto crystal attacks to take over the day-to-day running of it. I'll still oversee everything, at least for a while longer yet."

Noting his downcast expression, Shari moved closer and nudged his shoulder with her own. "The store will always be here for you, Jon."

"Thanks, Shari." His grin was sadder than she'd seen before.

"Tell me how you started it," she said, and moved to get some books from the hidden room.

"After I almost lost my insides one patrol, things got quieter. With less work to do, I figured it was a good idea to keep busy and earn my way. A bookstore isn't a necessity, so if Realm-saving took over again, Ronah wouldn't suffer for my absence. And there are always others who will help."

"Oh, I remember that. It was the first time I healed anyone," Shari said, pulling a vase from a shelf and peering at it. She shrugged and sent it over to the castle. She felt the rooms inside the castle shift and twist, making way for an office for the Guardian to work from. Another tricky bit of Innarn from the sentient isle, and a doorway connected Jonathan's home to his new workplace.

"Sorry?"

"Hmm?" Looking up, Shari caught Jonathan's slack-jawed expression.

"You were the one who healed me when I ran in front of Terrance, so he wouldn't be split in half by that trip wire?"

"I couldn't very well let you bleed out before you knew who I was."

Jonathan sat down heavily. "I thought I'd imagined you."

Shari wanted to giggle at the dumbfounded expression on his face but restrained herself.

"You healed me." He looked at her sharply. "Did I actually die that night?"

Tilting her head, Shari considered. "I think you did. I was only seven, but I had to call your soul back to your body. Mind you, Lissae helped quite a lot with that."

Burying his head in both hands, Jonathan grumbled. "Some Guardian I am."

"Hey. None of that," Shari scolded. "You are the best Guardian an Altoriae could have." The corner of her lips quirked up, and she peered at him over the stack of books in her arms. "Although a few less secrets would go a long way."

"I will endeavour to keep that in mind," he said dryly.

Getting to his feet, Jonathan helped her shift another stack of books over.

After hours of moving things around in the new office, Shari was thanking the deities that they had Innarn on their side. She couldn't imagine having to move so many books by hand.

"Well, I've got to get ready. Patrol tonight. See you tomorrow?" Shari asked.

"Will do. I'll meet you at the sh... here." Jonathan slumped slightly.

"We can meet at the shop, Jon. It's okay. Then we can grab a bite to eat from the tavern and come back here," Shari said. She had found moving out of home such a big change. Was still finding it a big change, even if the rest of the guild were good at giving her space. Most of the time.

"Sounds like a plan." His smile almost reached his eyes.

Tania tugged at her robes, and winced when Zana, Rakemyst's Linked, used her Air Innarn to push her hand away.

When she had agreed to be Ronah's Linked, she hadn't known it was going to be so *formal.*

In the back of her mind, Ronah chuckled.

If you had asked Tania a year ago whether she'd be comfortable not only living on a sentient, Shifting Island, but if she'd happily be the voice for said isle, fighting alongside the Altoriae and ensuring that the next convergence went smoothly, she would have run the other way.

But here she was, sitting next to Cyrus in a room above his lab on Talhan with Zana on her other side, the three of them staring into a huge Crystal Send and See screen at a diminutive being, planning the best way for Cantash to join with the other three isles.

Tania could only see the being from the nose up. Was the screen on their end was positioned too high? Or the aim was to focus on the wavy salt and pepper hair.

"Fire is the perfect mix of Air and Earth. And since Crystal is just another part of Earth..."

Cyrus scoffed. "A highly specialised form!"

On the other end, the little being scowled. "And beyond easy for anyone with half a brain to manipulate!" His hair was quivering with what appeared to be badly suppressed frustration when a voice spoke from off-screen.

"Thank you, Milo."

"But..." There was a huff, and Milo disappeared.

Footsteps came closer, and a being who was slightly taller than Milo approached the screen.

"Please excuse Milo. He's appointed himself my secretary but unfortunately lacks the skills to be one."

"Like passing along a message to meet the other Linked?" Cyrus asked.

"Exactly," the being on the screen laughed. Ze had auburn hair that was shaved on the sides and longer on top. A smattering of freckles sat over a turned-up nose. Bright blue eyes smiled at them. "Well met. I am Fenix, Cantash's Linked, Daen, and Fire Innarn Master."

Zana bowed her head, looking as serene and untouchable as always. "Well met, Fenix. I am Zana, Rakemyst's Linked. This is Tania, Ronah's Linked, and Cyrus, Talhan's Linked."

Fenix blinked. "Three isles joined already. I feel like this is leading towards something bigger." Ze grasped zir left lapel with their right hand, and something in the movement made Tania think it was significant.

"Your Milo wants a big Fire display," Cyrus said. Tania elbowed him in the ribs, hard.

"Milo is biased. He grew up around Fire Innarn."

"And you?"

"Much like the rest of us, I'm proficient in all types but can claim a mastery in Fire."

"What? Like, a school mastery?" Tania blurted.

Tilting their head, Fenix nodded. "I did advanced studies in Fire Innarn so I could better aid Cantash and fulfil my duties. Have you not done the same? Ronah is Plasma, yes?"

"I've only just found out I'm an Innarnian, really. Zana's been teaching me lots."

Something shuttered in Fenix's expression before they beamed. "That's brilliant! A new Linked—a new, *new* Linked. Just what we need to breathe life back into the stuffy formalities that so often dictate our lives. Don't you think, Zana?" Fenix barely let Rakemyst's Linked do more than open her mouth. "Alright, Tania. What do you think we should do for the joining ceremony?"

Grinning mischievously, Tania said, "Well, I was thinking..."

Teroupi

Rasshday—1am

Fifth day of the third week of Suncrest

Shari stifled the automatic huff of laughter as a tiny bird perched on one of Asterion's horns.

The minotaur snorted at her. Startled by the noise, the bird took to the air, chittering madly at them both.

Asterion grinned at Shari, who giggled again.

"Not here to bird watch, are we?" he asked.

"I know," Shari asked. "But it's nice to take the brief moments of joy while we can."

"Magic without being Innarn," he said, bending to pick up a snapped twig. Asterion nodded his giant bull head, and Shari fell into step with him.

They were tracking down a kedjum who was reportedly terrorising the locals around the Teroupi gateway. Jonathan had thought it would be a 'good experience' for Shari to see how long she could stand being on a Darker Realm for, and Asterion had offered to accompany her in case something went wrong.

Brushing through the tall ferns, Shari couldn't help but admire how peaceful the forest felt. Even if, behind her, Asterion was cursing up a storm as his horns got tangled in yet another vine.

46

The feathery creepers almost felt like they had a mind of their own, the way they wrapped around horns, hooves, and limbs alike. As Shari brushed away another thick tendril, she stilled.

The only description that locals had given them was the kedjum was wild, tangled, and unpredictable.

Tangled like a vine?

Rapidly, the surrounding vines flicked and writhed, coming to settle tightly around them, pinning their arms by their sides. A furry ball slowly lowered from the trees and blinked, four eyes staring straight at Shari.

She swore she could hear Asterion's heart beating from where she stood.

"Well met," she said.

The eyes blinked, and a tiny slit appeared in the fine fur. "Weeellllll mmmmeeeettt," it repeated. A long, flat tongue slipped upwards to lick its eyeball.

Shari stilled her shudder.

The kedjum tongue disappeared, and Shari tried a smile.

The creature smiled back. *Do Q'Aralide have more teeth than kedjums, or am I just biased because this one seems to think my face might taste good?!*

The creature propelled itself forward, aiming directly for Shari's head. She tried to duck, but with the vines... or limbs... of the kedjum wrapped tightly around her, it was impossible to move.

Fine fur tickled at her face and got in her mouth and nose as she struggled to turn her head away.

From behind the beast, there was a bellow. The kedjum stopped mid-lunge and backtracked, its grip on Shari going slack enough to allow her to drop free of the tangle of limbs.

"How in Lissae's name do I defeat a ball with legs?" Shari muttered. "Really, really long legs." Her eyes followed the thing she'd thought was a vine to where it connected with the fluffy ball with pointy teeth. "Remove them."

Asterion bellowed again, more muffled than before. There was the sound of thrashing and a low moan of pain.

A line of liquid fire sprang from Shari's left fingertips and up to the side closest to where five limbs fell from the head.

The kedjum shrieked, and its eyes narrowed, glaring at her as it drew closer before charging at her teeth first.

Right hand flaring out, she neatly severed the limbs on the other side and caught the free-falling fluff ball.

Whimpering, the kedjum's tongue flashed out and licked at the stumps she'd created.

"Sorry," Shari whispered.

"I'm not," Asterion growled as he stomped towards her. "It was trying to eat my face!" He snatched the ball out of her hands, and for a moment, Shari's heart raced, fearing he'd hurt it more than she already had. "Be safer with me."

"Why?" Shari asked.

The minotaur rolled his eyes. "Because creatures like this don't eat inked flesh. And if I bring you back injured when I could have prevented it, the Guardian will have my hide."

Eyeing the tattoos on his fingers, Shari tilted her head. "Does it work on Dark beings as well?"

"What?" Asterion was trying to figure out how to hold the kedjum without injuring it further and was avoiding her eyes.

"The ink."

"Best to ask Remmy or Torden from the Returned. They're the ones who inked everyone."

"What do you mean?"

Asterion removed a pouch from his belt, enlarged it, and gently placed the snarling kedjum inside. Hooking it back onto his belt, he gestured for Shari to take the lead. "When we were inside the pocket Realm, the only way to keep the other creatures from eating you was to have your flesh inked. The way they tell it, the others figured it out pretty quickly. Only, if you died in there, you returned to the state you were in before you arrived. Some sort of Innarn to keep Anriluka perpetually fed, or some rot."

"That's... you..." Shari shook her head. She'd unintentionally caused Asterion so much grief, denying him aid when he needed it not once, but twice. Sending him to places where he'd suffered so much.

"There's light, you know," the minotaur rumbled.

Shari glanced at him, and he smiled gently, the expression looking oddly at home on his bovine features.

"In every desolate place, in every dark time, there is light. You just have to want to look for it."

"Where was your light when I took it away?" Shari asked, her voice soft.

Asterion laughed. "You may be the Altoriae, but you aren't responsible for what happened to me, or anyone else. You do your job, and you do it well. And my light? Seeing one so tiny stand up for her mother."

Smiling around the threatening tears, Shari gripped his hand for a moment.

"Watching the joy of a child who wasn't afraid. And knowing that who I am now, what I look like, teaches those who matter to look beneath the surface for others."

"Asterion." Shari tried to ignore the lump in her throat, and she reached across to squeeze his hand again.

"Now, let's deliver this little beast and get back to more pleasant things."

"Like?"

"Hmmm, like making cookies with Eric, or helping in the castle garden."

"Are you enjoying life on Ronah?"

"I am," he rumbled. "It's nice having a bit of peace in my life, for however long it lasts."

"You don't think it'll last?"

"For all you walk the Realms, Altoriae, you miss a lot. Disturbances are running deep with many beings lately. Something is coming, and I fear it'll shake us all to the core."

There wasn't much to say about that. Shari had been getting the feeling for years now—with every battle proving harder than the last. Things were building towards something.

She just wished she knew what.

CHAPTER FIVE

Lissae

Rasshday

Tania was enjoying herself far too much.

"That B.I.R.D. is faulty." Temira, feared technomancer of Talhan, winced as the mechanical creature bounce off a wall.

Of course, it had nothing to do with the tiny bits of oil-crusted crystal Tania kept slipping to her assigned pet.

She grinned as the mechanical bird pecked at the saucer she had secreted amongst her mother's pot plants on the end table. It whizzed around the room, whistling off-key. Wings shaded with purple, it flashed brightly against the white furniture and the wooden walls. What her mum would say to finding they had another creature to look after in the house? Her smile grew. Tania's brothers were forever bringing home new animals to add to their menagerie, but this would be the first time she'd done so.

Temira had come to her house, ostensibly to talk about the upcoming joining of the three Shifting Islands to Cantash, but had presented Tania with the mechanical creature flitting about their heads.

"Useless thing!" Temira scowled at the B.I.R.D. "You were meant to have upgrades, not be so..." She broke off, ducking as the creature flitted over her head and blasted a new hole in the house's wall.

Smothering a giggle at the look on Temira's face, Tania crinkled her nose and the wall smoothed over again. "How did you upgrade it? I know Cyrus was talking about wearable crystal..."

Temira flinched at the word 'crystal' and scowled harder.

"Are you..." Tania stopped. She didn't want to ask if Temira was okay. How could she be after losing her oldest friend? And asking about crystal seemed like a similarly off-limits topic. "What upgrades did you make?" she asked instead.

For a moment, the scowl remained.

Tania leaned back, 'accidentally' clinking a pot against the saucer bearing treats for the hyperactive bird. It zoomed towards her head, swerving at the last minute to land amongst the leaves.

"Well, I thought I'd improved its proprioception and kinaesthesis, as well as minimising its physical distance between you and a threat. For instance, if I were to attack you, it should react." Temira seemed to pull her focus back to the room. "Best to test it then."

It was the only warning she had.

In that instant, Tania understood why there was fear in the eyes of those who dared to whisper *technomancer*. Temira twitched a finger, and Tania could feel her blood heating, fever-like chills breaking out across her body.

Before the heat could get worse, the B.I.R.D. flew in front of Tania and blasted the technomancer fair in the chest. The beam of light sent both her and the chair she'd been sitting in backwards into the wall with a cacophony of noise.

Without meaning to, Tania screamed and raced towards the fallen technomancer.

Blue skin paler than normal, Temira's neck was at an odd angle, her head haloed in a puddle of blood.

Tania screamed again. Frantically, she reached for Temira's wrist. She kicked the chair out of the way, allowing her friend more room to move.

Her vision blurred with tears. Tania grasped onto Temira's arm just as there was a horrific cracking noise, and the brilliant blue eyes of the technomancer flew open. They glowed for a moment, forcing Tania to look away.

Temira gently pushed Tania back and got to her feet. A negligent wave of her hand rightened the chair and cleaned the puddle.

The only evidence of the test was an indent in the wall where Temira had hit her head, and Tania sobbing next to it.

"Emotional distress will not get you out of joining with Cantash." The technomancer peered down her nose at the sniffling girl.

"You... your neck... I saw..."

"Ulnanians are stronger than Lissaens," Temira said. "And far longer lived than one would expect. Although, it seems I am coming closer to my end than I had previously realised."

"What do you mean?" Tania asked, wiping the tears and snot away with a handkerchief she'd pulled from her pocket.

"In my youth, you'd never have had time to see that I'd snapped my neck." The technomancer looked mildly annoyed. Was it because of a moment of weakness, or if, like her mother, Temira was contemplating how age slowed her down?

"It's happened before?" she said, struggling to fill the silence. It would be a long time before Tania would feel comfortable in a silent room again. Especially after holding Temira's wrist for that brief moment and not feeling a pulse.

"I am not what some would consider normal. Even amongst my own people, there were plenty who did not understand how I think. This was one way, at least, to test a theory."

"Well, I think you proved your theory right."

"Your temperature increased by three degrees."

"In about two seconds. The bird was quicker than most beings can react."

Sighing, Temira nodded. "I still think it could be improved upon. I will work on another. Shall I remove the faulty prototype?" Without waiting for an answer, Temira moved to pick up the bird from where it had landed on the side table. Fire blazing in her eyes as she stared at the dish, Temira gathered the B.I.R.D., scowled at Tania, and vanished without another word.

Too late, Tania remembered the oil-covered crystals.

Burying her head in her hands, she sobbed anew.

Jonathan smiled in greeting as Eva walked into Books 'n' More. "Well met, Eva of Talhan."

His newest employee snapped her heels together and thumped her first on her chest above her heart. "Well met, Guardian."

Just like when they'd met, she was wearing grey so dark it could be mistaken for black. Her short, bright blue hair highlighted the vicious burn along the side of her face and her missing ear.

"I'm so glad you've accepted the position."

"How could I not? I made a list of names, like you asked me, of those looking for work."

Jonathan took the list and looked it over. There were at least fifty names on it, written in cramped writing that spoke of how precious a commodity paper and ink were. "And how many are you in charge of caring for?"

Eva flushed but refused to look away from him. "I'm the eldest. If I don't, who will?"

"Good question." Jonathan ran a hand over his face, feeling much older than his years. "For now, we'll tackle the small things, like how to run the shop." He could see her biting the inside of her cheek. "And once you have a handle on that, you'll know how many others you'll need to employ to keep it running at the standard I expect."

Her gaze narrowed for a moment, but the set of her shoulders relaxed. "Sounds good to me. Where do we start?"

The bell over the door chimed, and Eva spun around, knives coming out of the sheaths on her lower back.

'Zhahyeem, Eva,' he sent. 'The chime is to let us know someone friendly has entered. Do you think the shop is unwarded?'

Slowly, she put the knives away and straightened.

Ignoring her blush, Jonathan smiled and waved a hand at their visitor. "First, let me introduce you. Lizbeth, this is Eva. She'll be taking over the shop. Eva, Lizbeth often runs the shop when I'm... incapacitated and no one else is available."

Lizbeth bowed her head. "Well met, Eva. I promise I won't give you a chance to use your knives."

"How can you tell?" Eva blurted.

It was only because Jonathan had known her as long as he had that he caught the tensing of Lizbeth's jaw. "I may be blind, but I'm not deaf," she said kindly. "And Innarn feedback gives me a clearer view of things than most sighted people."

'Like that book that shouldn't be in your office, Guardian. What is something so Dark doing on Lissae?' Lizbeth sent to him.

Snapping his gaze to his office door, he sighed and ran a hand over his face. Jonathan had a sneaking suspicion he knew exactly which book she was talking about.

"Do you..." Eva blurted and stopped. "I apologise. Well met. It's just. Reah lost her sight about three months ago. And I don't..." Folding her arms, Eva shrugged. "I've never... I don't know how to help her."

Lizbeth crossed over towards the girl, neatly avoiding the *From Ember to Flame* display. The latest book by Everon Castor was so popular, Jonathan was having trouble keeping it in stock.

"When she's ready, I'd be happy to help," Lizbeth said, reaching out but not quite touching Eva.

Grasping the older lady's hands as if they were a lifeline, Eva let out a choked sob. Bowing her head for a moment, Eva buried her emotions. When she lifted her gaze, her face was clear. "Thank you," she said.

"Why don't we let Jonathan disappear to do whatever Realm-saving thing he has planned, and I'll show you around?" Lizbeth smiled.

Eva nodded.

"I'll take my leave then. I'm only ever a send away." With a smile and a shrug, Jonathan slipped into the back room.

He was leaving his store in expert hands.

"Well met, Arilla," Anika said as she stepped up to the counter of the Quiver and Quill.

"Well met, Anika. How goes your day so far?"

"Slow." She pouted. Ever since her status as a Blank had been revealed, she'd been coming into the tavern to grab her lunch a few times a week. Arilla had been the only Blank on Ronah when she'd been growing up, and even though Anika had been a brat and a bully, Arilla never turned her away.

"Sometimes, slow days are good days," Arilla said gently and passed over a rutenberry shake.

"Thanks," Anika said, taking a drink.

Arilla picked up something in a cloth and started cleaning it again.

"What are you doing?" she asked, tilting her head to the side. If the move showed off the earrings that she'd designed from shells collected along Ronah's beaches, it was a bonus.

"Today is maintenance day." Arilla lifted the sword she'd been polishing, and Anika admired the gleam.

"Maintenance day? Is that the only thing you get to do with these?" The walls of the tavern had various weapons hanging on them, everything from bows to axes to swords of all shapes and sizes, as well as things Anika didn't even know the names of.

Laughing, Arilla shook her head. "Hardly. I'm the one who uses them."

"Wait." Anika sat back, almost slipping off her stool. "Blanks can fight?"

"Of course, we can." Arilla grinned and moved on to the next sword.

Anika watched and wondered. She'd been working on designs for weapons ever since the disastrous battle where she had broken the heel off her favourite shoes and used it to stab a bone-covered being who'd attacked her. The whole thing had left her shaken but determined to protect herself.

Never again would she be the victim.

Belfar was running for all he was worth. Sides aching, calves burning, and yet, the panting behind him spurred him onwards.

Ahead was the edge of the training island. Third largest of the floating islands above Rakemyst, it was where all the guards spent their days sparring and practicing to defend their elders, their island, and their Realm.

He had about ten seconds to make a choice. Belfar could keep running straight off the edge and fly downwards, or he could do another lap on top of the hundred or so he'd already done today.

Seven.

He could do this.

Five.

His wing was strong enough.

Three.

He'd be fine...

At the last second, he swerved, and the one chasing behind him careened off the edge with a shout.

The heavy beat of wings was followed by a string of curses. "Vebnah's breath, Belfar! I thought you had it this time!"

"So did I," Belfar said, sucking in heaving breaths.

Wolf landed lightly beside him. "It was one time," he said, gravelly voice gentle.

"One time I crash-landed after thinking I'd be safe to fly." He flapped his useless wing. "Crystal isn't as light as bone."

"Then infuse it with Air Innarn."

"Oh, I'm sorry. Why didn't I think of that? Not all of us are as talented as your niece," Belfar snarled.

Expression shuttering, Wolf pulled back.

"Sorry. Wolf, I'm sorry." Belfar leaned against a boulder, his wings drooping over the other side.

"Shari is exceptionally talented, but I was not expecting you to be like her."

Wolf moved beside Belfar, but not close enough to touch. The distance made him ache.

"Do you remember when we first signed up to be guards?"

Belfar couldn't help the wry grin that crossed his face. "Green as the autumn breeze, we were."

"Everything was hard then. Could barely get out of uniform before collapsing, only to get up and do it all again."

"RainbowMist had to be the strictest instructor we had."

"Mother was a terror," Wolf admitted. "But we got stronger, and things we thought were impossible when we started, we can do in our sleep now."

Some of those things Belfar had done in his sleep—or in a femto crystal-induced haze, at any rate. He'd injured people. Dozens of them, and he'd been unable to stop.

"Imbuing your new wing with Air Innarn now is just as hard as the first lap of this island was. It will get easier."

Biting back the words that threatened to rip from his throat, Belfar closed his eyes. Wolf was trying to be helpful. And his mate was right. That didn't stop him from wanting to scream out all the anger building inside. "I know." Pushing off the boulder and turning to look at the edge again, Belfar took a breath and leapt.

He almost missed Wolf cursing behind him as his crystal wing seemed to drag him down. Flicking his fingers out to call upon his Air Innarn, he whooped with relief as his wing finally worked. Toes skimming the tops of the tallest trees, he glanced to his side and smiled at Wolf.

It would take time, but he would heal.

Vebaday

Sixth day of the third week of Suncrest

Jonathan shuffled more papers into the pocket Realm he was using to transport his things to the Castle. Turning back to his desk, he paused. There was a denser, deeper shadow in the middle, almost as if there was something there that was sucking in the light from the room.

'Samuel? Do you mind having a look at this?'

It took a significant amount of effort for Jonathan not to touch the book-shape within the darkness. *'There's some sort of compulsion on it.'*

His apprentice was in front of him, between the Guardian and the desk. '*Blasted book!*'

Samuel was cursing up a storm, and if Jonathan didn't want to hold the *Hekkor Mafae* so badly, he would have been amused.

Waving a clawed hand, Samuel picked the shadow up and banished it back to the pocket Realm it was meant to be in. "I think we need to speak to the Datzal again," he said, eyes glowing golden for a moment.

"Do you think that is wise? The Datzal seems to have it in for you."

"Really?" Samuel lifted a brow. "I had no idea. Please, tell me how the annoying shapeshifter has made my life harder."

Jonathan rolled his eyes. "Sarcasm becomes you a little too well, friend."

"The Datzal was sent here to get under my skin. I'm not about to let ze have the pleasure," he said.

"But you fear the news."

Running a hand through his hair, Samuel snorted. "Wouldn't you? I know what it'll say: your murderous, devious queen demands you return to chair the most deadly council throughout the Realms. You, of course, have less than a twenty percent chance of walking out alive."

"I doubt those words will be used," Jonathan said. He took one more glance over his desk, and nodded, satisfied that he'd retrieved everything to do with the Altoriae or the guild.

"You don't understand, Jonathan. I've watched Oalark *eviscerate* beings for *blinking* out of turn. They couldn't blink, they didn't even have eyelids! And she still laid their bowels across the table like a festive garland."

Stopping to take a proper look at Samuel–creased brows, eyes almost sparking, and fingers tangled in his dark hair–Jonathan ran a hand over his face. "The Datzal might slip. Might give you more information than intended. If ze is so good at needling you, perhaps you know just how to get what we need from zir."

Samuel sighed. "One day, I won't have to be the bad guy."

Biting back words he'd regret, Jonathan thumped Samuel on the shoulder. "One day. But for now..."

"Now." Samuel gave a wry smile. "Now, I'm going to go make a bird sing."

CHAPTER SIX

Vebaday

The Datzal stood from where ze had been crouched on the cold floor of their cage. "Oh no. Has the big, bad priest come to make me talk?"

Samuel rolled his eyes.

Ze had clearly managed some Innarn to drop the room to a more comfortable temperature.

Too bad things were about to heat up.

"No words, priest? Jaileth got your tongue?" The creature cackled.

A red-hot shard of Innarn slipped through the bars and pierced zir side. The cackled stopped with a pained gasp.

"What do you know about the Dark Conclave?"

"More than you, I'd wager, for all the times you sat by the Queen's side."

Another shard, hotter than the last, hit its mark. It was met with a hiss this time.

"Our Queen knows what you've been up to, Sanithane. Knows where you've been and the company you've kept."

"Well, you'd be a lousy spy if you didn't keep your master informed," he said, seemingly bored. A third scorching shard streaked through the air.

The Datzal slipped to the side, and while the third shard missed, the fourth did not.

The spy howled, and Samuel fought to keep the grin off his face. "I'm wondering if you had any more messages for me?"

"Come closer, and I'll tell you."

"Oh yes," Samuel sauntered closer to the cage, but not near enough to touch. "Let me fall for the oldest trick in the book."

Slipping an arm between the bars, the Datzal swiped at him, and hissed again when ze missed.

"Nothing to say? No parting words of wisdom?" he said.

Ze merely shrieked.

"Very well." Stepping away, he turned and strode through the door, sending more shards through the bars and into the spy's tender flesh.

Zir howl echoed through the hall.

Samuel grinned. "I do like it when they sing."

Tania smiled at Collis as he bent over to pick up Esse, her mother's favourite blue-feathered chicken.

"She really is an escape artist, isn't she?"

"Yep. Thank you. I've been chasing her for ages. I swear she does it just so I'll run after her."

Collis laughed. Chicken firmly under his arm, he turned and guided Tania up the street back towards her house.

Smiling so hard, her cheeks hurt, Tania peered up at him. "I don't think I've properly heard you laugh before."

The grin fell from his face as if it had never been there. Tania was instantly sorry that she'd said anything.

"I haven't had much of a reason to laugh in the last... well. For far too long," Collis said.

"I'm glad you have a reason now. Are you settling in to your new place alright?"

"It's slow going. I've spent centuries with the rest just on the other side of a wall. Now we're scattered over Lissae." His long legs chewed through the distance, and they arrived at her gate before she could think of a reply.

"I grew up in the same village as my father's family. They're from the mainland. I didn't know until I arrived on Ronah that I was an Innarnian. It's odd to think that I could just... shift over there, spend the day and come back." Tania opened the gate and gestured him in.

"Why don't you?" Collis asked. He waited until the gate was closed before he put Esse down.

"Most mainlanders don't like different. Innarnians are different *and* powerful. Or, at least, we have access to a power they can't use or control. They're scared. And frustrated. Clearly, because we have access to Innarn, our lives are so much easier. They don't see the battles, the constant need to be on the defensive. How people worry if their loved one is going to come home from patrol or not." Tania sighed. "I know that there are a few big cities that have Innarnians, and there are some villages exclusively for us. But places like the village I grew up in, they're more likely to cast us out, if they don't kill us first."

Collis was silent for a while. He patted Esse, who shot him a rather unimpressed look and started pecking for bugs in the garden. "Your father's people would do that?"

"They'd try." Tania rubbed her arms, warding off a chill that reminded her of times gone past.

Standing, Collis rose and wrapped his arms around her. Tania relaxed into his embrace, marvelling at the feeling of safety.

From the comfort of a plush armchair in the castle's library, Samuel was lecturing her. "Even though the Dark Conclave is a diplomatic meeting of all the Dark races, the Q'Aralide Queen has long been the unofficial leader."

"Your queen," Shari said.

Samuel's eyes hardened. 'Not *any more. And it's more than my hide on the line if anyone from the Dark Realms is to find out about it.*'

Shari's mind whirled. She and Samuel had holed up, hoping to get her ready enough to face the conclave. "Alright." So many questions were begging to be asked. Maybe once they were back, she could. "Do we know when the conclave will start?"

"I'm expected to be there by the end of the week."

"Seven... we have seven days?" Shari spluttered. *How was she meant to learn everything she needed in less than a week?*

"There is a way we might speed the process up. But I'm not sure..." Samuel broke off and rubbed a hand over his face in a move that was eerily like Jonathan.

"So, you're older than the Shifting Islands and have the knowledge of twenty of my lifetimes stuffed in your head, but you think there's a way that I can know everything that you do?" Shari grumbled at him.

Heaving a sigh, Samuel rolled his eyes. However old he was, he really didn't act like it sometimes. "You don't need to know everything I do. But there are things that the Queen will test you on, depending on how you arrive."

"What do you mean?"

"There's... I can think of three ways we can do this. You shapeshift into the Datzal's natural form and take zir place in the proceedings. It's the most dangerous of the lot, as I've no idea how close ze is to Oalark.

The other option is we disguise you as a diplomat from one of the higher Dark Realms. Hopefully, someone Oalark has had few encounters with."

"Hopefully?" Shari butted in.

"My information is out of date and sorely lacking. Oalark may move at glacial speeds regarding some things, but her temper is that of a highly pressurised volcano–constantly threatening to erupt."

Shari snorted at the mental image.

"The third option is the one I'm leaning towards... and probably the one I'm most hesitant about."

He stared at something on the other side of the room, but whatever he was seeing, it wasn't the musty books on the shelves.

"What is this third option?" Shari said when it became clear he wasn't about to extrapolate.

"I ask a friend for help."

"A friend?"

Samuel sighed again. "I recently ran into one of my hatchlings. I'd like him to create a pocket Realm where you can safely reside in for the duration of the conclave but still be able to see and hear everything that occurs."

"And do you truly think I'll be safe in the pocket Realm of this hatchling?"

"Yes, I think you will be. Although I'd prefer to give you another form of protection, should something happen to him."

"What are you expecting would happen to him?"

"Oalark has no love for anyone, not even those she hatched. If she should suspect him of treachery, then his life, and potentially yours, would be forfeit."

"Why only potentially mine?"

"Always asking the hard questions," Samuel grumbled.

Shari was sure she wasn't meant to have heard him.

"Your reputation precedes you. Oalark would know that a fighter of your calibre is scarce, and she would do almost anything to get you in her grasp."

"And once she had me there?"

"Torture you until you didn't know which way was up and make you fight for her instead of Lissae. And honestly, do you think Lissae could stand against you if you were to fight on the other side?"

"There is no 'other side', Samuel. There is Lissae and everyone who tries to storm her borders."

He laughed mirthlessly. "The 'everyone' is the other side. I don't understand how you can fight for something but not understand what exactly you're fighting against."

It was Shari's turn to sigh. "I'm fighting for my people's right to be free. For them to make choices without someone else coming in who doesn't know us but still tells us what to do and how to do it. Jonathan can talk about how Lissae has a bunch of natural resources all he likes, but the reason I fight so hard is for the people."

Looking at her over his steepled hands, Samuel's golden gaze made it hard not to squirm in her chair.

"I saw how you were treated when I first got here. Why would you bother when others treated you so badly?"

"Because they had the choice to act that way. If Oalark took over Lissae, would she allow Anika to talk to her the way she'd speak to me?"

Samuel snorted. "No."

"Exactly. I'm not here to make Lissaens behave. My entire purpose is to make them safe."

Gazing at her for long enough that Shari wondered if it would be worth poking around in his head, Samuel finally responded. "What happens when one day they are safe? What would you do?"

Shari laughed. "I've been protecting Lissae for as long as I can remember. I doubt that there will be a time that she doesn't need protecting."

"Hypothetically, then. What would you do?"

"Relax?" She hated how the word came out as a question.

Smirking at her, Samuel asked, "How would you relax?"

"I... I don't know. Practice some more? Help run the tavern?"

"One day, I feel as if Lissae will let you rest. I just wonder if you'll be able to when that day comes." Standing, Samuel's smirk morphed into a sad smile.

Did he know something she didn't? "Until that day comes, I'm here to fight. And to keep everyone safe. Asterion had an idea that might help."

"Did he?"

"You've seen the tattoos that the Returned sport."

Samuel wrinkled his nose. "Inked skin."

There was a brief thought that if she got tattooed, at least Samuel wouldn't try to devour her. "Yes. Would that work against some beings at the conclave?"

Scrunching his face up as he thought, Samuel stared off at the same bookcase on the other side of the room again. "I believe so. There are always those who would rend your flesh from your bones merely for the joy of it and with no thought to sustenance. The beings at the conclave are more likely to be well fed, compared to the ones the Returned would have encountered."

Shoulders slumping, Shari sighed. "It was worth a shot."

"It was. As is my hatchling. Are you coming?"

"What? Now?"

"Best to meet him before he moves."

"Do you really think that he'll just up and go?"

"Every moment he's away from Altum and out from under Oalark's claw, is a moment spent fearing for his life. If he didn't move on shortly, I'd be ashamed of him."

"I have patrol first, but I can join you in the morning?" she asked.

Samuel sighed. "As soon as you get back."

"Deal."

"Do I get to know his name?"

"Jetonyx."

Chapter Seven

Vutolea

Zoeday

Seventh day of the third week of Suncrest

Shari groaned as she held the ice pack to the torn muscle on her shoulder. She'd forgotten how strong the nalparak were when she'd attempted to mount one by grabbing onto its massive antlers the way Anthea did. The Joratre always made it look so easy.

Anthea had called them in to help with a minor pest problem. It had been the perfect training exercise for some of the guild members. Teaching the Returned to work with the others was an exercise in patience.

Everything had been going well, until a wild nalparak had damaged the gateway, leaving them stranded on Vutolea.

The Joratre, of course, were gracious hosts, but Shari hadn't been able to get comfortable in the unfamiliar surroundings. In the deepest part of the night, she'd set a ward and escaped to the safety of her

Sanctuary, where she'd slept until her bones no longer ached with how tired she was.

Reappearing in the morning with the food she'd prepared, she let the smells waft over to the sleeping area. Groggy, her guild woke and sat down to eat with Anthea and her twelve wives.

To be fair, Shari was certain only three of the 'wives' were just that. The others acted friendly with Anthea, but the giantess didn't have the same spark in her eyes when she looked at them.

Anthea was moving amongst the guild, the tall woman hardly inconspicuous as she knelt by another group, offering food and drink to the weary fighters.

"How did you meet the Altoriae?" Amara asked as Anthea joined them.

White teeth flashing a smile, Anthea settled on the ground next to them. "Ah, that was quite a few years ago. This tiny slip of a thing wandered into the town, with skin so pale, we thought she was a ghost."

"I'm not that pale!" Shari spluttered.

Anthea held out her arm, midnight skin gleaming.

Rolling her eyes, Shari offered her own. Her olive skin had deep tawny undertones, and was a far cry from the white Anthea was claiming. Amara stuck hers out as well, and their host laughed.

"If the Altoriae was a ghost, we would have thought you an ancestor, come to haunt us for wrongdoings from thousands of years ago!"

"Do spirits get paler as they age?" Mu asked.

Shari shook her head. "Anthea is having you on. The Joratre hardly thought of me as a ghost."

"My elders believed her to be our salvation. And she has proved them right time and time again." Anthea patted Shari's arm, ignoring how the Altoriae tensed up and withdrew her limb.

"How so?" Amara asked.

"Your Altoriae has saved our Realm from those who see it as an easy stepping stone into Lissae. She's saved my life more often than some of my brethren." Anthea gave the Altoriae a fond look.

Before Shari could refute her claim, a discrete chime sounded, and she scrambled to her feet. "The Ducibus have completed their repairs. Finish up. It's time we went home," she announced.

Anthea snapped to her feet, helping the others to clear away the mess of having so many extra people in her home.

As Shari turned to say her thanks, a wave of Dark Innarn passed over her, and Samuel appeared at her side. Before she could blink, Anthea and all of her wives had the pointy end of their various weapons aimed at Samuel's head.

'*We must go to Jetonyx now. You've dallied enough,*' Samuel sent.

'*Couldn't be bothered to check in first?*' she scolded him. "Thank you for your hospitality. It appears the Guardian wants me back as soon as possible."

"He is no Guardian." Anthea's voice couldn't be shaking. The Joratre had shown her nothing but strength from the moment they met.

"Not yet." Samuel glanced down and looked up at Anthea from under his lashes. "I'm his apprentice."

Anthea sucked in a breath. It took a long minute for the weapons in the room to be lowered. She turned to the Altoriae. "You know his truth?" Anthea asked, her voice rough.

Shari nodded. "I do."

She just hadn't decided if she liked it any more than her host did.

Bazaven
Adonday
First day of the fourth week of Suncrest

Samuel stepped through Bazaven's gateway first. Glaring into the brightness, he sent out a tendril of Innarn to check if Jetonyx was still around.

There was an answering hum, and he motioned Shari to follow him. She did, closing the gateway behind her. Shading his eyes, Samuel set off due west towards the persistent tug that reminded him of Jetonyx's attachment to him while the hatchling was still in the shell.

Shari trailed behind, uncomplaining of the heat, the endless sand, or the blazing sun. She flicked a bit of Innarn at him, a little parlour trick that pulled on some of his shadow and used it to shade his eyes. It made things easier in the too-bright Realm.

Before long, they came to what looked like another gentle dune, but Samuel held his hand up, and Shari froze. His Innarn skimmed out, and Jetonyx erupted from the sand, showering them in grit as his poisonous breath washed over the shield Samuel had hastily raised.

'*Good to see you again, hatchling,*' Samuel sent, quirking his lips and scowling as he brushed the sand off.

'*Not a hatchling,*' Jetonyx sent back, his words a mumble. Catching sight of Shari, he perked up. '*You brought me a snack!*'

'*I am not a snack,*' Shari growled.

Jetonyx sank back onto his haunches, looking down at them. '*Why would the golden wyvern bring a mortal if not to feast on it?*'

From the look Shari was giving him, they would talk about this later. '*Jetonyx, may I introduce you to the Altoriae of Lissae? Altoriae, please ignore the manners of my hatchling. He hasn't eaten in far too long.*'

Tilting his giant head, and blinking his eyes, the hatchling lowered his maw and stared at Shari.

There was nothing quite like having all three eyes of a pitch-black Q'Aralide trained on you. Unblinking—unnervingly close, with fangs sharper than her favoured blade a hand span away from Shari's face.

'*Can't be,*' the black Q'Aralide finally sent, pulling back. '*Oh, it's a joke! So I can eat you!*'

He lunged forward, jaw snapping, as Shari whirled away. Pushing her Innarn out, she found the largest, nearest quadruped and *pulled.*

Jetonyx lunged again, and Shari danced closer to his belly, hoping to make it too hard for him to manoeuvre.

She forgot about the claws.

Giant wings came down to engulf her, and Shari hoped the beast appeared soon as she fell to the sand and rolled away from him—just in time for the quadruped to smack into his side.

Shrieking, the black Q'Aralide turned his head. Seeing his dazed prey—a massive bovine with two heads and a bulky belly that brushed the sand—he snapped, neatly biting clean through the beast's neck.

Shari tried her best not to flinch at the noise. And to push the wild, half-terrified-sounding voice that was shrilling, *could have been me!* to the side where she could safely bury it later.

'*Better?*' Shari asked.

Lifting his head from the belly of the beast, Jetonyx nodded, intestines hanging down either side of his maw.

She could feel Samuel's Innarn reach out, and he smacked the Q'Aralide on the back of the head. '*I taught you better manners than that.*'

'*Hungry. Sorry. No food for months.*'

Samuel's eyes were hard. '*No excuses.*' His send was just as hard as his eyes, but Shari caught the softening of his mouth as Jetonyx turned away to wipe at the blood ringing his maw. Clearly, he'd been worried about his... hatchling.

Shari crouched, resting whilst she could. '*Are you his father?*'

Both males turned horrified gazes on her. '*No!*'

Holding up her hands, Shari tried to show that she'd meant no offence.

'Q'Aralide don't work the same was as you do on Lissae. We all... well, most of us, share the same parents. One of my jobs was to raise the hatchlings and keep the next generation safe,' Samuel sent to her.

'It looks like you've done a good job, then.' Shari's send was as gentle as she could make it.

'There were many other jobs I was forced to do that were nowhere near as pleasant. The hatching grounds were an escape from the... duties I endured.'

'Were there many other good things?'

'Some. Mostly, it was all about how I could ensure that I would live to see another day. Or how soon I could get off-Realm to see the sun again.'

'There's no sun on Altum?'

'None. It's known as the Dark Realm for a reason.'

'Hilarious.' Shari rolled her eyes at him.

Jetonyx made a show of cleaning his face as he watched them.

'Well, you may have looked after the hatchlings, but I don't think you've passed on your menacing presence,' Shari sent, aiming to tease and break the sudden tension between the three of them.

Samuel seemed to hold his breath, and his forearms rippled as if he was preparing to shift. Was he doing so to protect her from words she was now wishing she could recall, or because he'd grown tired enough of her nonsense and thought the black Q'Aralide 's idea of a snack had some merit?

The hatchling licked his maw again and grinned. 'He tried. Held classes and everything. But the Golden Priest is feared even amongst our own kind.' Jetonyx flopped to the sand, grinding his belly into the warmth with a sigh. 'He let me chew on Helk's wing tips once, though. It was brilliant.'

'So Ridden Hall isn't the first time you've taught?' Shari sent to Sam.

'No,' Jetonyx answered. '*He was the best teacher. Strict. So strict. The Golden Priest would set us practicals to do and make sure that we could complete them before he'd let us move on to the next thing. Make us help the others. The Queen always grumbled about that. Said he was soft.*' Jetonyx's thoughts were coloured with the satisfaction of a good meal.

'Soft?' Shari looked at Samuel and snickered.

He glared back. '*I was hardly soft.*'

'*Were too. You let me heal after the acid falls when she would have pushed me to keep going. Did some of your magic to get me across when I could hardly move.*'

Shari tried not to snicker at the stunned look on Samuel's face.

'*You felt my Innarn?*'

'*You're not as subtle as you think you are,*' Shari and Jetonyx sent at the same time. The baby Q'Aralide raised his head, so he was eye level with her, and winked. She grinned back.

'*You two are going to be the death of me,*' Samuel sent, pinching the bridge of his nose.

Their grins grew.

'*But that is not why we're here. I have a favour to ask. One that I wouldn't if I hadn't considered all possibilities,*' Samuel sent.

Jetonyx sobered instantly. '*Can't make me go back,*' he grumbled.

'*I wouldn't ask if I didn't have to.*' Samuel stepped forward and cradled the massive head in his hands. It was only then that Shari realised the hatchling was shaking.

'But... *what if she...*' Jetonyx whispered.

'*The good thing is that I'll be with you the whole time. If you want to get out, we can,*' Shari sent.

'*And I'll be there too. I will protect you, as I always have.*' Something passed between the two of them, and Samuel looked disheartened for a moment.

Resting his chin on his wing claws, Jetonyx studied them both for what must have only been a minute, but felt much, much longer. '*I... I don't want to go home.*'

Samuel's shoulders slumped.

'*But I will, for you.*'

Samuel beamed at the younger Q'Aralide. Did he know just how much power he held over the hatchling? Shari couldn't decide if it was a good thing of not.

'*We can pick you up before we leave,*' Samuel sent.

'*Ha! No way. It would be safer for you to take me with you now.*'

The Altoriae looked at Samuel for guidance. Jetonyx didn't have anywhere near the control he did, and there was no way that she wanted him running loose on Lissae. '*How about my sanctuary?*'

Shaking his head, Samuel said aloud, "It would be too Light for him. But mine wouldn't be."

Hiding her smile at the thought of what an outstanding role model Samuel was, Shari nodded. He was scowling at her as if he'd heard what she was thinking.

Beckoning Jetonyx closer, Samuel flicked his fingers, and a great gaping portal opened behind them. As the hatchling moved, Samuel stiffened. '*We're being watched. Shari, get in. Make it look like you're fighting him and doing a terrible job.*'

Before she had the time to sigh at the ridiculous idea, Jetonyx pounced on her, careful to keep his claws from actually scratching. Shari shrieked, only half in surprise, and thrust out a palm—water bursting forth, harmlessly showering the Q'Aralide. The steam that rose from his hide made it look like she'd done more damage than a light sprinkle. Scrambling to her feet, she turned and looked at the black Q'Aralide, only to go pale as a golden one, twice Jetonyx's size, loomed over his shoulder.

'*I'm going to breathe, and you two are going to run. Straight into the portal.*' His tone left no room for comments.

The golden chest swelled, and Shari turned, bolting for the Dark portal. Glancing over her shoulder as Jetonyx was released from under a golden claw, and the younger Q'Aralide pounced after her, kicking up sand as he ran. Scrambling and almost tripping over her feet, she ducked and rolled just as Jetonyx reached her, seamlessly sliding through the open portal as a cloud of green gas passed over her head.

Shari used the same charm she'd used on Tocithas, making sure the gas wouldn't enter the shield around her face. It was a moot point. Jetonyx had skidded into the room after her, and the gas was pulled out, as if someone was breathing it in.

Then the world went dark.

CHAPTER EIGHT

Lissae

Adonday

First day of the fourth week of Suncrest

Skye was doing her best to become one with the white mist that was hiding the gaudy decorations on the edges of the room. Elder Chamele was looking down her nose at one of the other aides, scolding them for not bringing her tea at *exactly* the right temperature.

How in the name of Lissae has my life come to this? She dare not think about it, knowing that, for all her posturing, Chamele was more than likely to have another Innarnian on board who could read minds better than she could hide.

After their 'strategic retreat' from Talhan, the elders aboard the coal-hungry ship had done little but complain. They had hoped for more information, more crystal, more, more, more. Skye had never understood why mainlanders were so determined to get the things they couldn't have. Elder Suni, whom she'd been assigned to serve, picked at the slim offerings on the plate of treats. Everyone was living off rations until Chamele decided what she wanted to do next. And if she said attack, she'd have the full force of the others behind her.

What Skye really wanted to know was why they were so determined to gain control of the Shifting Islands.

As Chamele put down her cup, a shiver ran over Skye. It looked like she was about to find out something after all.

"The Shifting Islands have long been known to graciously host others, both of Lissae and... not." The scorn on the Elder's face was slight, but unmistakable. "With them moving into the Deep Ocean, they believe themselves to be all but untouchable. I, of course, know better."

Clenching her jaw, Skye kept her eyes forward. *I will not react. I will not react...*

"Did you know that refugees who are approved by the Guardian have been given space on the land *we* control? For free? Able to set up their little... villages as if they still lived in their home Realms?"

Elders around the room looked confused, and many started muttering. Chamele was talking about something that had been happening for almost as long as Lissae had been around. Otherwise, most of those in the room wouldn't be here at all.

"It would be so unfortunate if something were to... happen to some of those little villages." Crossing her ankles, Chamele picked up her cup again and smiled as the elders started chattering over each other, outlining plan after even more ridiculous plan.

"Set sail for Lawrgaea," Chamele ordered imperiously. "It is time, Suni, to get rid of some intruders."

Gulping at Suni's evil smile, Skye tried her best to blink the tears welling in her eyes.

She had to find another way to get a message to the Altoriae. It appeared the Council's plans had changed.

Samuel's Pocket Realm
Adonday
First day of the fourth week of Suncrest

Shari stumbled slightly as Jetonyx's wing caught her side. For the fifth time.

'*Why is his pocket Realm so small? If I can't fit in here, how can he?*' the baby Q'Aralide grumbled.

Really, calling someone a baby when they were towering over you was a bit of a misnomer. '*I think he uses this in his mortal form.*'

'*Wish I had a mortal form,*' Jetonyx grumbled.

Sighing, Shari conjured a chair and sank into a corner. '*Do you have a pocket Realm?*'

Jetonyx slumped onto his haunches, the bed underneath him creaking dangerously. Shari superstitiously sent a shaft of Innarn to strengthen it.

'*Yes.*'

When he didn't offer any more information, she sighed again. '*Do you think it would be safe for me?*'

'*I can make it one enormous battle, if you like.*' His eyes glowed, and Shari fought the urge to sigh for a third time.

'*If I'm looking out for you, I hardly think that's wise.*'

There was grumbling, and finally he sent, '*No fun.*'

Shari laughed, and Jetonyx raised his head at the bitter note. '*Not sure I know how to have fun anymore. I've been fighting for most of my life.*'

'*What does fun look like for you?*'

Why did all the Q'Aralides she meet seem so intent on her thinking about anything other than fighting? '*Fun is... swimming in the ocean and watching the sea creatures as they go by. It's finding the perfect move that incapacitates your enemy without causing more harm than needed. It's that tingle of Innarn when you shape it just right. What's fun for you?*'

Gazing at her for long enough that Shari almost forgot the question, Jetonyx huffed a sigh. '*Being free.*' The Q'Aralide turned his massive head away from her for a moment. '*But I like the things you've said as well.*'

She smiled at him and then startled as Samuel appeared between them.

Samuel smirked at her and put his finger on the flat of her blade before pushing it away from his throat.

'*Where'd that come from?*' Jetonyx's words were shrill.

Was wise to admit that she had moved before she'd even thought about it? Shari blinked, unsure if she should say anything.

'*You've gotten rusty, hatchling,*' Samuel taunted, but his gaze was on her as she sheathed her yellow blade.

Jetonyx grumbled again.

Samuel sent over the top of the hatchling's complaints. '*We're back on Ronah. I believe it would be wise for the Altoriae to make an appearance.*'

'*And me?*'

Who knew Q'Aralides could act like excited shem'ar young? Shari marvelled.

'*You will be our best kept secret.*' Before the younger one had time to complain, Samuel continued, '*The Queen has sent one of her Datzal.*'

Under his black scales, Jetonyx paled. '*I... I can be a secret.*' Even his send was shaky. '*But, please, can you make it bigger?*'

For a moment, Samuel looked uncomfortable. '*I wish I could. But...*'

'*My sanctuary has a sky,*' Shari blurted, and almost immediately kicked herself. '*You could. Sam, I know you said it was too Light, but it wouldn't be as painful as Bazaven. There would be room to fly and roam.*' And she could shrink the structures so there would be no way the curious Q'Aralide could get in.

Jetonyx turned wide, trembling eyes on Samuel, and Shari was glad she'd already put her blade away. She would have fumbled it at the look of pure, childlike wanting on the black Q'Aralide's face.

'What about food?'

Shari wrinkled her nose. 'If the conclave is in less than a week, how much would we need?'

'Oh, lots.' Jetonyx nodded wisely. Shari couldn't help but see tiny Eric trying to get more rutenberry cookies out of her.

'One more meal should be plenty.'

Jetonyx's head drooped.

Rolling his eyes, Samuel added, 'There will be a feast at the conclave for you to gorge yourself at.'

The hatchling perked up and hit his head on the ceiling.

'Better go now,' Samuel sent.

Nodding, Shari rose. 'I'll have to touch you to bring you through. If that's okay?'

Jetonyx nodded and bumped his head again. 'Anything so I can get some more space!'

"Samuel?" she asked.

His throat bobbed as he swallowed. "It's alright. I didn't want to invade your privacy."

"Like I haven't already done that to you," Shari scoffed. "Think of it this way. You're the only one who can tell me truthfully what Jetonyx needs. I don't want to do something that will hurt him."

Frowning, Samuel shook his head. "If I don't get back and tell Jonathan what's going on, he'll have my hide. I would be honoured to accompany you another time."

"As you will it," Shari said. Careful to avoid Jetonyx's fangs, Shari gently touched his face.

In a blink, they'd moved to her sanctuary.

Standing in the same clearing she'd made so long ago with Jonathan, Shari tried to look at the space she called her haven through fresh eyes.

Green trees, waving in the breeze. A trickling rock stream that led to a wider creek. And a bereni tree in the distance, which she'd based on her home... her childhood home. Closing her eyes, she concentrated and made the trunk smooth and impassable. No curious Q'Aralide noses could poke into things they knew nothing about.

Jetonyx made a sound of joy and, with a few ferocious beats of his wings, took to the sky.

Shari smiled. *'I need to get back too. Samuel and I will come with some food in a few days.'*

A whoop was her only answer as the black hatchling flew higher into the sky.

Lissae
Adonday

Arilla glanced at her father-in-law, who was mopping up the soup he'd spilled on his robes.

Ever since they'd reunited, SilverCloud had been appearing more and more frail. She'd never once seen him look anything less than immaculate, and now he seemed wizened and clumsy.

This was not the end a proud Ilutri would want.

Wolf and Calem, sitting across from each other, were determined to ignore the mess and spare the dignity of their father.

Catching her gaze from across the table, Belfar winked, and the soup syphoned away like it'd never been there.

Arilla smiled, and Belfar overlooked the way her lips trembled.

"Tell me what mischief my grand daughter is up to now?" SilverCloud asked.

Next to her, Calem gripped his spoon tighter. They'd mentioned Shari was off-Realm a dozen times in the last hour, but it didn't seem to stick in the Elder's memory.

"Oh, I haven't seen her today, but I'm sure it will be something interesting," Arilla laughed lightly. To be fair, interesting in Shari's world was not always a good thing. She dropped her hand to Calem's thigh, giving him a comforting squeeze.

"Do you think she'd have time to say hello to an old man?"

"You are hardly old," Arilla mock-scolded.

SilverCloud chuckled. "Don't pretend, Arilla. For me. I may be an old, dying man, but I know you are doing everything you can to protect me from a truth none of us can escape."

"What truth is that, Dad?" Calem asked.

"Time runs out for us all."

"Well, that's depressing," Wolf muttered.

"Depends which side of the clock you're standing on, I suppose," SilverCloud mused. The spoon missed his face again, but before the liquid hit his robes, Belfar pulled it away.

"I feel like a snack. Know anything good here?" Belfar asked, beaming at Arilla.

"Oh, I know the chef," she replied. "He's quite good."

Calem laughed, and a tray loaded with finger-foods floated towards their table. Savoury crackers rimmed the edge. A soft cheese flecked with red, a fiery orange dip, and red opaque berries sat on a green leafy bed.

Before Calem could issue his standard warning, Belfar took a cracker and a slice of cheese and slipped it into his mouth.

"The cheese has calromata in it," Calem blurted.

Belfar's face was slowly turning red. Beads of sweat dripped down his forehead as he swallowed with difficulty.

"Drink?" she offered.

The other Ilutri nodded, fanning himself.

Chuckling, Calem floated a rutenberry shake into Belfar's hand. He opened his mouth to drink, and a massive hiccup escaped. Eyes wide, he groaned and drank, holding the liquid in puffed-out cheeks in a vain attempt to cool his mouth.

Wolf reached across his mate and picked up a slice of the cheese. "Hmmm," he said. "Bit of a kick."

Incredulous, Belfar stared at him. Whatever he was going to say was lost to another epic hiccup. Scowling, he took another drink.

SilverCloud used a cracker to scoop up some of the fiery orange dip and bit into it, moaning with delight. "Oh, remember your mother's..."

"Narday night dinners," Calem and Wolf said together.

"She always used to add in the calromata so we didn't notice the burnt bits," Calem added.

"Not that it ever worked," Wolf said. He popped a red berry into his mouth and grinned.

Arilla didn't know how he could stand the spicy heat from them. They'd been selling more shakes than she could make since they'd started serving their Daen-inspired snack platter. The calromata berries were the heat on top of an already volcanic meal.

Calem laughed as he, SilverCloud, and Wolf finished the platter off.

"I'll make some more drinks," she said as sweat beaded on Calem's brow.

"I'll help," Belfar added.

Together, they rose and walked towards the bar. Arilla slipped behind it, and Belfar leaned over, scooping up the frozen rutenberries and the mortar and pestle to crush them.

"Solid food will allow him more dignity than liquid," he said.

Head snapping up, Arilla eyed Belfar before nodding.

"My parents..." he sighed. "My mother died of old age. If we survive to old age with our minds still intact, then our bodies won't be."

She glanced at the table, watching her husband and his remaining blood laugh at something. "I think it's the same for most races. It's just hard..."

"... seeing someone go through it. I know." He glanced at the mortar and pestle, a frown drawing his brows before he said, "For the Ilutri, though, we're creatures of the sky. Take that away, and what are we?"

Arilla's eyes watered. She hadn't thought of that. If an Ilutri's body started failing them, it meant that they wouldn't be able to fly anymore. "Ilutri are so much more." Her chin wobbled, but she reached over to snag the mortar from him and dumped the crushed berries into the milk.

"Some Ilutri, maybe." He sighed again. "And some, we've held up as the perfect ideal for generations. SilverCloud, without his wings..."

"Is still loved. And still cared for. Who needs wings when you can shift wherever you need to anyway?" Arilla asked.

Having moved to the Shifting Islands in her youth after being disowned, she'd never had to watch a parent grow old before. Never seen them wasting away. It took everything she had to paste on a smile and return to the table, drinks in hand.

Tania was hurrying to her meeting with Zana. "Late, late, I'm so late," she muttered. She scrambled across the bridge from Ronah to Rakemyst, shrieking as an Ilutri teen with silvery wings landed by her side.

"Sorry, didn't mean to scare you." Something about the way he was looking at her told Tania that he wasn't entirely telling the truth. "I'm Voxis. We've met before but were never properly introduced."

"Ah," Tania said. "You almost bowled me over then too."

"Well, I suppose we'll just have to stop meeting like this," he said, stepping closer.

"Or you could stop meeting me altogether," she muttered.

"Sorry?"

"Oh, excuse me. I'm late," she said, saccharine sweetness dripping from her words as she channelled Anika.

"I'll walk you," he said, and fell into step beside her.

Trying to remind herself that, as Ronah's Linked, it was beneath her to curse the boy. She lengthened her stride to get rid of Voxis sooner. He was prattling on next to her about something inane, and Tania wished for Collis's steady silence.

"Where are you heading anyway?" he asked, snapping her out of her thoughts.

"To see Zana."

"Brilliant! I haven't caught up with my aunt in ages," he beamed at her.

Internally, she groaned. Another reason she couldn't give him the slip.

He was chattering again, and Tania sent a swift query to Rakemyst, gently asking if the isle could speed their journey. Zana had wanted her to walk to their meeting, something about fit bodies and fit minds, but now Tania was wondering if it was because of the boy beside her.

As they arrived at the white tower in the middle of Rakemyst, Tania spotted his Linked tapping one finger against her crossed arms. The expression on Zana's face said she had nothing to do with her nephew's actions.

"Voxis, why are you keeping Ronah's Linked from our meeting?"

Tania had never heard Zana's voice as flat as that before. Voxis was in trouble.

"Oh, just showing her the way, Aunt Zana." Even his winning smile faltered under her unimpressed look.

"And did Ronah's Linked inform you of our meeting?"

Watching him glance at her out of the corner of his eye was amusing. He was clearly trying to decide if she was worth getting into trouble for with the formidable woman before them.

"Ah, ye... yes, Aunt Zana," he said, hanging his head.

For a moment, Tania was stunned. She had been sure he was going to throw her under the waves. As Zana's expression softened, she realised Voxis was still trying to play them both.

"He insisted on accompanying me," Tania said. "Wouldn't take no for an answer."

"Oh, you hardly protested," Voxis said smoothly.

Zana looked at them consideringly. "I suppose, since you've been such an excellent host, that you must join us, Voxis."

Doing her best not to groan, Tania followed Voxis into the building. As she passed Zana, the elder Linked winked at her.

"Ronah's Linked has progressed nicely since we first met." Zana gave her a small, barely there smile as she led them through the hall, deeper into the tower. "There is a type of Air Innarn she has yet to experience, but one I believe will be beneficial. I am grateful that you have chosen today of all days to join us, Voxis. You would make a most helpful subject."

Voxis's expression faltered for a moment, but his bravado carried him forward. "Of course, Aunt Zana."

'*He is my great nephew twice removed,*' Zana sent to Tania in a tight band. '*Forever claiming me whenever his need is greatest. Or when he desires to impress.*'

Tania sniffed. '*His behaviour has left an impression, alright.*' Her thoughts were a murky yellow–brown.

Stifling a smile, Zana opened a door and gestured them through.

"Wow," Tania breathed. She smiled as the word echoed back to her. "The acoustics in here are brilliant." The room was of round, white rock walls and a domed ceiling. Row upon row of white cushioned seats ringed the stage, where a perfectly lowered circle sat in the middle of the space.

"And they make this type of Innarn so much easier," Zana said.

"How so?" Tania asked.

"Acoustics, clearly."

Both Linked turned to glare at Voxis for interrupting them.

"Clearly," Zana intoned. "Go find a seat in one of the middle aisles, Voxis."

"Yes, Aunt Zana." He shot Tania one more leer before trotting down the aisle.

Holding out her hand, Zana raised an eyebrow at Tania, who grinned gamely and laid her own atop it. The next moment, they were on the stage. Zana flicked her hand, and the lights dimmed, one coming out to shine just on them.

'*Maintain your contact with my skin.*'

Nodding, Tania felt privileged. She'd never have thought that the private Ilutri would ask something like this of her.

Then Zana opened her mouth and sang.

Notes came out in a flurry, much like her racing towards the bridge. She could almost see a picture of the scene painting itself before her. The tempo changed as Voxis dropped from the sky, jumping a beat or two as her heart had when he'd startled her. He caught her gaze from his seat and winked at her.

The music changed again; the melody becoming grating and annoying. Voxis's expression drooped.

It turned sweet once she set eyes on the spectral tower before them, and sweeter still when Tania laid eyes on Zana.

The door to the room opened, and Collis slipped in. The music pouring from Zana's mouth rose around them as Tania's heart swelled with joy.

Out of the corner of her eye, she saw Voxis grinning smugly.

Tania only had eyes for the lanky Returned walking towards her.

Zana raised a hand and beckoned Collis closer.

The tempo increased along with Tania's racing heart as he approached.

As soon as the taller boy reached her, he held out his hand, and Tania reached out to grasp it.

White light poured from Zana's form, surrounding the pair even as her music rose, making Tania hurt from smiling so much.

Gently, Collis removed Tania's hand from Zana's, and the older Ilutri slumped, her mouth finally closing.

The music slowly faded away.

"That was amazing," Tania said softly.

"So, it's true." Voxis stood, and his face twisted as if he couldn't decide which expression to wear. Glaring, snarling, he settled on a tight grin. "Ronah's Linked has found her soul's match."

Tania blinked up at Collis.

He smiled down at her gently.

And they both ignored the noise when the door slammed shut.

She wasn't sure how long they'd stood there, staring into each other's eyes, before Zana cleared her throat.

"Not quite the way I'd intended you to find out."

"You knew?" They said together, voices echoing through the room once more.

Inthday

Second day of the fourth week of Suncrest

The Datzal glared at him as he shifted into the stone room.

"Come to free me or come to gloat?"

Samuel tilted his head. The creature looked even more gaunt than before.

"Perhaps I've come to end your suffering," he said.

The Datzal flinched.

Had they been on an even playing field, Samuel doubted that reaction would have shown. In a Realm that was burning the very soul of the Dark being, they had less restraint. Trapped in a Light cage was only speeding things up.

"So, there is something you want," he said.

"To serve our Queen." The words sounded forced.

"*Your* Queen."

"Traitor!" the Datzal spat through the bars.

"Hardly." Samuel started walking around the cage, careful not to get too close. "We are clearly not the same species, so *your* Queen can't be mine."

Staring at him from sunken eyes, the Datzal chuckled, then laughed. Ze laughed for so long, jet-black tears trickled down zir cheeks.

Samuel watched, mildly amused, as the Datzal reached out to stop themselves from falling and hissed as their hand touched the bar.

The room was oddly quiet. Stiflingly so.

"You have no idea, do you?"

"I know many things, and there are many more I have yet to discover."

Moving as close to the bars as they could without getting burnt, the Datzal glared at him. "Discover this then, great Golden Priest. We share an ancestor."

Raising an eyebrow, Samuel refused to take the bait. "Go back far enough, and we all share a common ancestor."

The Datzal rolled their eyes. "Your father was my grandfather."

Samuel laughed. "Are you suggesting that War'Jan started your line?" That wasn't what the spy was suggesting at all, but it wouldn't hurt to play along.

A devious grin crossed blurring features as the Datzal drew back. "Hardly. You, like me, can shapeshift. Can travel to a wider range of Realms. You, like me, bow to our true Queen."

The last, he noted, was almost a threat. "So, you are accusing the Queen of the Q'Aralide of being unfaithful to her bonded mate?"

"She is as true to War'Jan as he is to her."

So, not at all then. Samuel deciphered. "And our common ancestor?"

"My father was but a babe when his father disappeared. He never returned. Instead, the Queen came to grant us freedom."

Hidden inside sunken eyes was the truth.

Oalark had enslaved a race and made them do her bidding. Or die trying.

"And your grandfather?"

"His corpse was dangled over us. My father bartered for his return, as Oalark bled my grandfater dry on the egg he was said to have sired." The Datzal looked down. "My siblings swore revenge. They were felled one by one until there were but a handful of us left."

Samuel bit back his sigh. The story sounded like so many others he'd played the villain in. He was sure that the spy was trying to tug on heartstrings that had withered away long ago.

"The Queen trained us. She broke us, every bone and spirit, and rebuilt us to have a better purpose. To gather the information she needed to act against those who would harm her. Those like my grandfather." The Datzal raised their gaze and glared at him. "And like you."

"When had I ever shown that I was anything but faithful to the Queen?"

The laugh was as dry as the parchment-thin skin on their face. "See, Priest, my father's line carried the shapeshifting abilities, but my mother's line... She carried the ability to see into another's soul. And I can see yours. I knew, from the moment you left Altum, that you would find your path going against the Queen."

Here it comes, Samuel groaned internally.

"And I wish to join you."

Honestly, no imagination at all.

There was a growl from the shadows that Samuel recognised. His gaze slipped to the side and caught the two glowing points of light.

He looked at the Datzal and grinned. The scrape of bone on stone sent shivers down zir spine.

"Tempting, of course. How could I ignore such an eloquent speech?"

The Datzal's face remained impassive, but he could see the fire of glee lit in their eyes.

Slowly, to add to the ominous effect he was hoping to create, Samuel drew on the light sources in the room. Not in the cage, but everything else. He pulled towards him, allowing the room to grow dimmer until only the bars remained lit.

"The thing is"–Samuel stepped closer, knowing the glow reflected eerily across his skin as he allowed his scales to ripple–"I'm no traitor."

"Liar!" the Datzal spat.

"Be a good little captive and expire already."

"How are you going to..." Their words were cut off, and a shriek of pain filled the room.

Samuel sat back and watched the shadow from under his bed slip through the bars, its jaws solid enough now to latch onto the Datzal's throat. Impassively, he looked on as the spy who had tormented him for so long met their end.

'Jonathan, can you release the bars of the cage without coming in?' Samuel sent. He wasn't sure why, but as his shadow sat licking his chops and cleaning the blood off his now furry muzzle, Samuel had the distinct impression that he shouldn't share his fully formed friend with anyone else.

'*What happened to the spy?*'

The shadow paused in his cleaning and looked up, as if he'd heard the thought Jonathan had sent only to him.

'*They begged to die.*' Well, they might have, if their vocal chords hadn't been ripped out.

The Guardian's sigh echoed through his skull. '*Very well.*'

Bars of the cage melted away, and his shadow came to stand next to him, a heavy weight able to lean against him comfortably. Samuel looked down and ruffled the dark fur.

Eyes as green as the brightest leaves glanced back at him.

Shari's Sanctuary

Shari stood to the side and grinned as Jetonyx did a loop in the air above. The hatchling was clearly enjoying his time in her sanctuary.

Samuel had shifted in to check on his young charges. Once he'd arrived, however, he stayed standing where he was, taking everything in with wide eyes. "This... you did all this?"

Shari nodded.

"It's Darker Innarn than I thought it would be," Samuel said finally. "Much better suited to Jetonyx than Bazaven was."

"I'm glad."

"I think it's best if we had someone to watch over him, don't you?"

"I'm not staying in here until the conclave," Shari growled.

"No... no, that wasn't what I... I think I have just the creature for the job. May I?"

"If that mythical herd of fulni start rampaging through my sanctuary, I will not be happy," Shari warned.

Shaking his head, Samuel laughed. "No fulni. Well, I'm not sure what he is, to be honest."

"Fine. Try me."

Samuel moved closer to a bush and knelt. Was this Innarn she hadn't seen before? Shari crept closer.

Waving his fingers through the air, Samuel said a few whispered words, and two glowing green eyes appeared in the shadows under the bush.

"Zoomer?" Shari whispered.

The shadow moved in a blur, knocking the Altoriae flat on her back, long thin tongue whipping out to lick at her face with blurring speed. His jet-black body wriggled with happiness.

"Zoomer," she laughed. The palon slurped away her tears.

"You know this creature?"

Something in Samuel's posture had changed. Hardened.

"I did, long ago. Zoomer was my first pet. My palon. Anriluka..."

Samuel sighed. "Of course."

"Have you been looking after him?"

The weight of his gaze on her, even as she struggled to take hers away from the miracle currently bouncing on her chest.

"Yes." The word was clipped, as though he was afraid of her reaction.

"You are brilliant." She finally tore her gaze off Zoomer and looked at Samuel.

"I suppose you'll want him with you all the time, now." His hands were shoved into his pockets, head bowed like he couldn't bear to watch their reunion.

At his words, Zoomer froze. He looked between the two and slowly moved off Shari to stand by Samuel's side. The palon nudged Samuel with his head, whimpering.

"Somehow, I think he wants to see both of us."

Tension melted from Samuel, and he knelt to ruffle Zoomer's head.

'Snack?' Jetonyx had spied them and landed close enough to sniff the palon.

"No!" Shari and Samuel said together.

Samuel drew himself upright. "This is a creature of the shadows. Hurt him, and I will not be pleased." His eyes flashed golden, hand resting on Zoomer's head as the palon growled at the much larger Q'Aralide.

'Aww. You said I'd get a snack.'

"I did. And I have brought you one."

Jetonyx eyed Shari, who shook her head. "Really?"

Sighing, Samuel waved his hand, and four large nalparak beasts appeared.

'Lots of snacks.' Jetonyx sounded awed as the beasts ran. 'Thanks!'

"Children are always the same." Samuel shook his head. "Full belly, a safe place to sleep, and they're happy."

Shari grinned. "I'd say it's a bit more than that."

CHAPTER NINE

Lissae

Kerday

Third day of the fourth week of Suncrest

The Guardian was looking at him again.

Samuel lowered his book and raised his brow. "Yes?"

Giving him an enigmatic smile, Jonathan shook his head. "Nothing."

"Really?" Samuel stared at the other man.

Shaking his head, Jonathan said, "Shari told me about Zoomer."

"Shadow."

"Sorry?"

"I've been calling him the shadow under my... couch," Samuel admitted.

Jonathan mouthed the words.

"I couldn't very well tell Shari that."

"True." Jonathan looked down at the paperwork spread across his desk.

One... two... three... four...

"Why couldn't you tell her?"

There it is. "Do you think it would help her to know that I've seen the palon's insides? That I've been bringing back bones and limbs for it to gather enough strength to reform. That there's a possibility, or probability, I should say, that Zoomer, as she knew him, no longer exists?"

Rubbing a finger over his lips, Jonathan seemed to consider his words. "I think Shari knows..."

"I doubt it. You didn't see what she was like with the creature." *With my creature,* he wanted to howl. Instead, he gazed at the pages, hoping the Guardian would leave him be.

"Did you know he was Shari's?"

"No." The word escaped his lips and sounded exactly as sulky as he felt.

"The wonderful thing about Shari is that she's happy to share."

Samuel wanted to shout. To say that *he* didn't want to share. Couldn't he have someone to come home to who wanted to spend time with him?

He bit back a sigh.

Shari might be happy enough to share, but he wasn't about to ask her to do so.

In a different part of the castle, Shari sat with her ever-expanding guild. She wanted to go over their duties whilst Jonathan was distracted.

"And you have to make him rest. He's notorious for continuing to fight when wounded," Shari said, looking earnestly around the table.

"So that's where you get it from," Amara joked.

"He's far worse than me," Shari admitted. Well, Jonathan would say it was the other way around, but she was hardly going to tell her guild that. "Support Tania as Ronah's Linked. And there have been some disturbing reports that the mainlanders will launch an attack any day."

The group stopped laughing and joking.

"Seriously?" Talofa asked.

"Yes. I have someone giving me information, but ze's been quiet for a while now." Shari dared not send to Skye if she could help it, but an update wouldn't hurt.

"Alright. Look after the Guardian, support the Linked, watch out for attacks. Anything else?" Raven said, leaning against the door frame and looking like he was moments away from disappearing through it.

"Yes." Shari looked around the group, taking in those who had volunteered to join a guild they expected her to run after barely meeting her. "Look after each other. Make sure a healer is on each patrol, and one waiting at the museum. Sometimes, a send really is too far away."

There was a swell of murmurs through the room.

"I don't just mean on patrol, either. This is a lonely job. It's heart-wrenching, and back-breaking, and not something that should be attempted alone. Please, please take care of each other. Check in, bring food, make time to have fun together. It doesn't have to be all of you—that would be an organisational nightmare."

Someone laughed, and Shari grinned.

"It would mean a lot if you're all in one piece when I come back."

"We'll try," Raven said.

"That's all I can ask." Shari grinned back, hoping the others would take her cue and ignore the welling tears.

Tania grinned as the crystal in front of her hummed. It glowed gently, hovering above her practice board, before slowly lowering.

"Brilliant!" Cyrus said. Talhan's Link looked even more excited than usual. "You're a natural at this. What's your Crystal Innarn rating?"

"Rating?" Tania asked.

Cyrus pushed his hover chair away from the bench and looked at her over the thick goggles he'd donned. "Yeah, the colour of the orange bead on your bracelet."

Her eyes darted about his workshop, looking for a clue as to what he was talking about. There were half-finished machines, hunks of uncarved crystal, and buckets of bolts, but no bracelets.

"I... What bracelet?" The joy of getting the crystal to hover was shrinking under questions she felt she should know the answer to, but didn't.

"First day of school on the islands, you get your Innarn tested, and you get a bracelet showing your rating. The brighter the stone, the higher the rating."

"Um, is that when Lissae tests you?"

"Yeah."

"Lissae never tested me. The Mayor and the elders of Ronah did, but we don't have a high enough Crystal Innarnian." Tania felt mildly embarrassed at the lack, especially as Cyrus's face fell.

"Huh. Well, I suppose one of our elders could test you." He gazed into the distance, eyes focused on nothing. It was a look Tania was beginning to associate with sending to others. "Perfect! Great. Temira will test you."

Tania grinned. She and Cyrus chatted for a while. It wasn't long before Talhan's technomancer strode in, glaring as if she'd heard the thoughts in Tania's head.

"She's not been tested, and you're allowing her to access crystal?" Temira scolded him.

Cyrus shrunk a little under her fury. "I only just found out."

Breathing heavily out of her nose, Temira glared at him for a moment longer before turning to Tania. "Stand."

Immediately, she hopped to her feet.

Temira held her arms out to the side. A gently orange glow slowly crept to surround her. The technomancer towered over Tania, the lighter stripes in her blue skin picking up the orange, making her look ethereal and dangerous. Her eyes slipped closed. Temira held her hands out as if she was about to give Tania a hug, but she didn't move any closer.

"Best if you close your eyes," Cyrus whispered.

One of Temira's eyes opened and glared at them both before sliding shut again.

Nerves got the best of her, and Tania, trying not to chuckle, closed her eyes. She felt Temira's Innarn pulse through her very core. She was so busy assuring Ronah that she was fine, she almost missed the supernova happening in Cyrus's workshop.

Hissing as the foreign Innarn bordered on pain, Tania was brought back to a glow so bright that she could see it through her eyelids.

The pain and the glow faded. It took Tania a moment to blink away the spots behind her eyes. When she could see clearly, she looked up as the tail of Temira's coat snapping through the doorway.

"What... what just happened?"

"You're a pretty high-level crystal user. I think it reminded Temira of... someone else," Cyrus said, unable to meet her gaze.

Xani.

Bowing her head, Tania wished she'd had a chance to know Xani, Temira's friend and co-technomancer before she'd been possessed by rogue crystal determined to kill them all.

"Oh," Tania said. Suddenly, she felt quite small.

Cyrus slapped his hands on his thighs, making her jump. "You know what? We need a change of scenery. Why don't we grab Zana and finish up the plan for meeting with Cantash?"

Tania nodded, grateful for the distraction.

The pair wandered from Cyrus's workshop to the surface. Just as they left the building, Zana materialised to the side of the Techno Centre's entrance.

"I wondered when we were going to meet again," Zana said mildly.

"Come, I know a great little cafe where we can plan *and* have something delicious to eat!" Cyrus held out his arms, and Zana daintily rested her hand on one, while Tania looped her arm around the other.

Spending the rest of the day planning sounded like an idea. Especially if she could come up with a way to apologise to Temira while she was at it.

Narday

Fourth day of the fourth week of Suncrest

Samuel slowly made his way to the gazebo in the town square, Lizbeth resting one hand on his arm and prattling away about the best time to plant buds.

"And you should always ensure you turn widdershins three times before placing the julipa bud in the ground," she said seriously as they stepped into the shade of the gazebo.

Glancing down at his companion, he spotted the corner of her lips twitching, and he rolled his eyes. "Is that so?" he asked, voice as smooth as honey.

She laughed. "Ah, so he is paying attention."

Shaking his head, Samuel made sure she was seated first, then pulled a basket of food from his pocket Realm. "I do, occasionally, pay attention to others."

Lizbeth laughed again. "I'm sure." Her unerring hands helped to unpack the basket, filling plates with food as he poured their drinks. "How are you finding living by yourself?"

Samuel looked around the square. It was bustling, beings walking past, chattering as they made their way to the surrounding shops, and some with the same idea they had—a pleasant lunch in the warm weather. There had been reports of storms and a colder climate as the Shifting Islands came together. He passed her a glass and took a plate in return. "It is... odd. There are so many beings around. I find it eery to go home to silence." He took a bite. *And now I won't even have my shadow for company.*

"Your shadow?"

Son of a tuzar. He must have projected the last bit. Either that or Lizbeth really was a mind reader. "Not actually my shadow, but more a shade. He's been staying with me for a while, but now he's keeping someone else company."

Staring blankly at him, Lizbeth raised her eyebrows. "This must be someone you care about."

Thinking of Jetonyx, and how the hatchling had braved running away to help him, and Shari's wide-eyed disbelief at the return of her pet, Samuel tried for nonchalance and shrugged.

Patting his arm, Lizbeth smiled. "It's okay to care about others."

"I don't think he knows how," a female voice off to the side of the gazebo said.

Forcing himself not to lash out, Samuel instead vented on the food Lizbeth had piled onto his plate. Taking a large bite of some sort of eggy thing in a pastry shell, stuffed full of savoury herbs and with the barest hint of meat, he grinned with closed lips. She'd made it just for him then.

The female, wearing ridiculously tall heels, teetered into the gazebo as if she'd been invited.

Samuel glared at her.

She flicked her long, blonde hair over her shoulder. "Nothing to say?" she taunted.

"We're having lunch, Anika." Lizbeth sounded like a long-suffering host. "Unfortunately, only enough for two. Can we help you?"

Anika. The name sounded familiar. Sending his Innarn out, he brushed against her. A dense, blank space greeted him. "Ah. The rassu."

The girl bristled. "That's not what you said when we first met."

"I didn't say much at all. You were surrounded by your friends and came over to a group of Wisara I was with. You said 'Well met, gentlemen. You could be looking at the next Altoriae, but I'll never tell.' And then you winked."

"Well, I wasn't wrong. You could have been. I knew she was my age. And you latched on to me fast enough."

"I was hoping for an introduction," Samuel said, taking another bite. *'What is this?'* he sent to Lizbeth.

She responded with vague thoughts of thinking with his belly. *'Quiche.'*

'No, it's delicious.' He sent her a grin.

Lizbeth smiled back.

"I didn't come over here to rehash our first meeting," Anika fumed.

"Then why bring it up?"

Anika sighed. "I wanted to talk to you about your clothing choices."

Samuel took another bite, slowly chewing and swallowing. "What's wrong with my clothing?" He glanced down. Black shirt, black pants. It was movable, comfortable, and he looked good in it.

"There is more than one shade, Sammy." She reached over and snagged a rutenberry from the bowl.

He raised an unimpressed eyebrow.

"Sorry, Samuel." Anika rolled her eyes. "Colour would look good on you, and as the Guardian's apprentice, you need to look good."

"Menacing works just as well."

"You can look menacing in something other than black," she said. "Shari lets me make her clothing for the joining ceremonies now. You should consider doing the same."

"Why?"

"Because…" Blank or not, Anika's thoughts were loud enough for anyone who was looking to hear them. *The sad little girl who had been looking forward to her first pet, only to see them with someone else.*

The tentacle carrying a tissue and oozing soothing words into her mind. A promise made—what difference would a bit of time on Lissae for the tentacle owner, when she offered the chance for Anika to use Innarn? She would finally make her parents happy!

Her pet, dead. Now trapped in a promise she didn't want a bar of, but couldn't break.

Struggling with the foreign power. Forced to let the creature into Lissae. Living with the guilt, but not being able to admit it.

Wanting to make things right, but having only one thing she was good at. Staying up far too late at night, eyes blurring as she stitched together a dress for Shari, only to have the Altoriae shake her head. Trying again. And again, until she came up with a design the Altoriae could wear. The praise was still not enough to drown out the guilt thudding through her veins.

"Fine. Pick a colour, and I'll try it," he growled.

Anika blinked away the tears welling in her eyes and clapped her hands. "Fantastic! I'll have a few choices ready for our joining with Cantash."

"The joining that's happening at the end of the week?" Lizbeth asked, surprised.

"Of course."

Could his blind friend sense the brittleness he could see in Anika's smile? Ugh. He was going to have to be *nice*. "I have faith that Anika will have everything ready."

The girl beamed at him and rose. "Well, best get to work! I bid thee well," she said, and teetered off.

'*She's been touched by Innarn almost as Dark as yours, hasn't she?*' Lizbeth sent.

He chanced a glance her way. She was serenely sipping from a teacup. '*Yes. She has.*'

'*Anika will need all the friends she can get.*'

Fighting the urge to stand and storm away, he took another bite from the quiche. "Don't we all."

Rasshday
Fifth day of the fourth week of Suncrest

Ronah was calm, despite everyone on her surface rushing around with last-minute preparations.

Tania breathed in through her mouth, out through her nose, trying to let the frenetic energy filling her up subside into something useful.

In... Out... In... Out...

There was a tickle of warning. Someone familiar was coming up behind her.

In... seaspray and candlewood... Out...

A large, warm hand rested gently on her shoulder, and the buzzing along her nerve endings slowly faded until she could think again. Tania sank back into Collis's chest.

"Thank you," she whispered.

"I do not understand how you are so calm most of the time. There are a lot of... heightened emotions these days."

She laughed. "Heightened, or on display?"

Collis tipped his head in agreement. "Possibly both."

"I know that our population isn't what it was when you were a boy, but I think people have found that squashing their emotions isn't good for anyone, least of all the Linked." Tania had noticed that hanging around with large groups of the Returned left her weary right down to her bones, yet she could be around her... contemporaries? The ones who had been on the isle when she arrived. She wasn't sure what to call them anymore. But she could spend days with them without the same weariness. Although, the Returned had suffered more than anyone else she knew. Maybe her energy was helping to heal them? She couldn't begrudge them that.

"Do you have much left to do for the joining?"

"Most of it is in hand. Anika is taking care of my dress. Zana has my 'ceremonial robes'. Cyrus has the non-sentient crystals ready to go. And Ronah can't wait to meet up with her sibling again."

Under their feet, the ground rocked gently, and Tania laughed, tipping her head back to glance at Collis's face.

He was smiling at her, eyes bright.

Something twisted in her belly, and she did her best not to gasp. "Right. There are still the last-minute decorations, of course."

"Of course." He was looking at her fondly.

Tania blushed and tucked a strand of hair behind her ear.

Holding out his hands, Collis smiled at her. "Where would you like them?"

Tania pointed out the high spots she'd been leaving for him to decorate. How did a Linked go about asking someone to a ceremony?

For a moment, she thought about asking Zana and blanched. Asking the strict Ilutri Linked would be like talking to her mother.

She'd have to speak to Cyrus. Maybe he'd know.

"Don't slouch," Samuel snapped, a stinging line of Dark Innarn leaving his fingertips and landing sharply on her side.

Shari sucked in a breath and glared at him. "If I sat up any straighter, my spine would bend backwards."

"Oalark won't care. This lesson is in case something happens to Jetonyx. You can't be unprepared for the Dark Conclave's table."

Closing her eyes and breathing out slowly, she counted backwards from ten. "Tell me what I need to know to survive."

"Survival is not guaranteed at the Dark Conclave." Samuel slumped in his seat, running his hands through his hair. "If Oalark gets annoyed at the way you are breathing, at how loudly you blink, at the colour of the sky that morning, we could all be dead. *You* would be dead. Lissae can't save you from her."

"You'd be surprised at what Lissae can do." Shari smiled to hide her unease. Lissae had been quiet now. She'd thought she'd heard a groan every time Ronah joined with another Shifting Island, but that could be the thought of dealing with yet *more* people who knew her secret, who wanted to poke and prod her and see what made the Altoriae tick.

"Oalark will test you. One of the easiest ways is with food."

"Food?"

"She likes to serve living, squirming things. It's a sure-fire way of ruling out those from the Lighter Realms."

"Living... She makes you eat things that are living?" Shari felt her gut rolling at the thought.

"That reaction... right there—you'd be dead in your seat."

Shari groaned. "I don't even eat meat. How could... okay. Fine." Her chair skidded back as she stood. "Talhan has beings from all over Lissae. Surely someone has a wriggly vine thing for us to practice with?"

"Or..." Samuel shot her a look and waved his hand.

A bowl of soup appeared on the table.

"Sit."

Sliding back into her seat, Shari looked at the bowl warily. She glanced at Samuel.

"Eat."

Who knew a single-syllable word could sound so ominous? Gamely, she picked up the spoon and slid it into the liquid. A thin, grey tentacle reached out and grasped the side of the spoon. Something pulled, and an eye was blinking at her from the thick liquid. *Don't scream, don't scream, don't scream.* Gamely, Shari lifted the spoon, and the little creature clung on. Long, scaly tentacles joined a grey, bulbous body, topped with two enormous eyes that stared up at her, the whites showing. It took everything in Shari not to shudder. She started lowering the spoon, and the creature climbed onto it. Shari paused, looking at it and contemplating who could want to eat something so cute.

Then it launched itself at her face.

Shari shrieked, and the thing forced its head into her mouth. She fell backwards, chair and all, her head hitting the ground with a thud. Tentacles slapped against the inside of her mouth, and Shari gagged.

Across the room, Samuel was saying, "It wants to be eaten."

Shifting the thing away from her face and back into her soup, she stood, safely out of lunging range. "Wants to be eaten?" Neither of them mentioned how her voice trembled.

"They are raised watching their parents get eaten and believe they will be reunited with their family in the stomachs of others."

"That's..." Shari couldn't even find the words for how horrified she felt.

"That's the way Oalark will know you aren't part of the conclave. Everyone there will be delighted at the thought of tasting the dofi."

"So, they're a delicacy?"

"Yes." Samuel reached over and pulled her bowl towards himself. He raised the spoon just out of the liquid and the dofi obediently hopped on. Lifting it to his mouth, he opened it and swallowed the creature whole.

Shari looked away. She had no issues with those who ate meat. In some Realms, it was the only sustenance available. But she couldn't bring herself to do it. "How do I…"

"You are superb at shifting things."

She glanced his way in time to spot another dofi tentacle wrapping around his spoon. "I could shift it from my mouth into your stomach?"

Samuel grinned at her. "Exactly."

CHAPTER TEN

Vebaday

Sixth day of the fourth week of Suncrest

Beings scattered out of the path of the technomancer.

Temira turned to roll her eyes in exasperation with Xani... only for the B.I.T. by her side to cheep at her.

A reminder that she was alone again.

"Temira!" a voice called.

The tall, blue-skinned Techno-Innarnian turned, raising a hand to keep the glare of the morning sun out of her eyes. "Tania."

Ronah's Linked skipped up the path towards her, joy in every part of her being. "I'm so glad I caught you! Ronah said you were coming to check her crystals today."

Ignoring the flinch of those nearest them, Temira nodded stiffly. "I am."

"Brilliant! I wish I could watch, but I've got to get to school. Will I see you at the joining?"

"Do you want to?"

Tania blinked. "Of course I do."

"Then, yes. I shall see you there."

The young Linked beamed at her before scurrying away to join her peers.

Was I ever so young?

Turning back to her path, Temira marched on. There were a few scowls and mutters as she went, but nothing she wasn't used to. After a century, she'd learned to block them out. Cyrus had asked her to walk the improved B.I.T. around Ronah, but Temira couldn't see the point of it. Although, most beings seemed to avoid the training device, and not her, which was an agreeable change of pace.

Arriving at the castle, Temira found a likely spot to sit near the front door and settled down. She stroked the paving in front of her, and it split apart. A large, black crystal rose slowly from the ground. Why anyone would place the lode crystal in such an obvious spot had always been an enigma to her.

It hummed gently at her, and she hummed back. Placing her hands on the smoothed sides of the crystal, she could almost cry at how neglected it was. But she poured her Innarn into the glowing stone, bringing it back to full strength. Hands still on the lode crystal, she closed her eyes and sent out a pulse of Innarn. Crystals all over Ronah lit up dimly in the map the lode crystal was creating in her mind. She followed the paths, tending to each crystal, repairing cracks, polishing, probing, knitting the stone back together and re-powering them.

Long moments were spent re-teaching the crystals of Ronah to once more call upon the other elements for their power. Reminding them to keep their people safe. Ensuring that the ward crystals were strong enough to keep out the unwanted, and warm enough to let the loved through.

Temira lost herself in the thrum of the work, fixing, cleaning, replenishing, until her hands cramped and she fell back, done. The map slowly faded from her mind, and the bright lights that were the crystals winked at her, one by one, until they all faded away. And she was left in the dark.

"Hey. Are you alright?"

Opening her eyes, Temira blinked up at the speaker until her vision cleared.

The girl was only slightly bigger than Tania, but she sported the reddest hair Temira had ever seen. Dusk was painting the sky in pretty oranges and pinks. She'd been working with the crystals all day. "Drink?" she rasped.

"Oh. Oh, sure! Come on. Let's get you inside. I'm Amara, by the way," the girl chattered as she helped Temira to her feet and led her inside the castle.

She was deposited into a comfortable seat and had a moment of regret that she'd not asked for one of these before she started. Her bones were getting too old to be sitting on the ground all day.

Another being, a male, came and slid a cool glass of quass juice over to her. Temira took a grateful sip. "My thanks."

"I'm only sorry I couldn't get to you sooner," the redhead was saying. "I tried to, but your B.I.T. is, well, scary. Wouldn't let me near."

Temira raised a brow. Clearly, Cyrus had been tampering with the training device. It was not designed to guard.

"But you're just in time to see Shari changing!" Amara said.

Temira's eyebrows rose. "I have no desire to see the Altoriae get dressed."

Amara's cheeks went the same colour as her hair, and the boy who'd brought the drink laughed so hard, he fell back into a seat.

"Not dressed, changed. Like, changeling? Morphing her form."

"Ah. Yes, I would like to see that."

"Great, let's go!" The redhead jumped to her feet and led the way out of the room, tripping a time or two as she went.

"Getting dressed," the boy behind them chuckled. "She'd kill anyone who tried to watch that."

"As she should." Temira nodded solemnly.

The boy laughed again.

"I am one hundred percent sure that I do not need an audience for this," Shari grumbled.

She stood opposite Samuel on the training grounds. Half the guild and various others from around Ronah, Rakemyst, and Talhan littered the stands.

'They're curious to see how the Altoriae learns a new technique,' Jonathan sent to her. 'Have to admit, I'm curious too. I've never really helped you learn something new, only refined what you had already learned.'

"Still not a thing to be gawked at," she grumbled.

"At least your punishment is laughter and not a randy Queen sizing you up to see if you'd best be eaten or mated," Samuel said.

Shari blanched. "Ew."

"Exactly. It does up the stakes a bit, though."

"Ugh. Let's get started. How do you change?"

"Like this." Samuel was standing there one moment, and a giant golden three-eyed Q'Aralide was in his place the next.

Beings in the stand screamed.

Shari rolled her eyes. "That doesn't exactly tell me how to change. Just that you can."

Samuel shifted back. "Changing into your other form takes time. It took me decades to change so seamlessly. You don't need to change the entire way, just enough to blur your features if the hatchling's pocket Realm fails."

Sighing, Shari nodded.

"You are much like the hatchlings. You learn through watching others and then adapting what they do to suit your needs, yes?"

Thinking back through the different ways she'd learned how to do things, she nodded slowly.

"Writing it down, assigning gestures, using made-up words, none of it will help your focus. Enter my mind, and I'll change again. See what it feels like, how my cells change, what my bones do." Samuel was looking at her, and Shari had the sense he was seeing more than what was on the surface.

"I can do that," she said.

Catching his gaze, she slipped into his mind. His thoughts were well hidden behind a rolling wall she didn't want to get close to. Instead of peeking, she steadied herself and nodded.

Samuel shifted, just his hand at first. He held it out, and Shari had a moment of dual vision, where she saw through both of their eyes. Sliding hers closed, she focused again. Samuel changed his other hand, and Shari could feel the shift in his cells, feel his bones lengthening and reforming, feel the scales pushing through the skin, and the razor-sharp pain as the claws cut through sensitive fingertips.

"And back again." His voice sounded loud and far away at the same time.

Claws retracted, sliding painfully along the bones of his hand, scales pulled back, sizzling hot into his skin. Bones ground down, shortening back to the length that was somewhat familiar. Although there wasn't the constant feeling of too-tight skin standing too close to the open fire any more, there was a dull, thudding ache that seemed buried deep in his body.

She wasn't sure if it was from the change, or just from being on Lissae.

"Now you try."

Slowly, Shari detached herself from his mind and slipped back into her own. For a moment, her skin felt foreign.

Samuel had followed her into her head.

'Start on the cells,' he advised. *'Try to move them to what you want them to be.'*

For a long moment, Shari thought. She was a healer who had seen the insides of enough beings to know them with sufficient detail to change into them. Focusing on what the Datzal had looked like when ze'd been captured, Shari closed her eyes and willed her cells to change. She could see the way the organs had been stacked in the emancipated rib cage, the sunken eyes, the lank hair. There was a burning rumble in her cells, and Shari could feel them strain the longer she focused.

Something inside her ripped, and all she knew was darkness.

When Collis burst through the doors of the tavern, panting, Arilla was quite proud that she didn't hurl the cup she'd been holding at his head.

"Shari... Healers..."

At those words, she dropped it instead.

"Calem!" she yelled, halfway to the door already.

Her husband poked his head out of the kitchen doors, flour streaks on one cheek. "Yes?"

"Shari's at the Healers Centre?" It was half a question. At Collis's nod, she turned back to Calem, who had already disappeared.

Everything in Arilla wanted to run to the Healers Centre to see if Shari was alright, but there were customers in the shop, and from the smell, Calem was in the middle of cooking something.

"Go," Collis said. "I'll stay here and make sure everyone is helped."

Arilla nodded, handing him the towel she'd been using. "Thank you," she said.

Then she ran.

Lungs burning, and vowing to start up her morning runs again, Arilla took a moment outside the centre doors to breathe. Wiping her sweaty fringe out of her face, she entered the building.

Healer Edwards took one look at her and rose from behind the desk. "Follow me," he said.

Trying not to trip over suddenly shaky legs, Arilla followed Healer Edwards down one hall and along another until they arrived at the far corner of the building.

"Healer Holli and Healer Ribeck have stabilised the Altoriae," Healer Edwards said quietly as they entered the room.

Shari looked tiny on the bed, the colourful quilt seeming to emphasise how pale she was. Calem was by her side, holding onto one of Shari's hands.

"Thank you," Arilla said, as the Junior Healer slipped from the room.

"It was a training exercise," Jonathan said, making Arilla jump.

She moved to the bed and shared a look with her husband.

"Training? How did training leave Shari like this?" Calem asked.

Their daughter was covered in bandages.

"Shari was attempting to learn how to change her form." The Guardian sounded as emotionally tired as she felt.

Arilla couldn't bring herself to care. Not when Shari was lying on the bed looking like a museum exhibition.

"It may be best if she doesn't do that again," Arilla said softly. She'd... they'd never forbidden Shari anything to do with Innarn before, as much as it pained her. But if this was just from a training exercise, what would it be like when she succeeded?

"I warned her," another voice said.

Jonathan's new apprentice was standing in the corner, arms crossed tight over his chest, looking mournful.

"You were the one who taught her?" Calem's voice was deceptively light. Arilla reached over the bed and grabbed his free hand, shaking her head. She hadn't heard that tone in years, but she knew what it meant. Her ex-boyfriend and younger brother would remember too, if he hadn't knocked them unconscious thirty seconds after they'd heard him speak like that.

Calem gripped her tight and clenched his jaw.

She didn't let go.

"She fought to learn," Jonathan said.

Arilla glanced around and found the men were all staring at her daughter. Something about the looks they wore said that Shari would be protected wherever she went. Turning back to Shari, Arilla sank down beside the bed, stroking her forehead.

"If it's any consolation," Samuel said, "She did far better than I on my first try."

Gripping Calem's hand tighter, she glared daggers at Samuel. Shari waking to find the apprentice beaten to a pulp would not help matters.

"Coulda warned me," Shari rasped.

"Shari." Arilla's voice cracked. The men talking around her but couldn't take her eyes away from Shari's face.

"Mum." Shari tried to grin. "Dad. Well met."

"What happened?" Arilla asked softly.

"I... don't know. Was aiming for smaller. Some things I'm just not good at."

"And some things, you won't be trying again," Calem said, eyes hard.

Shari nodded. "Hol' on."

A green glow surrounded the bed, and Shari gasped—a harsh, rattly sound. Something went *snap* and there were a series of cracks before the glow faded.

"All better," Shari said. She grinned and went to sit up.

"You might be used to healing on a battlefield, and getting straight back up again, but you've just spent a huge amount of Innarn. You need to rest," Arilla said, gently pushing her back down.

"Between the joining ceremony and your... patrolling time off-Realm, it would be a good idea to listen to your mother," Jonathan added.

Arilla looked up as Calem shoot him a grateful look.

Shari wavered. Arilla sensed the absolute need for her daughter to get back up and keep going, and couldn't help the tears welling in her eyes. Shari really needed to rest, not go out and tear herself to shreds again.

"Fine. I'll stay in bed."

"A few lazy days sound just like what the healer would order." Healer Holli stood in the doorway, smiling at them. "I felt the pulse of Healing Innarn and figured it could only be one patient. Thought it best to check on you."

Stepping out of the way, Arilla walked around Shari's bed and rested her head on Calem's shoulder whilst Holli removed the bandages with a sweep of her hand.

Curling up and around Shari's bare arms was a single line of scar tissue. It was as if someone had tried to create a spiral out of her limbs and pasted her back together at the end.

Clenching her jaw hard, Arilla blinked away the tears. She didn't want Shari to see them and mistake her waterworks for pity. Because it wasn't. She was helpless in the fight her daughter was the leader in. And there was no way that she could stop the hurt Shari went through. And if her arms looked like this, what was the rest of her body like?

Shari raised her hand—on each finger, there was a spiralling red scar as well. They all met up near her wrist and wove together into the thicker scar on her arm.

"Huh." Shari seemed nonplussed. Closing her eyes, she glowed green again. When the glow faded this time, the scars faded into old white lines. She inspected her hand again and tipped her head as if she was happy enough with the results.

"No more Innarn use, you," Holli scolded. She touched Shari's hand and poured her Innarn into it, her healing a lighter green that seemed to settle under Shari's skin and made her glow from the inside. "You need to stay until the glow fades, and then you can return home. By walking. Or having someone else shift you. Altoriae or not, you need to rest."

Blinking up at Holli, Shari's eyes slipped closed. "Think you're right," she murmured, and her head fell to the side.

"The healing took a lot out of her, but everything is where it's supposed to be," Holli said softly. "She lost a lot of blood, but we've replenished it and have more shifting in as needed. All she really needs is rest, and gentle food when she's up for it. Shari being Shari, she'll be ready to go again in the morning. If she were anyone else…" Holli shook her head. "Well, just keep her as rested as you can. At least until the joining."

Calem shared a look with her. "We'll do our best."

✦

Kerday

Third day of the first week of Sunfall

"Why must you continue to try and kill yourself?" Cyrus asked as he entered her room in the Healers Centre. "When there are plenty of other beings who would like to claim the honour?"

Shari giggled, ignoring Samuel's growl and her mother's gasp.

"Well met, Cyrus. What brings you to my bedside?" she asked. There had been little bar mournful looks and a constant, silent stream of self-recrimination from Samuel since she'd regained consciousness three days ago.

"I come bearing gifts! Well, gift, singular." He rummaged around in his satchel and pulled a flat black box which he handed to her. "Something the technomancer and I cooked up." Cyrus glanced around

121

as if expecting Temira to pop up behind him. In a mock-whisper, he said, "She hasn't slept since your accident."

Shari grinned as she took the box. "Thank you." Lifting her hands to take the box didn't hurt nearly as much as having a drink had before. Recovery was slower than she liked, but she could still feel the thrum of Lissae's Innarn flowing into her. Gently setting the box in her lap, she wriggled to get comfortable, and opened the lid.

A wide silver cuff gleamed at her. Carefully extracting it from the box, Shari inspected it. There were tiny scales carved into the metal, reminding her of Samuel's form.

"The silver is coating black crystal. The scales mean there's more surface area, which helps when you do this." Cyrus took the cuff and slipped it on his wrist. Stepping back from the bed and abruptly raising his arm, Cyrus almost smacked his nose with his fist. The scales seemed to melt from the cuff, raising and lowering to form a pointed oval shield. "Hit me."

From behind the shield, there was a thud and an, "Ow!"

Giggling, Shari went to flick her finger, but her dad grabbed her hand and shook his head. Winking, he snapped his hand out, and the shield absorbed the yellow strike easily.

"It'll keep absorbing Innarn, and you can use it to power your Innarn shield." Cyrus turned, so she could see him. Bringing his arm down in a reversal of the abrupt movement of before, he faced her and slid the cuff from his wrist. "It will still absorb in this form but takes direct hits better as a shield. We've been playing with this on and off for years, but—" Cyrus shrugged. "Temira decided it was time to finish it."

"This is amazing. Thank you," Shari said.

"Temira's idea, really. She saw what changing did to you, and it shook her." Rummaging around in his satchel again, Cyrus pulled out a long silver chain. "This one is all Temira. She said putting it in a box was pointless, as you'd just take it out again, anyway."

Smiling, Shari took it carefully, looking at the rainbow shimmering pendant at the end of the chain. "Pretty, but I think it'd get knocked off in battle."

"That's the beauty—the chain is long enough to be a belt or go over one shoulder and under the other. The flat back means it won't rub or poke at you when you're moving around." Cyrus was practically bouncing on his feet. "The pendant is a forged fire crystal, designed by the technomancer to alter the shape of the wearer. She's been working on the prototype for months but perfected it last night."

"Wait…"

"She won't have to change again?" her mum asked, voice wavering.

"That's right. All you have to do is slip it on," Cyrus replied.

Staring at the pendant, Shari bit her lip. Changing her features had almost killed her. What if putting this on undid the healing? What if it knocked her recovery back, and Samuel had to go alone?

"Can anyone wear it?" Jonathan asked.

"It's not coded for one person, so they should be able to…" Cyrus didn't have time to finish the sentence.

Jonathan reached over Shari and snatched the chain out of her hand, slipping it on before she could stop him.

An eery shriek poured from the pendant, and the Guardian's arms flung out to the side, head snapping back as his mouth fell open. He remained suspended in the air before dropping heavily.

Shari sucked in a breath.

Gone was the slightly goofy Guardian she'd always known. In his place was a sunken, hollow-eyed being with a rib cage that was far too pronounced. Longer, spindly fingers came up to stroke the pendant, which seemed to have adhered to his greying skin. His bald head gleamed in the light, but his eyes seemed to absorb every speck of bright in the room.

Looking harder, she could spot traces of Jonathan in the shape of his nose and the quirk of his lips.

He inspected his hands, running them along his torso. "The change isn't visual then, but physical as well," he said.

Cyrus gulped and nodded.

Shari shuddered. Jonathan's voice sounded dull, as if someone had stuffed wool in her ears.

"We, ah, we wanted the wearer to feel the way they looked if someone else was to touch them." Cyrus, like the rest of them, seemed torn between staring at Jonathan's transformation and not being able to bear looking at him.

The Guardian plucked at the pendant. "It seems to be stuck."

An image of Jonathan trapped in the form before them filled her mind. Him lining up to get groceries while people nervously skirted out of his way, sitting down to a diplomatic meeting with the mainlanders, only for them to scramble out of their chairs and trample each other to get away from him.

"His Innarn feels Darker," Samuel said.

"That's part of it. It'll latch on to the Darkest being in the room and reflect their Innarn to them. He'll feel Darker to you, but Lighter to Calem."

"Clever," Shari said.

Jonathan's fingers were scrabbling at the pendant now. Through their link, Shari felt his heartbeat increasing.

"Say 'Life of Lissae' to release the pendant," Cyrus said.

"Life of Lissae," Jonathan repeated. For a moment, Shari didn't think it was going to work. Jonathan tried again, and the pendant pulled free. The Guardian melted back into existence—hair, flesh, colour returning as if it had never gone. "That is the most disturbing feeling," he said, shaking as if he'd just come in from a rainstorm. "It's odd to have my body twist, but not painful at all."

Clever Guardian. He knows what I'm worried about.

"It's not really meant for short-term use. Temira wasn't sure how long you would need to change for but was assuming you'd need to hold your form for days, if not weeks."

"Thank you. And please thank Temira for me," Shari said.

"She suggested not putting it on until you're somewhere no one else can see you. Just in case there are spies around," Cyrus said.

"Bit paranoid, the technomancer, isn't she?" Samuel asked.

"And you're not?" Jonathan said.

Samuel tipped his head and smirked.

"She's right, more often than not." Cyrus shrugged. Hefting his satchel, he grinned at them. "Just came to drop these off. Now I can go report to Temira you're in one piece and finish the final preparations for the joining. I'll see you tonight?"

The group nodded, and Cyrus gave them a jaunty wave as he left.

Shari eyed the pendant. She couldn't decide if the idea of another forced social event and meeting more people was better or worse than attempting to change her form again, even if she had an aide this time. "It really doesn't hurt?"

Jonathan shook his head. "Feels kind of like shifting, but when you stay on the spot. It's disconcerting, but no pain."

"No pain is good," Arilla said, plucking the chain away from Shari and tucking the sheets in around her shoulders. "You can't test it now. There's too many of us around. You'll just have to wait until you're better."

"Speaking of." Healer Holli was in the doorway, grinning at them.

Only Shari was close enough to hear the tiny groan escape from her mum.

"I've been monitoring your Innarn use. You've done exceptionally well, considering. And your levels are back up to baseline. Whilst I would prefer that you rest up for a few more days, the Guardian has informed me of the schedule you're on."

"Schedule?"

"Immediately after the joining ceremony, we're going to have to leave," Samuel said.

Changing. Changing is definitely worse.

CHAPTER ELEVEN

Narday

Fourth day of the first week of Sunfall

Fresh out of the Healers Centre and decked in the dress Anika had delivered to her bedside, Shari looked as put together as she was going to get.

"You're so grown up," her mum said, smoothing out the wrinkles on the sleeves of the dove grey dress.

Shari had never seen anything like it. The neckline was a wide 'V' starting at her shoulders and leading to the dip below her throat. Symbols for Plasma, Air, Crystal and Fire Innarn decorated the collar, cuffs, and hem of the dress. The back and sides of the skirt were wide and flowing. Shari did not know how Anika had managed it, but under the skirt was a pair of tailored trousers. The waist was angled down, but between her hips was a long bit of material that came to her ankles, making it look like a proper skirt if people didn't look too hard.

Anika had shown her how to shift the skirt parts away, so that she'd easily be able to fight in the outfit. And she'd even hid all but the toes of some stylish sephina boots. Having something on her feet that was immune to Fire Innarn sounded like a good idea when they were about to join up with Cantash.

"I feel like a showpiece," Shari grumbled. If she'd been going because she wanted to, it would be different. Instead, she would be on display again. Being the centre of attention usually meant someone was aiming for her. Shari could only hope that the attendants could focus more on the Linked and the joining than on the Altoriae.

"And you look amazing," her dad said.

Her parents had barely left her side since they'd arrived at her bedside. Was it because they hadn't had much of a chance to see her through earlier recoveries, or if they were just wanting to make sure she wasn't overdoing it? It felt like a bit of both.

"We'd best get going or we'll make the ceremony run late," her mum said.

"I could always not go? Samuel and I have... patrol after."

Calem's forehead furrowed. "Is patrol code for something else?"

Shari sighed. "We'll be off-Realm. I'm not sure for how long, but..."

"Is this where we tell you to be safe and use protection?" Arilla asked.

"I'm always protected, and I stay as safe as possible."

"Just how many times have you and Samuel gone on 'patrol'?" Calem asked, using his fingers to put quotes around the last word.

"This will be the first time..." Shari wrinkled her nose. "Are you trying to talk to me about sex?" she shrieked. "Ew. No. Zero interest. I'd much rather stab something."

"Just keep that in mind with Samuel," Calem said, frowning. Arilla laughed.

"Ugh! I'd rather be anywhere other than here if that's where your minds go."

Arilla slapped a hand over her mouth and turned away, shoulders shaking.

"We'll see you at the ceremony then," Calem said.

"Beat you there." Shari forced a grin and winked, shifting away before they could stop her. Slumping next to Jonathan, she allowed herself a moment to recover before he gently nudged her straight.

"Ready?"

Pasting on another smile, Shari spoke between her teeth. "For the battlefield, yes? To be paraded amongst the masses who would have been scrambling not to touch me a few months ago? Hardly."

"Well, you look the part at least," Samuel said.

Shari flicked her eyes towards him. It seemed like Anika had gotten hold of Samuel as well. He was dressed in a dark, just-light-enough-to-pass-as-grey sephina silk suit, silver embroidered Lissae symbols at his collar and cuffs.

"I feel like I've been branded," he grumbled.

Stifling a snigger, she chanced a glance at Jonathan. He was at the other end of the grey spectrum in a similar suit to Samuel's, so bright it could almost be mistaken for white. He, too, had Lissae's symbols on his collar and cuffs.

"It shows who your allegiance is to, without a soul having to ask," Jonathan said. He was the most relaxed out of the three of them, and Shari envied him.

"Are you sure we can't just sneak off now?" Shari asked. Samuel nodded. She felt the blood rushing to her cheeks and looked away. Zoemer curse her parents. Why did they have to mention sex? She didn't want to so much as kiss someone, let alone do *that*.

"You must be here for the joining, Shari. The Shifting Islands pretty much demand it," Jonathan said.

She sighed. *So much for skipping out.*

"Late, late. Why am I always running late?" Tania muttered. She slipped between Shari and Jonathan, coming to stand in front of them and between Zana and Cyrus.

Shari sniggered as Ronah's Linked shivered when Zana's Innarn brushed over her, settling her robes in place.

On the horizon, the sun was setting. As Shari squinted into the light, she spotted a black shape rising ominously from frothing waves with not a being in sight.

"That's Cantash?" Shari asked.

"The might of the Daens is well hidden behind Cantash's walls," Zana said.

Shari fidgeted and bit her lip. Samuel adjusted his stance, his arm brushing against her shoulder.

As they drew closer to the isle, Shari spotted the sheer black walls leaning inwards. Cantash looked like some long-forgotten deity had sliced the top of a volcano off and plonked it in the ocean, setting it to bob amongst the waves for an eternity. There was even steam rising from the centre. Shari was hoping it was all for effect, especially as the massive wall grew closer to them, before the islands shuddered to a stop and an orange glow flickering as part of the wall lowered towards them.

Opening her mouth, Shari wanted to call out a name, but she wasn't sure whose.

Before she could say a word, something nickered from beyond the lowering walls. Shari straightened like many in the crowd, craning to get a look.

"Oh, you're going to love this," Tania said, throwing her a grin over her shoulder before the three Linked stepped forward.

Four coal-black horses with their manes flaming burst over the top of the lowering wall, sparks trailing in their wake. Their riders held aloft what Shari mistook for jagged offcuts of rock. Red leaked down their arms and streamed behind them, while the tops glowed blue.

Torches. And the red wasn't blood, but thickly woven Fire Innarn. The four riders were using it to create rails along the sides of the wall that were almost touching Ronah's shore.

They were getting closer.

One pulled away, continuing along the line of where the wall was hitting the shore, while the others drew closer.

Fire Innarn streamed from the lone rider, dropping to the ground to create burning pillars that solidified and hardened to black rock. Startled, Shari realised ze was Cantash's Linked.

Her attention was captured by the horses galloping towards them. They turned, the three Linked before her stepped forward in synchronisation, each grasping the hand of a rider and leaping astride the flaming horses' backs. They galloped away, weaving their Innarn in with the others as they went, creating rails and stairs and supporting struts to keep the newly joined Shifting Islands together. The four Linked worked together, pulling the islands closer to each other, becoming glowing dots in the distance as the sun slipped below the horizon.

The glow went out.

Shari shivered.

As if it was a cue, the heavy tread of thousands of feet stepping in time sounded.

One step forward.

Reaching for the holster hidden under the side of her skirt, Shari wrapped her fingers around comforting grip of the handle of her short sword.

Jonathan reached out, gently tapping her wrist. '*Wait,*' he sent.

Another thousand feet stepped forward as one.

Muscles tensed, Shari bent her knees slightly, ready to move.

Another step.

She could feel Samuel gathering his Innarn.

Another.

'*Wait*,' Jonathan sent again to both of them.

And another.

'*It seems like a horrible idea to surprise us*,' Shari grumbled.

Samuel huffed beside her, like he wanted to laugh but dared not.

A rider on a jet-black horse was racing along the wall. A spark caught light, and embers ignited as fire burst forth from the fingertips of the Innarnian rider, who disappeared back behind the wall.

Something red from Cantash's side of the wall flew straight up into the sky.

It exploded into a burst of light and colour.

Fire kissed the sky, and sparks rain down, scattering without harm.

Shari glanced around and captured the awe on the faces of those closest.

"Fireworks," she chuckled.

"How is working with fire a good thing?" Samuel asked. He was still ready to fight off the lights in the sky.

"Fireworks are about colour, and joy, and celebration. Not about burning and pain." Shari turned and smiled at him.

He glanced at her, his gaze snapping back as another rose into the sky, colouring the Realm gold for a moment, and then looked at her again. "You lot have an odd way of celebrating," he said.

Giggling, Shari nodded. "I suppose I'll see a different sort of celebration soon enough."

From the dark expression Samuel wore, she regretted the change of subject. "Yeah. Soon enough."

"Not yet though," Jonathan said. "Now, we need to pay respects to Cantash's elders and greet their Linked."

"The joys of being popular." Samuel smirked

Shari rolled her eyes. She half wanted to be anywhere other than here. Despite the danger they were bound to face on Altum, surely it was safer *knowing* there were beings trying to kill you. Instead of wondering if someone in the crowd of well-wishers and gawkers was plotting her death? Pasting a smile on for the simpering crowd, Shari groaned. Maybe if she put Temira's fire crystal on now, everyone would leave her alone?

Four beings shifted in before them, panting hard and smiling even harder.

"Well met, Linked of the Shifting Islands," Jonathan said, bowing his head.

"Well met, Altoriae's Guild," Tania said, taking the lead and bowing her head. The other three Linked copied her. "May we present Fenix, Cantash's Linked."

Crystal lights flared to life around them.

Shari absolutely did not flinch, despite what Samuel would say later.

With the beach well lit, Shari could finally see Cantash's Linked clearly. Fenix was short, with fiery red hair and a warm smile. Hovering behind zir was a tiny being with wavy black hair and a clipboard.

"Well met, Altoriae, Guardian, Apprentice," ze said. "I look forward to exploring Ronah and the other Shifting Islands. This is Milo," ze nodded at the clipboard wielder.

Milo sniffed and attempted to peer down his nose at them. With his lack of height, it was a next-to-impossible feat.

"We'd be delighted to find a guide for you," Jonathan said.

"Oh, I'm pretty sure I can find my way around. Or, at least, I can annoy my fellow Linked until they get me lost and I need to find the way out by myself." Shoving zir hands into pockets, Fenix rocked back on zir heels.

"Does that happen often?" Shari asked, frowning. If the beings of Cantash were picking on their Linked the way those on Ronah had picked on her before her title was announced, she was going to have to take them to task.

Fenix laughed. "Hardly. Cantash is a purpose-built, ever-changing maze. If there's one skill we're good at, it's finding things."

The next batch of fireworks started, jumping high into the sky with a loud pop.

Shari jumped as well.

"That and Fire Innarn, of course." Fenix caught her gaze and smiled gently. "We're pretty good at that."

"I've noticed. Your fireworks are spectacular," Jonathan said.

"Would you agree, Altoriae?" ze asked.

"I... uh... Yes. Apologies, I'm a bit on edge tonight," Shari stammered.

"I can understand. Perhaps if I..." Fenix broke off, a frown marring ze's face for a moment.

The next firework rose silently into the sky and burst apart with nary a whisper.

"Beautiful," Shari murmured.

"Fenix is the best at such colourful displays." Milo sniffed.

"Indeed." Fenix seemed amused. "Now, may I escort you to Cantash? Ze's been waiting to meet you."

"I thought Cantash was male," Shari said, taking Fenix's offered arm and letting ze guide her down the stairs.

"Cantash, like me, is gender fluid. Ze prefers ze/zir pronouns. I'm happy with most but prefer they/them."

"Gender fluid?" Shari asked.

The muscles of Fenix's arm tensed slightly. "Ronah must be very sheltered," they muttered, low enough that Shari thought she wasn't meant to hear.

"I'm sorry. I've just never heard the term before."

"It means sometimes I feel like a male, others a female, and sometimes neither."

"Huh." Shari nodded at people as they walked past, heading farther along the main road of Cantash. "I suppose I have been sheltered. I've met beings who are one or the other, but never someone who switches between genders. I will use the pronouns you prefer."

Fenix relaxed. "Thank you. We'd both appreciate that."

"Do you... do people not..."

"Altoriae, there are plenty of reasons people like me, and it's *all* because of who I am." Fenix's grin was pure mischief.

"Oh? And who is that?"

"Cantash's Linked. Now—" Fenix spun, so they were standing in front of her and placed their hands on her shoulders. Gently, they pulled her forward two steps and one to her right. "Stand exactly here. Do not move. Let me show you what Cantash can do."

Shari stood, frozen. Samuel, who'd been led by Tania, was to her right, and Jonathan and Zana to her left. Cyrus came to a halt next to Milo.

"Ready?" Fenix asked.

"Ready." Shari nodded.

A rush of blistering heat made Shari want to flinch away and cover her face, but she didn't move. She watched in awe as the houses and building on either side of the road rushed past, twisting and turning as though they were riding some invisible river.

'We aren't just fire. We are magma. We are what awaits just under the crust of Lissae. And in a moment of weakness...'

A house brushed by, close enough for Shari to reach out and run her fingertips along the outer wall.

'We break through and show the world what we can do. But when our time is over, we disappear...'

With a sucking *pop*, all the buildings in sight disappeared.

'To ready ourselves for the next time our Realm, our people, our Altoriae, needs our help.' With Fenix's last words, the dwellings burst forth from the ground again.

Despite her brief journey through Cantash's streets, Shari could tell the buildings were in a different configuration than what they had been before.

"Welcome to Cantash," Fenix and Milo said together.

Shari grinned. From somewhere close by, someone started clapping, and she joined in, impressed. "I don't know of another island that could move so much mass around and make it look and feel so effortless," she said.

"Why, thank you. I'll take all the credit for that." Fenix grinned and bowed. The ground rumbled under their feet, and they sighed. "Alright, I'll take some…" 'Most…' "…of the credit. The rest, of course, should go to Cantash." *'Like, one percent.'*

Raising a hand to smother her laugh, Shari coughed and said, "I understand. Cantash has done a wonderful job, as have you."

Fenix beamed.

"And now, I'm afraid, I must steal the Altoriae away," Samuel said, coming to stand behind her shoulder.

"But you just got here." Fenix stepped to the side, and a curtain of shimmering heat fell, revealing mismatched tables groaning under the weight of loaded platters of food.

And the claws of a sedolic stretching Mitch's chest wide open. Breath shuddering from her lungs, Shari shook her head to clear it. "Can't we stay just a little…" she said, looking behind her at Samuel.

He nodded to the moon, sitting full and heavy in the sky. *'It's time.'*

Shari sighed. It would have been nice to replace some of the terrible memories with good ones. "I'm afraid we're on a bit of a tight schedule."

Nodding, Fenix said, "I suppose Lissae won't save herself anymore. We shall feast in your honour then and hold another when you return."

"I look forward to it," Shari said, having time to dip her head in deference before Samuel shifted them away.

In the doorway to the museum, Samuel shoved his hands into the pockets of his suit to hide how badly they were shaking. "Time to go," he said. Pushing open the doors, he glanced to Shari.

Shifting into her leathers, she nodded back and closed her eyes. Within moments, Jetonyx appeared on the Ducibus' side of the hall.

The curious hatchling sniffed at the air flowing through the gateway and sneezed.

"Rest," Samuel implored her.

Shari grinned. "I'll try to while I can." And she stroked Jetonyx's snout before disappearing into his pocket Realm.

Releasing a breath he didn't know he was holding, Samuel squashed his emotions and put them to the side. Fear had no place on Altum. "Ready?" he asked the hatchling.

Jetonyx shuffled, tail curling around his haunches as he sat back. '*Don't want to go*,' he grumbled.

"I know. Me neither. But this is our best chance."

Huffing a deadly sigh that was caught in the gateway's defences, Jetonyx turned and looked down the length of the hall, into the Dark that awaited them.

'*Still don't want to*,' he sent again and started walking slowly towards the end.

Samuel crossed the threshold of the gateway and changed. He took a step and stopped. What if the hatchling had been sent to set him up? Were assailants were about to appear out of nowhere and take him out?

Nothing happened.

'*Getting slow, old priest*,' the hatchling taunted, nerves making his send shaky.

Shaking his wings out, and his fears away, Sanithane strode after the impudent whelp. '*We'll see about that.*'

Together, the two Q'Aralide stalked towards the gateway to Altum.

A handful of others on their way to the Darker Realms skittered out of their way.

Was there actually a time when I enjoyed the stench of their fear? Before he could contemplate any further, they'd arrived.

Altum's door absorbed all light from the hall, jet-black scales only visible to those who knew they were there.

'*Behave,*' Sanithane cautioned.

Reaching out a claw, he opened the door and stepped through to the place he'd called home so long ago.

CHAPTER TWELVE

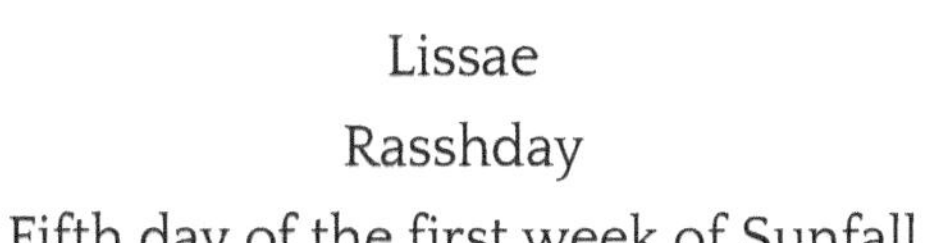

Lissae

Rasshday

Fifth day of the first week of Sunfall

Jonathan leaned back in his chair on the stage and ran his gaze over the children gathered in Ridden Hall's main area.

Liza, Headmaster of Ronah's school and mother of Ronah's Linked, had thought it was a good idea for Jonathan to make some sort of announcement to the students that Shari and Samuel had been teaching.

She had, in fact, tracked him down at the joining with Cantash and raked him over the proverbial coals, talking about how he was messing with the education of the next generation of Realm-savers by constantly asking her teachers to skip out because of other duties. And that if he didn't provide a replacement, she would be forced to ask both Shari and Samuel not to return. And, no, she didn't give a rat's hiney about any duties Shari had sworn to.

The Guardian had been both totally embarrassed and thoroughly impressed with Liza's impassioned speech, and had promised to talk to the students as soon as possible.

He just hadn't thought she'd meant today.

"... and I'd like you all to welcome the Guardian. He has some exciting news to share with us today." Liza led the applause as Jonathan stood and tugged his jacket straight. She turned and glared a warning at him before taking her seat.

Beaming, with a jaw clenched so tight it was painful, he took to the centre of the stage. "Thank you, Headmaster Hollingsworth." Looking out at the crowd, he wasn't sure he'd ever been that small.

"The Altoriae and my apprentice are both currently off-Realm on a training exercise at the moment. I will teach their classes until they return."

A hand raised.

Startled, Jonathan nodded before he'd thought about what he should do.

"Are they dead?" a childish voice asked.

"Did they get smooshed by the buildings moving around last night?"

"Are you going to let us play with knives?"

Behind him, the legs of a chair scraped and the children settled down immediately.

He didn't have to look to know Liza was giving them the same glare he'd received just moments before. "They are both fine and were in good health last I saw. No knives with me, but lots of Innarn instead."

There were a few groans and slumped shoulders. Jonathan bid them farewell before he fled back to his chair, wondering exactly what Shari and Samuel had been teaching.

Liza glanced at him and sighed as another teacher took the stage and started in on the more mundane announcements.

"They're going to eat you alive," she muttered to him.

Biting back a groan, Jonathan smiled at her. Was it too late to swap places with Shari?

Playing exchange student with the rest of her classmates was brilliant. The teachers had decided that the older years should swap around the schools on the different islands to get a taste for other ways of learning.

She loved her mother and Jordan, but getting away from the school they ran and being able to experience how Rakemyst, Talhan, and Cantash taught Innarn was exciting.

"I can't wait!" Tania said, gently bumping Collis's arm with her own. "I wonder if we'll learn how to control the air currents. Oh! Or the heat-curtain-thingy Fenix did last night? Did you try the calromata? It was so hot, I thought I was going to melt!"

Collis glanced down at her and smiled.

"I'd never let you melt." It was Zana's nephew.

"Uh, okay?" Tania wrinkled her nose.

"Well." Voxis glanced down, then up at her through his lashes. Biting his lip, he gave her a half-smile. "Maybe a little."

Tania elbowed Collis's ribs, rolling her eyes at the pure stupidity of the silver-winged Ilutri. Why would he want her to melt?

"Anyway." She turned back to Collis in a move Anika would be proud of. "Fenix said that the teachers of Cantash don't lecture so much as tell you what to do, then guide you through how to do it. Do you think that's how Shari learned?"

"I think the Altoriae is just a natural," Voxis said, voice loud enough to carry to their other classmates.

On his other side, Anika scoffed. "You think Shari was born knowing everything about Innarn?" She made a rude noise. "Clearly, you didn't see her latest training session."

Voxis looked at Anika and flinched so hard he stumbled backwards into Tania, who fell against Collis. "You're the b… b… Blank," he stuttered.

"Leave," Collis ordered.

The Ilutri teen tried to apologise and was met with Collis's scowl. Almost tripping over his own feet, Voxis scampered away from their group.

Anika stepped closer to Tania. "Are you alright? He practically knocked you over!" She brushed some imaginary dust off Tania's arm.

"I'm fine. Are you okay?" Tania asked. She would ignore the welling in the other girl's eyes if that's what she wanted.

"Fine," Anika said. "Besides, mister tall and inked here should keep him away for the rest of the day. When did you two get together?"

Collis stuttered, and Tania laughed. "Nothing official, but I wouldn't be opposed." She glanced up at Collis and smiled.

He grinned back.

"You two are sickeningly perfect together," Anika sniffed. "But, seeing as I was the one to point it out, I call dibs on designing your bonding ceremony robes."

It was Tania's turn to stutter.

"Deal," Collis said. "At least, it is if 'dibs' means what I think it means."

The two girls laughed.

Maybe I won't have to ask Cyrus about Collis after all.

Vebaday

Sixth day of the first week of Sunfall

"This is the second night in a row," Elder Shansky was saying, "That the mainlanders have failed to show up for patrols."

Jonathan pinched the bridge of his nose. "It is possible that they are just unable to reach us now. We are out in the Deep Ocean." He had been called to a meeting of the elders and new patrol leaders he'd set up. There were enough of them who wanted to attend—no doubt hoping for a glimpse of Shari—that they'd needed to use the conference rooms above the Techno Centre in Cantash.

"Giving them a pass?" Elder SilverCloud said. "No, there are enough Shifters on the mainland to easily transport them here."

"When was the last time we've heard from any of them?" the Mayor of Ronah asked.

There was some murmuring amongst those gathered, and it gave Jonathan enough time to look them all over.

Elders Thorne, Shansky, and Silverstone were present from Ronah, as well as Zac and three of Ronah's designated patrol leaders.

The elders from Rakemyst had their wings on display but pulled tightly back. SilverCloud seemed more comfortable with the situation than the other two elders. Wolf and Belfar sat next to two female Ilutri, all of them with stiff spines and matching blank expressions.

Belfar was garnering some looks from the Talhan delegation. Elders Jillon and her counterpart seemed most concerned, and they'd glared at Belfar until Temira had strode into the room and sat regally next to the scorned Ilutri. Despite the lack of small talk, the other elders seemed to take her presence by his side as a positive occurrence, and the glares lessened, mostly.

Talhan's patrol leaders were another matter all together.

Antya, Berrimon, Larn, and Neeth were whispering fugitively to each other and glancing at the Ilutri now and then. Whilst Belfar appeared serene on the surface, Wolf was not. He started growling, only stopping when Belfar put a hand on his arm.

The patrol leaders from Cantash seemed confused at the tension in the room, while their elders were oblivious or giving the others no mind.

They were muttering to themselves, trying to figure out the last time a mainlander saw them.

"Can we just—" Belfar said. The room fell silent instantly. "Apologies, but can we just address the fulni in the room?"

"There is no issue," Wolf growled.

The way Belfar sighed spoke volumes of how often he'd done it in Wolf's presence before. "Yes, there is. Me. I betrayed the beings of Talhan, and I hurt not only them, but the island as well. What can I do to make it up to you?"

"You caused no permanent injury whilst you were under the Crystal Intelligence's control," Temira said. She frowned as she looked around the room. "In fact, out of the beings present, only three can say that they were, at no point, under the control of the Crystal Intelligence. They are merely projecting their insecurities onto you." Laying her forearms on the table, she steepled her fingers and glared at everyone. "This, of course, is infantile and pointless. And will stop immediately."

Belfar lowered his head, but not quickly enough, as Jonathan had caught sight of the grin he wore. "You... I appreciate everything you have said, but if these feelings are left to fester, they will be decidedly unhelpful. The only recourse is to remove myself from the patrol roster."

"Nonsense!" Larn said. "You want to know why we stare and whisper? For us"—she gestured to the other patrol leaders—"it's because you did the near impossible. Do you know that while I was under the influence of the crystal, I cut my brother's arm off? And Antya, here, removed her younger sister's eye."

Antya looked down. The room was so silent they could hear the tears splash against the wooden table.

"We stare, because, yes, you broke bones and threw people around, but you didn't maim anyone for life or send them onto the Spirit Realm. You had enough control not to do the horrific things that we ended up doing. And we'd like to know how." Larn's chest heaved as if she'd run a mile. Her slouched hat sat slightly askew, a curl of dark blonde hair peeking out from under it.

"I..." Belfar looked both horrified and touched.

"May I suggest," Jonathan said, "That those who are interested, speak to Belfar after. Now, we must focus on the problem of the mainlanders skipping patrols at the moment."

"Can't remember the last time we saw them," one of Cantash's elders said. She was a tiny, fine-boned woman, with deep wrinkles from laughing so much and browned skin from being out in the sun. Or possibly from working too close to the forges.

"The mainlanders?" Jonathan asked.

"Yes. She thinks it was at the start of fall." The Elder jerked her thumb at her neighbour. "But I think it was well before that. Mind you, we don't get many coming our way at all. Strangers stand out."

As the Elder took her seat again, Jonathan noted just how short she was. Only her mop of white hair was visible over the tabletop.

"That Chamele is stirring up trouble," Elder Jillion grumbled. "She's constantly badgering us for more crystal at a cheaper price. Claims our stock is inferior!" He banged on the table, red-faced and grumbling.

"Elder Chamele is fast becoming a name I've been hearing too much of," Jonathan mused. "What do you know about her?"

"Nothing," Berrimon said. "After... everything that happened, I sent some scouts out to gather any information they could on her. It's as if she sprung up from nowhere about twenty years ago. She's slowly been working her way through the ranks. Anyone who has something bad to say about her either does a complete turnaround, or they just... disappear."

"I suggest we meet again in a week. Let me see if I can find out anything that will help us. If I do, we'll reconvene before then and decide how much of a threat Elder Chamele is to our relationship with the mainland." Jonathan sighed.

"I don't think they're the threat," Elder SilverCloud said. "I think she is."

From what he'd seen of the Elder so far, he didn't trust her as far as he could throw her. Jonathan sighed again and pinched the bridge of his nose. "I think you're right."

After saying his farewells, Jonathan walked from the meeting feeling disheartened. Was it not enough to keep Lissae safe from outside forces—now there was something odd happening on-Realm as well?

Frowning, he strode through the door, almost stumbling into another body.

"We have to stop meeting like this," Zac said.

Jonathan laughed. "I don't know. Seems like you're the highlight of my day."

Zac's eyes lit up. "Becoming smooth in your old age?"

"From memory, you're older than me," he laughed.

"Well, you should be nicer to your elders then."

Grinning at the teasing, Jonathan couldn't help but think of the discussion he'd just come from.

"Uh-oh, he's thinking too hard. Come on. Let's have some fun." Zac grabbed his hand and pulled Jonathan to the side of the doors. "Shift us to Cantash. I want to show you something."

Staring into Zac's eyes, Jonathan wavered.

"Friends go places together all the time. We're just two friends having an adventure."

"Until we're not," Jonathan said, his voice unintentionally husky.

Heat flicked through Zac's eyes. "Until we're not."

Taking the easier option, Jonathan shifted them to the middle of Cantash, safely away from the scramble of buildings.

"I want to show you something," Zac tugged on his hand and led him through the scramble towards the eastern side of the island.

"Have you been to Cantash before?"

"I've been all over. And I know some secrets that others don't." Zac looked at him and winked.

Ignoring the fluttering in his belly, Jonathan laughed. "I bet you do."

"Secrets like this," Zac said, and waved at the double doors before them.

They were nothing like the doors at the museum. These were mammoth, made of metal, and aged by both the weather and—near the handles—the touch of generations of hands. Set into the walls surrounding the island, the doors seemed ike nothing special, unless you could feel the thrum of Innarn that lay behind them. It was sending shivers along Jonathan's nerve endings.

"A good secret, right?" he asked.

Zac hid the flash of hurt well. "Yeah. Well, I think it's good. The Daen's are famous for their eobustus, flaming manes, coal-black coats, and hooves of steel. Yet, amongst all these buildings, do you see a single stable? Or a paddock for grazing? Any paddocks at all? Think of Ronah—every household has their own plot of land for growing what they need. Rakemyst has all their farming on ground level, with a scattering of houses and buildings, but most are raised up. Talhan has an entire sector of their isle that is just farmland. Cantash is just as isolated and needs just as much infrastructure as the others, but all you see up here are buildings."

Jonathan looked around. It was true. From his vantage point, he could make out most of the isle, and while there was the occasional spot of green on a balcony or rooftop, there was suspiciously little plant life.

"Okay, so where or how do they grow everything?"

With a flourish of his hands, Zac gestured to the massive metal doors.

"It leads into a wall, Zac."

Laughing, Zac grasped the handle and pulled it open.

Sweet-scented steam hit him in the face, and Jonathan puffed out a breath.

"Bet you're glad to be rid of the glasses now," Zac said, a slightly bitter twist to his lips.

"You have no idea," Jonathan said seriously.

Zac blinked owlishly.

"You two gettin' in, or you holdin' up the line all day?" a voice asked.

Jonathan glanced over his shoulder. An older man was leaning against a wall, a bulky bag resting by his feet.

"Sorry." Zac grinned. "He's a first timer. Wanted to give the Guardian the complete experience."

The man grinned, deepening his wrinkles and showing off pearly white teeth. "First timer? Want the tame tour?" He nodded to Zac. "Or the whirlwind?"

They glanced at each other, and Zac raised his brows.

"Whirlwind," they said together, and grinned.

"Follow me, boys."

Stepping to the side, they let the man pass and followed him through the doors.

They entered a huge box-like structure, and their guide let the doors close. The box shuddered and groaned before a swooping feeling had Jonathan grasping onto the railing attached to the walls.

"First thing. Only someone with Innarn can open them doors. Causes a few issues, as we've got Blanks, but we've rigged it so that a single Blank can enter with an Innarnian. Comes in handy. Second thing; I'm Mick. I check on the water for the sun in the afternoons."

"Water for the sun?" Jonathan mouthed to Zac.

He just grinned.

The doors opened.

And they were somewhere else.

Lush trees heavy with fruit lined a smooth, bricked path leading from the doors. A fine mist permeated the air, bringing with it the sweet smell of summer and ripe fruit. Looking up, Jonathan could hardly believe they were underground, but the proof was there in the rocky ceiling far above their heads.

"Don't hold the lift. Out we get," Mick said, and gathered his bag before heading down the track. "All our produce is grown here. Cantash filters water from the ocean and we use it not only in our wells, but in the special jets that keep everything at the right moisture levels. The animals have half the area, although the eobustus have half that. The rest are used for eggs, milk, and wool. A'course, there's the birds for bug control as well." Mick nodded to the side, where a tiny bird flew down to a fat black beetle on a leaf. A jet of flame emerged from its beak, and the beetle fell, burnt to a crisp.

A pointed snout poked out of a hollow near the base of the tree and sniffed the air. The creature shuffled forward, dirt-coloured scales making it blend into the trees surrounding it. Pushing its nose against the bug, it snuffled again before sitting back on sturdy legs, tail helping it to balance as the creature used its forelegs to grab onto the bug.

"That's an arustos, the tree custodian. They make sure our trees are healthy, and the caelonis fries the bugs for them. Arustos love nothin' more than fried bug," Mick said.

Sharp little teeth cracked the shell of the bug, and the arustos crunched its way through its meal.

"I've never seen one before," Jonathan said.

"Few have, unless you've been to Cantash's gardens. You can only find them here," Zac said.

"We got a bunch of critters you can only find here. These two, the dracovum, ignivas, and eobustus. Probably more than that, but the Cantash Five are the usual attractions. Come on. There's a new bunch of dracovum about to be released into the gardens. They're kept by the shed, so it's no bother to introduce you." Mick started down the path again.

Jonathan followed, craning his head to watch the caelonis fry another beetle for the sweet, scaled arustos.

Mick led them to the shed, an immense stone structure that was more hydro station than sun, situated in the middle of the farms. Great ziom blades turned on a wheel taller than Sanithane. The bottom half of it was hidden, presumably in the seawater under the island. It made sense to have the blades made of the strongest metal in the Realms with the amount of water they were moving. Sitting at the top of the structure was a massive glowing light. The ceiling of the immense underground room was some sort of reflective material, shining the sun evenly across the space.

"The dracovum are just to the side there. If you ask nicely, the keepers will point you in the ignivas's direction. Ask after the eobustus there and take a gander at the gardens while you're goin'. Gotta keep movin'. Sun doesn't keep itself warm," Mick said. "Nice ta' meet you both."

"Thank you, Mick. I bid thee well," Zac said, and Jonathan echoed his farewell, already eyeing the doorway to the promised dracovum.

Pulling him over with a laugh, Zac opened the door and ushered the Guardian in.

"Quick!" a voice from inside said. "This lot are eager to escape."

Hastily, Jonathan shut the door.

"Thank you," the smallest Daen he'd ever seen said. "Suppose you've come to see them."

"Mick recommended it," Zac said.

The tiny Daen sighed. "Very well. I'm Titch. Welcome to the draci. Come and meet our latest brood before they escape."

"Escape?" Jonathan asked.

Titch rolled his eyes. "Mick might like to think that we have some control over the lil beasts, but really, they have us all tangled around their tails." He lifted his hand closer to his face. "Don't you?" he cooed.

Sitting on the back of his hand, tail firmly wrapped around his fingers, was the smallest dragon Jonathan had ever seen.

"A draci?"

"Yes. These are fully grown dracovum. When they hatch, they're about the size of a pea. They take three years to mature into the draci, and only about a third of that time to cause trouble," Titch said.

The tiny draci was coal black, the same colour as Titch's hair, and had curls of smoke wafting from its nose.

"This lil one is more trouble than the rest. Got into a biff with the door and squashed his wing up good. He enjoys hiding in my hair most of the time, but comes out when visitors are here."

"Where are the rest?" Zac asked.

Tipping his head back, Titch raised his eyes to the ceiling.

Jonathan looked up and gasped. Hanging above them were thousands of tiny draci, tendrils of smoke drifting down as the little ones snored.

The one in Titch's hand squeaked. Jonathan looked back at him as he stretched out a serpentine neck, eyes firmly locked on the Guardian.

"Looks like you've got an admirer."

'No.' The voice was young and petulant. It reminded him of Samuel.

'Yes!' the voice sent.

"Who did you just think of?" Titch asked, voice serious.

"My... my apprentice. That send sounded a lot like a younger version of him."

'Mine!'

Titch laughed. "Looks like he's about to get a pet."

"He's... he's away at the moment. Patrolling."

"Well, this one isn't going to wait."

Indeed, the draci was stretching out, forelegs scrabbling in the air as it tried to reach him.

Jonathan instinctively held out his hands, and the tiny draci leaped into them, curling up in the palm of his hand neatly.

'*Will wait,*' the voice said.

"Do, ah, do you have a name?" Jonathan asked, raising his hand to his face.

The draci opened its eyes and wrinkled his nose before sneezing in his face, sparks shooting out of its snout.

With a yelp, Jonathan patted his face down.

Covering his mouth to hide his chortle, Titch said, "Sneeze. His name is Sneeze."

"Sneeze?" Zac asked.

The little draci yawned, showing his gummy mouth, and looked at Zac before giving a singularly unimpressed snort.

"Of course. What else would you be called?"

Sneeze trilled, and there was a scurry and a flutter from about them.

"Finally!" Titch exclaimed. "Alright, you lot. Come visit, but not too often, alright?" He waved his hands and muttered something.

The doors slid open.

Excited chittering filled the room. Jonathan and Zac ducked as thousands of wings beat hard as the draci dropped from their perches and flew into the gardens.

Titch and Sneeze sighed at the same time.

"You know, sometimes I think I have the worst of jobs. I mean, cleaning up after the lil' blighters ain't easy. Then, when their flame comes in, or they spark for the first time, or they whisper, mind to mind, it's the best thing in the world." Titch looked up at the empty ceiling. "Then there's today. When they're eager to rush off, and I'm left to start the cycle all over again with the next lot."

'*We remember,*' Sneeze sent. '*Never forget Titch.*'

Titch nodded. "And I never forget you." He sniffed. "I ah... Go the opposite direction to the way the draci are flying. You'll find the ignivas there. If you spoke to Mick, they'll be next on your list." Titch sniffed again, and reached forward to stroke a gentle, calloused finger along Sneeze's back. "Take care, you."

'*You.*' Sneeze stared hard at Titch for a moment

The tiny Daen's eyes welled. "Ember in my eye," he muttered, rubbing his face. "Bid thee well." And he was gone.

Zac and Jonathan stared after him for a moment.

"To the ignivas?" Zac asked.

"Lets," Jonathan said.

'*Up,*' Sneeze sent.

Jonathan lifted his hand up, and Sneeze climbed onto his shoulder, only slightly grumping that it wasn't the place he wanted.

Zac took his hand again, and they followed the path out, winding around the water-powered sun to the other side, and headed towards the far wall where they could see the occasional burst of flame.

As they walked, Jonathan huffed, the humidity making it hard to breathe. Casting a cooling charm on himself made Sneeze dig his claws into his shoulder and chitter angrily into his ear.

"Sorry, little draci," Jonathan soothed, and reached a finger up to stroke the creature.

Sneeze bit him.

Jonathan swore. "You are a perfect fit for Samuel, aren't you?"

The draci cooed in his ear, and Jonathan sighed.

Coughing to disguise his laughter, Zac nudged his ribs. "We're here."

At the end of the path was a glass wall. On the other side were trees with leaves the colour of flames. As they watched, a bird the same colour as the leaves rose from the trees. It's exceptionally long tail flared for a moment, and it opened its beak. The glass seemed to vibrate. Perhaps there was some sort of noise cancelling on it.

From farther away, another bird flew to join the first. The two danced through the air, sparks leaping from their tails each time they brushed.

On the ground, a keeper was following the birds, careful not to get too close, but catching the sparks as they fell.

"Enjoying the show?"

Turning, Jonathan smiled at Fenix, Cantash's Linked. Today, Fenix wore a dusky blue shirt that laced on the sides, and an old pair of brown, supple leather pants.

"Very much," he and Zac said.

"Do you know much about the ignivas?" Fenix asked.

Jonathan shook his head.

Behind them, Milo *tsked* over the top of his clipboard.

"They dance like this when they are happy. The sparks their tails let off are used to heal the trees. Growing underground takes a toll on our crops, but mixing in ignivas sparks with eobustus manure means our crops grow strong and healthy," they said. "People often confuse the ignivas with the phoenix, but they are night and day. Phoenix's *tears* heal and they burst into flames. Ignivas sparks revitalise, and they melt into a puddle before reforming."

"The Daens really are unparalleled in how they utilise Fire Innarn," Jonathan said.

Fenix smiled. "My thanks. We try our best to ensure our people and our creatures are given the best possible chances." Their eyes drifted to Jonathan's shoulder. "I would invite you to meet the ignivas, but today is probably not the best time."

Sneeze lived up to his name, and Jonathan idly patted out the sparks on his collar.

"Perhaps you'd like to see the eobustus?" Milo offered.

"Saving the best till last?" Mick, his bag nowhere to be seen, grinned at them.

Fenix's smile became fixed. "Always."

"I'd best take them then," Mick's smile was slightly mean.

"Fenix was informing me of the patrol schedule," Jonathan said smoothy. "Would you know it as well?"

"Don't reckon I know it better than Fenix does," Mick said, shoulders slumped. "Leave you to it then."

"What was that about?" Zac asked.

"There are many who do not believe that Fenix is suitable to be Cantash's Linked," Milo replied, glaring after Mick.

"What? Why?"

Gesturing for them to follow, Fenix started down a path they had yet to travel. "Cantash and the Daens are a matriarchal society. To have someone who doesn't conform to their ideal is difficult for some of the older generation."

"And so they take it out on you?" Jonathan asked.

On his shoulder, Sneeze grumbled.

"For all the good I do, I must work harder, and longer and be better to prove that I am just as capable as the last Linked," Fenix said. "It can be tiring."

"Who was the last Linked?"

Fenix glanced away.

"Their mother," Milo said.

"Ouch," Zac winced.

"Yes. She was wonderful, but that makes my job tougher. Still, Cantash wouldn't be where we are today without hard work. Or the eobustus." Fenix gestured at the paddocks ahead.

Coal-black bodies greeted them, the occasional flash of a fiery mane as they grazed on the...

"Is that lava?" Jonathan asked.

"Don't be ridiculous," Zac said, grinning. "It's magma."

"Magma."

Through the centre of the paddocks was a thick flow of magma. Rivulets branched off here and there, and the eobustus gathered around to eat from the molten rock.

"How are they not burning themselves?" Jonathan asked.

Fenix laughed. "You're asking how the horse with the mane of fire isn't burning?"

Jonathan chuckled. "Fair enough."

"Eobustuses are laid within the magma in thunder eggs. Once they've reached the required time and temperature, they hatch. They spend most of their first year swimming and playing in lava. As they age, they only require a daily feed of magma to sustain their internal heat." Fenix leaned on the fence and gazed at the eobustus.

"Why do they need to be so hot?" Zac asked.

"Two reasons. One, if you were born in a pool of magma, heat would be like home, yes?" Fenix asked.

Zac nodded.

"The second is more complicated. What is energy?"

Milo didn't wait for their answer. "Energy is heat. Add coal to the furnace to power a ship, add water to the fire to make the steam, add Innarn to the crystal and watch it power your lives. Eobustuses are a physical representation of that energy and heat transference. They use heat from their surroundings to gather energy, then they can convert that energy into other things. Movement, Innarn-boosting, running throughout the day without rest. Eobustuses are the fastest creature in all the Realms—provided they've had a good feed of magma, or the sun is at full strength."

"Okay, serious question. How do you hold on if they're that fast?"

Laughing, Fenix reached out and patted the muzzle of the beast who'd come to say hello. "Very tightly."

Sneeze harrumphed as more of the eobustus came to say hello.

As Jonathan patted one, he smiled a bit sadly. *Shari would have loved this.* His thoughts turned to how she was faring in the Darkest of Realms.

CHAPTER THIRTEEN

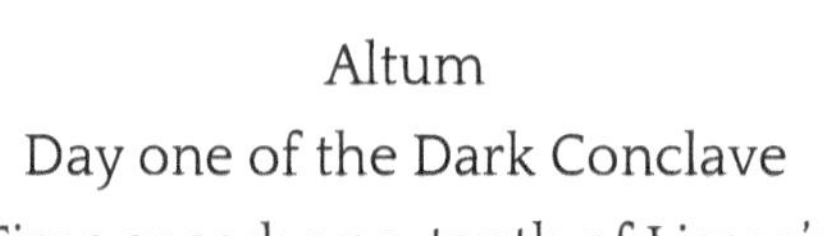

Altum

Day one of the Dark Conclave

Time speed: one-tenth of Lissae's

From thick square columns of sandstone hung tattered sheer red curtains, waving idly in a non-existent breeze. It broke up the monotony of the rough sandstone coloured walls of the huge rectangular hall. A long table in a slightly darker shade than the walls ran the length of the room. A hand span from the edge of the table was a finger-wide groove carved into the tabletop. It was filled with a thick red liquid that shimmered under the dull lighting of the room, moving sluggishly as if there was a beat.

Aeons of practice meant Sanithane no longer had to stop himself from hurling, but it was a near thing. The colour of that shimmering liquid was far too close to the shade of human arterial blood for his peace of mind. He shifted his focus instead to the occupants of the room.

There were ninety-nine delegates, elders from the Darkest races of the Darkest Realms, and their assistants, that made up the Dark Conclave.

On the opposite side of the curtains from the delegates, Sanithane was standing with a nervous Jetonyx by his side.

'*Breathe*,' he prompted his hatchling.

Jetonyx took a shuddering breath, only to gasp and choke on air when Oalark herself sauntered into the room, War'Jan trailing behind her.

Sanithane frowned as he looked at War'Jan. The leader who had inspired so much fear was peering around the room from rheumy eyes, cheeks and chest sunken so badly, his bones looked like they were just below his scales. All the flesh and muscle that had made him so formidable in Sanithane's youth had melted away, leaving a frail old Q'Aralide in his wake.

'*We merely await my priest, and...*' Oalark was sending.

The curtain parted, and Sanithane strode through as though he'd never been away. He didn't even dare think it, but a swell of satisfaction filled his chest as Oalark gaped at him.

'*Who's that?*' a feeble voice sent.

Oalark rolled her eyes. '*Clearly, my Golden Priest has returned.*'

'*Who?*' The feeble voice belonged to War'Jan. Just what were they playing at?

The Queen of the Q'Aralide growled, and a few delegates shuffled hurriedly out of the way as the pair settled at the table. '*And look,*' Oalark sounded amused.

Amused was not good. When the Queen was amused, it usually signified danger.

'*He's brought us a plaything.*'

'*My Queen, War'Jan, esteemed delegates.*' By the deities above, he wanted to scrub his soul with acid after dripping such flattery on the undeserving bunch. '*After searching the Realms, both Dark and Light, I come bearing glad tidings. I feared the legacy of the Gold would fade after my demise, and have been searching out a suitable replacement. Only one came close. May I introduce my apprentice, Jetonyx?'*

The hatchling bowed low into the silent room.

There was a warning rumble, and everyone held their breath. Face flushed under her pale scales, Oalark fumed at them.

'*E's a bit dark to be gold, isn't he?'* War'Jan warbled.

Oalark hit her mate over the head with her wing.

'So good to *have you back, my priest,'* Oalark sent.

'*Dead. I'm dead. We're dead. She's going to kill us dead.'* Jetonyx was babbling so loudly, Sanithane almost missed the Queen asking him to start the meeting.

'As *you will it.'* Sanithane bowed, and made his way slowly to the head of the table. '*Follow me and do* not *make eye contact with anyone,'* he sent to Jetonyx.

Stifling a whimper, the hatchling trailed him.

The gaze of every delegate in the room was on them, burning into his hide as he rounded the table. Sanithane took his time to settle onto his rest, and waved a claw to conjure a less ostentatious one for his newly dubbed apprentice.

'*Well met, and welcome one and all to the seventieth Dark Conclave.'*

Now, if they could all just stay alive to the end if it, he'd be happy.

Jetonyx's Pocket Realm

Shari wriggled her toes in the sun-warmed sand, letting the waves lap around her ankles. As she wrung the water out of her hair, she smiled. Jetonyx had clearly been paying attention to what she'd said when they'd spoken about having fun.

The baby Q'Aralide's pocket Realm had everything she needed. A wide sandy beach leading to a peaceful ocean, a hut with all the basic necessities. A training ground sat on the other side of the hut, big enough that it allowed her to move and practice, and try out a few new things on the never-ending supply of dummies.

She much preferred the dummies to Temira's B.I.T., even if they weren't as hard to knock down.

The weird thing about the pocket Realm was how utterly quiet it was. Waves on the shore were the only sound. The absolute silence was driving her to distraction, and, as best as she could figure it, she'd only been here a day or so.

"I'd give my right dagger to know what's going on out there," Shari muttered, more to hear herself talk than because she expected any sort of response.

Three massive screens popped into existence, and Shari shrieked. A great golden head glanced at her, both bigger than she'd ever encountered before, and yet smaller.

"Am I seeing through your eyes?" she asked.

The view on the screen bobbed, as if Jetonyx nodded.

"You are amazing," Shari said, and sank into the sand to watch what played out.

Altum

When Jetonyx grunted in the middle of the Roefill Ambassador's unending gratitude to the *clever, mighty, stunning, gracious Oalark,* Sanithane didn't know if he should be grateful or exasperated.

'*What are you doing?*' he sent.

'*Just looking.*'

The hatchling was going to be the death of him.

'Look *quieter*,' he snapped.

Oalark was staring at him.

'*Thank you, Ambassador. Are there any further matters to attend to before we take the oath?*' he asked.

A huge being from Eofix stood. Apparently, this ambassador needed to wax lyrical about the Q'Aralide overlords as well.

Sanithane refrained from resting his head on his claw. '*Can they seriously suck up any more than this? By what gods does Oalark have a delectable arse?*' he half-sent to Jetonyx.

A familiar giggle sounded in his mind, startling him so much, his scales rustled.

From the corner of his eye, Sanithane noticed Oalark looking over at him again and frowning.

'*Shari?*' he sent on the tightest band he could.

'*Still safe. Just watching the show.*'

Oh, for the love of toasted caltrop nuts. He was going to disembowel the hatchling.

Slowly.

He didn't dare relax as Oalark sank back into her rest, her claw coming up as she coyly glanced his way at the Eofix's words.

At last, the loquacious lump wound to a stop.

'*On to the oath,*' Sanithane said, jumping in before another delegate could go on for even longer.

As one, the entire party stood, the scraping of chairs and rests loud enough to cover up the mutterings.

Unless you were the priest.

And attuned to deception.

Unfortunately, for the one who'd just muttered a spell to make the next words out of their mouth false, he could not pin down who said it. Thankfully for them, he wasn't about to call attention to it, anyway. Any enemy of Oalark's could only help him get through this.

'Repeat after me. We freely come. Together, we can improve life. We seek not to betray the Dark, but to honour each other and give life to the next generation. We wish only to empower the Dark, and keep its secrets close to the hearts of those who attend.'

Voices rose and repeated the oath, and Sanithane wove his Innarn around them all. As much as he wanted to be lax and allow those who wished the gathering ill to slip through the cracks, he couldn't. Not with Oalark watching him as if she just needed the barest whisper of an excuse to end his existence.

Jetonyx's Pocket Realm

Shari watched on, safe in Jetonyx's pocket Realm, as the delegates obediently recited the oath after Samuel. His Innarn brushed against her, even where she sat.

Looked like she had secrets to keep, too.

Biting her lip, she wanted to reach out and let Jonathan gaze through her eyes, despite it being a bad idea. Not to mention draining. She'd never tell Jonathan or Samuel, but she was still feeling the effects of her attempt at changing her form. Laying back on the towel she'd conjured, Shari observed, and let her body heal.

There were so many unfamiliar races present, with three members of each one in the room. Thirty-three elders from across the Darkest of Realms, each with two attendants, except, of course, for the Q'Aralide. They had Oalark, War'Jan, Jetonyx, and Sam... Sanithane.

"Let's see..." Shari stared hard at the screens Jetonyx had provided, but she just didn't have enough information. Very few Altoriaes had ever been to Realms so Dark, and it appeared that, with each shade Darker, it was necessary to add more limbs in. Sure enough, tentacles writhing as they argued amongst themselves, were the U'tan delegation.

'*I'm sure you're all wondering,*' Oalark was sending.

Each syllable felt like a dagger through Shari's brain.

'*Why I've called a closed session of the Dark Conclave, rather than a full one.*'

There were murmurs around the table, but no one seemed game to question the mad queen outright.

'*It's simple, really.*' Oalark's grin made Shari shiver. '*We have a spy in our midst. One who is no longer keen to uphold the oath. One who seeks to turn everything that we've worked so hard for into ash. You!*' Oalark abruptly turned to Sanithane, pointing a wickedly sharp claw at him.

Shari's heart felt like it was going to beat out of her chest as the Queen glared at Samuel.

'*You will bear witness, my Golden One, to this deceitful, heinous act.*'

'As you will it, my Queen,' Samuel said, bowing his head.

'*And you.*' Oalark turned, facing Jetonyx fully. Her voice a dangerous purr.

Scrambling to her feet, Shari prepared to move, her blades appearing in her hands. What she was planning on doing, she didn't know, but she'd be ready.

'*You are in the perfect position to learn. You, my little hatchling...*' the Queen purred and leered at the screens.

Ugh. Shari fought against the urge to throw up.

'*Are about to learn what happens to traitors to our cause.*'

Abruptly, Oalark turned away from them, and Shari sagged with relief.

'*I believe we can rule out the Roefill and Eofix elders, as they were so eloquently singing my praises.*'

'*Perhaps it was a ruse?*' Samuel drawled, glancing at his claws rather than the row of paling faces down the table.

'*A ruse? And how should we test such a thing?*' Oalark rounded the table.

From the angle Jetonyx was sitting, she couldn't see what happened, and the hatchling was too busy shaking to dare look anywhere other than straight ahead.

Shari huffed, flopping back in the sand.

"This is like the worst drama in the Realms," she grumbled.

'*I'm sure my Queen knows best.*' Samuel's send was lazy, but Shari could feel the tension lacing his words.

'*Very well. Elder Ashbek of Roefill, give me your aide.*'

For a moment, Shari was confused. Oalark wanted help?

A shaking being with four legs and just as many arms stepped forward, sweat slicking her short, curly coat and soaking through her pale-yellow jerkin. '*Queen Oalark, how may I be of–*' The aide cut off with a shriek as Oalark slashed out with her claws and removed a limb.

'*Is Ashbek our spy?*'

The girl held the stub of her arm and sobbed, eyes glazed and unresponsive even as her Elder roared and lunged to his many feet.

Shari clamped her hand over her mouth.

She may have removed many limbs on the battlefield, but never had she done so in cold blood.

'*I am no spy, Queen Oalark. And my daughter is faithful to the Dark! As is my son!*' Ashbek pulled his other aide closer.

'*A limb hardly matters when the fate of the Dark is at stake,*' Oalark chided. '*Still, my priest is a capable healer, aren't you, golden one?*'

There was a rumble of agreement from Samuel.

'*If these are not the traitors, heal them,*' Oalark ordered, waving a negligent hand.

Elder Ashbek's daughter continued to whimper, hand plastered to the stump of her arm.

'*As you will it,*' Samuel sent.

Shari held her breath, but no Innarn streaked across the room, and Samuel held his position.

"What are you doing?" Shari wondered. He'd said that phrase a lot since they'd arrived. *As you will it.* "Oh, clever!" she said. His words were a subliminal message to the rest, that he was only carrying out the deeds Oalark wanted him to. But were the others getting the message? From what she'd seen, Shari wasn't so sure.

He held still.

Shari concentrated, but her ability to feel the Innarn outside the pocket Realm may well tip Oalark off to her presence, so she waited, and tried not to hold her breath.

It felt like hours but must have only been minutes. The Elder's daughter had swayed, the blood loss no doubt affecting her.

She saw, from the corner of Jetonyx's eyes, the great golden bulk that was Samuel rise. He made his way around the table, the entire room watching on with bated breath. After he laid a claw on the injured being, the delegates watched as her limb slowly regrew. Bone first, then the veins and arteries, muscles, and, by the sound of it, nerves.

The nerves were always when the screaming started.

He paused and looked back to where Shari presumed the Queen was sitting, before growing the skin.

The girl had passed out, slumping on her feet.

'The Roefill are not traitors.' Samuel turned and moved back to his spot at the table, careful to keep his eyes forward.

'*You must be very sure, my priest. Have you discovered who is?*' Oalark's thoughts were practically dripping with danger.

Holding her breath, Shari wasn't sure how he was going to answer. He'd been away long enough that Oalark surely had to make her own alliances and not rely on her enforcer, but to get rid of an actual traitor would surely do Lissae harm.

'*Elder Ashbek thinks of nothing bar how to help the Dark and how to ensure our victory. He and his are not the ones we seek.*' Samuel paused, and Shari shivered, hugging her knees to her chest. '*The ones we seek are more... devious in their thinking. It will take time to root them out, but I shall.'*

Shari's jaw dropped. "He just called an Elder slow." She snorted but hugged her knees harder. There was no way that he'd be allowed to get away with a comment like that, surely?

Oalark chuckled. *'You have yet to fail me, my priest.'*

"Ugh! I hate subtext!" Shari grumbled and flopped back on the sand. "Yet to fail... so don't fail me, or I'll have your hide?"

The pocket Realm rocked slightly, reminding her of when Ronah would laugh.

"Jetonyx, can you hear me?"

The screens dipped down and up.

A nod.

Burying her face in her hands, Shari resolved to keep her thoughts to herself. But there was no time to hide. Oalark was still interrogating the delegates, determined to find the traitor.

If there was no way to stop it, the least Shari could do was watch.

The flagstone floor became slick with the blood of many beings. As limbs, tusks, and flesh were removed or eaten in front of the horrified audience.

The worst part, though, was seeing how seamlessly Samuel changed into Sanithane, the most feared being in all the Realms, eager to meet out the Queen's punishment.

And there was nothing she could do to stop him.

Altum

Sanithane had never been more grateful to have had thousands of years to learn how to suppress his natural instincts.

Every slash of Oalark's claws, or whip of her tail, made him want to flinch and shy away from the atrocities she was forcing upon the delegates. Instead, he maintained his slightly bored air, and cleaned up her messes, watching as she sowed the seeds of dissent far more efficiently than he could ever have done.

At least six of the elders and eleven aides in the room were actively plotting against Oalark. It was unfortunate for them that it was in his best interest to give one of them up. Sanithane just had to pick the one with the plan least likely to succeed.

How two of the elders got to the age they now enjoyed, he would never know. They were broadcasting their thoughts so loudly; it bordered on painful. An Elder would satisfy Oalark's hunger better than an aide. She'd believe that cutting off the head was far more efficient than chopping up the body. But which one?

Zooghe's Elder dreamed about slashing her throat. Surely the tuzar knew the blade he had wouldn't make a dint in her scales? And Morreth's Elder was just as foolish, thinking he'd be able to slip some acid into her drink and watch the Queen writhe in agony before she died.

Oalark *bathed* in the stuff. A little sip was hardly going to do more than cause indigestion.

Tuzars, the lot of them.

As another aide lost a limb, Sanithane looked up. Zooghe's Elder had had enough.

'*My Queen!*' he sent, flicking an image of the Elder's thoughts to her.

'*Found you,*' Oalark purred.

It was a thing of terrible beauty, watching the white queen draw herself up and pounce on the unsuspecting Elder. His triangular head disappeared entirely into her maw, and his neck made the most satisfying crunch when she closed her jaws.

The sound did nothing to block out the mental screams from half the room.

Despite being a tuzar, Zooghe's Elder had been well liked, and over half the room was now actively plotting his former Queen's downfall.

He couldn't think of a better way to start off the conclave.

CHAPTER FOURTEEN

Lissae

Zoeday

Seventh day of the first week of Sunfall

Chamele hissed as her personal aberration wove Innarn into her skin, attaching the mask she wore to her face.

"For everything you can supposedly do, you can't make it hurt less?" Chamele snarled.

"Zhahyeem, Elder," the aberration said, wraith-like hands drawing away from her face.

The thing whimpered when Chamele struck out, the signet ring on her middle finger splitting the paper-thin skin of its cheek. "Don't use their words," the Elder snapped.

"Apologies, Elder." The thing moved away, wiping at the trail of blood dripping down its cheek.

Leaning forward, Chamele peered into the mirror, running her hand over the seam where the mask lay. It was, as usual, flawless.

"If it wasn't for your mother, you wouldn't have to be here, you know?" she said to the aberration. It had been right when the thing behind her had been old enough to walk and talk. Its mother had come out of nowhere and exploded. The Innarn backlash had melted Chamele's face to the point where she was nearly unrecognisable as human.

That was the day the white clouds had overcome her vision and shown her the way for a better Lissae.

She turned her head, studying her other cheek.

In a way, this was preferable. She would remain ageless now. Never again would she have to worry about wrinkles, or hair in the wrong places. Instead, her aberration would ensure her beauty for decades to come.

"Satisfactory, aberration."

It nodded, huddling back in its corner. Like it should.

Pleased, Chamele rose and straightened her robes.

Without looking at the corner, she said, "You may eat today." And swept from the room. She had a delegation to impress.

Arilla took a breath in and swung the sword, tip unerringly pointed at the training dummy's throat. Or, what would be a throat if it wasn't so blob-shaped. Or a bag of flour with a rough outline drawn on it.

"Dinner rush is about to start," Calem called through the door of the back room.

Sighing, Arilla wiped the sword down with a soft cloth and returned it to the stand. She'd be able to get an hour of practice after they closed.

Her skin itched at the thought. Everything in her said she should practise more, *more.*

Was this how Shari felt? The unending urge to keep practising, keep going, keep defending?

Still, hungry customers made for cranky ones if they were left waiting too long.

Pasting on a smile, Arilla pushed through the door and stepped out into the fray.

Hidden in the shadows of the darkened hall, Skye waited until Chamele strode past. Silently, she slipped into the Elder's rooms.

If she could just find something to prove that Chamele was unstable, then surely the rest of the council would abandon their ridiculous plan?

Hurrying, she moved over to the dressing table. The surface was empty apart from a jewellery box.

Someone as immaculate as Jinkor's Elder would have a lotion or two on hand. She is always so flawless.

"Thank you," a scratchy voice said.

Skye's eyes darted up, and she sucked in a breath.

The mirror reflected the corner of the room, where a shape draped in rags was huddled. Zir head lifted, eyes glowing a piercing blue.

"You're welcome?" Skye squeaked, heart pounding so hard, she was sure the being across the room could hear it.

The rags moved. Skye sucked in a breath.

There was a being under there.

Withered, bony hands reached out. "Thank you?"

"I... ah... what?" Skye turned away from the dresser and faced the being.

At least, she thought it was a being.

Skin pulled tight, the bones beneath showed clearly. Bruises darkened zir jaw and exposed shoulder, where the rag had slipped down.

"Food?"

"Right. Of course." Edging closer, Skye opened her pack and reached in. She had a corn muffin and an apple she'd been saving for lunch. One day without food wouldn't hurt her, but it might kill this poor being. Carefully, she placed the muffin in zir ands.

Ze looked at the muffin like it was all the riches in the world.

"Who are you?"

"Aberration." Delicately, ze picked a bit of corn out and lifted it to her mouth. Crooked yellow teeth took a careful bite, and ze hummed.

"Aberr…"

Heavy footsteps sounded outside the room.

Terrified, Skye glanced around. There was nowhere to hide.

The ragged being tilted zir head, and Skye shivered as Innarn flowed over her.

The door slammed open, banging against the wall hard enough to disguise the squeak.

Skye wasn't sure if she should move or not.

A guard, dressed in Jinkor black and red, strode into the room, staring contemptuously at the corner. "Elder says you're to be fed."

Both of them whimpered.

The being's hands were suspiciously free of the muffin. Pitifully, ze reached out.

The guard sauntered over. His belt was straining on the last notch, and his odour was more eye watering than the rotten food on the tray he carried.

"Oops," he said, grinning darkly as he tilted the tray. Dishes filled with rancid food tipped and spilled all over the being. "Clumsy me."

"Thank you," ze said, head bowed.

Laughing, he turned and walked away. "Eat up now," he said, roughly pulling the door closed.

Skye moaned, holding her nose.

Sighing, the being waved zir hand, and the mess disappeared, along with the smell. "Food," ze whispered, pulling the muffin out of the safety of zir robes. Breaking off a piece, ze then offered it to Skye.

"You have it," Skye said, shaking her head. She took an apple from her bag and held it out.

The being tilted zir head and looked at the shiny red fruit.

"You've... never seen an apple?"

Ze blinked.

Skye's eyes welling up. She didn't know what was going on, but no being should be treated like this. No *creature* should be treated the way she was. Forcing her tears down, she took a bite of the juicy red fruit and offered it to zir again. "You're not an aberration," she said. "You... you are strength. You are..." When she'd been a girl, and fallen over, her mother would tell her to stand up and continue with grace. "Can I call you Grace?" she asked, handing over the apple.

The being nodded. "Thank you."

"Okay, Grace, I'm not particularly powerful, but here." Skye took her crystal slab out of her bag and removed her metal comb from her hair. Running the sharp edge of the comb along the corner of the slab, she pushed her Innarn down through the metal and clipped off a corner. Careful of the sharp side, she held it out. "Keep this safe. Don't let anyone see it, okay? If something happens to you, or you need me, push your Innarn into the chip, and I'll know. The slab will glow and tell me."

Grace nodded and took the crystal chip. Reaching back and lifting the edge of the thin square mat she was sitting on, Grace then slipped the crystal under it, along with a meagre pile of things she must have collected through the years. Turning back, her glowing blue eyes fixed on her. "Go."

"But..."

Growling, Grace pushed against the air, and Skye felt herself moving to the door.

'I'll come back for you—I swear!'

She was out through the door and back into the hall before she could blink. Staring at the closed door, stunned, Skye wasn't sure what to make of the whole thing.

Someone cleared their throat behind her.

Jumping nearly out of her skin, Skye turned.

It was Chamele.

"Elder!" she simpered, sliding into the professional aide mask.

"Yes?" Her brows went up.

"My apologies. I was sent to see if you needed an escort, but when I got here, I didn't want to disturb you. And, well..." Skye stammered and blushed, looking at the ground.

Chamele waited a beat too long before she answered. "You could have knocked."

"I didn't want to wake you. It was a minor thing. Elder Suni wanted to check which tea you'd prefer today. I'd hate to disturb your beauty rest, I really would. You're just so flawless," Skye babbled. She glanced up through her lashes and immediately knew she'd said the wrong thing. Leaning in, she whispered, "You always look so graceful under all the pressure of your role. I really wish I could be like you."

The set of the Elder's shoulders relaxed. "Why, thank you. Keep following your elder, and maybe you will be." She smiled beatifically, and Skye purposefully didn't note that one side of her mouth hadn't moved. "And green tea, today. As always."

"Of course, Elder Chamele." Skye nodded and slipped away from the door. She scurried down the hall, praying to the Old Gods that her heart would stop beating so loudly.

"Aide," Chamele called.

Skye turned back. "Yes, Elder?"

"Did you enter my rooms?"

Eyes wide, Skye affected her most innocent look. "No, Elder."

Chamele lazily looked her up and down. "Good." She turned and opened her door.

Hoping that Grace had finished the muffin, Skye scrambled away from the Elder as quickly as she could.

She needed to get word back to the Altoriae about this as soon as possible.

Adonday
First day of the second week of Sunfall

Tania smiled at Fenix, who looked slightly nervous. Or maybe she was just projecting?

The Linked had arranged to meet at Fenix's house. As she had to finish the school day, Tania was the last one to arrive.

"Thank you for inviting us into your home, Fenix. I don't think I've been in a Fire Innarn structure before," Tania said. She took a seat on a colourful cushion placed before the low table and grinned at Zana and Milo, who were seated across from her.

Fenix blinked at her. "What do you mean?"

"Oh, well, I kind of found out recently that I'm an Innarnian—only found out when we moved to Ronah."

"When was that?" Milo asked.

"At the start of spring," Tania said with a shrug.

Cyrus and Fenix looked at each other, eyes wide.

"She had had quite an experience. Let us not forget that Tania may have insights into the way mainlanders operate." Zana may have looked totally serene, but Tania caught the uptick at the corners of her lips as the older Linked tried to hide her surprise.

"Start of spring," Fenix muttered, shaking their head. "Right, ah, these mainlanders, what do you think they want?"

"Crystal," Cyrus said darkly.

"Power," Tania shot back.

"Money," Milo said.

"Milo, you can take a break, you know?" Fenix grinned.

"There's still so much to do. The joining for the next island to organise, your exercise regime must be maintained, and you have a fitting with the Altoriae's stylist to prepare for tomorrow." Milo ran a finger down his clipboard, and Fenix sighed.

"I really don't understand why you follow me around, Milo. You're a decorated scientist! You've discovered things crystal can do that even Cyrus hasn't." Fenix glanced at Talhan's Linked. "No offence, Cyrus. Did you know Milo was the one who discovered the connection between copper and crystal longevity?"

Cyrus's jaw dropped. "Wait. You're *that* Milo?" He sat down heavily. "Just wait until I tell Temira I met you. She's going to be so mad she missed you!"

"What if Milo takes the day off being my shadow?" Fenix smiled gently at the tiny man. "And visits you at the Techno Centre tomorrow?"

Both men bounced in their seats. "That sounds like an excellent use of my time," Milo said.

"Oh, brilliant! I can't wait to see what you think of the latest gadgets." Cyrus grinned.

"I shall go prepare. I have a few things of my own that you may like to look over." Milo rose and scurried from the room.

"So, crystals and power. Is that not the same thing?" Fenix tilted their head.

"They don't want crystals to power things, they want to control people. Anything and everything they do is about control. Innarnians threaten that on so many levels." She so desperately wanted to wrap her arms around herself to ward off the chill that was creeping into her bones.

"And crystals will give them that sort of power?" Fenix asked.

"How much do crystals sell for?" Tania asked Cyrus. Zana and Fenix looked confused by the question.

"Small ones, forty gold pieces. Ones big enough to power a dwelling can go for five hundred," Cyrus answered.

"So, where I lived before, most people would get, say, ten gold per hour they work. Sounds like a lot, doesn't it? I always thought so."

"Ten gold is more than I've ever seen at once," Zana admitted.

"That's because Talhan, and correct me if I'm wrong, is the only Shifting Island who trades in currency."

"I'm pretty sure we are. Talhan has so many people from all over, it was easier," Cyrus said.

"But it's not. Think of it like this. If you work, say, fifty hours a week, that's five hundred gold."

Zana gasped, and Fenix's eyes went wide.

"Ah, but you have a family to feed. And food costs gold. There's one hundred gone." Tania was oversimplifying, but figured she'd make her point soon enough. "And you need a place to live. When you're only earning that much, someone else is most likely going to own your home, so you pay to stay there."

"Beings do that?" Fenix asked, frowning.

Tania nodded. "And it's not cheap. So, maybe half your weekly gold goes there. Healers, furniture, clothing, comforts, cleaning supplies, the morning paper—everything costs coins. At the end of it all, you'd maybe have twenty or thirty gold to save or spend on something you enjoy." Viciously, she shoved the memories that threatened to spill over away. Now was not the time to focus on what her dad would spend the family's extra coin on. "When a small crystal costs more than that, and a large one costs an entire week's worth of wages, it becomes out of reach for many people."

"How does that affect us?" Zana asked so innocently, Tania bit back her instinctive hurt.

"It's..."

"Do the mainlanders want to control the crystals to make them cheaper for their people?" Cyrus asked.

She laughed. "I doubt it. See, there are mainlanders at the other end of the scale, with those who make more money in a minute than most see in a lifetime. And not all of them want to help others. Chamele strikes me as someone who wants to get rich. Now, she could do it for a good reason, or maybe she just wants to keep the gold for herself. I'd say, from what you've said, it's more the latter than the former."

"And how can we stop them?"

Settling back in her seat, Tania grinned. "What defences do your islands have?"

Chamele sat back in her chair and stared out at the ambassadors before her. Through the white mist clouding her thoughts, she wondered if she could have gathered a more cohesive group. They were barely fit enough to be in her presence, let alone in the same room, and yet here they were, plotting to overthrow some of the most annoying, dangerous people on Lissae.

Someone had to save the wretched Innarnians from themselves, after all. Why not her?

"Do we have a plan?"

"We have the making of a plan, Chamele."

She raised a brow. The making of a plan was not what she was after.

"The decimation of my forces on Talhan's beach was..." Elder Gwyn started.

"If you say 'unprecedented' Gwyn, I will be disappointed in you," Chamele drawled. "We have long known the capabilities of the aberrations. This was merely a test. Now we know the results, we can experiment more."

"What do you mean?" Elder Suni asked.

Chamele looked Elder Suni directly in the eye and took her time, sipping on her tea. "Must I spell it out? Capture one of the beasts and run a series of tests. Find what will break them, then replicate it on a larger scale. It really isn't a hard concept to grasp."

The aide refilling her cup was shaking, although she managed not to spill a drop.

It was the same one who'd been outside her rooms.

"Does the thought disgust you, girl?" Chamele asked, sweeter than the honey she spooned into the tea.

"Only the thought of getting close to one of... *them*."

"A girl after my own heart." Chamele smiled, and the aide withdrew. "One or two of the beasts from each of our lands shouldn't be missed too much. Aim for those with few connections."

"And if someone asks about them?" Gwyn queried.

Tipping her nose into the air, Chamele said, "Say we put them to work."

Jonathan ran his hand through his hair. If he didn't know better, he'd say he was pining.

"Distracted?" Zac asked as he rounded the table. He caught Jonathan's gaze and took a sip from a glass before placing it on the table.

"Are you always going to do that?"

"Do what?"

"Test my drinks for me?"

Something hot flared behind Zac's eyes, but he kept his words mild. "I can't make up for what happened with the femto crystals, so I'll do it 'till you trust me again."

"And how will you know that?"

Lifting his own glass, Zac smiled. "I just will."

"The patrol groups are sorted," Jonathan blurted. He could feel the blood rushing to his face.

"Really?" Zac drew the word out. "Is that what has you so distracted?"

Taking a sip, Jonathan shook his head. "This is the longest Shari hasn't been bouncing around in my head since I discovered who she really was. It's disconcerting."

"Quiet, too, I bet."

He laughed. "Shari's sends are more images and feelings. A lot of colours usually. It took me years to decipher what it all meant. She does talk, but rarely."

"Is it the distance?"

"No, she's close enough." Jonathan took another drink and ignored the little voice in the back of his head chanting *liar*. Zac was right in that he wasn't entirely sure he could trust him yet. And the fewer people who knew where Shari was, the better.

CHAPTER FIFTEEN

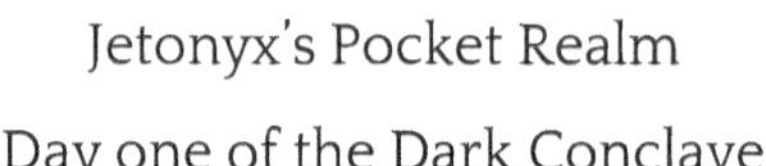

Jetonyx's Pocket Realm

Day one of the Dark Conclave

Shari sucked a breath in between her teeth as Oalark slurped on the innards of the Zooghe ambassador.

'Don't react. Her minions would express nothing but delight at the scene.' Samuel's voice sounded as an echo in her head—although she could barely hear it over the blood thrumming through her veins, demanding she take action. *'She uses this test to draw out the weak and the pretenders. Don't fall for it.'*

He was talking to Jetonyx.

'Something wrong, hatchling?' Oalark had taken notice, despite Sam's warning.

'There were so many ways I could answer that question, but which one won't get me killed?' Jetonyx was fairly shaking in his scales.

"Try: Your impromptu meal has merely reminded me of how long it's been since I last ate," Shari said aloud.

A distorted echo told her the black Q'Aralide had used her words.

'*Then, by all means.*' Oalark graciously waved a claw at the remains of her victim.

'*The marrow from the finger bones.*' Samuel's sharp send was at total odds to his put-upon sigh.

'*My thanks,*' Jetonyx simpered to Oalark, and stepped forward.

Swallowing bile, Shari watched helplessly as Jetonyx knelt. She sent a wordless apology to the Zooghe Elder as her host neatly sliced off the smallest finger. Swiftly, he parted the skin and flesh, removing the three bones and retreating to his spot.

Oalark lazily chewed the morsel of flesh he'd left behind as she watched Jetonyx snap a bone in two and bring it to his maw. He made an obscene slurping noise, sucking the marrow from the bone with delight.

Shari shivered.

'*My thanks,*' he sent again.

Appearing satisfied with his reaction, Oalark turned to see how the rest of the council had reacted to her sudden violent outburst.

Jetonyx slumped slightly, and looked out at the crowded room as well. Impressed that none of them were stupid enough to go against the Queen on her own ground, with a building surrounded by guards she commanded, Shari could still make out a few dark expressions. What excuse Oalark would use to get rid of them?

"Well, now I get why Sam and Jon were so worried about this." Shari dug her toes into the sand and sighed. "The Queen is totally, absolutely mad."

Head snapping around, the pale Queen glared at Jetonyx. "Make yourself useful, hatchling. Fetch my chest."

'*Chest? What chest? Where is the chest?*' Jetonyx sounded absolutely desperate.

Clear as day, the highest screen lit up with a totally different scene. It showed dark, pulsating chambers and, pushed haphazardly into a corner, a chest that seemed to writhe every time Shari's eyes slid away from it.

'As *you will it, my Queen*.' Jetonyx didn't sound nearly as confident as Samuel did, but she shooed him away all the same.

The scene played over as they walked outside, the view rocking with each step he took. Mammoth guards let him pass, clearly informed of his passage.

As he walked through the streets, Shari got her first good look at the Realm of Altum.

It was all movement. Slippery soft sighs of scales against flesh as a creature who defied all logical size constraints moved in undulating waves against something alive who made up the ground Jetonyx was walking on.

"The mountains are alive," Shari muttered. The movement was slow enough that from a curious glance one would not realise, but it was one that Jetonyx couldn't seem to take his eyes off.

'*That's how I know I'm home*.' Just from his send, Shari could tell he was smiling.

"Is everything alive in Altum?"

The view dipped and rose. Another nod.

Shari leaned back, trying to take everything in. The trees were bony spikes with calcified branches. Dwellings appeared to be made from the same flesh the ground was. Perhaps they were giant, hollowed out warts? She chuckled, her host ignoring the hysterical noise.

"A creature big enough to house the Q'Aralide race. The size of its brain must be enormous," she said. "Or incredibly small." She couldn't imagine how Oalark had enslaved such a creature. Surely, if it just turned over, they'd all be crushed?

Turning towards the largest dwelling they had seen so far, Jetonyx's claws curled as he carefully opened the door.

Inside the darkened room were the same red drapes hanging from open windows.

As Jetonyx passed through them, Shari saw what they were.

Skin.

They were made of flayed skin.

Shari was glad that her host had not included smell in his effort to let her know what was happening outside the pocket Realm. The stench must be horrific.

He moved deeper into the dwelling, through another set of doors, and into a room with the Realm's biggest bed.

So busy goggling at it, Shari almost missed the whimper.

Jetonyx didn't. His head snapped to the side, looking straight at where the noise had come from.

There were no torches or lights in this part of the dwelling, the area hid in shadow. Her host blinked twice, and it came into focus.

Cages ringed the wall of the room. Each one held a creature of a different species, all in various stages of undress. Some, by the dark liquid splattered on the bottom of the cages and the stumps they were cradling, were missing limbs.

One, closest to them, held a Q'Aralide even smaller than Jetonyx.

And it wasn't moving.

'Vice?' Jetonyx whispered, moving closer to the cage.

"Don't," a man croaked in the next one over. "Don't come any closer." He pointed a shaky finger at a glowing line on the floor. "Wouldn't wish this life on anyone."

'*What happened?*'

"Captures us, tests her theories, and then we end up like—" He jerked his head at the fallen Q'Aralide.

'*Is he dead?*' Jetonyx sounded detached. Had he had been friends with the unmoving Vice?

"Think so. Smells like," the man said. "Don't end up the same. Get what she asked for and get out. Lest you take his place."

Jetonyx was shaking again. He nodded hastily, and scampered to the other side of the room, well clear of the glowing silver line. Picking up the chest, he threw the man a nod over his shoulder and strode out.

"Wait!" Shari yelled.

He paused in the main room.

"We need to help them! We can't just leave them like that."

'*Vengeance takes time,*' Jetonyx sent to her.

No matter how she cursed at him, or what she said, he didn't turn back.

Shari fell onto the sand and cried.

Altum

Sanithane tried not to drum his claws against the table as Oalark decimated another elder. Honestly, how had half the fools who'd gotten the title survived long enough to earn it?

But with each slurp of entrails, Oalark continued to build enemies faster than expected. Goodness knows what she'd been doing for diplomacy whilst he'd been away.

"Now that's taken care of"—the Queen turned, the intestines of the Cradamull Elder dangling from her maw—"what was next on the agenda?"

She's either gone mad, or is doing it for the effect. Either way, he refused to react.

Glancing down at the parchment before him, Sanithane read, "Constitution amendments."

Oalark sashayed her bulk over to her rest, and lowered herself gracefully. She glanced at him and batted her eyes. "And they would be?"

A sudden, sickening realisation made him glad he'd not partaken in her feast. *She is trying to impress me.*

"I believe we can gratefully strike off the Zooghe and Cradamull amendments," he said, tipping his head to her.

She giggled.

The entire room seemed void of necessary air as he struggled not to throw up. He hoped that would be enough to prevent any more bloodshed. "There are three separate amendments to Article Two: Weapons Within City Borders. Three cities have asked for the following: Yrusri ask that spears and pikes be re-added after a two hundred year hiatus. Damiuth wishes for concealed blades to be withdrawn, and Otike proposes claw sheaths should be worn."

"Claw sheaths?" Oalark asked.

"They are the latest fashion." Otike's ambassador rose. An imposing, green-skinned giantess with golden caps on her prominent under tusks. She lifted a hand, and the claws protruding from her fingertips and her knuckles all bore the same golden caps.

Before Oalark could retort, Sanithane swallowed the build-up of acid in his throat and purred, "Very eye-catching."

Otike's ambassador flushed a deeper green, and Oalark growled.

"They would suit you well, my Queen." He smiled at her.

Oalark coughed and looked at the gold glinting on the ambassador's tusks. "Do you have samples?"

Dropping a curtsy, the giantess nodded and passed them around the table. "Of course, for the esteemed members of the council, we offer these to you freely. To the public, we would have to charge."

And there is the catch.

As the samples for Oalark made their way along the table, Sanithane caught a curious scent. Something bitter, and not quite familiar. A smell that reminded him of blood and pain and tears.

At the slightly too-wide smile of the giantess, Sanithane startled.

The Otike had done something to their samples.

Sitting back on his rest, he kept all three eyes trained on the giantess as she sank smugly into her seat, revelling in the thanks from those with tusks and claws. Eventually, she glanced at the Q'Aralides, and blanched when she caught him staring at her.

Jetonyx was reentering the room, and yet he didn't move his gaze.

"Do they suit me, my priest?"

Sanithane finally averted his eyes and glanced at Oalark. "The caps suit you perfectly, my Queen." He looked back to the Otike ambassador, who was doing her best not to gape at him.

He smiled, showing a few too many teeth.

She took a shuddering breath and nodded firmly.

Message understood.

Jetonyx's Pocket Realm

Shari didn't know what had happened in the short time they were gone, but they were down five more elders.

After what she'd seen in Oalark's chambers, she could only be grateful that their ending had been quicker than those the queen kept prisoner.

Jetonyx silently delivered the chest to the queen, then scampered back to his place behind Samuel's shoulder.

'I, too, *have a gift*,' Oalark said.

There was no need to look out of the screens to know the mad queen would be all teeth. The sound of a lock turning had Shari raising herself up, curious despite the horrors she'd witnessed.

Inside the chest were tentacled eggs, each softly writhing on a bed of green.

There were gasps of delighted astonishment all around the table as Oalark carefully lifted egg after egg out of their protective packaging.

"What are they doing?"

She wished she hadn't asked.

As the last egg found their owner, Oalark clapped her hands together. '*I know we've had a rough start to the conclave.*' She sounded genuinely unhappy by the fact.

"You were the rough start, you..." Shari broke off, unable to find a word hideous enough to describe her.

'*I thought it best we have a treat. Please, enjoy the dudrodie eggs, freshly harvested just two nights passed.*' Oalark smiled beatifically but reached out a claw and stopped Samuel from partaking.

All the others slurped theirs down, smiling and chattering.

Oalark turned to Samuel, the smile falling off her face. '*Not for us, my priest. These are just for our esteemed guests.*'

Something about the way she said it made the fine hairs on the back of Shari's neck stand up. "And I'm not even in the same room," she said, rubbing at her arms.

Jetonyx shuffled on the spot but made no move to leave.

Shari watched the ambassadors closely, but there didn't seem to be any signs of distress.

Still, Oalark looked far too pleased with herself to be giving a benign gift to the others.

'*Slow-acting poisons are her favourite.*' Sanithane's send to Jetonyx echoed.

Shivering, Shari almost wished she could turn back time and enjoy her blissful, naïve beach without having to witness the horror on the screens before her.

CHAPTER SIXTEEN

Lissae

Inthday

Second day of the second week of Sunfall

Fenix quirked a brow at the mirror and huffed. Smoothing the front of their tunic again, they turned to the side, checking the fit.

"Good enough." They tugged on the hem again. It was time to head to the garden. The market would happen tomorrow, and it was all hands on deck. Already, curious beings from the other isle had been dropping by to sample the Daen's wares and get a feel for what might be offered.

Tugging on the tassel next to the door, Fenix blinked the requisite three times, and murmured thanks to their home as they left.

Daens of all sizes and ages were in the streets today, scrubbing, sweeping, and cleaning to prepare for the markets. Carefully stepping over the puddles, Fenix pulled to a stop when they saw a crying child on a door stoop.

Kneeling, Fenix rubbed the young one's back. "What's wrong?"

"I... I stepped in a pubble!" She wailed.

"In a puddle?" Fenix asked.

Through the tears, she nodded.

"Well, why are you sitting and making more?" Fenix joked. "Up you get. Got to put it right."

They both stood, and Fenix reached up to pluck three thick leaves off the wirri plant that hung from the doorframe.

"How?" The child sniffed and wiped her sleeve across her nose.

"Oh, puddles are easy. Do you know why we hang wirri leaf in our entrance ways?"

She nodded and sniffed again. "To keep the bad luck out."

"And what is stepping in a puddle?"

"Bad luck."

Fenix nodded. "So, we find the puddle you stepped in..." They held out their hand, and the girl took it, leading them only a few paces from the stoop.

The child glared fiercely at the offending water.

Fenix tried hard not to snicker. Laughing at the old superstitions was just as bad luck as stepping into a puddle could be. "Now, how many times did you step in it?"

Two pudgy fingers rose.

Solemnly, Fenix handed over two wirri leaves. "Drop these into the water and say *aqua ineas.*"

"Aqua ineas," she said. The leaves fell from her fingers and drifted directly into the puddle, where the liquid soaked into the ground.

"No more bad luck."

Giving Fenix a gap-toothed grin, the girl hugged their middle and scurried away.

"How much bad luck would Cantash be in if their Linked stepped in a puddle?" a voice asked.

"Cantash will remove the puddles without me having to ask." Sparing a glance, Fenix noted the Daen from the Altoriae's guild was matching their strides. The road before them was curiously free from the water that had been used to scrub it clean.

"And why are puddles bad luck?" She pushed.

"Why would water be bad around fire?" Fenix shot back.

Thinking and walking were not in this guild member's strengths. Fenix pulled them out of the way of two carts and a pole before she processed the answer. "Water puts a fire out. I still don't understand..."

"You didn't grow up around here, did you...?" Fenix trailed off.

"Amara," she offered.

"Amara. Pretty much everything on Cantash relates to the flame. And anything that threatens it is viewed as bad luck. Because it is. We go cold if the flames go out. And hungry if the underground does. If the heart of Cantash goes out, we stop moving. It's happened before."

"But a puddle?" Amara pressed.

"Imagine trying to start a fire with damp wood. It takes time to dry out, but there are puddles all over from the rain. Just as you get a spark, someone steps in one too close, and the water splashes up."

"And the sparks go out."

"Exactly."

"Wow." Amara was unimpressed, if her flat tone was anything to go by.

Fenix looked around. People were skirting ladders and dodging puddles, leaving large chunks of the street free until Fenix walked by. They were followed by thanks as they grew closer to the gates.

"Ladders are a thing, too, aren't they?" she blurted.

"A thing? Well, you can't carry soup up one, but it's just poor etiquette to walk under a ladder. What if you knocked it?" Fenix shook their head.

"Cantash seems like the island of 'what-ifs,'" Amara said.

Laughing, Fenix pushed open the doors. "Cantash relies on a delicate balance to make sure our way of life is sustained. Over the years, it's meant a few superstitions have appeared. And they've been added to and adjusted until we have what we have today."

"Do you have one for everything?" she asked.

Pausing, Fenix gave their answer some thought. "Most things, but not everything."

Amara laughed. "Do you ever get used to them?"

"I've known nothing different," Fenix said, shrugging. They nodded to Milo as he trotted over to them, clipboard in hand.

The smile fell from Amara's face. "Lucky you."

"Where did you grow up?"

But the question got lost in the rumbling of carts exiting the doors.

"Thanks, Fenix!" someone called.

Waving, they turned to ask again, but Amara had disappeared.

Knocking on the doorframe to entice friendly spirits to follow the guild member, Fenix slipped into the elevator and sighed as it descended.

A Daen who wasn't superstitious. They hadn't thought such a being existed.

"Today's plan is quite simple, really." Milo's voice brought Fenix out of their daze.

"This morning, you're ensuring all the beasts are in the correct parts of the garden. A brief commune with Cantash, followed by a light lunch. In the afternoon, you have a meeting with the other Linked." Milo sniffed, as if he found the mere thought of the others odorous.

"Are you joining the technomancer today?" Fenix asked.

"After I see you safely to the gardens, I will. First, medicine." After thrusting a hand into the satchel hanging by his side, Milo withdrew a vial and held it out.

"Must I?" Fenix sighed.

"Yes. You know your mother made you take it every day for your health. Must keep it up."

Fenix glared at the blue liquid flecked with glowing yellow motes and sighed again. Uncorking the bottle, they wrinkled their nose. Downing it swiftly, they wiped their mouth to hide a grimace.

"Excellent." Milo smiled briefly before glancing at his clipboard.

'*Again!*' Jonathan broadcasted.

The two-hundred-and-fifty strong guild moved as one, flowing through the first defensive water pattern.

'*Now, air motus three!*'

Seamlessly, they flowed onto the next one, occasionally waiting for a member to correct their stance, or adjusting their neighbours as needed.

'*Fire defence six,*' Jonathan sent.

Interestingly, the Returned started moving through the motus he had yet to show them.

The patterns were older than he was. They were something he'd picked up from Joshua, the last Guardian, but he hadn't been aware that they were as longstanding as the Returned.

Feet stomped, hands flared, and voices rang out as those who knew the move guided the others through them.

There was something stunning about watching such a large group move as one.

'*Again!*'

He called three more times for a repeat before he was satisfied.

'*Stop! Take a two-minute break. You've all done well.*'

"Generous," Lizbeth said.

Jonathan chuckled. "Don't want them to become complacent."

"Good point. Why isn't Samuel leading the session?" Lizbeth leaned in closer.

"He's still patrolling," Jonathan said.

Lizbeth studied him, her sightless gaze moving across his form as if she was searching for something. "Do you know why I never mourned not having vision?"

"Because you were born without it?" he asked.

She laughed, a mirthless, hollow sound. "Because I can see so much more by looking through my other senses. My friend may be off-Realm, but he is not patrolling. And you, Guardian, need to learn to lie better. Especially with the mainlanders stirring up trouble."

"Who said I'm lying?" Jonathan tried.

"Fool me once, Guardian." Lizbeth rose and shook her head at him.

'Sometimes I'm not at liberty to say...'

"Then say that. But the instant you *can* tell me something, please do. I find I miss his company." Lizbeth clutched her bag closer and sniffed slightly.

"Well, I have something that might help with that. Meet me after the session is done?"

Studying him once more, Lizbeth nodded and walked sedately out of the training grounds.

"Uh, Guardian?" Mu called.

'From the top! Collis, take over calling the drills, please,' Jonathan sent. He had a shadow to trap.

Arilla shared a look with Calem as SilverCloud raised a trembling hand to adjust his robe. Collis had come straight from training, and had agreed to tend the tavern whilst they stole away with some of the other shop owners to sample Cantash's markets before the general populace.

As an Elder, SilverCloud had bartered his way in, offering some of the nectar collected by the honeyhawks. Despite their leisurely pace, the journey from Ronah to Cantash had worn on Calem's father. Long gone were the days when he would outlast them all.

"Go on ahead," SilverCloud said. "I'm happiest right here." He sat carefully on a bench, and Arilla grinned as the Daen vendors doted on him, offering the Elder the first pick of their produce. He looked at home, surrounded by the vibrant colours of the stalls and their holders.

"I worry about him," Calem said. "Between my father and Shari, it's a wonder we get any sleep."

"Sleep is for those who don't stress." Arilla smiled up at him, bumping her hip into his.

Calem smiled at her. "Or those who don't have a daughter whose favourite hobby is patrolling when she thinks we're asleep."

Moving to a stall that had bushels of bright red pears hanging from the wooden cross beam, Arilla gently tested one. "I don't know if I should be grateful we can't catch her sneaking out anymore, or more worried now we don't know what she's getting up to."

"Daughter troubles?" the vendor asked, wiping her counter down with a pale green cloth before leaning on it.

They nodded, grinning at each other.

"I have six, from ten to twenty years old. I would say it gets better, but I don't think I'm there yet."

The three of them laughed.

"Half of letting them go is making sure they're ready for the Realm. The other half is making sure the Realm is ready for them," she said, and winked.

"The Realms have never been ready for Shari," Arilla said.

"Shari... the Altoriae?"

"The one and same," Calem said.

"Praise be Adeon. Your girl has saved mine twice over!" After ducking under her counter, she bounced back out and reached across, handing them both a tiny candle. "You're here to shop, yes? Show these, and the others will give you first pick of their produce."

"Oh." Arilla shared a look with Calem. They'd decided long ago that they wouldn't take advantage of Shari's status. "Thank you, but..."

"The Altoriae has saved half the Daen patrols, or near enough to. We'll not have her parents leaving empty-handed!"

"Shari is big on treating everyone fairly. We'd love it if you would honour that," Calem said gently.

The stall owner paused, tears welling in her eyes. "She is the *perfect* Altoriae. Still, keep the candles. If you see something that will help her, please, let us know and use them."

"We will," Arilla said, smiling. She badly wanted to pat the woman's hands but it would come across as wrong to an Innarnian.

Keeping one eye on SilverCloud and the surrounding crowd, they moved farther into the market, sampling wares, and putting in orders for some spicy cheese and a new type of jam with a delicious tang to it.

By the end of the night, Arilla doubted she could handle one more taste test, or look at another tiny glass full of drink without her eyes swimming.

"Tired, love?"

"Home time," she agreed, leaning against Calem as he wrapped his arm snugly around her waist.

As they returned to SilverCloud, who was dozing against some brightly coloured cushions, Arilla smiled. She hoped Shari wasn't in too much trouble.

Kerday

Third day of the second week of Sunfall

Collis, sweat pouring down his back and making his shirt stick unpleasantly to his skin, finally called a stop to the training session.

"You are absolutely brutal!" Raven, formerly of Freeson, mopped his forehead.

"Collis is the best," Remmy said, patting him on the back and laughing when Collis glared at him.

"But, why him? No offence, but you're really young," Mu said.

Remmy snorted. "Collis might be one of the youngest Returned, but his soul is older than all of ours combined."

"I don't know if I should be offended by that or not," Collis said mildly.

"What do you mean?" Raven asked.

"Collis was the one who held us together. He was the one to make us safe, keep us informed, and when it was time, he was the one who led us out of the waking nightmare we were trapped in." Remmy conjured a glass full of water and raised it in a mock toast.

"You and I remember our time away very differently," Collis said.

"Really? You're going to try that? Alright." Remmy drained the glass and threw it to the ground before jogging up the steps on the side of the training ground.

Sighing, Collis waved his hand and reduced the glass back to sand.

A piercing whistle rang out across the grounds.

Everyone turned to find Remmy, standing above them in the stands.

"Returned!" he yelled.

Collis groaned.

The rest of the Returned cheered.

"Who held us together when we were gone?" Remmy shouted across the silent training grounds.

"Muran!" Collis called back.

He was drowned out by the sound of his name.

Remmy pumped his fist, whooping and stirring the crowd up.

"Who kept us safe?"

His name again.

"Who led us home?" Remmy was almost hoarse with shouting now, and all around them, the Returned were in a frenzy.

"Collis!"

"And who doubts his importance again?"

There was a smattering of laughter this time, and only a few people called his name, but it was enough for it to echo.

"We are going to pound who you are into your skull, Collis Iuvo!" Remmy pointed at him, a grin stretching so wide it had to hurt. "Because when we gave up, you were there. When we'd had enough, you were there. And when you don't believe? We'll be here. We always will."

The breath shuddered out of Collis's lungs, and he wiped away a different wetness from his face.

Tears.

CHAPTER SEVENTEEN

Altum

Day two of the Dark Conclave

Sanithane was going to kill the Altoriae if she didn't stop making snide comments about the Queen.

It made his job of looking bored by the proceedings that much harder when he was trying not to snicker. And the puzzle of how long the Otike had been planning this made him curious. What, exactly, did they have planned for Oalark?

He could only hope the poison coating the insides of the Queen's newest adornments was faster acting than the dudrodie eggs.

Shari was definitely a bad influence on him.

'The amendments have been agreed to, the gifts given. Does anyone else have any other business before we see to the main event?' Half-expecting Oalark to say something, Sanithane turned to her.

She demurely shook her head, eyes twinkling madly at him.

Someone is about to die.

For the first time since they'd entered the room, War'Jan stirred. '*I recently found out something interesting from the Grey Realms. Humans have these things called "trust exercises". Mostly rubbish things like falling backwards and trusting others around you to prevent imminent pain. I thought about doing a similar exercise over our acid rivers...*'

'*Acid rivers?*' Shari's send was thin, and a little reedy, but it was there, reminding Sanithane he was not alone in this madness.

Although, if he could choose, he would have prevented Shari from coming. No one needed to witness the horrors of the Dark Conclave.

'*But I thought there'd only be one strong enough to catch me.*' Oalark had broken in and was batting her eyes at Sanithane.

He took a sip from his goblet to disguise his shudder.

'*So, I came up with something else,*' War'Jan continued, as if his mate hadn't interrupted.

Guts churning, Sanithane idly pulled the poison from his system and shifted it directly into War'Jan's belly.

'*If you trusted us enough to drink from our goblets, you will be feeling the effects by now. Grytycide is, as you know, deadly.*'

Chairs scraping back were drowned out by the groans around the room.

'*Of course, there is only one cure for Grytycide. Isn't there, priest?*' War'Jan's milky eyes locked on him.

'*Two, actually.*' Sanithane grinned. '*One is dudrodie eggs, which have been incubated within our Queen.*'

Beings around the room were reaching into places, frantically shoving the squirming eggs into their mouths.

'*The other is to remove the poison from your system.*'

War'Jan was rapidly gaining colour, his pale hide turning mottled shades of green and brown.

Exactly how many beings had done the same thing Sanithane had?

'*How could you possibly do that?*' War'Jan scoffed, his send slurred.

'*Merely be adept at shifting, I would suppose,*' Sanithane sent, as if he didn't have a care in the world.

Oalark was glancing between them, horrified. In her newly bejewelled claws, she held the remaining egg.

War'Jan's hide started bulging out in places, lines of lightning streaking under his scales.

The Golden Priest smirked and raised his goblet again. '*It seems there are quite a few beings who are competent at shifting.*' He sipped lazily, allowing the poison to sit heavily on his tongue.

Eyes frantic, Oalark screamed 'No!' The Queen rushed forward, pressing the remaining egg into Sanithane's claws.

He gripped it carefully. Holding her gaze, Sanithane swallowed the egg in one go.

Right as War'Jan exploded.

Idly, Sanithane waved a claw. A shield sprung up, trapping the remains of the former leader of the Q'Aralide before he could ruin any more of the fine outfits in the room.

Screams trailed off as the ambassadors and aides looked around, stunned. A few who seemed to have misplaced their eggs had the same lines of lightning running under their hides. Sanithane blinked, taking as much of the poison from them as he dared.

'*Clean that up, please,*' he sent idly to Jetonyx, waving at the bubble that contained the mush of War'Jan.

'*How?*' Jetonyx sounded so young.

Pushing away his fierce regret about the years he'd missed spending with his hatchlings, he sent, '*Use your Innarn and dump it in the acid river. When we pass, we give back to Altum. Normally, we would wait. Big ceremony, lots of wailing by the riverbank, but his...*'

Something inside his bubble shield shrieked and popped.

'*... remains are still volatile due to the nature of the Grytycide. The sooner the better.*'

Trembling, Jetonyx took control of the bubble and guided it carefully out of the room. Many of the aides turned away with green tinges to their faces as the mess of blood and muscle passed them by.

Whirling to face the rest of the room, Sanithane bowed his head. *'War'Jan's sacrifice will not be forgotten. He wanted so badly for us to trust each other.'* He slowly made eye contact with the remaining ambassadors. *'That he was willing to pay the ultimate price. Let us take a break so that we may lay these bodies to rest and reconvene on the morrow.'*

There were murmurs of agreement, and the ambassadors who were left rose.

Two exploded before they reached their feet.

Aides from all over hastily came forward and gathered the bodies of their fallen. Sanithane hoped, for their sakes, that their Realms had not sent the brightest and best. Knowing Oalark's penchant for death and misery, they didn't usually. But something about this conclave was different, and Sanithane found he didn't like it one bit.

Oalark was standing above two of the Q'Aralide warriors—replacements for his friends long gone, if he was to go by their colouring.

'How could you forget to give War'Jan the egg? You knew it was necessary!' Spittle was flying from the Queen's maw as she screamed at them. By the way her Innarn was crawling around her, he'd best prepare another two eggs—this time, for their replacements.

But it would have to wait. Although he hadn't helped to raise these two, he would honour their passing enough to watch it.

Sitting back and letting the queen mete out her punishment, Sanithane sighed.

He'd have Shari to answer to later.

Jetonyx's Pocket Realm

Shari would not cry.

She wouldn't.

Not over a being who gave Sanithane a reason to hate who he was, and not over someone who ordered the removal of her head from her body.

War'Jan was the least likely being in all the Realms to deserve her sympathy, and yet, she couldn't stop the tears from spilling over.

Sobbing, she buried her hands in the sand and hung her head.

A memory of a meeting with the Mind Healer made her sob harder.

'All emotions are valid. You do not have to wonder why, but naming them can help.'

Scrubbing the tears away with the back of her wrist, Shari lifted her head and gazed at the screens before her.

Regret.

That was a big one.

Regret that she hadn't been the one to take him down.

Regret that anyone, no matter how foul, would die in such a fashion.

But her biggest regret was that Shari was almost certain it was Samuel who had shifted the final dose of poison to War'Jan and overloaded his system.

The last thing Jonathan's apprentice needed was another death on his conscious.

'To be fair, War'Jan was horrible, and if anyone deserves to die in such a way, it was him,' Jetonyx sent.

They'd arrived at the acid river, and Shari threw up a shield before she took a moment to marvel at the sight.

If she ignored the fumes, the yellow water rushing by could be written off as tannins. Although the foam from the nearby falls sizzled as it hit the shore, giving away the true nature of the liquid. Underneath the acid, grey worn scales had been polished to perfection. A grinding, grumbling sound came from closer to the falls. Shari had the distinct impression that the creature below the acid was not the same as the one who was causing it.

Maybe that was how Oalark had captured a beast big enough to house them all?

The thought went out of her head as Jetonyx gave the bubble one last push, and it plopped into the river, the acid eating through the shield almost immediately.

The blood, bones, and muscles writhed for a moment.

Hatchling and Altoriae gasped at the same time as the mess came back together, cloudy eyes looking out at them from sunken cheeks, a bone claw reaching for them as flesh started wrapping around it.

Scrabbling for Temira's present, she looped it around her waist.

The black hatchling froze, undecided on if he should help, run, or push the tyrant farther into the river.

'*Let me out,*' Shari sent, so firmly Jetonyx immediately reacted.

Forcefully ejected from the pocket Realm, Shari's head whirled. Gripping tight to the crystal the Technomancer had gifted her, Shari stumbled on the spongy ground.

War'Jan warbled at her, claws scrabbling at the bank of the river.

"One regret down," she said, and blasted pure Innarn right into the old Q'Aralide's face, sending him tumbling back into the acid. She watched, sheltered by Jetonyx's bulk, as the river ripped apart the atoms of the most feared leader of the Dark Realms.

'*You... you have to get back in. Sanithane said you mustn't be seen.*' The hatchling sounded both terrified and proud.

'*If Oalark was going to replace War'Jan, where would she go?*' Shari sent.

Jetonyx looked... well, even as a baby, he towered over her, his shoulders above her head. From the angle she was standing, pressed up as tight as she dared to his belly, it was hard to read his expression. By the tremors running through him, he was terrified.

'*Maybe we can get rid of them both,*' Shari wheedled. Although, to be fair, she didn't know if that was something the hatchling would go for again.

'*Then Sanithane would be safe?*'

'*And so would you.*'

He sighed and bowed his giant head. '*The hatching grounds.*'

'*Take me there.*'

CHAPTER EIGHTEEN

Lissae

Narday

Fourth day of the second week of Sunfall

"While the Shifting Islands are streaking across the Deep Ocean at a rate of knots, it makes things significantly harder for the Travel Innarnians to accurately pinpoint the landings." Chamele looked smug but hid it quickly at Jonathan's raised eyebrow.

Snug in a high-backed armchair in the library side room that he had claimed as an office, Jonathan couldn't help but feel a little disappointed. Crystal screens engulfed him, although all bar the one in front were black for the moment. This long overdue meeting with Elder Chamele was not going the way he'd hoped. She had recently put a limit on how far a Travel Innarnian could send someone, and it was messing with his carefully constructed patrol schedules.

"Really? That's why the groups haven't arrived for the last week?" The Guardian sat forward, staring into Chamele's eyes through the crystal screen.

She shifted her gaze to the side. "It's such a dangerous trip already. Surely you understand we can't risk our people any more than necessary?"

He bit back the instinctual urge to strangle the elder. Jonathan was half-sure that if he focused enough Innarn, he'd be able to do it through the screen and no one would be the wiser. "Unfortunately, the groups that have not arrived were tasked with training, as well as patrolling specific areas. Without them, everyone is at risk."

"Your little Altoriae can handle that." Chamele waved a be-ringed hand.

"The Altoriae already runs patrols of her own, and the Innarnians of the Shifting Islands are stretched thin as it is. Surely you wouldn't want any harm to come to our wonderful Realm?" Jonathan asked innocently.

Chamele bit back a hiss. "We cannot risk our people with such... unstable travel!"

"And we cannot risk Lissae being overrun by beings who would make travel the least of your problems," Jonathan shot back.

Gasping, and dramatically flinging her hand to her chest, Chamele asked, "Are you threatening me, Guardian?"

For a second, he thought he saw a cloud of white mist swirling around her head. Making a mental note to clean the screen after he was done, he answered, "No more than you threaten the safety of every other being on Lissae by refusing to lift the travel bans *you* put in place." He sat back in his chair as she stammered and stuttered. "Lift the ban, Elder. The only reason it's there is to stop Innarnians reaching the Shifting Islands when they're needed for patrol."

"I'll do no such thing." She scowled.

"Then I'll inform the rest of the council about your stance." He moved to cut the connection, but she laughed.

"They'll back me. The danger of travelling such distances..."

"Is the same as travelling to the next town over," he interrupted.

"Really, Guardian, there have been studies..."

Jonathan sighed. Out of view of the screen, he clasped his hands together to stop from pinching the bridge of his nose. "Studies that have long been proven faulty. I am living proof that travel over long distances does not harm, hurt, or corrupt an Innarnian."

"Can you prove that claim, Guardian?" Chamele's eyes narrowed, and her smile took a gleeful edge.

"The top Mind Healers of Lissae have cleared me. I check in with one every six weeks, minimum, as should every patrol member. The things that we see are not always pleasant, but we endeavour to make sure that our patrollers are well looked after."

Chamele's shoulders slumped.

As *if I'm going to give you a chance to discredit me.* Jonathan shook his head. "Last chance, Elder Chamele. Lift the ban."

"Very well. As soon as the Altoriae returns to train the patrollers, the ban will be lifted." She waved her hand again, as if the matter was sorted.

Working very hard not to grind his teeth, Jonathan shook his head. "The Altoriae does not report to you, Elder. She's about ten ranks higher than you. She, along with everyone else above your rank, has asked for me to ensure this happens. If not, we'll just have to change the way we do things."

Glaring at the screen, Chamele pursed her lips and asked, "What do you mean?"

"Currently, Travel Innarnians are based in fixed locations, on the mainland and Fixed Islands, yes?"

She nodded her head, looking like the last thing she wanted to do was agree with him.

"It makes for easier trade routes, quicker, safer travel for anyone who can afford it." Jonathan fought to keep his expression neutral. Elder Chamele was a fan of using her local Travel Innarnian to hop across to the next town for frequent shopping trips. "They could just as easily be based on the Shifting Islands. Of course, fees for everything other than patrols would skyrocket..."

The next part of his argument was drowned out by spluttering.

"You can't do that!" she shrieked.

"You aren't leaving me much choice, Elder. Lift the ban, or we will use the alternative."

"The council will never agree to this! You haven't even informed them..."

"See—" Jonathan leaned forward and, channelling his inner Samuel, allowed a smirk to settle on his lips. "That's where you're wrong." The screens behind him lit up one by one, showing various council members from across Lissae, all wearing expressions varying from annoyance to disgust. The Guardian was not naïve enough to think all those looks were aimed at Elder Chamele. But, at this moment, it was an effective message. "I spoke to the council before contacting you. If the ban isn't lifted, the Travel Innarnians will be reassigned. Permanently."

Chamele gasped, as did a few of the elders behind him.

"Now wait a minute," one was saying.

"Enough!" Jonathan's hand smacked down on his desk, and a few council members jumped. "Every day... every day since she was three years old, the Altoriae has risked her life to keep you safe. Do any of you have children? Grandchildren? Can you imagine what that's like, knowing your child is off, fighting to protect you? And what do you do?" He turned in his seat, eyeing every council member. "You make her job harder. Make her *work* for help. Help she needs to keep you safe." He snorted and faced Elder Chamele again. "When the Altoriae is away, I am the highest-ranking member of this council." He leaned forward again.

"And I am so *tired* of being out all night fighting, only to spend all day engaged in petty squabbles because all you can think about is what is best for you."

He sat back, ignoring the stunned expressions around him. "Lift the ban."

"I... I can't." Elder Chamele seemed every one of her years, and the mist swirled thicker around her.

"Then I will send out word of their reassignments." Jonathan slashed his hand, cutting his connection from the meeting. Pausing only to take a breath, Jonathan gathered his reserves and sent out a broadcast. '*Attention, Travelling Innarnians of Lissae. You are being reassigned. Please shift to the closest Shifting Island immediately and await further instructions.*' He set the message to repeat, bouncing from one Innarnian to the next, only stopping once they had arrived at their prescribed destination. Exhausting and annoying, but effective.

Sneeze dropped from his perch on the window to rest on Jonathan's shoulder and crooned next to his ear. Idly, the Guardian patted the draci. How much of a war had he just started with the mainlanders?

"Well, I think the Guardian has finally snapped," Fenix said, placing the last bowl on the loaded table. They had invited the other Linked back to their home to get to know one another outside of a formal setting.

Tania thought it was the sweetest idea, not to mention she was so sick of wearing formal robes.

Fenix's home was lovely. Made from orangey-red clay like most of the dwellings on Cantash, it was two stories, with the living areas on the ground floor. And the furniture seemed oddly out of place—mismatched, delicate pieces, all in the colour you'd find contained within a blue flame. The low, round table was groaning under the weight of the dishes piled onto it. The Linked were seated on bright blue cushions on the floor.

Tania idly wished she could make sinking to the floor in robes look as graceful as Zana did.

"What do you mean?" Tania picked up a chip and used it to scoop some of the green dip.

"He's just recalled all the Travel Innarnians," Fenix said. A tiny draci pattered down their arm and waddled across the table, scooching close and curling around the heated pot of calromata dip.

"Is that a bad thing?" Tania asked, frowning.

Cyrus nodded. "Trade routes will be shot, bandits will take advantage, and people could get hurt."

"Why'd he recall them then?" She bit into the chip and tried not to moan when the dip started setting the inside of her mouth on fire.

"Because we need to be safe, too," Zana said serenely. She carefully gathered a bit of the calromata dip on a chip and daintily placed it in her mouth.

Fenix raised their brows. "Hot?"

Zana chewed and swallowed. "Delicious," she said, and scooped up some more.

Tania felt like panting. Sweat was dripping down her face, and blood was rushing to her cheeks. Fanning herself, she took a grateful swig from the glass Fenix handed her.

Cantash's Linked was trying their best not to laugh, but the tiny shakes of their torso gave them away. She had never been so glad to be purposefully ignored before. It felt like her insides had turned to lava.

"That's... Wow. Only the ones who truly love calromata like that dip. It's bad luck *not* to put it out, but still." Fenix shook their head.

"Bad luck?" Cyrus asked. He was eyeing the dip but moved onto something a little less deadly.

"Cantash has a lot of... superstitions. Don't wear white, or whistle at night. Don't step in a puddle, or forget to make your bed. Take heed of the fable, but don't take the…" Fenix smacked Cyrus's hand, where he'd been nudging the draci. "… draci off the table."

"And if you do any of that?" Tania puffed, drinking again as cool air invaded her mouth and set off another wave of prickly lava heat. *When will the burning stop?*

"Bad luck." Fenix leaned forward. "Or worse."

"What could be worse than bad luck?"

"Death, dismemberment, hauntings." Fenix shrugged. "Surely you have superstitions too?"

"Don't pull crystal from the ground," Cyrus said. "Not without asking."

"And if you do?" Fenix tilted their head.

He sat back in his chair, plate loaded with delicious-looking food. "When I was a child, I was told that if we tried, Talhan would eat us."

"Did you ever try?"

He laughed and held his hand up. Shaking the sleeve of his shirt so it slid back to his elbow, he pressed something on the cuff around his wrist.

And his finger fell off.

Tania shrieked.

Cyrus laughed. "I tried. Cut my finger on an exceptionally sharp piece of crystal. I always ask now, and it's a great teaching tool." Balancing the plate on his knees, he picked his finger up and popped it back on.

"Prosthetic?" Fenix asked.

"One of Temira's."

"Brilliant! Do you get a lot of sensation in it?"

"Some. Enough that I can feel pressure, mostly. Not great with temperature. What about you, Zana? Any superstitions?"

"From a young age, all Ilutri are told not to eat meat, or our feathers will fall off." Carefully, she skewered a piece of raw fish and dragged it through the calromata dip.

"Does fish count?"

Zana's eyes sparkled. "Oh, yes," she said, and popped the morsel into her mouth.

"I swear, if you spontaneously moult, I'm going to scream," Tania said, pointing her spoon at the Ilutri. The burn was going, but she couldn't feel the inside of her mouth anymore.

Laughing, Zana said, "There is a reason behind all superstitions. For the Ilutri, meat reacts differently with our digestive systems, making us markedly heavier. Those who patrol will eat lots of fruits, vegetables, and grains, and typically drink quass juice, or some other carbonated liquid, because they believe the bubbles will help their flight. Personally, I've tracked the myth back to an Ilutri who was exceptionally allergic to a protein in meat, and it caused him to moult."

"But the myth lived on," Fenix said.

"And became part of our everyday lives. We cannot mindlessly obey what our elders tell us is best without looking for ourselves first." Zana speared another piece of fish.

"Tania?"

"Oh, um... I don't really know any of the superstitions from Ronah..."

"What about from where you grew up?" Fenix asked. "I don't think I've ever heard any mainland ones before."

Tania's eyes darted around the room. The other three had never spent significant time away from their islands before. How could she tell them what the kids at her old school had whispered? "Oh, um... don't cross your eyes on a full moon." It sounded benign enough, right?

Cyrus laughed. "Why not?"

"Um..." Tania shoved a slice of fruit in her mouth and shrugged.

Zana glanced at her. "Did you ever do it?"

"Every chance I got." The words sounded joyful enough to disguise the bitterness from the taunting she'd endured.

"And did it work?" Fenix asked.

"Yes."

"Tania, what was it?" Zana asked softly.

She lifted her knee and hugged it miserably. "If you do, you'll become an Innarnian."

Fenix sucked in a breath and choked on a bite of food. Cyrus leaned over and patted them on the back.

"Do mainlanders really not like us all that much?"

"I don't think it's that they don't like... Where I grew up, there were none. My mum went there as an outreach teacher and fell in love. By the time she found out she was pregnant, it was too late for her to leave. My father... well. He had ways of keeping her... keeping us there."

"But you got away?" Fenix came closer, stroking Tania's back.

"Yeah. Grandad showed up and kicked some arse. Took the lot of us away. Except for two of my siblings who refused to leave," she sighed, and looked down. "It's been hard, going from not knowing any of this to discovering all of it. I'm still figuring out where I fit in."

"We'll help you," Fenix said fiercely, slinging an arm around her back.

Tania leaned into their side. "Thank you," she whispered.

Temira stared at the tiny being invading her workshop.

"And you are?" she drawled.

"Milo." The ridiculous being straightened to his full height, the top of his wavy hair barely reaching her waist. "Secretary to Cantash's Linked."

"Why are you here?"

"I was invited."

She continued to stare at him until he fidgeted.

"Fenix suggested that my expertise could be utilised here." His knuckles tightened around the clipboard by his side.

"Did they?"

"Cyrus was quite excited to learn of my discoveries regarding copper and crystal longevity."

"Ah." Temira's thoughts whirled. The connection between copper and crystal had transformed her own work. To talk to the one who had discovered that... "Let me give you a tour."

Milo sniffed and peered up at her. "I'd be honoured."

Rasshday
Fifth day of the second week of Sunfall

'*He's easily startled, so we must be quiet,*' Jonathan sent to Lizbeth. Slowly, he eased open the door to Samuel's house and checked the coast was clear. '*Come on in. Mind the creaky...*'

Too late.

Lizbeth stepped into the entryway, right onto the creaky board. Eyes wide, she froze on the spot as Jonathan swiftly closed the door.

Something in the shadows at the end of the hall snarled.

The fine hairs on the back of his neck rose, and a shiver left bumps all over his skin.

"Oh, aren't you the sweetest!" Lizbeth cooed and plopped to the floor.

The snarl changed to a whine, and a creature he was still hesitant to call a palon crept forwards.

"He's... ah... well..." Jonathan rubbed a hand over the back of his neck.

"He is stunning," Lizbeth said.

Slowly, the creature made its way towards them, sniffing the air as it went.

'Samuel has been feeding him bones and meat, so he'll gain strength. Said he came straight from the shadows.'

"Oh, and you look like you are still part of the shadows, don't you, little one?" Lizbeth's voice was soothing in a way that Jonathan couldn't mimic. At least, not in his terror.

Bright green, intelligent eyes peered up at him, and the beast huffed.

Jonathan, feared Guardian of Lissae, absolutely did not jump.

No matter what Lizbeth's snickering implied.

'As you can tell, I'm a tad twitchy around him. The first time I tried to feed him, he tried to take a chunk out of me.' Jonathan would not mention it was from his arse, and no, thank you very much, he was not going to the Healers for that. Nor was he explaining the resulting scar due to him treating it at home.

Lizbeth chuckled, and the beast ran forward, the front set of paws landing on her shoulders, the other four squarely in her lap to get traction as he bathed her face with a long, thin tongue.

For a moment, Jonathan wondered how he was going to explain to Samuel that his pet ate his friend, but the beast settled down before he could properly formulate the right words for *sorry, your creature made of shadows ate the first person on Ronah to be kind to you.*

"Let me guess, you'd like me to take care of this gorgeous creature for Samuel?" Lizbeth asked.

"Well, he's kind of... not just Samuel's."

Sightless eyes turned his way.

"This is Zoomer. Or, rather, the Returned version of Zoomer."

"He survived?" Lizbeth gasped, burying her hands in his fur.

"But he's... changed. He's not quite the palon that Shari fell in love with. Not since his time in Anriluka's pocket Realm."

"We are the sum of our experiences." Lizbeth rested her forehead against the inky-black fur of Shari's lost pet. "And I would be happy to add looking after this lovely creature to mine."

Jonathan sighed in relief.

He could only hope things went that easily for Shari and Samuel.

Chapter Nineteen

Altum

Day three of the Dark Conclave

There were plenty of times over the years that Shari had been grateful for the Guardian's insistence that shielding become as automatic for her as breathing was.

This was one of them.

Leathers black enough for her to sink against Jetonyx's hide and not stand out gave her a slight edge. In her bones, Shari could feel Jetonyx's nervous chittering. Reaching up, she stroked the rainbow jewel Temira had gifted her, ignoring the way her fingers had changed and the dull grey colour of her skin. The cuff from Cyrus glinted in the low light, the only thing that had the potential to give away her position. *Well worth the risk,* she glanced down at it.

'*Think about what you're doing for the Queen. About how you're a good Q'Aralide who goes above and beyond,*' Shari sent.

'*She's going to eat me... or worse.*'

Before the conclave, Shari would have put his words down to child-like hysteria at disappointing a parent figure.

Now she knew better.

'*You're doing this for Sam... Sanithane,*' she sent, hoping it would work.

'*Sanithane.*' Jetonyx sighed and ushered her into a cavernous room. Pointing a wing claw at the far wall, they walked towards it, but stopped as another set of claws scraped over the stone behind them.

'*What are you doin' in here, hatchling?*'

The hatchling turned, Shari scurrying under the curl of his wing.

A scarred vermillion Q'Aralide glared at Jetonyx out of two good eyes, the left one an oozing, slitted mess. Shari wished she'd ducked under the other wing.

'*Master Warrior Helk.*' Jetonyx bowed.

'*Well?*'

'*The Queen sent me to...*'

'*The acid river. Long way from here, hatchling.*' Helk sniffed.

Shari held her breath, hoping the warrior wouldn't discover her.

Jetonyx slumped onto his haunches and ruffled his wings. Shari, gripping tightly to her tenuous perch, could only hope that Helk put her fingertips down to some sort of scale malformation. Or that she was simply too small to notice.

'*I... War'Jan...*' Jetonyx lowered his head.

But Helk's snapped up. '*What about War'Jan?*'

'*Something happened at the conclave. Poison? It was a test, and...*' Jetonyx shrugged the shoulder closest to Shari, shifting her with his wing as if her weight were nothing.

'*Did War'Jan tell you to go to the river?*' The big vermillion warrior looked confused.

'*The Queen ordered War'Jan's remains to be cast into the river,*' Jetonyx sent.

Helk's eyes widened, his jaw dropping, showcasing row upon row of razor-sharp fangs. A green gas seeped unbidden from his mouth. Before Shari could blink, Helk had moved, holding Jetonyx by the throat and pushing him into the wall, pinning his wings and crushing her.

'*War'Jan's remains?*' Helk's send was low and gravelly. '*Think carefully, hatchling.*'

'*I saw it. Everyone saw. War'Jan is with the ancestors.*'

From the way Jetonyx was pushing further against the wall, Shari could imagine the bigger Q'Aralide using his bulk to intimidate. A larger part of her mind was taken up with how she was going to get out of this. She dared not use her Innarn, lest Helk sense it at such close quarters. And there was literally nowhere to go, wrapped as she was in a black leathery wing, with a wall on one side and a terrified hatchling on the other.

'*You came!*'

The send was lighter, feminine, and it made Shari's skin crawl.

The press eased off, and Jetonyx let out a grunt as Helk stepped away.

Before Shari could so much as get her breath, she was sucked back into the pocket Realm.

'*Clever hatchling,*' Shari sent, along with as many soothing thoughts as she could.

'*... found the hatchling here,*' Helk was sending.

'*Oh, clever one,*' Oalark cooed.

Shari felt nauseous as the Queen of the Q'Aralide parroted her words. *Did she hear?*

'*You wanted to make sure the next lot of hatchlings were safe, didn't you?*'

The screens above the ocean flickered and blinked back to life in time for Shari to see Oalark cross the room and scratch Jetonyx under the chin.

'*You shouldn't be rough with Sanithane's replacement.*' Oalark ran a claw lightly along Jetonyx's shoulders as she circled him. '*We want him to stay with us, after all.*' The Queen leaned closer and pressed her maw against Jetonyx's snout.

Deep in the corner of his mind, the hatchling whimpered.

And Shari was the only one to hear it.

Using War'Jan's abrupt demise as an excuse, Sanithane shook himself off and adjourned to the rooms set aside for him as Chair.

They were not, as he'd half been expecting, as spartan as the ones where he grew up. Instead, lavish decorations in polished ziom and gleaming golds offset the bone-coloured walls and red, suspiciously wet rugs on the floors.

Stepping carefully, he avoided the rug, not wanting to know what creature the skin had been taken from.

To absolutely no surprise, the Otike ambassador was hiding in the shadows of the room, watching him as he moved towards the sink and washed his claws and maw.

Refusing to acknowledge her, Sanithane retreated to the table and sank into the rest, feeling every single one of his years. If she tried to douse him with hydrusfel, he was going to be annoyed.

'*She's gone mad.*' The ambassador seemed to recognise his tactics, sending him mental images of Oalark's reign without his guiding hand.

Cities wrecked. Families ruined. Realms where the very air was on fire.

Over everything, a film of dripping blood.

'*Taking from the sole survivors. Or the souls of the dead, sometimes. The ones she didn't torture to insanity first.*' The ambassador paused. '*We never realised how much control you had over her until you were gone.*'

The question, although unasked, was left hanging.

'*I did not leave by choice,*' he rumbled.

The ambassador stalked forward, the gold on her tusks gleaming in the low light. '*And yet, she welcomes you back now. Flirts with you openly. Perhaps she caused War'Jan's… demise.*'

'*Oh yes, it had absolutely nothing to do with the others who syphoned the poison into his gullet.*' Sanithane refused to take responsibility when he knew there were at least a dozen others who'd done the same as him. '*Should have picked a slightly different target, perhaps.*'

'*As if she's not warded to the Mother Realm and back,*' the ambassador laughed. '*I do think she'll be the only one to mourn him.*'

Ignoring the mention of Lissae, Sanithane summoned a glass and a bottle of Shemmegote Stinger that was hidden in the rafters of each of the rooms and poured the smoking green liquid into the glass. After a pause, he summoned another glass, poured, and offered the second drink to the ambassador. She went to take it, but he pulled it back. '*I don't make a habit of drinking with people whose name I don't know.*'

'*Zirgha,*' she sent, taking the drink from his hand.

As her fingers touched his claws, he received more images of the conclave, minus Oalark, gathering and trying to decide the best method of dealing with the mad Queen.

They had only come up with one option.

'*Can she be helped?*' Zirgha asked. She sounded almost plaintive.

He could remember her, from conclaves passed, laughing and schmoozing with Oalark like they'd been the best of friends. Zirgha was no stranger to meting out violence, but the Otike had to have a reason for it. During his absence, Oalark had long since forgotten that, and had done worse than push one of her staunchest allies away.

'*You would do this to her?*'

Flushing a darker green, she scowled at him. '*She knew my trouble conceiving. Knew how badly I wanted a brood. And yet she laughed in my face as her claws stomped my unborn children into the blood-soaked ground.'*

Oalark would never live past the end of the conclave.

'Is there another way?'

Raising his brows, Sanithane drowned his drink in one go, relishing in the alcohol's burn. *'If there is, I don't know it.'*

Deep down, hidden away where no one would hear, he thought, *Let's go kill a queen.*

CHAPTER TWENTY

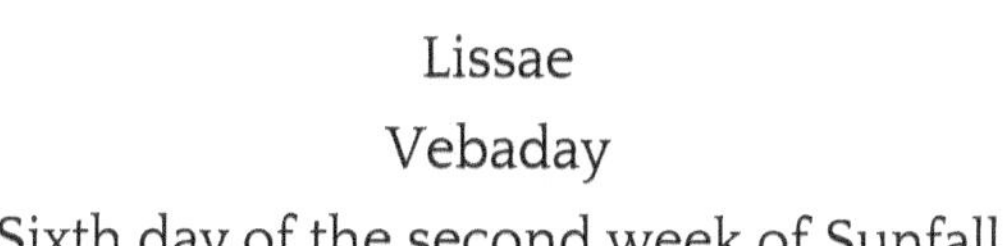

Lissae

Vebaday

Sixth day of the second week of Sunfall

Belfar landed hard and took a few stumbling steps forward. Frowning, he glared over his shoulder at his softly glowing wing.

"You alright?" Wolf asked, clapping a hand on his back.

A quick glance showed the rest of their patrol group studiously not paying them any attention.

"Fine," Belfar said, trying his best to appear as breezy and unruffled as normal.

"Alright." Wolf gave him another concerned look and nodded. "Pack it up, you lot. Make sure your weapons and armour are clean before you leave! See Varlee if you need healing. And Charin will check your weapons before you go."

The others grumbled, but Belfar ignored them all. After sliding the quiver from his back, he slammed it on the bench in the patrol prep room and scowled.

Checking the weapons used to be *his* job.

Since when did having a crystal wing make him incapable?

Shrugging off Wolf's concerned gaze, he peeled his chest plate away and glared at the blood splatters. He half wanted to just use his Innarn to blast the mess, but knowing his luck, it'd be mangled beyond repair.

Slumping onto the bench, Belfar huffed. He picked the chest plate up and started cleaned it, ignoring the way his greaves were cutting into the back of his knees.

Charin sank onto the other end of the bench as Varlee tutted at him. Patiently, he stared at his wife as she held his jaw in one hand and traced over his fractured eye socket with her index finger. There was the buzz of intimate sending. Charin loosely grasped Varlee's wrist and gave her a dopey grin as the swelling went down.

Belfar averted his eyes, feeling like he was interrupting a personal moment, even as the rest of their patrol group flittered around the room. He was in his own bubble. None of the others dared come close lest they fall to his bad temper.

After the night they'd had, Belfar couldn't exactly blame them. He'd seen the look in their eyes after he'd wrenched the strilite's arm out of the socket. And when his fist had slammed into their next attacker's temple, there had been more than one indrawn breath. The stench of fear from his patrol group had overpowered the decaying leaves of the forest they'd been checking.

Scowling as he polished his chest plate, Belfar wished they could go back to the time before he'd been infected with femto crystals and torn through the beings of Talhan like they were leaves on a tree. Would he be able to forget? And how could Wolf possibly have forgiven him?

After setting the gleaming chest plate aside, Belfar unstrapped his greaves, using the movement to ignore Wolf as his mate sat beside him.

"Dinner at the tavern?" Wolf asked.

"Don't think I'm fit for polite society." Not when he could still feel the crunch of bone breaking under his fist.

"You'd really say no to Arilla's cooking?"

He grunted. Wolf bumped his shoulder gently. Belfar took a deep breath and wiped the scowl off his face. "Calem is the one who cooks at the tavern."

Wolf groaned theatrically. "I'd forgotten that. Maybe we should just stay in."

Belfar grunted again and flexed his hand, looking at his split knuckles. How hard had he hit that strilite?

"Oh, let me get that for you." Varlee took his hand, ignoring his flinch, and ran gentle fingers across the swollen flesh.

Silently, Belfar sighed as the wound knitted together and his hand returned to normal.

"Good as new," she said. "I'm glad you were with us tonight. I dread to think what would have happened if you hadn't been."

"You would have handled it," he said. "You managed for weeks without us."

It was Varlee's turn to glare.

Charin spoke before his mate could. "Are you kidding? Our injury rate went through the sky with you away. There's a reason that you two oversee the rest of us."

"You need to stop seeing yourself as a liability," Varlee said, poking his chest. "The things you've gone through have a way of changing your outlook."

"We worry about you," Charin added, running a soothing hand over Varlee's ruffled feathers.

"We all worry about you," Wolf added. The furrow between his brows that Belfar had spent so long admiring from afar was out in full force.

Some of the stiffness melted away, and Belfar took a breath. "I know I haven't been..." He wasn't sure how to end the sentence. Hadn't been himself? Had swerved so far from the happy-go-lucky Ilutri they'd known?

"It's alright to ask for help," Wolf said.

Belfar nodded. "I... help would be..." He hung his head. All his words seemed caught inside his mouth, but refused to tumble out.

Wolf enveloped him in a hug, with Varlee and Charin joining in to surround him.

For the first time in an age, he felt safe.

Zoeday
Seventh day of the second week of Sunfall

Skye had been trying to send to the Altoriae for days, with no response.

Elder Suni would not be retiring for at least an hour. The elderflower brandy had been poured, and the trays of biscuits had been set out. Clasping her shaking hands together as the Elder for Lawrgaea dismissed her, Skye bowed and slipped from the room, resolutely staying to the required halls and away from Elder Chamele's quarters.

No matter how much she wanted to check on Grace.

Skye forced herself to stroll casually past the guards, spine straight and eyes ahead. She did not blink as she walked by the guard who had dumped the rancid food on Chamele's captive.

Schooling her expression until she was safely in the closet-turned-room afforded to all the aides, Skye sighed as she flipped the outer locks. The sparse room was hardly comfortable, but she kept it neat, the stack of papers she may need to refer to safely in the reed basket on the far side of the simple bed. She was thankful that the winter chill had yet to set in, as the lone blanket was thin enough to make her wish she could freely use her Innarn to warm herself up. As it was, she had to lay her travelling cloak over the top. The rest of her clothes were in a tiny trunk she could carry on her back.

Glancing at her crystal timepiece, Skye huffed and sat on the too-firm mattress. She had about twenty minutes to come up with some sort of plan, and another forty to rest, if she was lucky.

Common sense said that if she could not send to the Altoriae, then she should contact the Guardian. But how was she to do that without arousing suspicion? The Guardian's title had long been taboo amongst the zealots on the mainland, and trying to contact him was next to impossible without someone picking up on the send. Skye was experienced enough to know there were unscrupulous Innarnians chasing a quick bit of coin and willing to sell out their own kind. She had no master she could rely on, which meant directly sending to him was out of the question.

Clenching her fists, Skye gently thumped them on her thighs and flopped across the bed, almost smacking her head into the thin crystal slab that held today's newspaper.

Muttering impolitely, she nudged it out of the way, scowling when it lit up at her touch. The front page of *The Shifting Island Sentinel* was an image of fireworks bursting over Cantash, and a grim Altoriae next to her smiling Guardian. Underneath was an advertisement proclaiming *the best calromata in all the Shifting Islands!*

An ad… Perhaps the Guardian read the Sentinel?

Scrabbling for her quill and paper in the basket, Skye ignored the scattered documents fluttering around her.

What to write?

Chewing on the end of her quill, she dithered for a moment. But she really did not have enough time.

She could go for subtle, or…

The Skye guards the Grace of the mainlands, held captive. The Guardian is needed to keep both safe. Save Lawrgaea. Save the Grace.

Forty minutes before Elder Suni would be back.

Quietly, Skye put her final copy on top of her trunk and tidied the other documents. She redid her hair, straightened her clothing, and remade the bed.

Sitting on the edge, feet firmly on the floor, she reached one shaking hand out to the advert she wanted to run in tomorrow's paper. The other hand fumbled in the pouch on her belt, pulling out the correct amount of ziom beads. Hoping she wasn't short, Skye wrapped the beads in the paper, and in a shaking hand, wrote the address on the outside.

Chamele, for all she disliked Innarn so much, had exceptional wards around the entire town. They would alert her to the moment Skye did any sort of Innarn, although there must be exceptions in place for Grace.

Was the trek across the compound, the risk to sneak into an elder's chambers, all to get Grace to send the message for her worth it?

There was no guarantee of success that way. At least, if she were to send the message herself, it would get through—even if that meant a few days in the dungeons. Surely someone like Chamele had dungeons? Perhaps she could play the whole thing off as the crystal slab malfunctioning? That could work.

Before Skye could talk herself out of it, she flicked one finger across the slab until she got to the submissions page.

A quick glance at her timepiece showed twenty minutes, max, before the Elder would stride into the room.

Pressing the paper against the submissions button, Skye held her breath as the crystal sucked the little package in, beads and all.

Expecting pounding footsteps, Skye sank back on the bed and held her breath.

Silence.

She waited another five minutes before allowing herself a tiny grin. Perhaps she'd gotten away with it after all.

Five minutes after her allotted hour, Elder Suni stumbled through the other door, hiccoughing and smelling as if she'd bathed in brandy.

Skye rose and smoothed her skirt, letting her smile melt away.

Time to get back to work.

Nittany

Zoeday

Seventh day of the second week of Sunfall

Collis looked at his patrol group and rubbed at the soot on his arm.

Talofa giggled and pointed to his nose.

How could the tiny Uleulan be so cheerful after they'd almost been burnt alive? The forest surrounding Nittany's gateway was still smouldering, curls of smoke wafting high into the evening air and obscuring the sunset.

There was something to be said about the nightmare pocket Realm they'd been trapped in. Even through all the times of trying not to get eaten, it was decidedly less stressful than knowing how permanent his end could be if the flames had licked a little closer.

"You have some on your nose," the Uleulan said, her single eye gleaming with mirth.

It would be the height of rudeness to point out that Talofa was absolutely covered in soot, so he refrained, even as he used his Innarn to wipe away the bit on his nose and on her exposed skin.

She grinned in response and went to say something.

Something brushed against the half-burnt branches, and both snapped their heads around to look. Talofa's water shield was up and ready before Collis could send to her.

Staff in hand, he motioned for the others to stop. The glowing red end of his weapon did little to settle him as whatever was making the noise sunk to the ground, crispy leaves rustling in its wake.

'*Can you see?*'

'*It must be tiny.*'

'*There's nothing there.*'

His patrol group were sending to each other, tightening the net around the invisible beast. Perhaps it was the one that had set the Nittany's forest on fire?

There was a shuddering gasp from Talofa.

Turning, Collis spotted a cloud of ash whipping around the slight girl, her shield doing nothing to protect her.

Brows drawn in a frown, Collis pushed against the cloud and felt something Light inside it push back.

'*Dark Innarn shield, now!*' he commanded. Instantly, the rest of his patrol group poured Dark Innarn into him. Collis gathered it, scraping the head of his staff along the ground in a sweeping arc, using the line it created in the ash to point the Innarn at Talofa's feet. It swirled up and around the four-armed girl, and pushed out from her skin, surrounding her.

Something in the ash shrieked, and the cloud surrounding her exploded.

Talofa fell bonelessly to the ground.

Rushing forward, Remmy picked up the Uleulan. Holding her securely, he nodded.

Collis, brow still drawn, motioned the others to head for the gateway. Pushing his back against Remmy's, they slowly trudged towards safety. All the while, Collis was trying to figure out how to explain to the Guardian that he'd almost lost one of his new group members on their first patrol out.

Lissae

Zoeday

Seventh day of the second week of Sunfall

Chamele settled into her chair, ignoring the drooping reflection in the dresser mirror for the moment.

Someone inside the building had just used Innarn.

It wasn't her aberration, but another.

A smile crept over her face, sagging grotesquely at the corners.

Perhaps capturing one of the beasts was going to be easier than she expected.

CHAPTER TWENTY-ONE

Altum

Day four of the Dark Conclave

Sanithane, a glass of Shemmegote topped up once more, stood tall as he spoke to the delegation from Damiuth.

'*My priest, there you are!*' Oalark's shrill send had everyone in the room turning. She sashayed through the crowd of beings, who practically leaped out of her way, a significantly smaller shadow following. And bringing up the rear, his old tormentor, looking significantly worse for wear.

'*My Queen,*' he replied, not letting his thoughts show how bitter those words now sounded inside his skull.

'*We found your... replacement wandering, all alone.*'

The look on Helk's face said that he noticed her slip. The warrior's eyes cut to Sanithane.

The priest curled his lip in a brief sneer.

Helk didn't realise the expression was due to the frantic send from the hatchling meant to be under Sanithane's command.

'*I entrusted Jetonyx to guard the entrance of the cavern, lest anyone nefarious slip by.*'

'*That's a job for warriors,*' Helk grumbled.

'*And yet, Jetonyx got farther in than any other, correct?*' Sanithane rumbled.

'*Almost to the doorway,*' the hatchling confirmed.

Sanithane raised his brows.

Helk flushed.

'*You were guarding the eggs?*' Oalark was looking at Helk like he hung the moons.

'*Of course,*' he sent.

She sighed in a way that was worthy of Shari's school friends.

With their crushes.

Hiding his shudder, he nodded at the Damiuth ambassador. '*We were just discussing...*'

'*Retiring for the night,*' Oalark purred.

'*If you wish to retire, my Queen, it is probably for the best. You've had a long day, with the loss of your mate. We will figure out how to best honour War'Jan.*' Mostly by roasting Oalark alive, but what the deluded queen didn't know wouldn't hurt her.

Yet.

Oalark pouted at him. '*Why talk when we can retire? Together.*'

'*As Chair, my duty is to ensure all diplomatic efforts of the conclave go smoothly, my Queen. Duty must come before pleasure.*'

With the look she gave him, Sanithane could tell they were thinking of very different forms of pleasure.

In lieu of anything better to do, he sipped from his drink, the Damiuth ambassador leering at him.

'*Of course. Don't take too long.*' Oalark gave him one more disappointed look and turned away.

'*What about the hatchling?*' Helk asked.

'*Leave him. He can watch a master at work.*' Oalark winked over her shoulder at Sanithane and swayed out of the room.

Helk gave him one last scowl and followed their leader.

'*What in the Nine Hells has come over her?*' Jetonyx asked.

'*Language,*' Sanithane idly sent, staring at the passage the Queen had taken. Sanithane sniffed the air. The same bitter smell that had coated the claw sheaths wafted behind her.

He turned to look at the back of Zirgha's head.

Was she trying to make the Queen infatuated with him as some way to get rid of them both?

Jetonyx's Pocket Realm

Shari clasped her hands over her ears, singing loudly to cover the noise from the screen.

She didn't care how childish it made her. If she had to watch Oalark make one more overtly sexual pass at Samuel, she was going to yak.

The beach below her jostled, and she chanced a peek from under her lashes.

Oalark was leaving.

'*We need to get back…*'

'*Do you want to die?*' Jetonyx broke in. '*I don't! I'd rather grow to get my colours, thank you very much! We wait.*'

'*Wait?*' Shari asked.

'*Yes.*'

'*How long?*'

'*Until Sanithane says it's safe.*'

Huffing, she rose from the sand and dusted off her clothes. Slowly, she started on the first-level air motus set, monitoring the screens in front of her.

She'd cornered Belfar and Wolf on one of their mopey days and asked if they could teach her how to do the air motus their students were taught. Whilst her Innarn was instinctual, it didn't hurt to know how others learned. They had gone through the main ten sets with her in only a day, rather than the years it normally took. It left them both shaking their heads.

Shari smiled as she moved on to the second-level set. Wolf would be devastated, and a little proud, to know that she had already figured out the flaws in this set and adjusted them. The first four sets of each motus were foundational, and there were three moves in the second-level set that were off. It would explain why some Ilutri were struggling with casting the air net. When she got back, it was one of the first things she planned on fixing in the lessons she taught.

She took her time, moving slowly through the rest of the sets, ensuring each raise of her arms or sweep of her leg was perfect. It wouldn't do to be teaching the wrong thing. Wiping the sweat from her brow, Shari wandered over to the hut and poured a drink. Lifting the glass, she turned to see what was happening in the outside Realm. Half the room was empty, the ambassadors having decided that if their host had left, it was safe to do so as well.

Samuel lifted a brow at Jetonyx. *'Go to the hatching grounds. Let your tag-along out. Have her infuse the eggs with her Innarn to keep them… strong.'*

Frowning, Shari took a sip. The inflection on the last word was wrong. "What does he mean?"

Jetonyx sighed at her but lumbered away. *'The Queen is doing bad things to the eggs. It's time to make sure they don't suffer any more.'*

Outside the hall, a vermillion tail was swishing around the corner. The black Q'Aralide paused, and Shari could feel the fear running through him.

"You can do this," she said, and settled on the floor of the hut to stare at the screens once more, trying hard not to think about what Samuel was asking her to do.

Altum

Sanithane sighed as Oalark's pale claw wound around his chest from behind. It was followed by the rest of the Queen as she tried to rub up against his side again.

The sneaky Queen had waited in the outer chambers to waylay him as he left for the night.

'*My priest, I fear I must retire. Walk me to my chambers?*' she sent.

Somehow, admitting he'd rather gnaw his own tail off would, unfortunately, give the wrong impression. Well, not wrong, but it would leave him short a limb or two. Or she'd remove his head.

'*I believe Helk is waiting to escort you, my Queen,*' he sent instead, and guided the clingy Q'Aralide to the doors. Sure enough, Helk was waiting outside.

'*What's wrong?*' Helk sent, frowning.

'*The Queen would like to retire.*' Sanithane forcefully removed her from his hide. There would be nightmares in his future. He skilfully transferred her claws over to Helk.

The warrior flinched slightly.

Oalark gave a breathy sigh and draped herself over Helk. '*My warrior.*'

Swallowing the meal that threatened to return, Sanithane dipped his head and left the smirking warrior with the Queen.

He had to find Zirgha and figure out what she'd done to those claw sheaths.

Ambassadors scattered before the bulk of the Golden Priest as he made his way directly towards the Otike representative.

'*Zirgha.*' Her name was a loaded question in his thoughts.

'*Priest.*' She bowed her head.

'*Tell me, those claw sheaths are so fetching. How are they made?*'

A sly smile crossed her face, but those around them looked the wrong side of terrified.

'*Are you impressed with our handiwork?*'

A low growl left his throat.

She laughed. '*Q'Aralides are always such prudes!*'

Sanithane's smile became fixed. '*Did you ever meet Ruker? Or Gazn?*'

Zirgha shook her head, as did the ambassadors closest to them who'd stopped to listen in.

'*Both proud Q'Aralide warriors who decided, in their youth, to see what the pleasures of the flesh were all about.*' Sanithane paused. '*They are the reason my own kind fear me.*'

Paling to a lighter green, Zirgha asked, '*What did you do?*'

He could still hear the rattle of the chains, and feel the sting of Light Innarn. '*Under orders, and before everyone, I pulled their still-beating hearts from their bodies.*'

A flash of navy, the same colour as Ruker's scales, caught his eyes, and his head snapped to the side, tracking an ambassador who was leaving for the night.

'*Did you enjoy the act?*'

Looking down his snout, Sanithane sneered. '*Like most of my childhood, it was kill or be killed. And mercy was weakness. Weaknesses needed only one thing.*'

'*To be eradicated.*'

He hadn't heard that voice since the death of Jonathan's predecessor. Slowly, he turned.

Jaileth stood behind him, smirking. '*Miss me?*'

Looking warily between the gold and bronze Q'Aralide, Zirgha didn't seem to know if she should go or stay.

'*Jaileth*,' he sent.

'*Mate*,' she replied. '*It has been far too long. Eaten any good Guardians recently?*'

He barely recognised the hollow laugh as his own. '*What brings you to Altum?*'

'*Let's call it... for old time's sake. I see you've made some new friends.*' Jaileth looked down her snout at Zirgha.

The Otike ambassador smiled... or snarled... It was hard to tell.

'*Ambassador Zirgha, this is Jaileth, a fellow priest and my soul match. Jaileth, Ambassador Zirgha from Otike has developed some new claw sheaths.*'

The bronze held out a dainty claw. '*Pleased.*'

Zirgha bowed her head over the claw, knowing better than to take it. '*We are honoured by your presence, Jaileth.*'

'*I hear claw sheaths are all the fashion in Otike.*' His mate was smooth.

Fifteen years ago, when he'd last seen Jaileth, he had feared for her sanity. She'd collapsed into madness and become almost unrecognisable. And yet he was meant to believe she had turned herself around and was now not only able to mingle in polite society, but get a double-crossing, traitorous ambassador to give up carefully guarded secrets?

'*Oh, they are. My partner loves them. Especially if they are dipped in isoiglabrane first.*'

'*Isoiglabrane?*' Sanithane had heard of it before but couldn't place where.

'*It's quite a powerful aphrodisiac—I'm sure you remember, dear.*'

The Otike ambassador was looking between the two, a frown on her face. '*It's made from the crushed leaves of the crystal forest in Saundun.*'

Saundun. Days and nights of nothing but being entangled in each other's wings. Was it chemically induced? Was that why he'd felt so... different after? Sanithane turned disbelieving eyes towards his mate.

'Ah, *he remembers*.' Jaileth couldn't hide the bitterness in her tone.

Biting back a scowl, he scanned the room. Jetonyx had left for the hatching grounds, and Sanithane couldn't be gladder. He didn't need a witness for the conversation he was about to have.

As much as he wished he could join them, Sanithane could only hope he hadn't giving Jetonyx and Shari an impossible task.

CHAPTER TWENTY-TWO

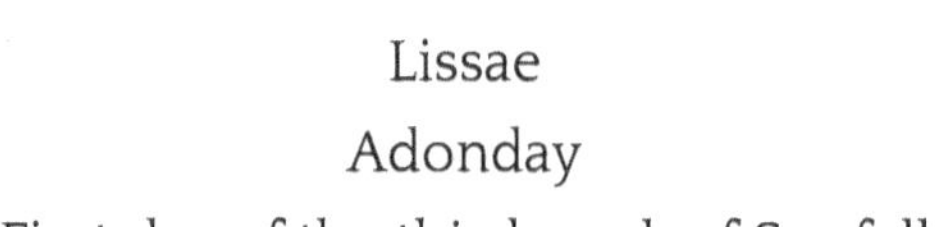

Lissae

Adonday

First day of the third week of Sunfall

Low growling greeted Lizbeth, vibrating through the walls of the hall as she slipped inside to Samuel's house.

"Well met, dear one," she breathed. "I've come bearing gifts of food and pats."

The growling broke off, and a curious chirping took its place. Detaching from the shadows, a beast that felt smaller than she remembered slunk forward.

Sinking to her knees, she held out her hand, fingers curled to her palm. Sending out waves of Air Innarn let her see Zoomer creeping closer, belly to the ground.

A thin tongue rasped across her knuckles, and Lizbeth gave a huff of laughter. "There you are. Now, I suppose you'd like some food? Do you have a bowl?"

The palon nosed into her basket, snuffling in search of the promised food.

"Guessing that's a no." Lizbeth pulled a hunk of meat out of the basket. She'd traded the butcher on Cantash a bundle of wool for it.

Zoomer glanced up at her expectantly.

"Sit," she said.

He tilted his head.

"I know Samuel may not have had time to train you, dear one, but you must have manners. So, before you get your food, you need to sit and wait. Can you do that? Sit," Lizbeth said.

Giving her a long, unimpressed look, Zoomer plopped onto his hindquarters.

She smiled and patted his head, then laid the hunk in front of him.

He sniffed at it for a moment before tucking in, the meat disappearing quicker than she expected.

Belly finally full, Zoomer lay next to her, eyes glazed.

"Oh, you needed that. Didn't you, dear one?" she cooed. Leaning against the wall, Lizbeth idly patted his back.

Zoomer's eyes slid close, and they lapped up the quiet together.

The head of the guard snapped to attention as he entered the briefing room, his gaze falling on Chamele.

"Yes?" Suni asked, looking up from the map spread across the large table, her finger pointing at an easy entry point their forces could access.

Ignoring the other elder, he turned to Chamele. "The ships are loaded. We only need your authorization to go," he said.

Chamele stood taller as every gaze fell on her. She was silent for a long moment. Now the time to give the order to attack had arrived, she was having second thoughts.

"These aberrations are draining my country dry, and you dawdle?" Suni asked in a low voice.

Tilting her head down to hide a grin, Chamele breathed out through her nose to calm herself. "Merely considering the implications. It's all so real." She raised her head.

"Real?" Suni looked at her and scoffed. "The way they are living off my generosity, my land, my *people*, is real."

Chamele, vision free from the white cloud that usually obscured it, sighed. "And the way they fled to the safety of your lands is real as well."

"Now is not the time for second thoughts," Ben broke in. "Now is the time for action."

Sucking in a breath as the familiar white settled around her again, Chamele nodded. Looking at the head of the guard, she said, "You have my leave."

Raven was running through the forest, the crisp evening air keeping the sweat from drenching him.

The pounding of his feet was muffled by the dirt path, and the noise from the others in the guild trailing behind him. Rounding a corner, he came to a clearing and spied a teen he vaguely recognised, clumsily swinging a sword.

Pulling off to the side, he allowed himself to snap a twig.

Shrieking, the teen turned, sword held in a grip too awkward to be threatening. Staring at him with wide eyes, it took the others crowding into the clearing before she lowered the sword. "Uh... well met," she stammered.

"Well met," Raven said, wiping his brow with the back of his hand. "Doing a spot of training?"

She glanced at the sword and back at him. "Yes?"

"Oh, that is so good, Anika! I'm still not sure how to use a sword properly," Tania admitted.

Raven dragged his eyes from Anika's top to her toes. He recognised the name, but it took him a moment to place it. She was the one who was designing the Altoriae's official outfits.

"I heard Arilla trains regularly. She'd have to, in order to keep all the weapons down in the tavern in good condition," Tania said.

"I know." The blush was leaving Anika's face.

"Sword work is one thing, but being fit enough to swing one is another. Want to join us for the rest of the run?" Raven offered. He ignored the withering glare from Mu.

The blush returned, but Anika nodded. "I'm not much of a runner."

"I won't let you fall behind." He smiled. He gestured to Mu, who rolled her eyes and started off down the trail.

Tania looked at Raven for a long moment but moved off when Collis lightly touched her elbow.

"Shall we?" Raven asked.

"What should I do with this?" She hefted the sword.

Raven grinned and held out his hand. She passed the sword over without stabbing him, and he slipped it into his pocket Realm.

A glint of something sad flicked over her features before her expression smoothed out. Turning, she sprinted down the trail after the others.

Laughing, Raven took off after her.

Jonathan settled into the chair at his new desk in the castle library, grumbling. The desk was just taller than his old one by a finger's width, which meant he was knocking into everything. He placed his mug of azehal down and touched the newspaper crystal slab to activate the screen.

A knock sounded on the open door.

Glancing up, Jonathan smiled at the minotaur. Asterion looked only mildly out of place in a green, button-up cardigan and brown flared pants.

"Mind some company?" Asterion asked.

"Not at all," Jonathan said, gesturing at the rest of the library. "I've just stolen away to work on some correspondence."

Asterion peered at the glowing slab. "And catch up on the news?"

"Exactly," Jonathan said. "A guilty pleasure. Although some days it feels more like a chore."

"Oh, I understand." The twist of the minotaur's mouth was unexpected.

"Finding it hard to settle in?" Jonathan asked.

"A bit. Lissae differs greatly from Atlantis. You are more advanced in empathy, but less in technology."

"Honestly, I'd take the former over the latter any day."

Asterion laughed. "Me too. But I do miss the news of the latest upgrades and newest breakthroughs."

"Have you had much luck finding work?"

"I scour the paper, but no." Asterion looked down and sighed. "I check each day, but there is not a lot of call for someone with my... talents."

"By talents, I'm assuming that you mean..." He gestured to his head.

Asterion nodded and reached up to stroke a horn, a mournful look on his face.

Wishing he could do something more, Jonathan held out the slab. "Why not have a look while I answer some letters? The *Shifting Island Sentinel* is a favourite for keeping up with the news from the islands."

"Thank you." Asterion crossed the room and took the slab before retreating into a chair near enough to Jonathan's desk, but far enough so he couldn't read anything on it.

The sound of papers shuffling, a quill scratching, and gentle tapping filled the study.

Working his way through the pile of papers on his desk, Jonathan got a third of the pile sorted before Asterion cleared his throat.

"Uh, Guardian? You might want to look at this." The minotaur rose but waited for Jonathan to clear a spot on his desk before he approached.

Placing the slab on the desk, Asterion tapped a manicured nail next to an advertisement.

The Skye guards the Grace of the mainlands, held captive. The Guardian is needed to keep both safe. Save Lawrgaea. Save the Grace.

"Does this mean anything to you?"

Jonathan shook his head but ran a finger over the words. Plasma sparked from the slab and jolted his hand. "Ouch!"

"I think the message is meant for you." Asterion said.

"I think you're right," Jonathan admitted. "Now, to figure out what it's actually saying."

"If I may?" Asterion offered.

"Of course." Jonathan pushed the slab back towards the minotaur.

Together, the two worked silently. It was peaceful to have another working in the same space as him who lacked Shari's frenetic energy. He only had a few pieces of paper left when Asterion bellowed softly.

"Got it. Someone in Jinkor. They have included a nifty little piece of tracking Innarn you should be able to access now you know what you're looking for."

"Jinkor?" Jonathan frowned.

"What is wrong with Jinkor?"

"There's a particular elder there who is... opposed to Innarnians. She's been working steadily to pass laws designed to limit us."

"Do you suspect a trap?"

The corners of his mouth twisted down. "These days, everything feels like a trap."

"Do you know this Skye and Grace?"

"I know a Skye who was an aide for the Lawrgaea elder, but I'm not sure who Grace is."

"Is it worth walking into an attempted trap to save them?" Asterion asked.

Jonathan ran his hand over his face. "I don't like the idea of leaving innocents to suffer. But I'm not sure I can take the risk of retrieving them at this stage."

"There is a way, but it may not be palatable to you," Asterion said.

"Try me." Jonathan grinned up at him.

"I go in your place. In disguise, as you. If I am captured, you are still free and know the trap wasn't worth it."

"Where does that leave you?"

"With horns and hooves sharp enough to inflict pain on those who would deceive you," Asterion rumbled.

The Guardian laughed. "You have proven capable of protecting yourself, but I dislike the thought of you putting yourself in danger."

"We can set limits, and I can carry a tracking device."

Sitting back in his chair, Jonathan raised a hand to push up glasses that weren't there anymore and ended up rubbing his temple to disguise the movement. "Can I ask why you are determined to put yourself in harm's way?"

"What else is there for me to do? There is *one* family on Ronah who would allow me to look after their child. Others shy away or flat out flee from the sight of me. I'm struggling to find my place here. And I know"–Asterion raised both hands to rub the sides of his neck–"that it will take time. I know, I've done it before. The minotaur who doesn't fit in anywhere."

Jonathan sighed. "And I'm the fisherman's boy who was whipped every time I spoke incorrectly, whose master put a lump of ice into my throat and almost killed me. It does take time. And you have challenges

I didn't. If you're wanting to make Ronah your home, I'm more than happy to help. Just not if you're going to risk your life at every turn."

Asterion lowered his hands and said, "I trust you to keep me safe."

It had been a long time since someone had so baldly stated their faith in him. "Well. How would we go about achieving the disguise?"

The minotaur sat back and grinned.

Inthday
Second day of the third week of Sunfall

Arilla perched in the seat opposite SilverCloud and slid a cup across the table towards her father-in-law. "Thought you might like something to drink," she said.

"Thank you." SilverCloud smiled.

She grinned back, ignoring the faint lines of pain around his eyes. He took a drink, and Arilla relaxed as his pain faded.

"Delicious. What is it?"

"Calem's special brew. We've been giving it to Shari to help when she returns from patrols," she said.

"What made you think that an old man who hasn't even been close to the Ducibus' Hall in quite some time would need such a restorative?" he said shortly.

"Mother's intuition isn't just good for telling me when my tight-lipped child needs help—it's also good for recalcitrant elders." She smiled to take the sting from her words.

SilverCloud stared at her for a long moment, then he laughed. "Fair enough." He took another drink. "How is Shari going?"

Arilla tilted her head. "She's off-Realm at the moment."

"I thought..." SilverCloud frowned into his mug, the confusion written on his face.

"She'll be back soon enough," Arilla said easily. "Drink up. I'll see if Calem has finished the pastries you like."

"Thank you," he said distractedly.

Rising, Arilla smiled easily and headed for the counter, brows drawn in contemplation. She weaved through the full tables, nodding to the headmaster of Ridden Hall and the Thorne elders as she went.

Before she could slip into the back room to check with Calem, Anika cleared her throat. Pasting on a smile, Arilla turned. "Well met, Anika. What can I get you today?"

"Well met, Arilla. I was hoping... That is, do you offer... um..." Anika trailed off and chewed on her lip. Her hands twisted around the handle of an unfamiliar blade.

"Sword lessons?" Arilla asked.

"Um, yes?"

Arilla gentled her smile. She remembered what it was like to be the only Blank on an island filled with Innarnians. "I'd be happy for you to train with me."

"Really?" Anika squeaked.

She nodded.

From behind Anika, the headmaster asked, "Can we join in? I'm rather rusty, and I don't think Jordan has swung a sword in his life."

Liza's husband laughed. "I'd be lucky to know which end is pointy."

"Sure. The more the merrier. I can ask the Guardian if we can use the training ground. More room means less chance of encountering the sharp side of someone else's blade," Arilla said.

Laughing, Liza nodded. "What time would suit?"

"Maybe before school? Or on the weekend?" Arilla glanced at Anika, the teen looking pale at the thought of her headmaster joining in on sword lessons. "A rusty sword is better than not having one," she said. "And sometimes, it's good for the teacher to become a student again."

Anika's grin was tiny, but she nodded. "Mornings work for me."

"Perfect. Why don't we meet here around six and we can go over to the castle? I'll speak with the Guardian tonight."

"Thank you. I bid thee well." Anika gave her a stilted half-bow and weaved through the tables to the door.

"We'll be there." Liza grinned, ignoring the groan from Jordan.

Arilla laughed.

"Giving yourself more work, love?" Calem asked, as he came up beside her with a plate of pastries.

"Is it work if it's helping someone else?" Arilla asked lightly.

Calem huffed, but his smile said he wasn't upset. After placing a kiss on her cheek, he slipped past and headed to his father's table.

What had she signed herself up for?

CHAPTER TWENTY-THREE

Jetonyx's Pocket Realm
Day four of the Dark Conclave

Shari wanted to grumble about being sent away right as Jaileth, the bronze Q'Aralide, had arrived. Something about the way she moved set off warning bells.

Jetonyx fled as soon as Samuel gave him an excuse.

'*We're to do what Sanithane says,*' Jetonyx sent in response to her questioning. '*He wants you to push Light Innarn into the eggs in the hatching grounds.*'

Sitting back, Shari was quite glad there was no one around to see her dropped jaw. '*What? All of them?*'

'*Something has happened.*' The hatchling was fretting as he wound his way back to the hatching grounds, careful not to be seen.

"And that something warrants genocide?" Shari hissed. For beings that hatched into the blackest of rooms on the Darkest of Realms, it would be akin to murder.

The hatchling said nothing as he slipped through the final, thick door, sealing it behind them. Shari could feel him shaking.

Before she could plan an argument, she was standing on the black sands, staring at the elaborately decorated plinths that rose from the ground like reaching, bony fingers. Each bore a singular, glowing egg, the lights fading into the distance. Columns on both sides, and running in two rows down the centre, went on so far that she couldn't see the end of them.

'*Just how many eggs are here?*' Shari asked.

'*Too many. With these, the Queen could raise an army,*' Samuel sent directly to her. '*Someone has poisoned her, and she is beyond help. If you don't, she will harvest their Innarn to fuel her own.*'

Grimacing, Shari sighed. '*Alright. I'll see what I can do.*'

The plinths were spaced far enough apart for one large Q'Aralide body to safely pass through. Shari made her way into the middle of the room slowly, the eggs providing the only light. The room was made of stone, instead of flesh. '*To use Light Innarn on such a scale would be foolish. I may as well leave a calling card saying I'm here.*'

'*Just be quick.*' For the first time since he'd proposed this ridiculous plan, Shari could hear the pain in Samuel's thoughts.

'*You don't want to cause them pain, do you?*' she asked gently.

'*Of course not! It was my job to care for them, to raise them and nurture them.*'

'*Can't we take them somewhere safe?*' she begged.

Samuel sighed, the sound echoing in her head. '*You can try.*'

Shari stepped up to an egg. The light around it dimmed. "Not you, huh?" She moved deeper into the room. Some eggs glowed brighter, some dimmer.

A curious Jetonyx appeared by her side. '*What are you doing?*'

Shrugging, Shari sent, '*Searching.*' Moving past another egg, she ran her fingertips over the shell, and heatless fire swirled around the base of the egg, flaring brightly. "You?" She moved away, and the flames licked out, one reaching around her wrist and pulling her back. "Alright."

Slowly, using both hands and a fair chunk of Innarn, she lifted the massive egg from its plinth.

'Where are you going to put it?' Jetonyx asked.

'Oh, for the love of...' A wail like she'd never heard before cut off the rest of her thought, and the room shuddered.

'Whatever you're going to do—do it fast!' Samuel sent.

Cursing, Shari shoved the egg into her sanctuary, hoping it would be safe. The wailing continued. 'Run!' she sent to Jetonyx, and took off.

The hatchling fled, with Shari on his heels, weaving in and out through the eggs, flinging tendrils of Light Innarn at them as she went.

'We need to shift,' she sent.

'I can't,' the hatchling wailed.

'We need somewhere safe,' Shari sent to Samuel. An image of the corner of the room where all the delegates were came to mind, and Shari pulled in a breath. She'd have to shift them both and immediately move to Jetonyx's pocket Realm. "Piece of cake," she muttered, placing a hand on the black Q'Aralide hide and pulling them to the suggested spot, cleaning him off as they went.

'What are you doing, hiding behind your wings?' someone sent to Jetonyx as Shari disappeared into the pocket Realm.

'The noise!' Jetonyx moaned, and Shari found she agreed. Below ground, the wailing had been horrific, but above the ground, it was deafening. The hatchling cautiously lowered his wings from around his head and peered out at the rest of the room.

All the remaining delegates were in various stages of distress—some curled into balls on the floor, others with appendages firmly clamped to ears. A few lay twitching, eyes unseeing, as viscous fluid poured from facial orifices.

'*Who dared to take one of my eggs!*' Oalark, in fine form, descended upon the group, brushing red from the sides of her maw.

In the privacy of Jetonyx's pocket Realm, Shari allowed herself to feel the terror the queen was radiating, even through the screens.

The ground rumbled in tandem with her shrieks, and the wailing finally stopped.

Oalark paced before the delegates, squishing those who hadn't been able to rise under her claws. '*Where is my egg?*'

'*My Queen, have you been down to the hatching grounds? Perhaps one has rolled off?*' Helk asked from the doorway.

The pale Q'Aralide turned and snarled at him.

Safe in a totally different Realm, Shari allowed herself to shiver. The look in Oalark's eyes was not one she wished to have trained on her.

'*My eggs don't just roll off.*' Acidic spittle flung from her maw, splattering a few unfortunates. It sizzled against their shields.

Unfortunately, it seemed the delegates did not expect the Q'Aralide Queen attacking with her teeth.

Shari winced as she bit one ambassador's torso straight through. His lower half remained stable for a moment, the three legs propping up the remains of the torso, before collapsing in slow motion.

Altum

Day four of the Dark Conclave

Sanithane slid over to the Queen's side. 'Come, let us sort this out. Perhaps we can trace an Innarn signature from the hatching grounds?'

Oalark nodded feverishly, and stalked out of the room, tail swishing dangerously and slamming into the doorframe. Sanithane and Helk glared at each other but followed the Queen along.

At the entrance to the hatching grounds, Oalark paused and sniffed the air. *'I can smell the Innarn! Someone from the Grey Realms was here! Here, in our most sacred place!'* She stormed into the room, snout raised as she sniffed about.

'Shall we help?' Helk asked tentatively.

'If you stand in the doorway staring, I'll remove your hide from your flesh one agonising stripe at a time,' Oalark growled.

'That's a yes,' Sanithane translated, and started sniffing on the other side of the cavernous room. What he found disturbed him far more than he thought.

Plinth after empty plinth stood at the back of the room. Rows upon rows of nothing, where there once were healthy, thriving eggs. *'My Queen?'* he sent.

Oalark was by his side so quickly, he wondered if she'd shifted. She glanced out at the empty expanse at the back of the room blankly.

Like she expected nothing to be there.

'You found something?'

'I seem to remember more eggs?' Sanithane asked.

She scoffed. *'You must be addled by the wailing. This was never full.'* Turning her back, she stalked towards the empty slot in the middle of the room.

Sanithane's gaze wandered to the side wall, where there were another three empty plinths.

Just what had Oalark been doing whilst he'd been gone? And where were the missing eggs?

Helk sidled up next to him. *'Is the Queen okay?'* he sent in a sharp, brief burst.

'I'm more concerned with the eggs. Why are there so many missing?' Sanithane had taken care of these grounds, of these eggs, for more than a thousand years. They had been his everything, and he knew the ins and outs of the hatching grounds better than any of his kin. Last time he'd

been here, almost one hundred and fifty years ago, every single plinth had been full. And, yes, just over a dozen eggs had been hatched, but it didn't explain where the rest had gone. He looked at Helk, and the two turned to watch as Oalark gripped the empty plinth in the middle of the room and roared, the sound drowning out the wail.

Vermillion scales twitched.

'*Hear that sound a lot?*' Sanithane asked.

'*Every moon rise. At least,*' Helk replied.

'*The wail or the roar?*'

'*Both.*'

Oalark scooped up an egg on the other side of the empty spot and ripped the shell clean apart before lowering her maw and feasting.

Blanching, the nest enemies looked at each other and silently swore not to say a word. They prowled the back rows, ignoring the cracking of shells and the wailing and roaring, until Oalark, belly bulging, waddled over to them.

'*Thank you for your service. I believe it is time to retire for the night.*' Oalark, for the first time since Sanithane had returned to Altum, sounded sane.

Helk glanced at him.

It was everything Sanithane could do to keep his scales arranged in a neutral expression. '*As you will it, my Queen,*' he sent.

'*Helk, with me,*' Oalark ordered.

Silently, the vermillion warrior followed Oalark from the room, glancing back once at the Golden Priest before leaving him in the darkness with the glow of the eggs around him.

The click of his claws echoed on the stones as Sanithane took the time to travel down every row. What had once been home to five hundred eggs now housed a little over ninety. There would have been more at the start of the night.

It was time to hunt down the one he'd left in charge of the eggs, all those moons ago.

Istaniern.

CHAPTER TWENTY-FOUR

Lissae

Kerday

Third day of the third week of Sunfall

Chamele swept through the halls, ignoring the guards and the phalanx that followed her, tugging on the chain in her hand. Her personal aberration, thick metal collar around its neck, stumbled but didn't fall.

Chamele tugged harder.

It tripped, landing hard on bony knees.

The guard directly behind it gave a kick with the clawed metal toe of his boot—all in the name of helping the beast to its feet.

No one remarked on the wound that started weeping, although, as the beast scrambled to its feet, a few guards side-stepped the trail of blood left behind.

"Well?" Chamele asked.

The aberration raised a shaking hand and pointed to the door of the room Elder Suni from Lawrgaea had been assigned.

A quick glance at the polished silver inlay on the wall to ensure her mask was flawless and Chamele glared down at the hunched beast on the end of her chain. "You'd best be right," she snarled, motioning to a guard.

The bulky man nodded to another, and the phalanx took up position around the door, Chamele standing serenely at the end. He glanced in her direction, and she nodded.

It was all the approval he needed. The door caved in with a single, well-placed blow, and the guards poured through the opening to line the walls of the room.

Suni was slumped across the enormous bed, snoring the way only the truly drunk did.

"Is it her?" Chamele asked her aberration.

Wide eyes looked up at her. There was the barest, hesitant nod.

"Do it," the elder ordered.

The head of the guards drew his sword and sliced through the deceitful elder's neck, decapitating the aberration before she could wake from her alcohol-induced slumber.

Suni's slack-mouthed expression didn't change, even as her head rolled slightly now nothing anchored it to her body.

A shriek from the open aide's doorway alerted the guards, who turned, weapons in hands, to face the intruder.

The false elder's aide was staring at the bloody scene of her former mistress, shaking hands over her gaping mouth.

"And her?" Chamele asked, looking down at the chained beast by her side.

Slowly, the aberration shook her head.

Chamele sighed. "I suppose that you'll have to join my aides now," she said, making her tone as soothing as she could. Inside, she seethed. She had trusted Suni. Had believed the elder wanted to rid Lissae of the aberrations as much as she did, and yet, Suni had betrayed her.

At her words, the guards stowed their weapons away. Two of the men moved to strip the bed, using the sheets to cover the still-bleeding corpse of the traitor.

The aide made garbled noises. "I... Elder... What?"

Sighing again, Chamele tempered her tone. Maybe the aide would prove to expose more of Suni's plans if she could keep her onside. "Your elder was false. Innarn was used in these very rooms. We fear"–Chamele allowed her hand to flutter up to her heart–"that Suni may have plans in place to waylay the army we send to Lawrgaea. Did she speak to you?"

"But..." The aide gestured to the guards, now heaving the wrapped corpse from the bed.

"How did we know? You remember our plans to capture an aberration?" Chamele said gently, making her eyes as big and innocent as she could. "Well, I knew it would work because I'd already done so. Capturing one in the wild is far different from having a traitor walk my halls, you understand?" She chanced a glance at the dripping sheets as the guards hoisted the beheaded aberration away.

"I..."

The poor girl was simply stunned. She was staring at the beast on the chain with horror.

"I remember you were afraid to come into contact with them, but I have this one well in hand." Chamele tugged on the chain again, and her aberration stumbled to squat by her side like a dog.

The aide blinked, her watery gaze drawn back to the bed. "May I retire? I do not feel... I..." She took a shuddering breath. "If I can't tell who is false and who is not, perhaps it is best for me to go?"

"If you wish to do so. Of course, with the Travel Innarnians being recalled, your journey home may take months." Chamele was not at all fussed to be rid of the girl. One less mouth to feed at any rate.

"I have your leave?" The aide glanced back at her and drew away with a gasp.

Self-conscious, Chamele reached up to touch her face. The corner of her mask was slipping again. "Take your time to gather your things, but yes, you may go." She turned and strode out of the room, tugging her aberration along behind her.

Narday

Fourth day of the third week of Sunfall

Collis was glaring at the map rolled out on the table of the tavern. It was the quiet time, when most had been in to eat and drink and the next wave of customers wasn't due to start for about half an hour.

"What's got you in such a twist?" Remmy asked.

"I was thinking about walls," Collis said.

Remmy looked at the map. "Walls?"

"Cantash's defences are solid walls. Rakemyst and Talhan's cliffs will make it harder for sea-borne projectiles to hit. Our weak side is Ronah. Here—" Collis pointed to the long stretch of beach on the eastern side that extended down along Rakemyst. "If someone from the mainland was going to attack, it would be from there."

"So, what do you want to do?" Remmy asked.

"Walls," Collis repeated.

"What? You want to fortify the whole beach?" Remmy yelped.

"It wouldn't take much," Collis argued.

"It wouldn't..." Remmy said. He stood back, crossing inked arms over his chest, and glared at Collis. "You miss it," he accused.

Looking up from the map, Collis frowned even harder. "What are you talking about?"

"The constant adrenaline from living in a world where you could be torn apart at any moment. Building and rebuilding to drain every bit of

Innarn, only to rest and do it again." Remmy shook his head. "It's not the answer."

"Don't you feel it?" Collis said lowly.

Remmy raised his brows.

"The constant buzzing under your skin, like your Innarn is about to burst out."

The other man didn't answer, but his eyes slid away, and he gave a sharp nod.

"I think... We were there for three lifetimes. I think we built up a bigger reservoir, or tolerance for large capacities of Innarn. And"–Collis lowered his voice–"I'm scared that if I don't use it, it will escape my control."

Scrunching up his face, Remmy sighed. "There are a few others who have said something similar," he finally admitted.

"Maybe we should help. It feels like there's a war coming. This one is just on our side of the doors."

Sighing, Remmy leaned over the map. "Tell me what you're thinking."

Collis grinned. "Well..."

Jonathan glanced away from the draci on his desk. "Next!"

Sneeze clambered to the top of the paper pile, and Jonathan considered investing in some sort of bed or cage for the draci. The tiny creature glared as if he could hear his thoughts.

A rotund man dressed in blue silk and covered in gold chains waddled into his office in the castle and lowered himself into the seat on the other side of the desk. "Well met, Guardian," he said jovially.

"Well met, Fortesque. How have you found your relocation?"

The man grinned from beneath his large, white moustache. "Quite pleasant. I haven't been home to Talhan in years!"

"Any trouble settling in?" Jonathan asked as he pulled the man's file from the slowly dwindling stack. He was determined to get through the last of the Travel Innarnian interviews today, trying to touch base with all of them and ensure they weren't having any issues being reassigned.

"Oh," Fortesque waved a hand, gold bracelet flashing. "Nothing a bottle of Lawrgaea wine won't cure!"

"Any backlash?"

"Well..." He leaned forward and tapped the side of his nose. "My new neighbour does not like when I sing." The affront in his voice took Jonathan aback.

"Sing?"

"Yes! She says I sound like a walrus! The *nerve*."

"I'm sure you have a marvellous singing voice," Jonathan started.

It was all the encouragement Fortesque needed.

He started to... make noise. With grand passion.

The Guardian wished he could plug his ears. Sneeze had no such qualms and was burrowing under the paperwork as swiftly as he could.

As Fortesque drew breath for his next note, Jonathan burst into applause. "Brilliant," he said dryly. "Perhaps we can ask an Earth Innarnian to thicken the walls of your dwelling? Better acoustics for you," he said with a wink.

"Oh, brilliant. Fantastic idea, dear Guardian." The man beamed so hard his moustache wobbled.

"I'll get someone on that right away." Jonathan made a note in Fortesque's file and duplicated it onto the list off to the side. "Is there anything else I can help with?"

"No, dear Guardian, but I'll be in touch if I have any other issues." Twisting in his seat, he peered at the doorway, where the silhouette of the next Innarnian in line could be seen. "It seems like you're quite the busy man." Rising from his seat, he gave a little bow. "I bid thee well."

Jonathan nodded his head. "I bid thee well," he replied, grateful for such a brief check-in. As Fortesque left the room, the Guardian placed the file in the completed pile. No matter how quickly these meetings went, it never seemed to grow, and the 'to be done' pile still felt exponentially large.

Poking his head out, Sneeze sneezed, and Jonathan absently batted away the sparks from Fortesque's file.

"You need an assistant," the next Travel Innarnian said instead of a greeting. The tall, willowy Ilutri fairly floated into the room, gracefully sinking into the chair Fortesque had just vacated. "Aharny," she offered. "Formerly of Dento."

Raising a brow, Jonathan looked at her. "Are you offering?"

She scoffed, an oddly harsh noise for such a slender being. "Hardly. Unless an observation counts?"

He laughed. "Unfortunately, my apprentice is busy with other tasks."

"Not an apprentice," she said. "An assistant."

Although his immediate instinct was to deny such an idea, the Guardian sighed when he glanced at the overflowing pile. "I have to admit it, the idea is quite tempting. How are you settling in?"

Aharny took the change of subject in hand. "Quite well. It's nice to be home."

"Are you finding everything to your liking?"

The Ilutri looked at him. "Why are you wasting your time asking us if we're happy with our accommodations? Surely, someone else is free to check in with us."

"I like to welcome all new residents to Ronah," Jonathan said, repeating the same lie he'd been telling all day.

"Except, I'm not a resident of Ronah," Aharny pointed out.

He glanced at her file, spotted the green glow, and put it aside. "This is true. But some find a sense of comfort in the welcome."

The look she gave him spoke volumes. '*The mainlanders are furious,*' she sent. '*They are planning an attack. Jinkor has become the base of their operations, as their elder is quite... charismatic.*'

'*Is she?*'

'*Chamele is a danger to any who have so much as a spark of Innarn,*' Aharny sent. "I suppose some do. But I would like to get back to work, if I may?"

"Of course, thank you for your time," Jonathan said. '*If you have anything else, please let me know.*'

Aharny stood and smoothed out her skirt. '*Only that, of all the beings on the mainlands, she is the one who terrifies me the most. A powerful leader will order reluctant troops to fight, a charismatic one has their people willing to die.*' She smiled, although it didn't reach her eyes. "I bid thee well."

Jonathan dipped his head as she slipped out of the room. He glanced at the files again, and not one of the embedded crystals he'd borrowed from Cyrus showed any sort of lie.

The draci climbed up his arm and crooned in his ear. Absently, Jonathan ran a finger along Sneeze's back.

Fighting with the mainlanders was one thing, but with a war coming for the Shifting Islands from both sides of the doorway, they would need all the help they could get.

Tania smiled at Collis as they crossed through Ridden Hall's gates.

"I'll be so glad to get the Realms assignment done! Do you have any idea where the Niverwell Ranges are?" she asked.

He smiled down at her, but didn't answer, a distant look in his eyes.

"I feel like I should know this, but for the life of me I can't remember," she said, looking up at him.

Plucking the books from her arms, Collis hummed. Tania had the distinct feeling he hadn't even heard her.

"Of course, Esse could tell me," she said, grinning. "Chickens have an innate understanding of these things."

He nodded and hummed again.

"Collis," Tania said, "What's wrong?"

"He's planning." One of the older Returned fell into step with them. "Needs to exercise his Innarn more, and he's wondering about the best way to do it."

Collis shot the man a dirty look.

"Oh, there's so much you can help with!" Tania said, a bounce in her step. "The last of the new houses still need finishing up, and there's the preparations for the convergence to be done. Is there something you're wanting to work on?"

"Actually..." Collis rubbed a hand across the back of his neck.

The older man bumped his elbow into Collis's ribs. "He wants to build a wall."

"A wall?" Tania asked, confused.

"There's a weak point in our defences," Collis said.

"Is there?" Tania frowned. She tried to think about where a wall in the museum would go.

"Yes. Around the island."

Tania wrinkled her nose, trying to picture how they could wall off the entire museum to protect Ronah. "I suppose it would work, but how would the patrols get in?"

Collis shot her a confused look. "The Travel Innarnians have already moved, so it shouldn't be too much of an issue."

"But would they climb the wall around the museum? If there's a door, that would just be another weak spot, wouldn't it?"

He smiled at her indulgently. "Not around the museum—around the Shifting Islands. A wall running the length of the beach, but one that can be raised and lowered as needed."

"Ooohhh. That makes a lot more sense." Tania giggled a bit, imagining Zana clambering over the wall she'd been picturing. "Something like that would take a lot of Innarn."

"Exactly." Collis smiled fiercely.

Asterion stepped behind a swarthy four-armed man who was waiting outside the door to the Guardian's office.

The man turned, a smile on his face and welcome on his lips. The words failed to form as his smile dropped and he glanced up at Asterion's horns. He nervously chuckled, and snapped his head back around without saying anything, skittering closer to the door, as if the Guardian was going to protect him from the big bad minotaur.

Keeping his expression peaceful, Asterion clenched his fingers around the scroll case in his hand. If he tried to sigh, it would come out of his bull nose louder than intended and cause more alarm to those around him.

More than once, it had made him wonder if the transplant had been worth it.

A being with bark-like skin rambled passed them, and the four-armed man strode inside, with only a singular backwards glance.

Considering his state of distress, Asterion was quite impressed.

There was a wait of ten minutes, and he reappeared at the doorway. When he saw Asterion again, he paused.

"Guardian, would you like me to remain?"

Jonathan's voice came from inside the room. "No need. Send the next being in."

"It's…" The man glanced at him again, his lower hands clenching and unclenching. He looked over his shoulder. "It's a minotaur."

"Asterion?" The Guardian sounded closer. Sure enough, he appeared just behind the man. "Brilliant! I was hoping you'd be back. Come on in." To the other man, he said, "Thank you, Lerryn. Please reach out if you have any more problems."

Lerryn looked rather flummoxed by his dismissal, but left the room, squeezing to the far side of the wall to get past Asterion.

The minotaur ignored him as best he could.

"I'm so glad you've been able to free up some time to help. Your expert opinion is sorely needed," Jonathan said, loud enough for his voice to carry after Lerryn.

Asterion shot him a look and stomped over to the visitor's chair near the desk. "Don't bother. Beings like him fear what they don't know, and pretty words won't change it."

The Guardian came around the desk and held his gaze. "I will always bother."

The minotaur nodded and looked away, taking a moment to clear the unexpected lump in his throat.

Moving to a table off to the side of the desk, the Guardian set about making them hot drinks. Fire Innarn casually sprung from his fingertips to heat the water he'd poured into cups. The fragrant aroma helped to settle Asterion's nerves.

"I'm assuming you've come to discuss your plan?" Jonathan asked as he turned and handed him a cup.

"Yes, here." He passed over the scroll case. "I've outlined the basic idea behind the process. It's a little difficult, as we are different builds and heights. But I spoke to the technomancer, and she gave me something that can help with the illusion."

Uncapping the case, the Guardian slipped the scroll out, placed it on a stack of files, and perused it whilst sipping his tea. "This is incredibly well thought out. Most plans come half-hatched and verbalised. And your writing is impeccable." He went to put his cup down on the overflowing desk and sighed. "I don't suppose you're still looking for work?"

Cup halfway to his mouth, Asterion's brows drew together. "Sorry?"

"Someone mentioned the idea of an assistant to me." The Guardian glanced at his desk. "I'm thinking that's rather a good idea."

"It would help?"

"More than help. It would free me up to do what needs to be done, instead of bureaucratic fighting and dealing with ridiculous policies designed to entangle or stop us."

"Perhaps after this rescue, if you still think the plan is good, we can discuss it again?"

"Brilliant." The Guardian grinned at him.

CHAPTER TWENTY-FIVE

Altum

Day five of the Dark Conclave

Istaniern was elusive.

Sanithane had tried asking her nest mates subtly, to no avail. The pearl-coloured Q'Aralide was tiny, and quite adapt at hiding, if what he was gathering was correct. When questioning them outright, he garnered looks that made him wonder if she'd woven some sort of Innarn over everyone that made them forget her existence.

If she had done it for herself, would she be willing to do it for others?

Would she do it for him?

Sighing, Sanithane put the impossible question out of his mind. One missing hatchling was all he could handle right now.

Striding through Altum made him grind his teeth.

For a visitor, his home Realm would appear as just the right balance between awe-inspiring and terror-inducing.

Fresh hide curtains fluttered in windows, but the grime that covered the glass shouldn't have been there. Discarded bones and debris were piled against most of the buildings, and the stench of fermented meat, rather than the sweet smell of a fresh kill, permeated everything. The buildings had lost their sheen, and everything looked closer to grey instead of the red he remembered. Mould and moss grew in cracks and crevasses.

There was a general air of neglect over everything.

Altum looked tired. And old.

After the events of the day, none of the ambassadors or their staff were game to take to the streets. They had secreted themselves away, no doubt determined to preserve those who were left. He half wished they could call in replacements, but the doorway to Altum was closed for the rest of the conclave. Only the Q'Aralide and possibly Shari would be strong enough to get through to the Ducibus' Hall.

The few Q'Aralide he came across were so downtrodden, that had he not had questions about Istaniern or Jetonyx, they never would have looked his way.

Even the proud warriors appeared tired as they dragged back exceptionally small kills.

A patch of darker shadow lunged at him as he passed by two buildings, and Sanithane swore. He was lucky his hatchling didn't get toasted.

'*Where have you been?*' he growled.

'*There's...*'

He didn't let Jetonyx say another word. Grabbing the hatchling by the scruff of his neck, Sanithane marched him back to the relative safety of his quarters.

'*Do not leave. If anyone attempts to enter, send to me immediately. And if it's the Queen...*' Jetonyx looked at him with enormous eyes. '*Run. Hide. Do whatever you need to do to get away from her. Understand?*'

The hatchling nodded.

With Jetonyx safely sequestered in his quarters, he found he couldn't stay still. Time to revisit an old haunt.

In a whirl of gold, Sanithane stalked from the room. There was only one place on Altum that he could trust the Queen not to go, and he needed to see if anyone else was using it first.

His trip through the tired building was quicker with a destination in mind. At the edge of the acid river, he looked down. The beast underneath the frothing liquid was still happily feasting on what was left of War'Jan. The expanse that had once seemed impassable was barely more than a hop for him now.

On the other side of the bank, Sanithane stuck his head into the cave that he'd whiled away half of his early years in.

Only for a streak of Dark Innarn to glance across his maw.

Pulling back, Sanithane had to admit that Jonathan's constant hammering about having a shield up was the most likely reason he still had his face.

'*Well met,*' he rumbled, rubbing a claw along his snout.

'*Stay back.*' The sender was young and trembling.

'*Istaniern?*'

'*I'll not suffer the same fate as my keeper.*' Another streak of Innarn shot out of the cave, wild and untamed.

'*Who are you, little one?*'

'*Your worst nightmare,*' the being in the cave tried to growl.

Sanithane bit the inside of his lip, trying not to laugh. Settling down on his haunches, he laid his head on his forepaws. '*Oh no, I'm so scared.*'

The growl grew louder. '*You should be!*'

A jet-black head, smaller than Jetonyx, hesitantly poked out of the cave entrance. The tiny Q'Aralide eyed him askance. '*You don't look scared.*'

'*Oh, I'm terrified,*' Sanithane sent, and smiled.

She squeaked and disappeared back into the cave.

'Why're you here?' the little one asked.

'An answer for an answer,' he replied. 'Tell me your name first.'

Her tiny face peered at him out of the gloom. 'I don't have one. Istaniern was...' Her lower lip trembled. 'She was eaten before she could give me one.'

Well, that explained things.

'And you've been surviving out here by yourself?'

The hatchling nodded.

'How many others are there?'

The trembling gave way to acidic tears. 'I'm the last one.'

Sanithane experienced a flash of memory; War'Jan and Oalark descending on the nest room, fragile bodies giving way to snapping jaws.

And he'd been powerless to stop it.

'She tried to stop them—didn't she?'

There was a nod, and her eyes narrowed into a glare.

Innarn shuddered through his body, but he trampled down the fury he was feeling.

Snippets of the Queen in the nest room, and in the hatching grounds, eating the eggs before they'd even become whole beings.

She needs to be stopped.

'How can you stop her?'

Startled, Sanithane looked at the little one. 'Leave that up to me.' Rising, he stretched his legs out, careful to keep his wings out of the falls. 'Are you staying here, little one?'

She nodded.

He frowned. 'I may not be able to come back for you. Would you like to go somewhere safer?'

Onyx eyes stared into his soul. 'Give me a name first.'

This tiny, fierce hatchling needed a name that would remind her of her strength. Of her tenacity, and her will to survive in a Realm where everything was stacked against her doing so. 'Tormorylth.'

She smiled, the movement slow and painful-looking on hide stretched too thin for one so young. Tentatively, the hatchling crept out of the cave, keeping low to the ground.

Sanithane reached a claw out. '*I'm going to shift you. I have a friend, another hatchling, who has a safe space for you. But you must not eat the beings there. I will provide food for you.*'

Tormorylth looked at him. '*What sort of food?*'

'*What have you been eating?*' It was easy to peer into her memory and feel the growling of her belly and the frantic scrabble of tiny claws on rock as she struggled to catch even the measliest of bugs for her next meal. The long nights of licking the moss on the cave walls, and hoping that when it combined with her tears, it would fill the ache that never seemed to go away. '*There is plenty of food for you to try. For now, I'm going to use my Innarn to hide you. Stick close to my side and don't wander off.*'

She nodded solemnly.

And he hated it. Hated that his race was born to fear the very ones who should have been protecting them.

Turning back to the river, he felt her pause.

'*I can't make it over,*' she whimpered.

'*I'll help you, Tormorylth.*' Sanithane stepped across the river. Looking back, he eyed the hatchling and drew a circle on the riverbank with his claw. A bubble surrounded her, floating the startled hatchling safely to his side. '*Now, stay close,*' he sent as he dismissed the bubble.

Tormorylth sank into the shadow at his side.

He made his way slowly back to his quarters, trying to allow for shorter legs to keep up with his stride. No one stopped him, or even glanced his way. Sanithane didn't know if he should revel in the ease of their passage or be disturbed by it.

'*Jetonyx, we have a guest. She will need to join your other one,*' he sent. It was far better to warn his other hatchling than to startle them both into a fight. '*Please have some food ready for her.*'

There was slight grumbling, as if his charge had woken from a nap, but he could feel the older hatchling rising.

His doorway was in sight when Jaileth stepped into his path.

Tormorylth froze. Sanithane draped a lazy wing over her. She was so frail, it looked like nothing was there.

'*How goes my mate on this fine night?*' Jaileth asked, bronze scales gleaming in the lamplight.

'*Tired. Much the way the rest of Altum is looking,*' Sanithane replied.

'*Awww, don't be like that.*'

'*The last time we spoke, you cursed my name and tried to rend my wings. What other way would you expect me to be?*'

Jaileth stepped up to him, brows raised and eyes earnest. '*You know I would never normally do that. War'Jan, he was mucking about with stuff, injecting us. It made us mad.*'

'*And yet you were the only one I came across who tried to hurt me.*'

'*The Queen, San, she's...*'

Mindful of the hatchling burrowing into his side, he raised a brow and glanced around. There was one warrior at the end of the street, and another two houses over. Both were close enough to listen. '*Bring your friends along, did you?*'

Jaileth startled. '*Can we talk?*' She gestured towards his quarters.

'*She tried to get in, but your wards held,*' Jetonyx sent.

Suddenly, he was hit with a longing to return to Lissae. Where double speak and triple-crossing was done with the good of the Realm in mind.

'*I am tired, Jaileth. Can it wait until the morning?*'

His mate bowed her head. '*You know that every second we waste...*'

'*Tormorylth, I say this to keep you safe,*' he sent in a short, sharp burst. The hatchling dug her claws into his side. They did little to hurt his hide, but the sharp pinpricks helped to ground him. '*Is a second when the good of Altum, the Q'Aralide, and our Queen will regret.*'

Jaileth stepped away from his hard gaze. 'I see.' Her words were stilted. For a moment of abject horror, Sanithane feared that he had read her so wrong. But the tiny claws dug in harder. '*I'll leave you to rest.*'

Biting back his instinct to call her back to him, Sanithane stared after her. Cylanthar's bells of destiny rang loudly in his mind.

Was the ages-old deity was laughing at his predicament, or glad to see his mate leave?

The moment her bronze tail turned the corner, Sanithane slipped into his quarters, Tormorylth still plastered to his side.

Chapter Twenty-Six

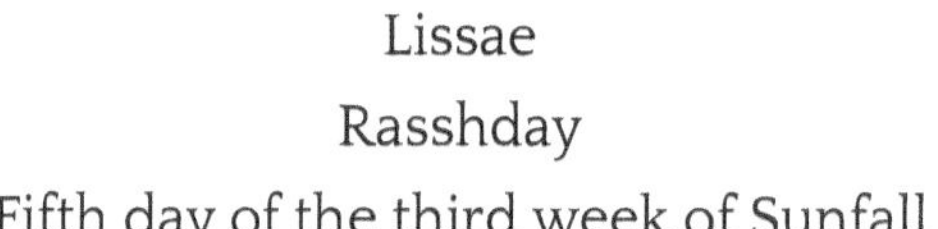

Lissae

Rasshday

Fifth day of the third week of Sunfall

Arilla's eyes were wide as she took in the assembled beings milling around inside the public entrance to the training grounds.

Word of her sword lessons seemed to have gotten out. Anika stood off to the side, a somewhat guilty expression on her face. The Hollingsworths were there, as were quite a few of the displaced from Talhan who'd been hanging around Ronah and doing odd jobs for anyone who'd hire them. No Ilutri, of course, and only three from Cantash if she knew the mark of the leathers they wore. All up, there were twenty beings holding wooden practice swords with varying degrees of discomfort.

"Right. Uh, well met, all. The Guardian has said that we're free to use the training grounds here for an hour in the mornings, three times a week. I think that's plenty to start with. Before we begin, I was just wondering who has had any experience with a sword?"

Liza put her hand up, as did a thin man from Talhan with a slash along the side of his face.

"Excellent. Come out to the front, please. You'll be helping me today. I didn't expect quite so many of you," Arilla said.

"Sorry," Anika burst out.

"Don't apologise. Any who want to learn are welcome." Arilla smiled. "Now, number one lesson—don't get hit."

The guy with the scar pointed to his face and nodded. A few people in the group sniggered.

"Number two, if you haven't used a sword before, your muscles won't be used to it. That's the main thing that we'll be starting with. There's plenty of room, so if we line up, it'll make things easier. Hold the sword in your dominate hand and raise it like so." Arilla glanced down the line. "Excellent! Now, the boring bit to start. Place your dominate foot forward, and your back foot pointed slightly to the side. Leading with the blade of the sword, I want you to make twenty short cutting motions forward. Like this." She demonstrated. "Keep the blade of the sword aimed at the thing you're cutting towards. Liza and, uh..."

"Ciaran," the scarred man offered.

"Ciaran will watch and correct as you go." Arilla turned to her two helpers. "Mind you, if you want to practice as well, feel free."

"I will," Liza said. "But I can do this and walk around at the same time. I think I'm too rusty not to start with the basics."

"I'll check on technique. I'm a bit more comfortable using a blade than the others," Ciaran said.

"How comfortable?" Arilla asked, arching a brow.

He smiled. "This"—he gestured to his face again—"is an old wound. I've learned how to dodge since then."

"Up for some sparring after?" she asked.

"Absolutely."

With the help of Liza and Ciaran, Arilla found it easy to adjust the techniques of the others, suggesting a wider stance here, more wrist action there, or a different way to hold shoulders.

"Another twenty!" Arilla said.

There were groans, but they did it easily.

"And a bit of a break. Ciaran?"

The scarred man was at the other end of the line. He hefted his sword and started running at her.

Arilla stepped away from the others and braced herself. Ciaran leaped into the air. The windup for his overhead swing was so blatant, she considered letting it connect, but dodged out of the way at the last second. She swung as she moved, the flat of her sword hitting his back. Ciaran stumbled but recovered enough to turn and strike again.

The dull *thunk* of wood meeting wood made a few of those gathered gasp. Arilla ignored them, parrying as she and Ciaran moved around the grounds. The other man was pretty good, for all that he broadcasted every move with massive build-ups before his swings.

Changing tactics, Arilla went on the offensive, rapidly striking and pushing Ciaran until his back touched the wall around the grounds.

"Yield?" she asked, blade against his throat.

"Yield," he panted, grinning at her.

She stepped back and bowed, Ciaran bowing back.

"And that is your aim," she said, turning to the group and wandering towards them.

"To yield?" a teen from Talhan called out. A few of his mates laughed.

"To fight long enough to get away. You don't have to be the strongest to wield a sword, or the bravest, or the fastest. If you can master the basics, it'll give you a good idea of what to do if someone comes at you with a blade."

Arilla was close enough to hear Anika mutter, "When, not if."

"Pair off, and try to hit your opponent's sword. Twenty strikes each. Try to focus on varying the strength of your blows and aiming with the midpoint of the sword."

The group milled around a bit before they partnered off. Thuds rang out as wooden blades connected, and there were muffled grunts and laughter as the group helped each other out.

Moving amongst them all, Arilla corrected their technique again, adjusting grips and widening stances.

After the first lot, she said, "Everyone move one to your left. Those on the end of the line, join together, and repeat the exercise with your new partner."

By the end of the session, even Anika was sweating, but most were beaming with delight at getting at least one strike in on their opponent.

"Have a break tomorrow, or keep practising striking, and we'll meet up again the day after to work on the next stage. Great work, all! I bid thee well." Arilla gave her best smile as the others filtered out, Anika leading the way.

Arilla stared after her, worried.

Skye had very little to pack.

It didn't stop her hands from shaking as she smoothed over her travel cloak. Everything she'd brought with her was all ready to go, including the incriminating crystal slab at the bottom of her basket. Was it poor form for her to rummage through the elder's belongings? There may be something that would help ease Skye's travels, but was it worth the risk when Suni was considered a traitor?

She'd have a quick peek and find out.

Carrying her portable trunk by the top handle, Skye released a shaky breath. Taking the two steps to the doorway that led to the dead elder's room, Skye trembled as she spied the trail of blood leading to the door.

My fault.

Elder Suni had been a bigot and an all-round horrible person to those she considered lesser. And Innarnians were worse than lesser in Suni's view. Despite the elder's wish to eradicate all 'aberrations', it still didn't mean she deserved to die.

Trying to block the blood from her mind, Skye moved slowly around the edges of the room, poking through the papers on the desk and rummaging in the large wooden wardrobe. There were a few more modest travel garments secreted amongst the frippery and finery Suni had typically preferred. Gathering two of the plainer dresses and three of the shirts, Skye tucked them into her pack. Suni's travelling cloak was slipped in as well, along with four square handkerchiefs and a leaf-patterned spring scarf that Skye had always admired. She glanced at the shoes lining the bottom of the wardrobe, knowing that even if they hadn't been two sizes too big, they were all hideously unpractical, and bound to fall apart before she'd even reached the docks at the edge of the town.

Moving on to the dressing table, she ignored the potions and lotions, but gathered up the cosmo-shell-inlaid brush set. It would fetch a pretty coin or ten, and the elder had many more like it at home. Taking the long way around to the far side of the bed and ignoring the pool of drying liquid on the mattress, Skye stopped when her toe hit a bottle and it rolled away towards the open doors of the tiny balcony.

Frowning, she carefully picked it up and sniffed the uncapped opening. The elderflower brandy Suni had so enjoyed had been laced with something bitter.

"Had to make sure she'd sleep," came a scratchy voice from behind her.

Skye gasped and whipped around. The mound of blankets that she'd assumed had been thrown to the side shuddered and moved.

Grace peered out of a gap through one swollen eye.

"Grace?" Skye whispered, falling to her knees.

"She knew about you." More of Grace's face appeared, all of it mottled with bruises. "Suni and Elder both."

"Cham...?"

A frail hand shot out of the blankets and held up a warning finger, cutting Skye off mid-word.

Nodding her silence, Skye gently took Grace's hand and skimmed careful fingers over rice-paper-thin skin. "I need to go, before Cha... *she* suspects me. Come with me?"

"Leave?" the scratchy voice trembled.

"And never come back." Skye's harsh whisper was a direct contrast with her touch.

"Am I interrupting?" a deep voice asked from the direction of the balcony.

Skye shrieked, falling backwards and scuttling away. Grace disappeared back into her mound of blankets.

"Forgive me. I did not mean to scare you." The man stepped into the room and held his hand out. Something around his head shimmered slightly.

Heart pounding, Skye looked at his hand, her gaze travelling up his arm until it rested on his face.

The same face that had stood next to the Altoriae, smiling on the front page of *The Shifting Island Sentinel*.

"Guardian?" she whispered.

Grace poked her head back out of the blankets. "Elder comes," she warned.

"Elder?" the Guardian asked.

Gaze swivelling to the mess on the mattress, Skye fumbled to her feet, grabbing her basket and trunk, and holding out her hand to Grace. "We need to go, Grace. You can't end up like Suni."

Far too slowly for Skye's peace of mind, Grace extended one long, spindly limb and grasped onto her hand.

As she got to her feet, Grace's one good eye gazed at the door.

Skye wasn't sure if it was her heart thumping out of her chest, or boots pounding through the hall outside.

"She comes," Grace said.

"And we go," the Guardian said. Carefully, he laid a hand on each of them as the door to the former elder's room slammed and bounced against the wall.

Whipping her head around, the red of the guard's uniforms and the distorted expression on Chamele's face were etched into Skye's memory before they were shifted somewhere else.

Chamele rushed through the door of the traitor's room. She glimpsed a man with obscured features reaching down and wrapping one hand around the traitor's terrified aide and the other around her personal aberration. Between one step and the next, they vanished.

"No!" she screeched. Carried by her momentum, she slipped on the trail of blood the aide had yet to clean. Arms pin-wheeling, she fell backwards—hard. Holding her hand to her aching head, the startled gasp of a guard did little to help the ringing in her ears.

"Elder, your face..." he said, eyes wide and filled with horror.

Time seemed to slow as she moved her other hand to her face, feeling the edges of the mask she'd worn for so long peeling away from the ruined flesh underneath.

"What did he do?" she slurred.

"The aberration on the balcony did this?" The gruff voice of the head guard helped to identify the man as her vision blurred and doubled.

"Yes," she rasped.

Blinking away the stars dancing around her head, she caught the glance between two of the other guards.

"Sneaky. Must have trapped the door," she said.

"She was the first one through," the head guard said. "Well? What are you waiting for? Call a Healer! The elder needs help."

His words were like drums against her skull. Allowing her head to loll, Chamele tried to stifle the bile threatening to rise. "Make sure... the attack... goes ahead," she groaned out, before the blackness closing in on the corners of her vision overcame her.

Wolf paced outside the Mind Healer's rooms, unable to sit still.

Belfar had been inside for the better part of the morning and had yet to surface. The Healer had to have a strong privacy ward up, because he couldn't hear a thing. Not that Wolf wanted to invade Belfar's session, but his concern was making his worry increase.

Pacing around the outskirts of the room bled off little of the tension knotting above his wing joints, but it did help. Before Wolf could start on the next side, the door opened and Belfar stepped out, eyes puffy, but a small smile on his face.

"See you next week?" the Mind Healer asked.

His mate nodded.

"Brilliant. Same time then." She smiled. "Take care, and if you need anything, just send to me."

"Thank you," Belfar rasped.

Wolf sucked in a breath. Behind the privacy ward, Belfar had been crying.

The healer nodded to them both and disappeared back into the room.

"Take me home?" Belfar asked.

Gathering his mate into a tight hug, Wolf said, "I'll race you there?"

Wolf's heart soared when Belfar kissed him on the cheek and softly countered, "Beat you there." But he made no move to break away.

"We could go together," Wolf said.

"Together." Belfar nodded, giving him another small smile.

Hand in hand, they walked out of the Mind Healer's offices and along the manicured garden outside. The winding path was shaded with large green leaves and dangling white flowers. Here and there a honeyhawk flittered around, collecting nectar. They followed the cream stones to the hedged-off flight platform. Another Ilutri was arriving on the round paved area, slowly coming to a landing before taking a second path towards the offices with a nod in their direction. Belfar moved to the platform and squeezed Wolf's hand before letting go.

He moved right towards the edge. "Do you know I can remember everything that I did when I was under the crystal intelligence's influence?" Belfar said.

"Really?"

"I can remember heading straight for a cliff in the Earth Provence of Talhan and thinking I should jump. Apparently, the crystal didn't figure wings into the equation," he said with a twist of his lips.

Wolf wasn't sure what to say. *I'm glad you're here. I love your wings. I love you. Please don't forget to fly.*

"Never been more thankful for them, I think. Even if one isn't real anymore."

"You're real," Wolf blurted.

"But this—" Belfar waved his crystal wing. "This is not."

"Tis," Wolf argued. "It's just a highly advanced prosthetic."

"And makes me half an Ilutri," Belfar spat. Then he rubbed his eyes. "Sorry."

"Don't apologise for feeling," Wolf said.

Belfar stared over the edge of the platform for a while, ignoring the comings and goings of the others. When he was ready, he turned to Wolf and offered a wan grin.

"Home?" Wolf asked.

Belfar nodded and leaped into the air. "Race you."

Wolf barked a laugh and flew after him.

CHAPTER TWENTY-SEVEN

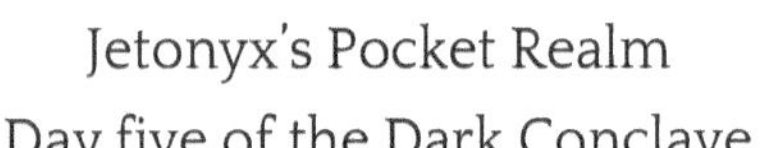

Jetonyx's Pocket Realm
Day five of the Dark Conclave

Shari watched through the crystal screens as Samuel entered his quarters, moving stiffly as if he had been wounded. Sitting up, she gripped the hilt of her yellow blade with no remembrance of calling it to her side.

'*Sanithane?*' Jetonyx was fairly trembling with worry.

'*Easy, little one.*'

At first, Shari thought the send was aimed at her host, but Samuel lifted his wing.

Half expecting a weeping wound, Shari startled when a tiny hatchling tumbled to the ground.

The minute creature glanced around, and on spotting Jetonyx, tried to growl.

The Altoriae of Lissae did the unthinkable and dropped her sword. Hands flew to cover her mouth, even though the others wouldn't hear her squeal at how cute the rumpled creature looked.

Jetonyx shuffled and lowered his head, nosing the hissing creature curiously. *'Do I know you? I don't think we've met.'*

The little hatchling hissed and swiped razor-sharp claws across his nose.

Partly smothering a laugh, Jetonyx rubbed at his snout as if she'd injured him. *'Feisty! What's your name?'*

'She needs to join your other guest.' The send was aimed at her as well. Hastily, Shari banished her blade. Samuel lowered his great, golden head, waiting until the new arrival turned to look at him warily. *'There is another, who will take care of you. She is not a snack.'*

'Is she in trouble?' the little one asked.

Samuel laughed and glanced at Jetonyx. Shari had the feeling that he knew she was watching. *'She's trouble, alright. Now go, and listen to the other. She will protect you.'*

Shari huffed out a breath. A tiny part of her was resentful of being given another soul to care for and watch over, but as the little Q'Aralide materialised beside her, all those thoughts drained away. The hatchling was clearly malnourished; her ribs were far too prominent and her belly almost non-existent. Her hide was pulled painfully thin over her knobbly spine.

'Well met,' Shari sent softly.

The little one spun to face her, a snarl on her lips.

'I will not hurt you.' Shari held her hands up, palms out, with her fingers curled in, trying to make herself as non-threatening as possible.

She plopped to the ground, her hindquarters barely indenting the sand. *'Where are your wings? And your fangs?'*

'I'm not the same race as you.'

The little one—*'Tormorylth,'* Samuel supplied—stared at her.

'I don't think you could hurt me if you tried.' Tormorylth sniffed and stood again, the smell of the fresh meat Sanithane had shifted into the

pocket Realm clearly calling to her. With barely a backwards glance, she raced towards the food and started wolfing it down.

Blinking, Shari couldn't decide if she should be glad Tormorylth wasn't scared of her or offended that she didn't come across as threatening. To be fair, if the little hatchling was comparing her to the queen, she should probably be glad she didn't alarm the little one. '*Don't eat too fast*,' Shari warned.

Tormorylth only glanced over her shoulder but slowed the rapid shovelling of food into her mouth.

'*It's been a while since you've eaten, hasn't it?*' Shari asked, carefully approaching the hatchling.

Growling, Tormorylth moved so she would be between the food and Shari.

'*Oh, you don't have to worry. That's all for you*,' Shari said, wrinkling her nose as she caught sight of the rivulet of blood dripping down the hatchling's chin. '*I've got my own food. But little meals are good when you haven't eaten for a while. I can keep the rest of it fresh for you, if you like.*'

Cheeks full of food, Tormorylth looked at her warily and nodded, slowly backing away from the carcass.

Lifting a hand, Shari wiggled her fingers, freezing the food in time and preventing it from spoiling. '*Wait an hour or two, and you can have some more.*'

'*More?*' Tormorylth mumbled as she chewed slowly.

'*Yep. Lots of little bits of more, until you can eat as much as you want in one sitting*,' Shari sent easily. Settling down in the sand where she could see the hatchling and the crystal screens, Shari offered a friendly smile. '*How did you get here?*'

Random images flicked through her head. The thoughts echoed from Samuel as he explained to Jetonyx how he'd found the tiny hatchling.

Shari found herself grateful for the countless patience that waiting on endless battlefields had given her.

'*Samuel?*' she sent at the end of Tormorylth's tale. '*What are we going to do to stop the queen?*'

When he turned to look directly at the crystal screens that were Jetonyx's eyes, there was no doubt he was looking directly at her this time. '*Every monarch has to come to the end of their rule, eventually.*'

More images flicked through her head—the scene he'd come across in the hatching grounds, Helk's admission, the Queen's serenity after eating the eggs.

Rage like she'd never felt flared through her.

'*Eventually better be looking like some time tomorrow,*' Shari all but growled.

Tormorylth gave her an approving grin. '*Spoken like a true Q'Aralide.*'

Shari didn't know if she should be offended or flattered.

'*Why are you hiding? Sanithane said you're trouble.*'

Coughing to disguise her chuckle, Shari flicked a glance at the crystals. All three of Samuel's eyes seemed to laugh at her. '*I... ah... I wouldn't really be welcome here.*'

'*Like me.*' Tormorylth plopped down again, with all the grace of a toddler. '*Is there somewhere you are welcome?*'

A bit of Shari's heart seemed to break for this tiny, deadly creature who'd known only fear and pain. '*Yeah. My home is pretty welcoming. I live in a Realm where it's...*' She wanted to say, 'where it's okay to be yourself,' but could that really be true for Tormorylth? She was so young, and so Dark. It was painful for Samuel to just exist on Lissae, but for Jetonyx and Tormorylth?

It could very well be a death sentence.

Chapter Twenty-Eight

Lissae

Vebaday

Sixth day of the third week of Sunfall

kye's fingers tightened around her pack in one hand as Grace squeezed the other. Looking around, it took her a moment to realise something.

We are safe.

Far out of the reach of Chamele and the guards, far away from those who gave them names like *aberration*, she could finally relax.

Or she would, if Grace would stop growling at their rescuer.

"Thank you so much for getting us out of there," Skye said, squeezing Grace's hand back gently. She could feel the bones just under the other girl's skin.

"Don't thank me. Thank the Guardian," said the Guardian.

Frowning, Skye's gaze darted around the room. "Aren't you?"

His face shimmered for a moment, and two curved horns sprouted from his forehead.

Grace's free hand shot out, a glowing purple Innarn shield springing from her fingertips.

The minotaur froze.

"I'm not the Guardian, but I am his friend. He asked me to bring you to safety. To Ronah."

"We're on Ronah?" Skye asked.

"You go now." Grace scowled at him.

Skye had the horrid feeling that Grace was moments away from making minotaur soup. *Does he know that tilting his head makes his horns gleam?* Her thoughts spun as she gently reached out and placed her hand over Grace's.

"Would it be possible for us to talk to the Guardian, please?" Skye tried her best court manners.

The minotaur bowed. "Of course." He, quite smartly, backed out of the room.

Grace didn't drop the shield.

"We're safe," Skye crooned. "Safe on Ronah."

The plasma faded away as quickly as it had appeared, although it left a wake of static behind.

It flared like lightning in Grace's eyes as the real Guardian walked through the door.

"Well met," said Jonathan Baun, youngest Guardian since Ogea Geolk in 3745. First to stand up to the combined questioning of the Elders of Lissae and keep his Altoriae's name a secret for years.

She squeaked.

Grace grunted.

Clearing her throat, Skye tried not to hyperventilate. She'd never thought she'd actually have the chance to meet the man she'd been unofficially working for. "I... um... well met, Guardian." She wanted to squeal and jump up and down, but Grace's death-grip on her hand reminded her of where they'd come from.

"Are you the one who sent the message?" His voice was gentle, for all his Innarn was humming just under the surface.

"Yes!" she blurted, and cleared her throat again. "I mean, yes, that was me. Fiona said that it was important that you know when the mainlanders were planning on moving against the Shifting Islands, and the Altoriae wasn't replying to my sends, and I haven't been able to get hold of the network for months..."

"Network?"

"Of Innarnians spying on the mainlanders," Skye said.

There was no recognition in the Guardian's expression at all. "Why don't we get comfortable, and you can tell me all about it?" He turned and led the way out of the room.

"Food?" Grace said in a whisper so low it tickled the fine hairs on her neck.

"Would you like something to eat?" he asked.

Skye wasn't sure if he had exceptional hearing, or he was the perfect host. "Yes, please. We're famished."

She waited until they were seated on comfortable lounges with platters of finger foods on the table before them. Grace looked at the food, shifted her gaze to the Guardian, then back to the platter again. Taking a plate, she loaded it with a few morsels and scurried into the corner.

The Guardian watched her go, before turning back to her. "So, you're a spy?"

"The good kind," Skye said. "Fiona set up a network a few years ago. Most of us have just enough Innarn to get by, but our levels are so low that we can be mistaken for Blanks. It allows us to gain positions within influential households to see if they're as tolerant as they make out."

Lips thinning, he nodded and took a sip from his teacup. "And whose household were you a part of?"

"I was an aide to Elder Suni," Skye said. Blinking away the picture of the blade swinging from Suni's neck, she reached forward and placed a few biscuits on her plate.

"Was?"

"Chamele had her killed."

"Killed?"

It felt like there was an echo in the room.

"Yes. Grace"–Skye tipped her head towards the huddled form in the corner–"saved me. And then you... or your minotaur saved us both."

"Asterion is hardly *my* minotaur. But he is my friend."

A chunk of cheese, some savoury biscuits, and a tiny bowl of fruit rose into the air and floated over to Grace.

The Guardian watched their progress in silence. "Is Grace part of this network?"

"No, she was Chamele's prisoner. I don't actually know what her name is. They only called her..." Skye gulped, her throat closing up. She didn't want to say the horrid word.

"Aberration," Grace said hoarsely from the corner.

Brow raised, the Guardian looked shocked. He drank from his cup again. "Was it the immediate threat that made you leave?"

"That and, well, I've been trying to reach someone else to confirm it first. But Krystal hasn't responded in weeks, James is nowhere to be found, and even Feon has just vanished. I haven't heard from anyone in months."

"Confirm what?"

"The mainlanders are planning a war."

Going on dusk, the major port in Lawrgaea was a hive of activity.

A sailor standing on the deck of his boat on the outer port cracked his back and lifted his head, wiping the sweat from his brow. Catching a thick scent on the air, he turned curiously and looked out to sea.

Something was burning on the edge of the horizon.

"Fire!" he cried before his mouth caught up with his brain. What could burn out there?

The captain heard his cry and echoed his thoughts.

As they watched, a horde of coal-powered ships belching black smoke appeared, lining the horizon as far as they could see.

"What in the name of Lissae?" the captain swore.

Cries of 'fire' came from other boats as well, and the entire port watched, silently, as the massive black ships descended upon them.

As they grew closer, the ships drew into an arrow formation, the lead one coming to rest neatly at the largest dock. Gangplanks were thrown between the ships as makeshift bridges, until it looked like a giant, metal jungle had sprung up in the port in a matter of minutes.

The sailor stared at the Quartermaster—a weedy man with a balding head—whack his hat on and stride over to the lead ship as crewmen in full armour started marching along the dock.

He couldn't hear what was being said, but the sailor had a bad feeling in his bones. Wave after wave of armoured men stomped from ship to ship, down the dock, and towards the town.

"They ain't sailors," he muttered.

"Soldiers, every one of 'em," the captain said.

Glancing at the town, where the faintest sound of screaming was echoing off the old brick buildings, he shuddered.

"What's goin' on?"

The captain hitched his pants higher. "Reckon someone's just declared war."

Zoeday
Seventh day of the third week of Sunfall

Arilla wrung her hands around the dishrag as Calem broke up another argument.

The fifth one today.

Tensions were high, and all the Innarnians on the island were buzzing. Even she could feel it.

There were more wary looks, more snapping, more anger than she'd ever seen on the Shifting Islands. It was uncomfortably reminding her of the town she'd grown up in.

Another couple entered the tavern, stopping just inside the doorway to bicker.

Raising a hand as if she could ward off what was about to happen, Arilla took a step forward as the door opened and someone stepped up, bumping directly into the bickering pair.

Harsh words were exchanged between the trio. The shorter one turned to rouse on the newcomer. The taller one's hand slid to the small of his back, gripping the handle of a dagger.

Arilla surged across the room. She slammed her blade against the dagger as the taller one swung. The clang echoed through the tavern, and all conversation stopped.

"No," Arilla said. "This will not happen. Weapons away." She glared at the newcomer. "All of them."

The harsh buzz of Innarn faded somewhat, and the one with the dagger gave her a sheepish look.

"Sorry," he muttered.

Sheathing her sword, she sighed. "I know the whispers from the mainlands are scary. But we are, and always will be, stronger together."

The ones closest to the door nodded and drifted back to their own conversations.

The trio all apologised again, and made their way to the counter, standing at opposite ends.

"At least they aren't glaring at each other," Calem said as he came over to her.

"Or bleeding on the floor. I'd hate to mop again," she said, trying to disguise the fear in her eyes when she looked at him.

Calem dropped a kiss on her head and neatly pulled her to the side as someone else barrelled through the door.

Ronah's Linked stood before them, panting. "Ronah said you needed help?" She blew a hunk of silvery hair out of her eyes.

Glancing at the trio, Arilla smiled grimly. "All sorted, thank you."

Tania followed her gaze. "For the moment. It's the bad vibes, stirring up everyone. Like sitting on an ant nest. I have a suggestion, though. I've recruited some of the Returned to help me. We're putting calming wards and crystals onto doorways and entrances to public areas."

Arilla frowned. "Isn't that a bit morally grey?"

The couple at the end had started to bicker again.

"It will not stop those who really want to express their opinions, but it'll help to keep public displays of..."

The guy with the dagger plucked it from his waistband again and used it to pin his companion's hand to the bar. The other man howled.

"That," Tania finished flatly.

"Do it," Calem said and strode off, scolding the daggerless man, whilst a healer snapped at the howler to hold still as she fixed his hand.

"Great!" Tania bounced on her toes. "Collis will do it before he starts his shift. He's just finishing up next door."

"Thank you," Arilla said softly. She wanted nothing more than to wrap Shari and Calem up in her arms and keep them safe from the world.

It would have to wait until Shari got back.

Whenever that would be.

Chapter Twenty-Nine

Altum

Day six of the Dark Conclave

Sanithane woke up on the wrong side of his nest.

Or maybe he was just infuriated.

Staring into the polished surface in the bathroom of his far too opulent quarters, he bared his fangs and almost wished for clothing so he could adjust something. That way, one thing in his miserable life could be put right.

Straightening, he growled, low enough that the hatchling sleeping in the next room wouldn't hear it. Sanithane wished it was as easy as Shari thought it would be to just go in and remove Oalark from existence. But the Queen hadn't been around for as long as she had without learning a trick or two.

Yet, this time, most of the conclave were prepared to get rid of her. How many of her actions lately were an act designed to pull in the unwary, and how much of it was her mental decline. Who knew what effect eating your unborn would have?

As he roused Jetonyx and the sleepy hatchling stumbled past him to get ready, Cylanthar's bells chimed in his head.

Today, something was going to change.

The delegates from the Dark Realms appeared more collected this morning. Overnight, the table had shrunk, so the missing seats were not as obvious. Some aides had stepped in for their fallen ambassadors, and others were left floundering, not sure who they should support.

Sanithane eased into the room, striding to the head of the table under the Queen's watchful gaze. There was a spark of intelligence back in her eyes.

How long would it last?

'*I believe we were about to move on to the next item on the agenda?*' Oalark asked serenely. As if she hadn't spent the last few days indiscriminately massacring beings for breathing wrong.

Behind him, Jetonyx flinched.

Oalark took no notice.

Perhaps her fountain of youth was wearing off quicker than anticipated? Glancing around the table and waiting for them to settle, Sanithane let his eyes slide over Jaileth, who sat almost opposite him at the other end.

'*Of course, my Queen,*' he said, and glanced at the parchment. '*The next item is the takeover of the Mother Realm.*' He could only hope that Shari wasn't listening to this.

'*I've seen this pattern happen before.*' Oalark tapped her claw caps on the table. '*The Mother Realm is active, her protections strong, but over the years, she weakens as the birth of a new Realm is nigh. Lissae…*'

In the back of his mind, where his link to Shari sat, Sanithane felt the Altoriae sit up and take notice.

'… is weak. Her defences are but one puny Altoriae, and her Guardian. Although patrols are regular, my spies have successfully crept into Lissae and are reporting back to me. In fact, one sits at this table right now!' Oalark looked on smugly as the delegates glanced around, trying to determine who was Grey enough to step foot in such a Realm.

Sanithane held his breath. Did she know what he'd been doing? Or was there another spy he hadn't been aware of?

Jaileth waved a claw, bringing all attention in the room to her. She gazed directly at him and smiled with more teeth than necessary.

Behind his strongest shields, Sanithane swore.

'The beauty of my spy is, of course, that she didn't need to set a claw on the disgustingly Grey Realm. All she had to do was sit back and watch through her mate's eyes.' Oalark smiled, turning her gaze to him.

Carefully affecting a bored expression, Sanithane raised a brow.

'Our Golden Priest has been busy earning the trust of the Altoriae and her Guardian. Through his eyes, I have been able to see what absolute bumbling fools they are.'

What in the name of Cylanthar was Jaileth doing? He could feel Shari stirring through their link, threatening violence that was totally impractical in their current situation. There was no way that she'd be able to tear Jaileth's scales off without Innarn Darker than the Altoriae was capable of.

'Sanithane continues to guide them in the wrong direction. He even rescued the last of the fulni, which the keepers are busy breeding, so that we may once again enjoy their offerings of flesh, after Anriluka so selfishly took them from us.'

The entire room started talking over each other, some leaping to praise him, others growling at the U'tan ambassador, who slunk in her seat. If Anriluka had still been around, there was no doubt she would have been eviscerated.

Shari's growl echoed off the back of his skull.

'I believe, with Sanithane's continued help, we will overrun Lissae with no difficulties. The Altoriae is but one, untrained, impetuous girl, and the Guardian is stuffy and out of date with his fighting methods.' Jaileth was laughing as if she knew Shari was calling her all the swear words in the Realms. Perhaps, if the twitch in her brow was any sign, she did.

'Excellent. If the Altoriae is as incompetent as you say, we should easily be able to take over...'

'Now, hold on!' The U'tan ambassador was over her embarrassment. 'This so called "incompetent Altoriae" took out Anriluka, one of the best U'tan strategists in eons. Surely, we need to look more into her fighting methods and get a feel for...'

'Luck.' Jaileth cut her off. 'It was all luck. Had the Altoriae not had the aid of a prophesy, she wouldn't have succeeded.' The glance at her claws was a little overdone, in Sanithane's opinion.

The U'tan ambassador blustered, but Zirgha, on the other side of the table, shot her a look.

'Do you truly think Lissae is vulnerable enough?' the Otike ambassador asked serenely.

'Lissae, as my Queen has rightly pointed out, is in the end phase of birthing a new Realm. Birth, no matter what your species, is painful. All the Mother Realm's concentration is focused inwards, and thus, like any mother about to give birth, she is vulnerable.' Jaileth looked just as serene.

Zirgha frowned. 'Few mothers have a general to defend them. There are stories of the Altoriae single-handedly wiping out the Dark Army when we tried to attack through Neharne.'

Oalark waved a claw as if she hadn't stood on the battlefield and watched the soldiers under her command die in droves. 'Exaggerations, as most stories are.'

'You were there, were you not?' the U'tan ambassador asked. 'We lost hordes of Korvie and Xanterians with nothing to show for it.'

'*In war, the armies must always have fodder.*' Oalark ignored their concerns, her claw sheaths flashing in the light.

'*And yet, it is always us who supplies the fodder, and you who gains the spoils.*' The U'tan ambassador had clearly had enough of the Queen's games.

The room fell preternaturally still.

Oalark gazed at the U'tan ambassador for one long moment after the other. No one dared to move.

After an age, the Queen of the Q'Aralide's laughed, the joyful sound shattering the silence.

All around the room, delegates looked at each other in shock.

The U'tan aides were surreptitiously checking their ambassador for missing tentacles. Personally, Sanithane wanted to see if her nut of a brain had been scooped right out of her gelatinous head. Just yesterday, her words would have had her eaten before she could have muttered 'help!'.

'*We may get the spoils, but I am, as I have always been, generous with them. If my trusted spy believes it is time to move on Lissae, then I must agree with her. Now, I just need to know who is brave enough to lend the might of the Q'Aralide some more...*' The Queen's joyful tone dropped as her smile took on a sinister twist. '*... cannon fodder?*'

One by one, ambassadors stood to pledge their army to the Queen's aide, until all but the U'tan and Otike delegates stood.

'*How do you plan on splitting the spoils of this particular battle?*' Zirgha asked.

Oalark looked at her for a long moment, and Sanithane caught the flare of madness creeping into the Queen's gaze. '*Jaileth?*'

'*It is theorised that, when a Realm gives birth, land masses that are floating in its womb, in this case, an ocean, are forced together and out of a portal big enough to expel them into another Realm. Currently, Lissae has...*' Jaileth paused and looked at him. '*Seven?*'

Sanithane, feeling sick, nodded. He had a feeling he knew where this was going.

'*Seven such land masses.*' Jaileth nodded back to him.

In the back of his mind, he could hear Shari whispering, '*The Shifting Islands.*'

'*These naturally grow and expand until they fill the Realm. There would be enough room for many of us to relocate, providing that we can ensure one of ours is first through the portal.*'

'*The Q'Aralide will need one, but you are welcome to... come to an agreement regarding the others.*' Oalark leaned forward, as if she hoped the ambassadors would start ripping each other to shreds.

'*And why do you need the exclusive use of one?*' Zirgha asked.

A push of Innarn was directed at the Queen, and Oalark sent before she could censor the words.

'*Altum is dying.*'

CHAPTER THIRTY

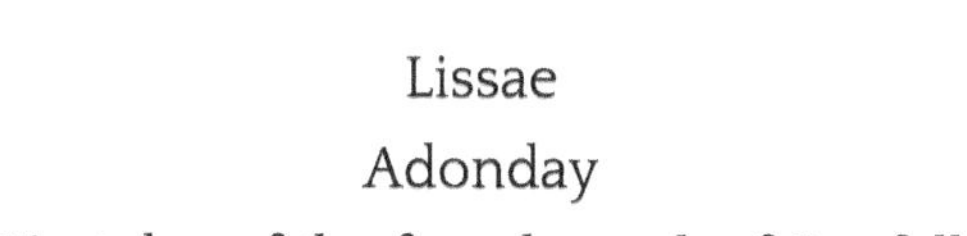

Lissae

Adonday

First day of the fourth week of Sunfall

The abduction of her personal aberration meant Chamele's mask had well and truly slipped.

Guards had been sent out to the best seamstresses in Jinkor, with orders that the woman make something that would not chafe her sensitive, raw skin.

Chamele was still deciding if the seamstress had lived up to her reputation. She had come up with a thrice-damned opaque veil, stylishly draped to hide the worst of her burns.

From the gasps and horrified looks the delegates were sending her, it wasn't working very well.

Gathering calm around her like a shroud, Chamele held her head high as she walked into the Blue Room. A favourite of her departed mother's, it was decorated in pale blues and creams, with gold accents and fine, tawny flowers native to Jinkor's beaches.

Usually, the space reassured her, but today, with Ben's wrinkled face smoothing in shock, she was knocked off kilter. Gwyn, seated opposite him on the long lounge, trembled and turned away to face the empty fireplace.

To his credit, Ben recovered first. "Who did this?"

"Our traitor set some traps." Chamele allowed her voice to waver and snuck a hand under the veil to wipe away a non-existent tear.

"I still find it hard to believe that Suni would betray us so," Gwyn said, knuckles white around the delicate handle of a teacup.

"Suni had us all fooled." Chamele sank gracefully into the single seat off to the side, glad the veil hid her wince.

"And she had accomplices?" Ben prodded.

The head guard, now permanently hovering just behind her left shoulder, answered before she could stop him. "From outside. He abducted two women from Suni's rooms."

"What are we doing to recover them?" Gwyn asked.

Chamele hissed and played it off as her if burns were hurting. "The attack force has been tasked with their retrieval."

"And you think this outsider is from Lawrgaea?" An aide handed Ben a mug with froth on the top. He drank deeply, the white foam sticking to his thin moustache.

"Suni's home providence, and she sets traps just as our forces are close enough to attack. If she had succeeded, you would have called everything off," Chamele said, careful to keep the contempt from her voice.

"Do we still want to go ahead with this plan?" Gwyn glanced at her, the liquid from her teacup spilling over onto her trembling hand and into the saucer.

"We must," Chamele whispered. "The last thing I would want is for another to end up like me."

After clearing his throat, Ben took another pull from his mug, eyes sliding away from the others in the room. "Besides, our forces have landed. I sent the messenger bird out this morning. They have orders to attack at dusk."

Hidden by the veil, Chamele smiled.

Lynn, the elder of the Ofanahni refugees, stared out at the gathering dust cloud on the horizon. Theophania, a visiting elder from the Teeldrit settlement two dunes over, turned to her in concern.

"Too early in the season for a sandstorm," she said, worry making the wrinkles lining her face deeper.

"Can you tell what it is?" Lynn asked. As much as she connected with the water running below the sand, Theophania could sense the movement of a single grain and know what caused it.

Theophania's brilliant green eyes drifted closed, and she swayed in her seat. Mere seconds later, she snapped her eyes open, gasping. "An army. On the march. Heading our way."

We've only just stopped running. Lynn scrambled to her feet as swiftly as her old bones would let her. "How long?"

"An hour. Perhaps a little more," Theophania said.

"Go. Evacuate your settlement. We'll follow shortly." Reaching behind her, she started gathering her iron-grey hair into a sturdy knot on the top of her head. Now was not the time to have hair flying into her face.

Theophania paused, halfway out of her seat. "They crossed the land bridge from Lawrgaea. We're the first settlement the army will come across, but not the last.

Lynn swore. "I think we need to contact the Guardian."

Nodding, the other woman rose and held out her hands. "Together?"

Grasping the Teeldrit's wrinkled fingers, Lynn dredged up feelings of water, and pushed her Innarn towards Theophania. *'Guardian!'* they chanted repeatedly.

'Well met, refugees of the desert. How may I assist?' The Guardian's soothing voice was a balm she'd not expected.

Ignoring the tears of relief streaming down her face, Lynn let out a shuddering breath as Theophania sent images of the army she'd seen.

Thousands strong.

Grim faces.

Sharp blades.

Bearing down on them.

'Gather your kin. Go through the doorway. You will be safe,' he replied.

'The others...' Theophania started.

'We have sworn to protect you, and we will. Have heart,' the Guardian replied. *'Use the doorway,'* he sent again, and the connection ended.

Chest heaving, Lynn looked at Theophania, who was staring over her shoulder.

Turning, she blinked. There was a doorway that hadn't been there a moment ago. "We must leave," she said. "Go. Go!"

Theophania drew her hijab up, gathered her skirts, and swept out the door at a run.

Following the other elder, Lynn waited until the whirling dervish containing Theophania was past the walls. She started yelling into the streets. "An army approaches! Gather your things. We must flee!"

With only thirty in their village, it was the work of no time to get everyone and their belongings gathered.

"Hurry, hurry," Lynn said, pushing them towards the new door on the outside of her house and eyeing the dust in the distance. She fancied she could see the smudge of black uniforms but was hoping it was a trick of the light.

A few sobbed, another cursed as a herd beast excreted near their feet. A babe cried as his mother ineffectively tried to shush him.

"Go, go," Lynn urged. Slowly, the queue lessened, and she was the last one left.

Hand on the door, she paused.

There was a high whistling noise, and she looked up, tracking something long flying through the sky. It arced, and started racing downwards. Lifting a hand to shade her eyes, Lynn looked directly at the thick arrow as it hit on the grassy hill just outside of the village.

The *boom* rattled her bones and set her teeth chattering. Her ears were ringing, and no other noise could make it in.

The Realm shook again, and Lynn stared in horror as the building on the very outskirts of town exploded. Chunks of clay rained down around her.

A grey-hooded figure appeared in her line of vision. She had the sense that ze was saying something, but she couldn't hear.

She couldn't hear.

Preying to the water gods, she let go of the door handle. The world shook again, and she was falling.

Falling.

Tommie was catching her.

Struggling in his grasp, Lynn got to her feet and turned. She needed one last look...

The door was gone.

The army of Jinkor crested the orange dune and started work setting up the ballistas.

They worked efficiently, powering through the motions, despite the less than ideal footing.

Arrows as wide as a man were loaded, and the lever was tightened, cranking the shaft into release position.

Standing tall, his chest puffed out, stood Captain Rappen off to the side, eye pressed against the farscope as he conferred with a marksman.

"Ready!" he called out.

Soldiers snapped to as the marksmen scurried into position.

"Aim!"

Stepping forward, the marksmen adjusted the angles, preparing the shot.

"Fire!" the captain screamed.

The first bolt left the ballista, whistling through the air.

Captain Rappen scowled as it landed on an unoccupied hillside. "Aim!" the captain called again.

Hasty adjustments were made to the second ballista.

"Fire!"

Whistling through the air, a cheer went up from the soldiers as the bolt hit a building, sending chunks of masonry flying.

Something shimmered on the other side of it.

Spittle flew from Captain Rappen's mouth as he shrieked, "Aim!"

The third and final ballista was adjusted.

The shimmering seemed to increase.

"Fire!"

Streaking through the air, the bolt hung, suspended for a second too long, before ploughing into another building. Deafening cheering dominated the hillside.

"What are you waiting for?" the captain yelled. "Charge!"

Slipping down the dunes, soldiers swarmed the town.

Cheers and battle cries turned to shouts of anger as they realised the Innarnian interlopers had escaped.

Striding through the town, Captain Rappen scowled at everything in sight. "Search it. Then burn it to the ground."

"And if there are survivors?" a lieutenant dared to ask.

Captain Rappen turned his cold, silver gaze on the man. "What survivors?"

"Yes, Captain." He gulped, and scurried away.

Hidden at the top of the next dune over, the Guardian of Lissae glared down at the army crawling through the former Ofanahni settlement.

By his side, Zac placed a hesitant hand on his arm.

"Have the Teeldrit been evacuated?" Jonathan's voice was colder than Zac remembered hearing.

"Yes, they're all out." Zac strove to keep his voice even. Watching the wanton destruction of the tiny village had shaken him as well.

"And the patrollers?"

"The mainlanders are all off-Realm, and the Shifting Island Innarnians have all reported."

Jonathan's jaw tightened. "I don't want a war."

"None of us do," Zac soothed.

Hefting his crossbow, the Guardian sighed. "But if they want one, well." His gaze was harder than it had been when the crystal intelligence had sought to control him. "Who am I to deny them a fight?"

"You're a good man," Zac argued.

"At the moment, I don't feel like one."

"I, uh, heard there were sword lessons here?" Skye said, glancing around the wide-open space of the training grounds.

A bronze-skinned woman about her height wandered over. "Keep going," she urged the group, who were waving their wooden swords around with looks of intense concentration. "Well met," she said. "I'm

Arilla. You're welcome to join us if you like. It's nothing formal, and more of a basic, starters guide."

"Well met," Skye said, blushing. It seemed her manners had been left behind in Jinkor, somewhere on the mattress soaked with Suni's blood. "I'd love it. If it's not too much bother."

"Course not," she said, and pulled another wooden sword from the pile near the entry. She went to pass it over, and froze. "What happened?" she asked, her voice suddenly softer.

Skye looked at her with wide eyes. "What do you mean?"

"There's a heaviness around you." Arilla stared at her for a long moment. "Sometimes, swinging a sword is good for what ails you." She held it out again.

Taking it with trembling hands, Skye nodded.

"But other times," she said in that same gentle voice. "Talking is far better for you."

Bursting into tears, Skye dropped the sword.

"Oh, child," Arilla said, moving to comfort her. Only to end up with Grace, Innarn crackling around her, with her hand thrust towards Arilla's chest.

The sword teacher froze. "Well met," she said.

The students didn't seem to realise anything was amiss, and kept waving their swords. Skye stifled a hysterical sob.

"No," Grace rasped.

Arilla backed away and knelt. "I would never hurt you, or your friend."

Shuffling back, Grace bumped into Skye. "No," she said again.

"Grace," Skye said gently, moving so she was to the side of the crouching Innarnian. "I'm okay. I've been having a bit of a rough time, you see." She kept her voice low and soothing, but spotted the way Grace's eyes flicked towards her and back to the sword teacher. "I kind of felt that it would be a good idea to defend myself. I'm not so great at that."

"My job," Grace growled.

"Oh, Grace," Skye sobbed. "Your job is to get better, to live and be free."

Eyes large in her thin face, Grace looked up at her. "Free?"

"Yes. Free to choose what you want to do. Not to be forced to obey someone else's command. Free to be you."

"I can choose?" Grace said.

"Yes, yes, absolutely," Skye said, blinking back the tears welling in her eyes.

"Protect you." Grace pouted at her and moved so she was between Skye and the sword teacher again.

Arilla was glancing at the pair of them with mild amusement written on her face. "Perhaps you would feel better about your friend taking lessons if you were to watch a few first, Grace?"

Head swivelling to take in the students, Grace nodded. She waited until Arilla rose and walked back into the training grounds before she shuffled forward, guiding Skye to stay behind her.

Although she felt like throwing her hands up and calling the whole exercise a bust, Skye eventually settled in, hoping she'd be able to learn by merely observing.

It seemed like it was mostly just practising cuts. When the students were told to pair up, Skye craned her neck, hoping to see something interesting. When the first dull thud of wood on wood sounded, Grace flinched and grabbed Skye's hand. She held on, loose enough for Grace to escape if she needed to.

Glancing at her protector, Skye smiled. Grace was utterly absorbed.

It really didn't look so hard.

"Well done. You've all made some great improvements." Arilla's voice carried across the grounds. "Break again tomorrow, but we'll meet here the day after."

"What about a demonstration?" a well-dressed girl asked.

Arilla glanced over at Skye and Grace. "Maybe next time."

Groans from the students rang out.

Hanging her head, Arilla sighed. "Wait here." She trotted over to them but stopped a respectable distance away.

Grace still growled at her.

Cheeks burning in mortification, Skye tried to stutter an apology.

"No need," Arilla said kindly. "I know what it's like to want to protect someone precious. I just want to let you know that a demonstration is a bit more active than the training we've been doing. Grace, you might feel safer putting a shield up. I'll try to keep the action away from you, but please know that we don't want to hurt you or your friend."

Not turning away from Arilla, Grace squeezed Skye's hand.

"Practice is important when learning a new skill," Skye whispered.

Hesitantly, Grace nodded.

"We'll try to stay?" Skye asked.

Grace nodded again.

"Thank you." Arilla bowed. "If you feel safer leaving, that's fine, too." She smiled and jogged back to her students. "Alright. A quick demonstration," Arilla said. "Any volunteers?"

The well-dressed girl stepped forward on heels that looked far too thin to hold her weight. "I want to see what a sword is like against something shorter."

"I'm not sure if we're ready for that, yet." Arilla glanced their way again.

Skye beamed, trying to show her support.

"Arilla, please. I want to know..." Her voice faded from Skye's ears, and a few of the students closest looked at the girl in shock and awe as she continued to speak in hushed tones.

Throwing them another glance, Arilla puffed her cheeks out and nodded. "Alright. We can try that. How realistic do you want?"

"As much as you think I can take." The girl looked grim.

"Come into the middle. Grace?" Arilla asked, her voice still gentle despite the distance between them. "Would you mind creating a large dome around Anika and I? It should keep us in, but others out. And at the first sight of blood, it comes down."

"But..." Anika started.

"No buts." The sword teacher stopped her immediately.

Skye chewed on her lip, as the dome materialise, sealing teacher and student inside.

Twirling a real sword in her hand, Arilla looked every inch the competent blade wielder as she circled the inside of the dome.

Anika was breathing hard enough for it to be noticeable from where Skye sat.

"You've got this," she whispered.

Grace squeezed her hand tighter as Arilla lunged forward. Shrieking, Anika skittered out of the way, stumbling in her towering heels.

Crouching, her hands wrapped around her ankles. When Arilla struck again, Anika launched herself upwards, a dagger in each hand, held in a crossed position to catch Arilla's blade.

"Excellent!" Arilla yelled.

Shrieking, Anika pushed her teacher, and started a rapid series of thrusts and stabs, making the older woman dance away from her.

Parrying and dodging, Arilla wove her way around the inner dome, avoiding all of Anika's jabs.

She was relentless.

Skye found herself on the edge of her seat, fingers curled tightly around Grace's hand.

It was Grace who noticed it first. She lifted her free hand and pointed at the student.

Anika had tears running down her face.

Skye bit her lip. What had happened to such a young girl?

Thrusts were becoming more erratic now, and stabs were sloppy. A few times, Arilla leaped out of the way in pure feats of athleticism.

Pushing forward one last time, Anika screamed.

And the dome dropped.

The grounds were quiet.

The thud Arilla's knee made as it hit the dirt seemed to echo in Skye's blood.

"No, no, no, no," Anika was saying, getting louder with each word.

Skye, one hand gripping the back of the seat in front of her, gasped, and raised her other hand to cover her mouth.

Grace had blinked out of existence, and was crouched by Arilla's side, snarling at Anika.

'Gozochas.' Skye scrambled out of her seat and down the stands, rushing to the trio in the middle of the field.

"Sorry, sorry, sorry," Anika was sobbing.

"Here." Skye gently pulled the distraught girl away.

Stick-thin hands were plucking at the hem of Arilla's top, but the teacher gently stopped her.

"Brilliant job, Anika. Remember to stay focused on the fight, not on the past. You are a formidable fighter," Arilla said. Her mouth was tight with pain, but her words were still gentle. "Keep practising."

Some came and wrapped kind hands around Anika's shoulders. The others crowded in, but Arilla shooed them off. "Look after her," she said.

There were more than a few concerned glances, but the crowd thinned out, leaving only Arilla, Grace, and Skye.

"Well," Arilla said. "That's going to leave a scar."

"Heal you," Grace said.

"Oh, you are sweet." Arilla smiled. "But it won't hold. I'm a Blank."

Skye looked at her in shock.

"A lift to the Healer's Centre would be appreciated though."

Grace sighed and, lightning quick, reached forward and plucked a hair from Arilla's head.

"Ouch!"

A sharp laugh escaped before Skye could stop it. "You don't flinch when you get stabbed, but hair-pulling is where you draw the line?"

Arilla huffed.

A basket appeared by Grace, who sank to the ground and crossed her legs. She plucked at Arilla's shirt again, and this time, the sword teacher allowed her to lift it.

Wincing at the angry red line, Skye stared, fascinated, as Grace used water from the basket to wet a cloth and clean the wound. The hunched Innarnian seemed oblivious to Arilla's hiss and flinch. The hair twisted into something finer as it passed through the water, but she had to look away as Grace started sewing Arilla's wound together with it.

Reaching out, Skye took hold of Arilla's hand, and the sword teacher grabbed on tight, callouses rubbing against Skye's smooth skin.

Banishing the materials, Grace sat back, her lips a thin line as she looked at Arilla in fear.

"That's a neat trick," Arilla managed. She ran her fingers lightly over a cloth Grace had stuck over the wound. "You could teach Shari a thing or two."

Slowly, she stood , giving Grace plenty of time to skitter away.

"I have to head to the tavern, but if you'd like to join me, we can break our fast together?"

Skye looked at Grace, whose eyes were darting between the two. "Breakfast sounds wonderful. I don't think Grace and I have had much of a chance to explore Ronah yet."

As they went to leave the training grounds, they came across Anika standing just outside the entrance, daggers hidden inside her heels again.

"I'm so sorry!" she cried.

"I'm fine. You just glanced my side. Grace stitched me up, good as new. We're going to get some food to help wear down the adrenaline. Would you like to join us?"

Wide eyed, Skye looked at Arilla. She needed to learn diplomacy from a woman who could be so gracious to the one who stabbed her.

"I... uh... yes, please," Anika said in a small voice.

Grace pulled Skye forward and pushed her to the head of the group, stepping between the teacher and student.

"I don't know where to go," Skye protested.

Arilla laughed. "Just follow my directions," she said.

The unlikely quartet headed off.

Chapter Thirty-One

Jetonyx's Pocket Realm
Day six of the Dark Conclave

Three paltry words.

That's all it took for the delegates of the Dark Conclave to descend into madness.

Shari mind span at the thought.

Could Jaileth's theory be right? Could Lissae really be the Realm who had given birth to all the others?

There were stories the Wisara Lore tellers used to whisper about a Mother Realm intent on protecting her fledgling children. Could that really be what had happened? What was happening?

Were the Shifting Islands about to become their own Realm?

A scaled head prodded her side, and Shari glanced up.

Tormorylth, unaware that Shari's entire world had been flipped upside down, nudged her again. *'More food?'*

Scrubbing her hands over her face, Shari rose. Sightlessly, she staggered towards the carcass and waved her hand, cancelling the time lock on it.

'*Thanks!*' Tormorylth descended on it with relish.

A quick glance at the screens showed the conclave was still in an uproar.

Sinking back to her knees, Shari poked at the sand, drawing meaningless patterns in it. If the bronze Q'Aralide was right, it would explain so much. Why Lissae had been so withdrawn, why the attacks were more frequent, and why tensions were increasing everywhere.

But why did no one on Lissae know about this? Was it because the last time it happened, all those with the knowledge of it had disappeared along with the islands? Which Realm was the last to be created? Or born? Perhaps Jonathan would know.

'*Done now,*' Tormorylth said, licking her maw clean.

Flicking her fingers, Shari recast the time lock on what was left of the food. The hatchling, she noted idly, had been quite good at pacing herself without a reminder.

'*Why are you sad?*' Sated, the tiny black hatchling wandered over to her and leaned against her side.

Shari, careful of the wicked-sharp claws at the end of her wing tips, wrapped a loose arm around Tormorylth. '*I just found out that my Realm was not quite what I thought it was.*'

'*Me too! I thought everyone would try to eat me, and then Sanithane came and saved me.*'

Looking out at the screens to the giant golden shoulder blocking part of the view, Shari sighed. Was Samuel going to save the day for Lissae as well?

Or was he going to be the one to doom them all?

Altum

Sanithane sat back on his rest, stunned.

Altum was dying?

Snatches of visions filled his head. The mountains' sluggish movements as opposed to how fluid and graceful they had been in his youth. How tired and wrecked the streets and dwellings looked. The layer of grunge that seemed to permeate the very air. Oalark's tenuous sanity.

That something as simple as a planned poison had brought down War'Jan.

His home was dying.

And Oalark's plan to fix the problem was to take over Lissae.

A Realm he'd sworn to protect.

Oalark was scowling at everyone, her tail lashing in an unsurprising show of annoyance. Her Innarn lashed out, and the ambassadors shrank in fear. *'This is old news. Why do you think we have been working so long to get to Lissae? Altum's death is nothing more than a blip on the timeline.'*

A blip.

That is not what he would call the destruction of his childhood home.

'Lissae is vulnerable at this stage of the birth. And she will only get more so as things progress. We do, however, have a limited window. Sanithane?' Oalark turned to him, and for a wild moment, he thought about not answering.

'Yes, *my Queen?'* Sanithane blinked, the only sign that he was shocked that he'd kept his send level.

'How long do we have?'

'I am unsure what the parameters are,' he sent. It was not like he could say that there was no way he was about to give them a time frame.

Oalark's tail flicked dangerously, and she narrowed her eyes. *'Jaileth?'* she sent, without taking her gaze from him.

His mate smirked. '*If the Shifting Islands continue to join at the same rate, the birth of the new Realm will happen as summer turns to autumn.*'

With Jaileth sitting in his head, there was little he could do to keep the information away from the Queen. '*Surely there is an easier target?*' Sanithane sent without thinking.

Oalark's Innarn lashed out, and he shuddered as tiny slices appeared all over his hide. '*Q'Aralide don't go for easy. We go for the best.*'

'*Of course, my Queen.*'

Zirgha met his gaze over the expanse of the table, the worry she held clear.

'*How do you suggest we proceed?*' the U'tan ambassador asked.

'*Another army, made up of our finest. History tells us that when Lissae is about to expel the new Realm, the gateway in the Ducibus' Hall will be unprotected. That is when we must strike.*'

Carefully, now Oalark was distracted with the planning, Sanithane healed the multitude of cuts. Opposite him, his mate smirked, the claws on one hand clicking together as she watched his wounds fade away.

'*You plan on getting an army together to bottleneck them into walking through a gateway? Are you asking for fighters or fodder?*' Someone scoffed.

'*No, no, it could work.*' The U'tan ambassador leaned forward. '*If we had a few beings in position, ready to shift armies in, we could sneak through whatever guards they have in place...*'

Jaileth, gaze still on him, laughed and cut her off. '*The Lissaens barely realise how important the hall is. Their guard is a single, middle-aged woman.*'

The U'tan smiled. '*Even better. It is a shame the Eni were wiped out. We could have used one of them to replace her.*'

'*One of my Datzal should be able to replace such incompetence.*' Oalark waved her claw.

Sanithane wanted to cut it off.

He refrained.

Shari seemed to whisper in his ear, for all she was safely locked away in Jetonyx's pocket Realm. *'Her information is out of date. Keep it that way.'*

Several other ideas were thrown out and rejected. The idea for using the higher Dark Realms as fodder was agreed upon, seeing as they wouldn't lower themselves to join in the conclave.

No one made a mention that they were all here by invitation only, and that very few would want or be able to set a claw on Altum without express permission from the Queen.

'So, we have advanced scouts go in, shift the army, and then what? Attack?' another ambassador was asking.

'Exactly.'

'What about the Grey Army? And the Light Realms have not been quiet either. Atlantis staged an attack on Lissae only a moon ago!' The U'tan ambassador was better informed than she should have been. Unless they, too, had spies on Lissae.

'The Grey Army can barely organise a parade,' Sanithane drawled. *'And Atlantis did not have anywhere near the power needed to overtake the Mother Realm.'* He wasn't entirely lying. Although, if Shari had not been there, it would have been a different thing all together. It took more focus not to turn and look at Jetonyx. The hatchling was allowing Shari to see everything that was going on in the conclave. He half thought it had been a good idea until this topic had arisen.

'Perhaps it would be best if we wait until they are just about to join with the last island? Their focus will be on the joining, and not the gateway.' Jaileth looked at him smugly.

He smiled back, too many fangs showing as he thought about the best way to eviscerate her from the inside out.

Smug look falling, his mate sent, *'Unless our Golden Priest has a better idea?'*

'No, *just thinking how good it will be to not have to pretend anymore.*' Sanithane didn't mention the rosters and patrols he was mentally scheduling and planning to give to Jonathan as soon as they were back. The idea of the Q'Aralide loose on Lissae made something ache near his hearts. The utter devastation his kin would cause...

'*Brilliant!*' Zirgha was saying. '*If the priest agrees, then we should celebrate. To our plan coming to successful fruition!*' She raised a glass, claw sheaths glinting in the light.

'*Don't drink.*' The send was so short and sharp, he couldn't pinpoint who it had come from.

Raising his glass with the others, Sanithane lifted it high before bringing it to his maw and using his Innarn to syphon the drink directly into the Queen's belly.

Oalark belched, and whatever sanity had been in her eyes, fled.

CHAPTER THIRTY-TWO

Lissae

Adonday

First day of the fourth week of Sunfall

In the distance, someone was wailing.

Jonathan looked at Zac, who gave him a sharp nod and gripped the handle of his scythe tighter.

Shifting closer to the noise, Jonathan used the shattered corner of a building to duck behind. Peering around, he spotted the wailer, dirty and bloody, clutching at the still body of another. And totally oblivious to the platoon of black-clad soldiers heading his way.

Apparently, they'd been unsuccessful in evacuating everyone from the hamlet.

There was a *bang*, and the wailing stopped.

Gritting his teeth, Jonathan pushed his back hard against the crumbling wall. The sound of the soldiers was getting closer. He had to move.

Had to go.

Any time now.

Revenge, he reminded himself, *would not help the dead.* No matter how badly he wanted to dish it out.

His job was to get the beings of Kafehara Hamlet to safety.

Not revenge for a life cut short.

Pushing his Innarn out, Jonathan sought any other survivors.

Dots on the map in his mind showed his patrol group. They were blinking in and out as they gathered those around and whisked them away.

A crunch just around the corner warned him to go.

Shifting without a sound to the final Innarnian, he landed in the middle of a group of soldiers.

Should have checked for Blanks as well.

They whipped around, long barrels pointed at him.

"Got me," he said. Hands held loosely by his sides, he let them glow.

Maybe he had a bit of time for revenge after all today.

The joined Shifting Islands were buzzing with activity.

Tania hurried towards the temporary building the Returned had helped to build on Ronah at the end of Summer Close.

Refugees were flooding in from the mainland as the Guardian and his patrol teams plucked them out of the way of the soldiers closing in.

Coming to the building, the first thing that hit Tania was the smell of smoke and burnt hair. The building was big and airy but filled with the sound of whimpers and foreign languages.

Skittering to a stop next to Zana, she sent, *'What do you need me to do?'*

Even amongst the confused and wounded, Rakemyst's Linked radiated peace and calm. *'We must heal them, test them to see if they will be true to our isles, and then help them.'*

'*There are so many,*' Tania sent, looking out on the veritable sea of beings.

'*And more to come,*' Cyrus sent grimly.

"Best get to work," Fenix added as they joined the group.

'*How are we going to fit everyone in?*' Tania wondered.

'*Akoren is mostly uninhabited. The Wisara live under the island, and he has a few delegates, but that's it. Plenty of viable space. I'll reach out to his Linked and see if they can join us,*' Cyrus sent, hefting a crystal screen and slipping away for some privacy.

Tania took that as her cue to get to work and started towards her station.

Fenix stepped into her path, a serious look in their eyes. '*These beings have been through a lot,*' they sent. '*I know it's going to be hard, but they don't want our tears. They need our strength.*'

Shuddering, Tania glanced around, taking in the green-skinned woman with a gash on her forehead rocking a child who was almost too big to be held; an expressionless four-armed man leaning against a pole, one hand buried in the palon's fur by his side; the teen who was wandering between the makeshift beds, scanning every face hopefully.

'*Okay. Yeah. I can do that,*' Tania sent. Fenix nodded, and they moved to their respective tables.

The first being who approached Tania was the mother she'd noticed before.

"Well met," Tania said.

She frowned in confusion.

"Send instead," Zana, from the table on her right, advised.

'*Well met.*' Tania tried again.

'*Ah. Well met. We come from Kafehara Hamlet. Told to see the Linked?*' The woman's send was slightly disjointed, as if the words were being parsed and run through a translator.

'That's me translating,' Ronah sent to her. 'Haven't had time to teach you how yet.'

'Oh, thank you!' Tania replied to her island. 'I'm Ronah's Linked. Have you seen a healer?'

'For child, yes.'

'You have a cut,' Tania said, swiping at her own forehead.

'Is nothing.' The woman shrugged. She seemed to want to add more but refrained. 'Somewhere to rest?' she asked instead.

'Use your Spirit Innarn to determine her true intentions, and if she is not a threat, send her to Rakemyst. There is a temporary city going up until we can join with Akoren,' Ronah advised.

'May I scan you?' she asked. The woman gave a sharp nod. Tania sent a gentle wave of Spirit Innarn out and could see bone-deep sadness and the desire to rest. 'Welcome to the Shifting Islands. I wish we had met under different circumstances, but for now, there is a place for you on Rakemyst. Would you like me to shift you?'

The woman shuddered as she held back a sob. Slowly, she nodded. 'My thanks,' she sent.

Smiling gently, Tania shifted woman and child out.

The man standing behind her moved forward, and Tania started the spiel again.

The sound of clapping made Tania look up.

Applause filled the tent as the patrollers were shifting in, one by one.

"They're done?" she asked.

"Looks like," Cyrus said.

Beaming from beneath sweaty, dirty faces, the patrollers moved amongst those who they'd saved, clapping backs and bowing, checking in on beings from all over the Realms.

They really had a wide variety of races present. The Ofanahni and the Teeldrit were the least affected, having gotten out before the attacks had really begun. But the Vladine, Sivote, and Diaxampal had suffered serious wounds and losses. There was still, if Cyrus was right, the refugees from Greonilae to come, and Tania dreaded to see how they had fared.

Looking at the familiar faces moving amongst the new, Tania frowned. "Do you see Jonathan?"

"The Guardian?" Cyrus scanned the crowd, brow furrowed. "No, I don't see him."

Spotting the one person she thought would know, she called out, "Hey, Zac, where's Jonathan?"

Zac's shaggy head snapped up, and he glanced around. "Jon?" he called out.

A few beings around him looked at his yell, but no one answered.

"Jon?" he tried again.

The other patrollers were searching now too, but no one had seen the Guardian.

"For the love of Lissae," Zac sighed, and shifted away.

"I hope he's alright," Tania said.

"He's the Guardian. Why wouldn't he be?" Fenix said.

Tania snorted. "Jonathan and Shari both have trouble staying safe when they're on Lissae. Off-Realm, they're forces to be reckoned with, but here." She sighed. "That's... questionable."

"Really?" Fenix leaned forward to glance around Cyrus. "They both seem... I don't know. Confident? Capable?"

"Pains in the..." Tania started.

Zana cleared her throat.

"Right. Uh, next?" Tania asked.

Four newly settled beings later, and she was worrying.

"I wonder what's taking so..." She cut off as someone new shifted back in, supporting the slumped form of another.

Zac, holding up the bleeding Guardian by a shoulder and his belt.

"Found him," Zac said.

"Oh, Jon!" Tania scurried from behind the desk, beating the Healers to the Guardian's side. 'Ronah?'

'What? Oh. Why does he think he's invincible? Skin, blood, and bone make him a lot squishier than me.' The island obligingly covered Jonathan in a green, healing glow. 'Maybe I should just change him into an island, and the only danger he'll have is from seacows tickling his underside.'

Hands over her mouth to stifle her grin, Tania sent, 'Please don't turn the Guardian into an island. We kind of need him in human form at the moment.'

Grumbling, Ronah subsided.

Tania wasn't sure for how long her isle's silence would last.

Zac sank down to a vacated bedroll, carefully lowering the Guardian. "Jon?"

Slowly, Jonathan blinked away. "Hey," he said, grinning dopily up at his rescuer.

"Hey. Back with me?"

"Always." Jonathan reached out to stroke Zac's face, and almost poked the other man in the eye.

Catching the Guardian's hand in his own, Zac smiled. "What happened?"

Jonathan blinked a few more times. He glanced around, and grimaced when he saw Tania. "They have weapons designed to hurt us. Some sort of modified crystal that can drain Innarn."

Cyrus swore.

Tania vaguely remembered him talking about something he'd developed. "Crystals talk to each other, don't they? Can you call them all back?" she asked.

"I can try," Cyrus said, standing abruptly. Pausing, he looked at Zana.

"Go. If you can stop this before it gets worse..." Rakemyst's Linked broke off.

Nodding, Cyrus scurried away.

CHAPTER THIRTY-THREE

Altum

Day seven of the Dark Conclave

There was something comforting about having a tiny being asking for food when your world was falling down around you.

Shari smiled, although it felt more like a grimace, and flicked her fingers, lifting the time lock again. Tormorylth bounded over to the carcass and started her next tiny feast.

The Dark Realms were planning on attacking Lissae.

Lissae, the sentient Realm who had chosen Shari to protect her. To be her last protector before she gave birth.

To a new Realm.

The Altoriae felt lost for the first time since she'd been a child, agreeing to protect Lissae so no one else would come close to losing the ones they loved.

Didn't I fail spectacularly at that? The might of the Dark Realms was about to come knocking on Lissae's door.

Tormorylth nudged her head under Shari's arm, a few pieces of fruit in her claws. '*Is this your food?*'

'Yes.' Shari looked at it blankly.

'*Does it taste good?*'

'I *think it does.*' Why, exactly, was she talking about food when her Realm was about to burn?

'*Do you know, I thought I was going to die?*' Tormorylth had juice dribbling down her chin.

Shari hugged the tiny Q'Aralide closer to her.

'*Sanithane came and saved me. He's big and scary, but nice too. I didn't think any of them were, but he is.*'

Silently, the two watched the screens as the meeting ended, the conclave apparently happy with their plans to take over Shari's home.

'*Don't be upset. If Sanithane can help me, maybe he can help you too?*' Tormorylth solemnly offered Shari a piece of fruit.

If only it were that simple.

Sanithane watched tiredly as Oalark swept from the room, and the others cleared out.

Jaileth and Zirgha both sent him secretive smiles, and he hid his snort through long practice.

Just what was the Otike ambassador playing at?

Waiting until the last one left, Sanithane sent a burst to Jetonyx. '*Take our guests back to my quarters. Stock up on more food.*'

The hatchling nodded and strode from the room with a confidence he'd been lacking amongst the sand dunes of Bazaven.

For the first time since the discussion about attacking Lissae started, Sanithane gave a genuine smile. He allowed himself a moment to bask in the success of his hatchling before rising. He had an ambassador to interrogate.

Using his Innarn to pull the shadows around himself, Sanithane groaned as he changed form. On silent feet, he slipped unseen through the main part of Altum and towards Zirgha's quarters.

Pausing outside her door, he pulled the shadows closer and slipped in as her aide left. He'd never been more thankful that his mortal form was so small compared to his natural one.

Zirgha was seated, looking at something on a table too high for him to see. She stood about twice his height, and he felt rather childlike. As he wondered if this was what Tormorylth felt like, Zirgha shuddered.

Arms and head flung back, the Otike ambassador's mouth opened wide, a mist pouring from it. Swirling in the mist was an Innarn so Light, it was painful.

Sanithane shrank back into the corner as the ambassador's body slumped to the ground, lifeless.

Without getting closer, he could tell she'd been dead for quite a while. The smell gave it away.

Panic was setting in, but Sanithane steeled himself. What could have possibly killed off Zirgha without them noticing?

The mist hovered near the ceiling, flashes of plasma darting through it in time with the sends he could feel drifting through the air.

As if the night could get any weirder, there was a pounding on the door.

Another plasma flash accompanied a send in Zirgha's thought patterns. '*Enter.*'

Oalark stepped through the doorway and over to the table. She looked down at Zirgha's body and sighed. '*Another dead one. I was hoping to get some claw sheaths in a different colour.*'

The mist drifted lower, and Oalark's eyes went white.

'*Oh, there you are, Zirgha. Napping at the table will age you horribly.*'

Sanithane frowned as Oalark converse with the mist.

'*Oh, I don't know. My priest has been awfully standoffish lately. I don't think he'd take kindly to being borrowed.*' Oalark laughed.

The plasma seemed to flash brighter and faster the longer the conversation continued, and by the end, Oalark wasn't speaking any language Sanithane had ever come across.

From his place by the door, Sanithane noted footsteps getting closer. Sending a trickle of his Innarn out, he realised the aide was returning.

Eyes unseeing, Oalark's head snapped towards the door as well.

If he hadn't been watching it, Sanithane wouldn't have believed it as the mist pulled away from Oalark's head and seeped back into Zirgha's mouth.

It was, unfortunately, believable that Oalark pounced on the aide and ripped a limb off the shrieking being.

Sanithane wasn't entirely proud as he used the distraction to escape the fake ambassador's quarters.

He needed to figure out what had just happened.

Shari absolutely would not pick on Jetonyx for jumping when Samuel burst into his quarters, the door bouncing off the wall.

'*I need to speak to Shari,*' he sent.

The Altoriae raised her brows and looked at Tormorylth. The tiny hatchling shrugged.

'*I can hear you just fine,*' she sent. She wasn't entirely sure it was safe for her with that much Q'Aralide pacing around.

'*Zirgha is not who she says she is,*' he blurted. '*She's dead. Well and truly dead. And something is using her as a... as a skin suit.*'

Shari shared another look with the hatchling by her side. '*That's disturbing.*'

'She's doing something to Oalark, but I think she might have done it to the other ambassadors as well.'

'He's panicking,' Tormorylth said, sucking the marrow out of the end of a bone.

"Yup," Shari said. 'I'm pretty sure the other ambassadors are all just terrified of Oalark. Not that I can blame them. What do you think she's doing to her?'

'I... I don't know. I've never seen anything like it before.' Sanithane's eyes were wide and frantic. Shari could feel his Innarn reaching out as he added layer after layer of protection to his quarters. 'But, I've heard tales.'

Tormorylth snuggled closer to her side.

'What sort of tales?' Shari asked.

'Long ago. The Head Priest before me spoke about Light beings who fed off Innarn. I think that's what she's doing to Oalark.'

'Feeding?' Jetonyx asked.

'Exactly.' Sanithane looked grim. 'Do not go anywhere alone. And if Zirgha or her aides approach you, leave. Make whatever excuse you need and get back to me. All of you.' The lines around his maw were tight, and he only marginally relaxed when the three of them agreed.

'I don't think there's anything like them in the handbook,' Shari sent. 'I can't remember Jonathan mentioning them either.'

'From what Izarrk said, they were old. Older than Lissae, older than Altum even. The tales had something about not needing a body anymore. And the mist that poured from Zirgha's dead mouth proves the theory.' Sanithane slumped against the door, as if his very bulk could keep the mist that so terrified him out.

'How could something so Light survive down here?' Shari wondered.

'By draining the oldest, most powerful being around. Oalark.' His voice sounded defeated.

Shari shivered.

Beside her, Tormorylth pressed close, whimpering. '*I don't like it.*'

'*What do you mean?*' Shari asked, running a gentle hand over the trembling hatchling's scales.

'*Sanithane is scared.*'

CHAPTER THIRTY-FOUR

Lissae

Inthday

Second day of the fourth week of Sunfall

Triage was full.

And Temira hadn't sighted her bed in thirty-six hours. To be fair, most of that was because she hadn't slept for twenty-eight hours before the refugees started flooding the techno centre.

She felt old, right down to her bones.

As she could currently see the bones inside the fourth leg of the Diaxampal, she would keep going.

Snapping her fingers, she waited for the slap of the femto crystal disc to land in her hand.

Nothing happened.

Glaring at Milo, she snarled, "Dish. Now."

"Oh. Right, sorry." The tiny Daen fumbled on the cart, and hastily grabbed a disc.

The wrong one.

"Too small," Temira snapped.

Milo sniffed and started tearing through the carefully prepared supplies, mixing them up.

The sudden flash of memory—a grey, smiling face, silently laughing with delight as they watched the femto crystals work for the first time.

Xani.

Scowling fiercer, Temira reached past Milo and plucked the correct size from the cart. "The disc must be no less than an inch smaller in circumference from the initial wound."

"Oh!" Milo looked stunned. "That's why…"

The Daen rambled as Temira cracked the disc and slapped it on the leg. As badly as she wanted to see the job finished, there were more patients waiting to be seen.

Another Diaxampal with pale, clammy skin and unfocused eyes, waited on the next stretcher. Pressing firmly on the abdomen, Temira ignored the flinch.

"Vial. As long as your finger," she said, and held out her hand.

If Xani was not here to read her mind, Temira would have to learn to speak it.

She shuddered at the thought.

Fenix was clambering up the side of the mountain on Cantash's north-eastern edge in the dark of predawn, sweat dripping from their brow.

Yesterday had been hard.

To see so many broken bodies and wounded souls had made something deep inside them ache. The burn of their muscles as they climbed was a pleasant distraction.

Reaching the top, Fenix wiped their forehead and sighed. The crashing waves down below had a calming effect, and they sat on the peak to meditate.

Eyes closed, Cantash's Linked went through the mental exercises designed to refocus and reflect until the golden light of the sun bathed the back of their eyelids.

Slowly, Fenix rose and stretched their arms to the sky, opening their eyes when their body was fully extended.

Only to spot black clouds streaming from the horizon.

'*Cantash?*' Fenix asked.

'*Yes, my Linked?*' Cantash answered.

'*What is that?*'

'*It is outside of my range. And I can feel... nothing from them.*'

A shiver raced along their skin. '*Thank you,*' Fenix said, even as they shifted away.

They needed to find the Guardian.

Now.

If yesterday was bad, today is worse, Tania thought.

She and the other Linked had worked through the night to get the refugees settled in their temporary homes. Rakemyst's population had swollen by six thousand overnight, and from what Fenix had just sent, they were about to get quite the unfriendly visit.

All she wanted to do was crawl home, snuggle up in her bed, and go to sleep.

Immediately, she felt guilty about thinking anything of the sort. She had spent the day speaking to beings who would never again see the homes they'd worked so hard to create after being uprooted from their birth Realms. They would have the comfort of not only their beds, but the feeling of safety that they'd already had to carve out once, upon arriving on Lissae.

Stumbling over her own feet, Tania paused, leaning against a crystal pillar.

If only she could close her eyes for a moment.

Someone stepped towards her, blocking the light. Opening eyes she hadn't realised had closed, Tania glanced up.

"Well met, Collis," she said around a yawn.

"Well met, Ronah's Linked." He held out his arm for her to take.

Wrapping her hand around his forearm, Tania allowed Collis to guide her through the town, towards the mayor's office where Jonathan was waiting for them.

"Did you get much sleep last night?" he asked.

"Sleep? Ha. None. You?"

"Very little. But I am used to surviving on less," he said.

Tania gave him a look.

Collis sighed. "We had a guard schedule. Four hours on, four hours off. Most nights, there would be twelve hours off, but towards the end, things got a little busy."

"It's feeling busy now," Tania said softly.

Glancing down at her, Collis nodded. "There's a similar taste in the air."

"A taste?" She wrinkled her nose.

"Desperation."

"Ugh. Sorry I asked," she said as they climbed the stairs.

He laughed, but it was a mirthless sound.

Quietly, they entered the office, the tempting smell of azehal drifting out to greet her.

Seated around the long table were the Linked, the elders of the four joined islands, the mayors of Ronah and Cantash, and someone new who Tania didn't recognise.

"Come in. Take a seat and a drink. We need to figure out our next move before the mainlanders' ships arrive," Mayor Pratt said, his normally cheerful countenance solemn.

Tania and Collis did as they were bid.

"What's the plan?" she asked.

"Collis has suggested fortifying the beaches of Ronah and Rakemyst with the same sort of walls as Cantash," Fenix said.

Tania whistled. "That'll take time, and a fair few Earth Innarnians working together, won't it?"

"Not really. We've had lots of practice," Collis said. "But I'd require your approval to go ahead."

"We?" Tania's nose wrinkled in confusion. "Oh, right." *The Returned.* "Yes, go! There's no one better." She grinned at him.

Rising from his seat, cup in hand, Collis bowed to Tania and those gathered at the table before taking his leave.

"Rather old-fashioned, isn't he?" asked the person Tania didn't recognise.

"He's from a different time," Tania said, staring after him. She took a sip of her drink and sighed as the hot liquid seeped into her bones.

"Different time?" the stranger asked.

"Not important," Jonathan said. "How goes the preparation for the refugees?"

The stranger sighed. "It's been a long time since Akoren has held this many beings. And there is a wide variety of requests that I fear we may not be able to accommodate. We are trying our best."

He's Akoren's Linked. Tania blinked and took another sip, not wanting to interrupt the meeting for an introduction. One would happen soon enough.

"Is there any way that we can speed up the joining?" Mayor Pratt asked.

"Ginorti is currently already on her way. Akoren is as well, but is much farther out," Fenix said. "We can push the islands as much as possible, but I fear that the ones who have already joined need to focus on defence and not speed."

"What if the Returned helped to speed us up? There would have to be some Water Innarnians amongst them," Tania said.

Jonathan looked at her over the top of his cup, only a scratch above one eyebrow remaining from his fight yesterday. A tiny black dragon was nestled in his hair. It did little to take away from his serious expression. "Do you think that could work?"

Tania looked at Zana.

The older Linked nodded slowly. "If some were moving the currents in our favour, whilst others worked to delay the ships, the Linked could help the Earth Innarnians to fortify the boundaries."

A small part of Tania saddened at the fact that her morning was filled with talk of war and defence, whilst others were going about their day like nothing had changed. Taking another sip, she tried to reframe the thought. *I'm helping to save lives. I'm preventing others from worrying.*

She'd think about the cost later.

"Who are these Returned you keep mentioning?" Akoren's Linked asked.

The Guardian plucked the draci from his head and placed the creature on his shoulder. He took a breath.

It looked like he was about to dismiss the other man again.

"They're our hope," Tania blurted out. "In more ways than one. They were stolen by Anriluka to fuel her Innarn." She didn't miss the shiver or the cursing from the others in the room at the mention of the U'tan's name, but Tania continued, "And against all odds, most of them survived centuries, honing their skills in the hopes of finding a way back home. Back to Lissae. And they did. Their story tells us that even now, as another monster approaches, we alone hold the hope of making it through to a place where we're safe and free again."

Akoren's Linked looked at her with wide eyes. "Sounds like some pretty important beings to have around."

"They really are." Tania smiled.

No one mentioned her tears.

Jonathan stood on top of the mountain range that used to be Ronah's beach and stared out to sea at the ominous clouds of black smoke.

The ships were getting closer.

Zac leaned against his shoulder.

Together, they took in the sea spray, the scent of the ocean burning Jonathan's nose in a way that would always remind him of home and phantom fish.

"Do you think they'll really attack, knowing that the might of the Shifting Islands is behind us?" Zac asked.

"Oh, they will," Jonathan said. "And when they fail, they will start going after Innarnians on the mainlands. I've already got the Travel Innarnians working on shifting in as many as they can to Akoren and Vannali. Ginorti has some space as well, and honestly, the influx isn't as large as I thought it would be. It seems like, over the last decade, most Innarnians have been driven away from the mainlands."

Zac turned his head to stare at him. "And you're mad you didn't realise sooner," he said flatly.

"I should have!" Jonathan said, throwing up the hand that wasn't linked with Zac's. "I heard the mutters from those coming to patrol. Saw what the mainlanders were capable of in my youth, and wanted to give them the benefit of the doubt."

"They aren't all bad," Zac said. "Some are quite nice."

The need to rant was strong, but Jonathan refrained. There would be time enough when everyone was safe to wonder where the *nice mainlanders* had hidden whilst their neighbours had been hunted. "I think the plan is actually working," he said instead.

"The Returned are insanely powerful," Zac said, looking over at the next ridge where a team of Water Innarnians were working tirelessly. "Do you think it will be enough?"

Jonathan clenched his jaw. "It'll have to be."

CHAPTER THIRTY-FIVE

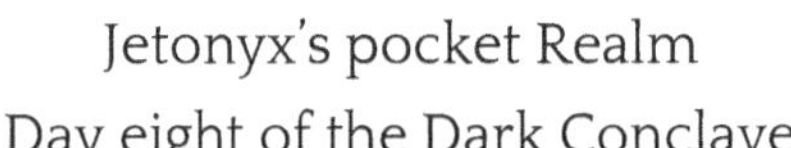

Jetonyx's pocket Realm
Day eight of the Dark Conclave

It took a great deal of talking to get Samuel to return to chair the conclave the next morning.

Shari couldn't believe they'd done it.

They were back again, Jetonyx standing, slightly bored, behind Samuel's shoulder. The Golden Priest gazed imperiously at the ambassadors as they slowly filled the room, the noise of their chatter making their numbers seem more than what they actually were.

Oalark, as usual, entered the room last. Whatever Zirgha had done to her last night was still clearly affecting her. The Queen stumbled and swayed her way to the front of the room, squashing two aides against the wall as she went and tripping over her trailing wings.

From the icy feeling emanating from Samuel, he was not impressed.

'Today's agenda. Taking over Lissae.' Oalark's send was slurred.

For the first time, Shari felt sorry for the Q'Aralide Queen.

'*We spoke about Lissae yesterday,*' the U'tan ambassador furrowed her brow. It was an odd look for a creature made predominately of tentacles.

Oalark lurched forward, but caught herself on the edge of the table before she could fall. '*And we shall talk about it again today. And the next, until we have a solid plan of attack and a way to secure a new home for us all.*'

Around the table, ambassadors looked at their neighbours, trying to figure out how to answer the Queen. Even stuck inside Jetonyx's pocket Realm, Shari could read the room and see the exact moment when they realised the reasonable, diplomatic Queen who'd appeared before them yesterday was no longer. This was the mad creature who'd decimated their ranks at the start of the conclave, and not one of them wanted to be on her bad side.

'*Of... of course,*' the U'tan ambassador sent.

Shari would have laughed if she didn't feel so bad for them.

Beside her, resting on the sand, a sated Tormorylth rubbed her full belly. '*Small meals are good,*' the hatchling said.

Turning to smile at her, Shari almost missed the flash of movement. Snapping her gaze back to the screens, Shari gaped as mist poured out of Zirgha's mouth. The body of the Otike ambassador was, in the gory light of day, at the decomposition stage. Yet none of those around her seemed to notice.

'*Sam,*' Shari sent.

The table had erupted, and beings from across the Dark Realms were shouting and throwing things. Innarn was being flung around indiscriminately, but Shari kept her eyes on the mist above Zirgha.

'*Samuel,*' she tried again.

No response.

Pushing her will against Jetonyx, she bid her host to look to his left.

Tendons and scales were flared out on the golden Q'Aralide beside them. Samuel's Innarn was bristling as he did his best to block the attacks aimed their way.

'*Samuel!*' Shari all but screamed.

He didn't so much as flinch.

Cursing, Shari pushed up from the sand and started pacing. There was nothing she could do from here. Trying to push her Innarn through Jetonyx would be futile, as the pocket Realm was designed against that. Just forcing Innarn straight into the room from so far away would be like accurately throwing a needle from one end of Ronah to the other. It wasn't going to happen.

Glancing at Tormorylth lazing on the sand, Shari sighed. There was only one choice.

She was going to have to go there herself.

Altum

Sanithane could not believe how quickly the ambassadors descended into fighting, squawking miscreants.

Well, maybe he could a little. Especially with how Oalark had been acting recently.

His sole focus was on Jetonyx and the precious cargo the hatchling carried. If he could keep them safe long enough for the others to wear themselves out, they could escape.

At least, that's what he'd thought until the white mist floating above Zirgha's fallen body caught his attention.

While he couldn't be sure what or who the mist was, it was clearly bad news. For now, it was staying still, but tendrils were unfurling and caressing against the others in the room. Thankfully, Zirgha and the mist were at the other end of the table, and Sanithane had some time before it would reach him.

'*If we've covered something and come up with a plan, we don't need to go over it again and again!*' someone was saying.

'*Oh yes, we'll invade Lissae with our finest some time before the last island joins. Clearly, that's a stellar plan and nothing can go wrong with it,*' the U'tan ambassador shot back.

'*Plans don't have to be convoluted to work! Look at what happened to your best strategist. Turned to goo by a teenager who had more luck than sense!*' An ambassador lunged across the table at the U'tan, held back by their aides.

The mist above their heads seemed to laugh.

'*Without contingencies, there is nowhere to turn when things go wrong,*' the U'tan argued. Several beings around her were nodding in agreement, even as the one closest palmed a knife.

Sanithane rolled his eyes.

This was going to go down in the Hekkor Mafae as the bloodiest, deadliest conclave in history.

He found he wasn't all that inclined to stop it.

The mist, however, was intent on spreading. It covered a good third of the ceiling now, tendrils poking and prodding about half of the totally unaware ambassadors.

Keeping his shields up, he sent a passive wave of Innarn, making it seem like it came from the Queen. '*Enough!*' the send boomed, making many at the table clutch their heads.

Helk stood in the doorway, chest heaving and a spear clutched in one hand.

A tendril reached down and brushed against the side of his head.

The warrior's eyes, normally the same vermillion as his scales, turned white.

He hefted the spear, glaring at Sanithane.

'*You have done nothing to keep the Queen safe!*' Helk's send was so loud, several aides whimpered as they pressed back against the wall. He took no notice. Raising the spear, the warrior took two running steps, crushing the Ferah ambassador as he used her chair as a boost to get onto the table, and threw the spear.

Sanithane raised a bored brow as the pointed wooden shaft flew towards him.

A gentle brush of Air Innarn saw the trajectory change. And before the warrior could cry out, the tip of his spear pierced the Q'Aralide Queen's hide, slamming through her rib cage and sending her staggering.

Pinned by the spear, Oalark's shriek sent the rest of the room to their knees.

The warrior by the door, now surrounded by his compatriots, was horrified.

For a moment, Helk's gaze met Sanithane's, fury giving way to pleading before one of his own lashed out and took off his head with a scythe.

Beings everywhere were screaming.

The poor ambassador at the end of the table was covered in blood. Her aide was trying, ineffectively, to clean her off.

Others were attempting to run from the room, only to smack into the wall of warriors blocking the doorway.

The mist was pouring back into Zirgha's open mouth. How had none of those around her noticed a corpse in their midst? Perhaps another property of the mist?

Sanithane turned slowly to face his Queen.

Oalark was plucking at the spear, seemingly unable to use her arms properly. It had gone straight through her ribs, piercing one of her hearts, and into the wall behind her. She looked at him and reached out.

'*My priest,*' she sent, her maw opening and closing as bubbling blood dripped from it.

"I think he hit one of her lungs," Shari, in her Datzal disguise, said.

Glancing down, Sanithane swore.

The Altoriae had joined them.

CHAPTER THIRTY-SIX

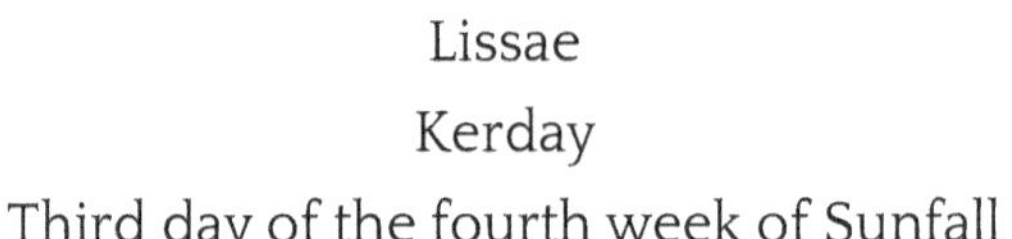

Lissae

Kerday

Third day of the fourth week of Sunfall

A gentle breeze drifted through the window, causing Chamele to hiss. Every brush of air against her skin felt like fire was racing through her veins.

It was nothing compared to their devastating losses at Lawrgaea. How could the entire attack force of the Fixed Islands be so thoroughly defeated? Of course, she badly wanted to blame Ben and Gwyn for their lack of forethought and commitment to the cause. Suni, in death, was a suitable scapegoat. It would be easy to spin the story that the traitor had gotten the word out.

If only her personal aberration had not been abducted, it may have been able to offer some protection for the attack forces. Balefully glaring at the pallet that had once held it, Chamele stormed over. Shrieking, she fell to her knees and, ignoring the pain in her hands, tried to tear the thin blanket to shreds. Panting as searing tears fell across her scarred cheeks,

Chamele gave up and started tossing parts of the meagre pallet behind her.

Something glinted in the very corner of the room.

Scrubbing the tears from her eyes and cursing, Chamele shuffled closer. There, tucked tight against the grotty baseboard, was a sliver of crystal. After prying it free with aching fingers, she held it up to the light.

Reflected in it was a face too smooth to be her own.

Frowning, Chamele rose and wandered sightlessly through the mess she'd created, her gaze trained on the crystal in her hand.

Cautiously, she lifted it to her ear.

A voice that was not her own murmured something too quiet to make out.

Snapping her gaze to the tiny rock in her hand, she squinted at it harder.

And in the reflection, the face of the Guardian drew closer.

The Elder of Jinkor smiled.

She knew who had stolen her aberration.

Now she just had to get the beast back.

Slowly, Jonathan approached Grace as she huddled in the corner of her room, perching on a blanket she'd dragged from the bed and bundled up. Skye hovered in the doorway, twisting her hands together. Her gaze was burning into the back of his head.

The malnourished Innarnian tilted her head. "Not the same," she said.

"No," Jonathan replied. "I'm not the one who rescued you."

"Look like him," Grace pointed out.

"Yes. It was a bit of a trick. We weren't sure if it was a trap," he said with a twist to his lips.

Grace blinked up at him, but didn't move from her hunched position.

To be fair, he wouldn't really know what to say to that either. "I was wondering if you knew anything about the plans for the attack on the Shifting Islands?"

"Kill the aberrations," Grace responded automatically.

"Aberrations?" Jonathan frowned, but refrained from turning towards the spy standing off to the side.

Holding her hand up, Grace called forward a little ball of plasma and twisted it neatly between her fingers. "Aberrations."

"We call them, us, Innarnians," he said.

She blinked at him.

"Is there anything that you can think of which would help us keep that from happening?"

"Must happen," Grace said earnestly. "Need to wipe it clean."

Jonathan sighed. "What if we don't want to die?"

"Like Suni?" Grace tilted her head.

Glancing to the side where Skye was hugging herself, he rose a brow. "Elder Suni?"

"Chamele had her beheaded. In her sleep," Skye said.

Jonathan wasn't sure if she was bitter that the elder didn't get a choice, or that it had happened. "Did she want to die?"

"No," Grace said.

"Then, yes, like Suni."

"Dead," Grace said.

He looked at Skye for help.

"Grace," Skye said and came closer, sitting cross-legged at the edge of the mat, far enough to be outside arm's reach. "You said you would protect me, didn't you?"

She nodded.

"Chamele thinks I'm an aberration."

Fire, literal fire, danced in Grace's eyes. "No." Her voice was stronger than anything he'd heard her say so far.

"She would go through everyone on the islands to get to me, wouldn't she?" Skye pressed.

"Yes," Grace admitted.

"How can we stop her?"

Jonathan blinked, and for the briefest moment, Innarn as strong as Shari's swirling around the broken girl.

"I help," Grace said.

Skye grinned at her. "Thank you."

Rasshday
Fifth day of the fourth week of Sunfall

Zana, looking every inch the proud Ilutri, stared grimly out at sea. Despite their best efforts, the mainlanders' ships were gaining on them.

"What do we do?" Tania whispered.

"Hold them off."

"How?" Fenix asked.

Tania was glad that she wasn't the only one feeling uncertain.

"As best we can," Cyrus answered.

Swallowing her whimper, Tania nodded. "As best we can," she repeated softly.

Lots of thin, straight things flew through the black clouds of smoke, cutting the air like an over-large arrow and landing in the water just outside of the island perimeter.

It took Tania a moment, to realise something was wrong.

The breeze had stopped.

The islands had come to a standstill.

"Cyrus," she asked, her voice higher than she intended. "Did you track down those Innarn dampeners?"

"Most were too far away to... oh. Oh! Do you think they're using the dampeners to hold us in place?"

The ships were rapidly getting closer, and she could make out the line of the smokestacks on them now.

"Yes! Yes, they're using the dampeners!" Tania almost shrieked.

"Cyrus?" Zana asked.

"Got it," Talhan's Linked said as the ships fired their second volley.

Tania could feel it the moment Cyrus pulled the dampeners out of Ronah's soil. It was as if a ziom weight the size of the castle had been lifted from her shoulders.

The islands shot away, the breeze making all four Linked stumble to keep their footing.

It was rather comical, really, the rate that the mainlanders' greatest naval threat appeared to be retreating into the distance.

The force of the wind swallowed their sighs of relief.

"I wouldn't celebrate just yet," Fenix said, and pointed.

Although the islands were moving fast, the ships had been saving some of their fuel, and the clouds of smoke that had them all so worried were still dogging them from the horizon.

"Either they'll run out of fuel, or we'll exhaust ourselves." Fenix glanced over at the closest group of Returned.

"Let's just hope they run out first," Zana said.

Ronah jolted, like she'd stopped dead in the water.

Arilla looked up, eyes wide as she stared towards where Calem and his brother were holding the border for Rakemyst. Not that she could see anything from inside the tavern.

Worrying at her lip, she lurched and grabbed onto a table as Ronah started moving again, right as Anika burst through the doors.

Even when the girl had scratched her, Anika never had so much as a hair out of place, her makeup always perfectly applied. Now, she had as many as four stray hairs, and rings of black around her eyes where it looked like she'd cried and tried to scrub the tears away.

"They won't let me fight!" she sobbed.

"Oh, Anika," Arilla said, and opened her arms.

She flew into them, sobbing against Arilla's shoulder.

She patted the teen on the back. With all the fear and uncertainty permeating the very air of the Shifting Islands, Arilla couldn't help but hope that Shari was safer wherever she was now.

With the Returned scattered along the new wall protecting Ronah, Jonathan stood on the highest point with Asterion, surveying their efforts.

Black puffs of cloud were retreating into the distance.

Still, he worried.

"Success!" Asterion grinned at him, the brisk sea breeze ruffling the fur on his face.

"I'm not sure if I'd say that," the Guardian admitted. "For a moment there, I thought they would be on us." If he unfocused his eyes, he could see the massive amounts of Innarn the Returned were pushing into the water to move them along.

"Yet we got away."

"But it was a close call," Jonathan replied. He didn't know if it was his unease that was prompting the argument, or that he felt unsatisfied that the ships were still after them.

"It will be enough," Zac said as he joined them.

Quietly, the Guardian looked out as the ships grew smaller and smaller. Glancing at Zac, he sighed.

And allowed himself to hope.

358

CHAPTER THIRTY-SEVEN

Altum

Day eight of the Dark Conclave

'*What are you doing?*' he growled.

Sanithane moved so his bulk would cover the Altoriae and glanced around. As the shock of seeing Shari wore off, he scanned the room. It was just as frantic as it had been before her appearance. No one had noticed the fresh addition to their midst.

'*You were rather outnumbered. Thought I'd give you a hand.*' She was so casual about the whole thing.

'*You can't be here,*' he hissed. '*Go back.*'

Shari looked up at him, glaring. '*Did the mist get you, too? Don't be ridiculous.*' Ignoring him, she turned to the Queen and the black blood bubbling from the wound. '*I think I can heal her.*'

'*Why?*' Samuel sent on a narrow band.

'*Because she's not really in control of herself. And I kinda feel sorry...*'

Oalark growled and spat, the sizzle of her acidic blood landing by Shari's boot.

'*Maybe not.*' Stepping closer to the Queen, Shari asked, '*Do you really want this to be the way you die?*'

Despite her lungs filling with blood and only one heart pumping, Oalark managed to glare.

The Altoriae looked conflicted. '*It doesn't feel right leaving you like this.*'

'I'd... sooner... eat you... than... have you...' Oalark wheezed, blood pouring down her chest and eating away at the floor by her claws. '*heal... me... cestoray...*'

'*Altoriae, actually,*' Shari sent back.

Slumping, the life went out of the Queen's eyes.

Sanithane and Shari had a moment to glance at each other, both glad and terrified that the mad Queen had died.

Looking over his shoulder, the smile dropped from Sanithane's face.

'*Get behind me,*' he rumbled as he twisted around.

Something in his tone made her obey before she was even conscious of moving. Another time, he'd tease her about it.

"What's wrong?" she whispered.

'*Shadow Bringer,*' Sanithane growled.

Before them was a creature in the shape of an overly large canine, made from white wisps of shadow. Its glowing opalescent eyes locked onto Shari.

'*Begone!*' Sanithane ordered, waving his claws in a complicated gesture.

The canine growled back.

Shocked, Sanithane rocked backwards.

"What's a Shadow Bringer?" Shari asked warily.

The creature disappeared. Sanithane caught the same fleeting glimpse of white out of the corner of his eye that he'd been seeing the whole time they'd been on Altum. '*A bad omen. A being of Light Innarn that someone sent to track you. They are usually intent on killing the being*' *they're set upon.*' He frowned, turning to stare as the dog reappeared on Shari's left.

'*They can also be set to protect a being,*' Jetonyx offered.

'*And what do you make of this one?*' Samuel asked.

'*This one...*' He sniffed, his nose twitching. '*This one, I'm not sure. Gathering information, perhaps?*'

Disappearing in another blink, the creature was gone.

Before anything more could be said, they were interrupted by heavy claws scraping against the stone floor.

'*Have you healed her?*' It was the warrior who'd sliced Helk's head off. Dangling from his claws were two ambassadors, knocked out cold.

Turning, Sanithane carefully tucked Shari under his wing as unobtrusively as he could. '*I tried, but... Helk's aim was true.*'

The warrior glanced at the slumped body of the Queen and raised his head to howl. The other warriors stopped rounding up the recalcitrant delegates and joined in.

Under his wing, Shari stirred. Glancing down at the puddle of blood was eeking closer to them, Sanithane sent, '*Have your warriors prepare her body. And contain the ambassadors in their quarters. Something like this should not be spread to the rest of the Realms.*'

'*Yes, Head Priest.*' Bowing, the warrior then turned and started barking orders.

Using his distraction, Sanithane shifted Shari back to Jetonyx's pocket Realm, bearing her complaints with a grin.

Until he lifted his head and caught Zirgha's gaze on him.

The Otike ambassador smirked as she was led away.

Sanithane, Golden Priest and newly appointed leader of the Q'Aralide, shivered.

Jetonyx's pocket Realm

Shari seethed as she watched the procession for the Q'Aralide Queen from the safety of Jetonyx's pocket Realm.

The ambassadors were there in resplendent glory, looking tiny next to the bulk of the Q'Aralide who passed the plank that bore the body of their former leader claw over claw.

Samuel, at the end of the line, looked tired. As the plank reached him, he used Innarn to carefully tip the Queen into the acid river.

She slid in without a single splash.

As one, the Q'Aralide rose their voices. The haunting melody painted a picture across Altum's sky of a Queen who ruled by force, but cared for her charges, who ruthlessly sought the best, and took pleasure in meting out the worst.

The ambassadors stood silently as the entire Q'Aralide race paid their respects to their leader. Even Zirgha's mist stayed firmly inside the Otike's animated corpse.

The song faded away, and one by one, with bowed heads, beings began to leave. The gates of Altum were due to open, and none wanted to be trapped here any longer than they had to be.

Not to mention the warriors had made it clear they had overstayed their welcome.

Jetonyx moved slowly over to the Golden Priest, who was talking to Jaileth.

'*Are you staying?*' Jaileth was asking.

'*No. I'll leave Altum in your capable claws,*' Samuel sent.

The bronze Q'Aralide laughed. '*You leave me this dump whilst you go on adventures to the Mother Realm, where you know I can't follow.*'

Samuel smirked and caught Jetonyx's gaze. '*Someone has to make sure the Altoriae doesn't catch wind of what happened.*'

'*Do you really think she's that smart? Seems like all she knows is how to fight.*' For someone born to a race who delighted in overpowering others, Jaileth appeared to be unimpressed with Shari's prowess.

She wasn't sure if she should be flattered or offended.

'*You'd be...*'

The ground under their feet rumbled, cutting him off.

Cracks appeared on the riverbank, and chunks of suddenly decaying flesh started falling into the acid.

'*What's happening?*' Jaileth sent.

Holding his wing out and guiding Jetonyx away from the river, Samuel glanced around.

"What's happening?" Shari asked.

The hatchling copied Samuel, and Shari gasped.

The buildings of Altum were collapsing. Tremors from the river had travelled quickly and were splitting the very ground around them. Walls shuddered before falling, and beings all over were calling out in distress.

'*I think Altum was connected to the Queen's life force. Or she was connected with it. Either way, the Realm we called home will not be around much longer. Get everyone out.*' Samuel looked at Jaileth, and shook the bronze Q'Aralide as she stood there, gaping at him. '*Now!*'

Taking to the sky, Jaileth started broadcasting, but Shari paid her little attention.

'*What do you need us to do?*' she sent.

Staring into Jetonyx's eyes, Samuel sent, '*Tormorylth. Are there any others like you?*'

The little hatchling shook her head.

'*She says no,*' Shari sent when it became apparent that fear had stolen her voice.

'*Then, Jetonyx, go.*'

Shari was proud that her trembling host stood his ground. '*What about the eggs?*'

Samuel cursed and turned to stare at the hatching grounds on the other side of the river. '*I'll...*'

A massive boom cut him off, a cloud of dust making them choke and cough.

When Jetonyx opened his eyes again, the buildings on the other side of the river were nothing but rubble.

If Shari had thought the words Samuel had used before were bad, they were nothing compared to what poured from his mouth. The utter devastation in his expression was enough that she started to say something about the egg she'd liberated.

Before she could open her mouth, the ground under their feet crumbled and sank.

It was only by the grace of their wings that the two Q'Aralide weren't pulled into the acid river.

'*Fly!*' Samuel ordered.

Turning, the two aimed for the gateway at the other end of Altum. The surrounding mountains were writhing, and the movement reminded Shari of death throes, even if the beast dying was bigger than any other she'd encountered before.

The air was full of dust and screams. More Q'Aralide joined in the flight, winging their way towards the exit.

As the closest one dropped to the ground to open the gateway, an endless cave was appearing to the side, teeth bigger than the nearest Q'Aralide protruding from it.

Shari screamed a warning.

The cave—a mouth—snapped shut, and the Q'Aralide disappeared with a sickening cry.

Another, not seeing the fate of the first, tried to get through, and was eaten by the mountainous creature.

'*Sam!*' she sent.

'*It's the only way out! How are we going to get out?*' Jetonyx was babbling.

'*Samuel!*'

The Golden Priest pulled to a stop, hovering well out of reach of the hungry mountain. '*I never knew they could do that,*' he muttered.

Another Q'Aralide tried and failed to get past the jaws. They were swallowed, along with three of the delegates who'd been trying to hide behind him.

One sneaked by as the mountain crunched through another escaping party.

'*I'll distract, and you...*'

'No!' Jetonyx, Shari, and Tormorylth cried together.

'*Let me out,*' Shari sent to Jetonyx.

Her host glanced down. The ground under their feet was a mass of cracks big enough to swallow her whole.

'*Trust me,*' Shari sent.

He peered at the monster guarding the gateway as blood sprayed from its mouth.

Another Q'Aralide down.

There was a squeezing sensation, and Shari was free-falling. Using Air Innarn to right herself, she pushed up before hovering safely above the churned-up ground.

Taking in a breath, she tried not to choke as dust coated the inside of her mouth. Acid froth from the roiling river permeated the entire area and started eating into her skin.

'*Ready?*' she sent, as steadily as she could. There was no way she'd be able to wait any longer if they weren't. One hand on the cuff Cyrus had created, Shari gathered her Innarn and shifted the three of them straight into the Ducibus' Hall. Gasping in the clean air, she fell and bounced off Jetonyx's side.

Behind them, screams and cries from Altum's open gateway echoed through the hall.

The Ducibus on duty stood, wringing ze's hands as tears leaked out from under their hood.

Running feet pounded as a group with wild eyes streamed towards them.

Samuel, wings unfurled to hide both of his charges, glared at the unseeing ambassador who broke through the gateway, using the death of another of his kind as cover.

'*We need to leave,*' Shari sent as gently as she could.

The golden Q'Aralide was torn, but Shari could feel something was about to happen, and she wasn't sure it would be good for Samuel to witness it.

'*Sam... Sanithane, we need to leave,*' she tried again.

Turning his head, he nodded. '*Sorry,*' he sent. Jetonyx shrieked before he disappeared. '*He'll be safer in your Realm than here.*' Sanithane shrank into the form that Shari was more familiar with. '*Bit less conspicuous this way.*' He smirked.

'*Here.*' Shari unsnapped the cuff from her wrist and slid it onto Tormorylth's foreleg. '*Safer for you to go to my Realm too, okay?*'

The tiny hatchling nodded, and Shari shifted her away.

She looked up as Samuel threw one last glace back at his dying Realm. Exhaustion lining his face, Samuel turned and started the long trek back to Lissae's gateway, tugging Shari along behind him.

Shari's head snapped around as a blur of green skin and golden caps tumbled through Altum's gateway.

A tiny being in a grey robe bustled over to her. '*You are not on the same path...*' Thanks to the magic of the Ducibus, the hall fell quiet and the body of Zirgha disappeared.

She wasn't sure if it was a good thing that they were unable to see the others traversing the hallways, or a bad thing that they couldn't be sure who had survived and who hadn't.

Either way, the silence seemed oppressive after the battle.

Sneaking a glance at Samuel, Shari sighed. *How did you comfort someone who'd just seen the destruction of their entire Realm?*

CHAPTER THIRTY-EIGHT

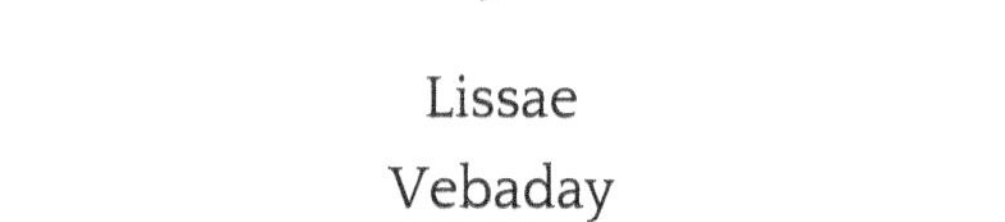

Lissae

Vebaday

Sixth day of the fourth week of Sunfall

The Quiver and Quill tavern was bursting at the seams with the exhausted, elated defenders.

Tania couldn't keep the grin off her face as another cheer went up as someone toasted to leaving the mainlanders' ships in the wake of the islands.

Laughing, she swung around a table, dodged past Fenix, and practically fell into Collis's lap.

"Well met!" She grinned up at him as if she hadn't just gone to get another drink of water.

He smiled down at her.

The doors opened as the Cantash group swarmed in, bringing with them a fresh blast of noise and tired joy.

Leaning her head against Collis's chest, he rumble something against her ear, but Tania was too tired to listen to what he was saying.

He eased her hair out of the way and started stroking her back, chatting to someone who was sitting on the other side of the table.

Letting her eyes slip closed, Tania dozed for a moment, enjoying the comfort and peace they'd worked so hard to achieve.

There was a tiny tug on her consciousness, but she brushed it away.

'Help.'

Scrunching her nose, Tania whimpered slightly.

'Help.'

Somewhere inside the whisper was a word.

'Help.'

That was the word.

'Help.'

Yelping, Tania jerked upright, almost smacking her head into Collis's chin.

'Help.'

She met Zana's gaze across the room, the astute Ilutri looking every bit as ruffled as Tania felt.

Ginorti was in trouble.

Captain Rappen grinned as the green hills of Ginorti came into sight.

"Ready the ballistas," he ordered.

Sailors scrambled to do his bidding.

This one was still ripe for the taking, even though the islands that had already joined had gotten away.

The tavern was a mess.

Arilla Dawn couldn't care less.

After the outburst from the four Linked, tables had been pushed back, chairs overturned, and drinks spilled in haste as everyone had rushed to see what they could do to save the Shifting Island that was under attack.

Something numb and cold had settled into her bones, so she did what she'd always done in times of stress.

Sharpened her weapons.

Rising from her seat at the counter, she mechanically walked to the next in line and took the sword down off its mount on the wall before carefully carrying it back to her sharpening station.

"Time for bed, love," Calem said.

"One more," Arilla replied.

"They'll be here tomorrow."

"Will we?" she asked, meeting his gaze.

Calem sank to his knees by her side. "Yes."

He said it so earnestly, she couldn't help but be touched.

"Take me home," Arilla whispered.

After carefully removing the sword from her hands, Calem gathered her in his arms and hugged her tight. Guiding her out of the tavern, he lifted her effortlessly and took flight, winging his way to their home.

Snuggling into her husband's chest, Arilla sighed.

If only Shari was back, the Realm would feel like a safer place.

Ducibus' Hall

Walking away from Altum seemed to take an age, but Samuel didn't dare look back.

Turning her around, Samuel guided the Altoriae towards the very middle of the hall, where the gateway awaited them.

Samuel had never been so grateful to see the double doors of Lissae before. He glanced down at Shari and smiled.

"Almost home," he said.

It was true. Lissae had felt more like home than Altum had for a long time.

A part of him would always mourn the passing of his Realm. The place where he'd grown up, where he'd learned how to harness his Innarn, how to change his form, and made allies that would see him through his darkest years. But another part was almost glad that the place where most of his torment had taken place was gone.

Samuel wasn't entirely sure if it was because of Oalark's death or Altum's destruction, but he felt lighter and freer than he had in centuries.

"We will need to figure out how to explain Jetonyx and Tormorylth to Jonathan," Shari said. "They can't be cooped up in my sanctuary forever."

He glanced down at her fondly, before looking back at the doors that represented freedom. "I'm sure the Guardian will be understanding. After all, he has to be with you as the Altoriae."

There was a gasp, and Samuel laughed.

Silence.

Samuel turned, and Shari was no longer at his side. "Shari?"

He spun around. "Shari?"

The Altoriae was nowhere in sight.

"Shari!"

Pushing his Innarn out, he swept the hall for her.

Nothing.

The Altoriae was gone.

A

Aberration – A slur used by mainlanders to refer to Innarnians.

Adonday – First day of the week on the Realm of Lissae. The other days are **Inthday, Kerday, Narday, Rasshday, Vebaday,** and **Zoeday.**

Aestques – Beings native to Tocithas.

Altoriae – Protector of the Realm of Lissae. Traditionally a female role, although there has been one male Altoriae. Previous Altoriaes have included Kay'imi, Muran Curtis, Jali Thorne, and Fiona MacAde. Forces of nature cannot kill her. They must swear to uphold the seven duties of the Altoriae.

Altum – The home Realm of the Q'Aralide.

Apprentice, The Guardian's – The Guardian's Apprentice is to take over the role of Guardian once the current holder of the title falls in battle or dies of old age.

Arustos – A small mammal native to Cantash. These tree custodians live in hollows near the base of trees. They have a pointed snout, dirt-coloured scales, sturdy back legs, sharp teeth, and a strong tail. They use their forelegs to grab onto bugs, which their companion Caelonis fries for them.

Aqua ineas – A phrase used to counter the bad luck of stepping into a puddle.

Atlantis – A Grey Realm with a predominantly human population, Atlantis is famous for its Techno Innarn and wide variety of Innarn-powered machines.

Azehal – A drink favoured by the Guardian. A rutenberry-flavoured stimulant drink, typically served with sweetener and milk.

B

Bazaven – A Light desert Realm. Native beings include the **Sylpans** (See: Sylpan) and the **Ofanahni** (See: Ofanahni).

Bereni trees – Trees that are grown to be used as buildings. The size and design of the tree can be controlled by an Innarnian or by one of the sentient islands.

B.I.R.D. – Stands for "Bio Instructor for Relative Distance." Designed by Xani of Talhan to ensure beings would stop bumping into things if they were absorbed in their crystal slab. The B.I.R.D. device acts as both a guide and a guard.

B.I.T. – Stands for "Basic Innarn Training." A device created by Temira of Talhan, it is designed to test the user's abilities without anyone else getting hurt.

Blank – A person who can't use Innarn.

Books 'n' More – A store on Ronah that the Guardian runs when he's not saving the Realm of Lissae.

C

Caelonis – A tiny bird native to Cantash. They can produce a jet of flame from their beak. They typically use the flames to fry beetles for their arustos companions.

Calromata – Red, opaque berries with the approximate heat level of lava. Favoured by the Daens and native to Cantash.

Canak-Maku – A Grey Realm, which is home to the minotaurs.

Castle, Ronah's – The centre point of Ronah and the traditional home of the Altoriae, the Guardian, and their respective families.

Cosmo shell – The pearlescent shell of a deep water crustation native to Lissae. Used in decorative objects and jewellery. Incredibly expensive because of the difficulty of harvesting the shell from the long-lived creatures.

Cradamull – A Dark Realm. Oalark eats their elder during the Dark Conclave.

Crystals – Hold energy, which is turned into electricity. Often installed in clusters to gain more power and last longer. Different coloured crystals do different things. White Crystals are used for communication. Black Crystals gather power, and Orange Crystals connect currents to create fences. Crystal necklaces are given to young children and Blanks for them to manipulate the crystals.

Curses – Several curses are common on Lissae, including: Adeon's fire; By the Life of Lissae; Ke'ra's Flash; Zoemer's Rocks; Rasshnae's Floods; Vebnah's Breath; Na'reh's Ghosts. Other curses from the Realms include: ketarr; dathae; tuzar's arse; tongue of a Ne'fora; whale's arse; basalt-chewing, hemmit-loving buzzard; cestoray; slime vattar; hanotqe; slime-filled cedore; feseor; gozochas; thrice-damned; fizzpot; trusnuck.

D

Daen – A short, fierce, and loyal race with amazing control over the Fire Element.

Damiuth – One of the Dark Realms.

Datzal – A Grey shapeshifting race conquered by the Q'Aralide and used as spies by the Queen.

Deities – Lissae has six Deities who are said to have lived on Akoren. See: **Beings and Creatures: Adeon, Ke'ra, Na'reh, Rasshnae, Vebnah,** and **Zoemer** for more details.

Denfur – A race of gelatinous beings

Dento – A fixed island on Lissae. Home of the Kumaru.

Diaxampal – Refugees from the Grey Realm of Daixam, now living on Lissae.

Dofi – Native to the Dark Realms, the dofi are considered a delicacy. Small creatures with a grey, scaly body, long tentacles, and two enormous eyes, the dofi have limited intelligence. They are raised watching their parents get eaten and believe they will be reunited with their family in the stomachs of others.

Draci – Tiny dragon-like creatures that grow no bigger than a human's palm. The draci are native to Cantash, and those who have not found a being to bond with live in the gardens.

Dracovum – The hatchling stage of the **draci**.

Ducibus – The Ducibus guard the gateways between the Realms. No one really knows what they look like, as they all wear dark cloaks. There is a theory that they come from different Realms and comprise many races. They ensure the safe travel between Realms and that those who aren't meant to get through, don't.

Ducibus' Hall – The place between Realms, guarded by the **Ducibus**.

Dudrodie eggs – If these eggs have been incubated within the Q'Aralide Queen, they can cure **Grytycide** poisoning.

E

Earth – A Grey Realm with ley lines like Lissae. Once the home of Atlantis before it split away to form its own Realm. Also home to the myth of the minotaur, and most of the readers of this series.

Elders – Those who have, through age and experience, survived the Realms long enough to guide their people. They also act as advisors to the mayor.

Elements – Lissae has seven major elements that Innarnians can manipulate: earth, air, fire, water, plasma, spirit, and technology.

Eni – Malicious shapeshifters, able to permanently assume the form of influential figures to summon others of their kind to possess the subjects they have gained. Seriously Dark beings, the Eni are rarely seen out of the Dark Realms. The Eni mentally 'piggyback' their prey before assuming their form. They were wiped out by the thirteenth Altoriae during an unsuccessful attempt to take over Lissae. References from the Eni's time on Lissae can be found in the **Eni Inside**. See **More to Read**.

Eobustus – Native to Cantash, the coal-black equines with manes of fire are a physical representation of energy and heat transference. They use heat from their surroundings to gather energy, then convert that energy into other things–movement, Innarn-boosting, running without rest. They are the fastest creature in all the Realms–provided they've had a good feed of magma or the sun is at full strength.

Eofix – A Dark Realm home to huge beings.

F

Farscope – A device predominantly used by sailors and explorers on Lissae to view things at great distances.

Fempar – A creature the size of a medium dog, it had six legs, antennas, and it was the only thing on the Realms that could pierce a Q'Aralide hide. Now extinct.

Femto crystals – The latest in healing technology for Talhan. They can help a patient recover from any damage they've sustained and decrease recuperation time.

Ferah – Humanoid beings with cat-like features, including fur, tail, whiskers, and claws.

Freehorne – The Guardian's hometown.

Fulni An animal similar to Earth's buffalo, but carnivorous and with two heads. The last fulni herd went extinct over two hundred years ago. Their tails are attached to a major artery, and if the tail is removed, they will bleed out in seven seconds.

G

Glamour – A type of Innarn used to hide or disguise things. Typically cosmetic in application, glamours are favoured by those with heavy scarring or blemishes.

Greonilae – Refugees from the Grey Realm of Greon, now living on Lissae.

Grytycide – A deadly poison with only two cures—removing it from the victim's system or ingesting Dudrodie eggs.

Guardian – The rank for the person who oversees training and caring for the Altoriae, and for Lissae. In cases of emergency, the mayor and elders defer to the Guardian.

H

Healers – Similar to Earth's doctors, they heal patients who are sick or injured, usually using Innarn, although they also use the old methods.

Healers Centre – Also called the Hospital. A place on Ronah or Rakemyst to go when sick or injured.

Hekkor Mafae – A book about Dark Ones. The Guardian is extremely uncomfortable about having it on Lissae. The Guardian's Apprentice has banished it to his personal pocket Realm more than once.

Hospital – Also called Healers Centre. A place to go when sick or injured.

Hulios – A fixed island on Lissae.

I

I bid thee well – A traditional phrase when two or more people part ways.

Iabovar – A Grey Realm, home to the stunning Niverwell Ranges. The Realm where the Chirea made their base camp.

Ignivas – Birds native to Cantash.

Inthday – Second day of the week on the Realm of Lissae. The other days are **Adonday, Kerday, Narday, Rasshday, Vebaday,** and **Zoeday.**

Isoiglabrane – A powerful aphrodisiac made from the crushed leaves of the crystal forest in Saundun.

Ilutri – Winged humanoids from Lissae. They are usually found on Rakemyst and are high-level Innarnians. They include some of the finest archers on the Realm.

Innarn – (said Inn-*ar*-n) Predominately elemental magic which is present in all Realms to varying strengths. Innarn is split into three major groups: Dark, Grey, and Light. Each variant of Innarn has its own specialties. See **Elements** for more information. There are other disciplines of Innarn, including Animal, Crystal, Mental, Realm, Time and Travel.

Innarnian – (said Inn-*ar*-ni-an) A person who can use Innarn.

J

Jinkor – A fixed island on Lissae.

Joratre – A race native to Vutolea. Of Amazonian build, the Joratre have jet-black skin and live in polyamorous relationships.

Julipa bud – Native to Lissae, this fleshy plant is notoriously difficult to maintain.

K

Kedjum – Native to Teroupi, the kedjum is a wild, tangled, and unpredictable ball of fluff and teeth.

Kenorvia – A continent on Lissae.

Kerday – Third day of the week on the Realm of Lissae. The other days are **Adonday, Inthday, Narday, Rasshday, Vebaday,** and **Zoeday.**

Kinaesthesis – The sensation by which bodily position, weight, muscle tension, and movement are perceived.

Knarec – Acclaimed archers with arrows strong enough to hurt a Q'Aralide.

L

Lawrgaea – A continent on Lissae.

Libertatia – Home to pirates from across the Realms, Libertatia is regularly patrolled, although its gateway is rarely opened.

Linked – A soul joined with that of one of Lissae's Shifting Islands. As the Shifting Islands are sentient, it was decided long ago that they should link with a being on their island to ensure that they remain in touch with the current needs of their population, and not remove themselves from the trials and tribulations of everyday beings.

Lissae – A Grey, sentient Realm who is defended by the Altoriae. Consisting of six continents, seven sentient Shifting Islands, and multiple fixed islands, she is home to ten races. She is said to be a Mother Realm. There are two moons in her orbit.

Lissaen – A person who lives on Lissae.

Lore Keeper – The Eldest of the Wisara is given the title of Lore Keeper and charged with passing down the tales of Lissae to those on the

Shifting Islands. This is typically done as payment, and called the Tales of Lore.

M

Mainlanders – A name for those residing on the mainlands or fixed islands of Lissae.

Morreth – A Dark Realm.

Mother Realm – The only Realm capable of giving birth to new Realms. Highly guarded and sought after.

Motus – The movement used to create Innarn. One must have thought, intent, and movement correct for the Innarn to work. Motus can be an individual construct, or a widely recognised form. Forms of motus used: Air; Sleep; Wind Blast; Wall of Stone.

N

Nalparak – Massive, antlered beasts native to Vutolea.

Narday Fourth day of the week on the Realm of Lissae. The other days are **Adonday, Inthday, Kerday, Rasshday, Vebaday,** and **Zoeday.**

Neharn – A desert Grey Realm with two suns.

Nindonia – A fixed island on Lissae. Home of the Zindara.

Nine Hells – The name given to a particularly nasty set of nine Realms.

Nittany – A Grey Realm with a forest around its gateway.

Niverwell Ranges – A stunning mountain range on the Realm of Iabovar. The range has a myriad of tiny, naturally created holes going from one side of the range to the other. It allows for the static build-up of two elements, creating a whistling noise. Local legends claim the noise is caused by the souls of the departed.

O

Ofanahni – Native to Bazaven. The Ofanahni are typically oppressed by the Sylpans, whose brutal and inconsistent justice system makes their lives difficult. A group of Ofanahni refugees has settled in the desert region of the continent set aside on Lissae for refugees.

Otike – Green-skinned giants with prominent under-tusks, clawed fingers, and knuckles.

P

Palon – Native to Lissae, the palon is a small, six-legged creature descended from wolves. They have soft fur and long tongues, with a preferred diet of insects.

Patrol – Any Innarnian resident over fifteen is required to help the Guardian and the Altoriae patrol the Realms to watch for any potential threats. The Linked, elderly, and Blanks are not required to patrol.

Permian – A Grey Realm.

Pocket Realm – A small Realm that is attached to a larger one.

Prime – Non-binary equivalent of prince or princess.

Proprioception – Perception or awareness of the position and movement of the body.

Q

Q'Aralide (said Que-*ral*-die) – A vicious Dark race who wield Spirit, Earth, Plasma, and Air Innarn. Approximately thirty feet tall, their social status depends more on their colour and abilities than anything else. Apart from their Innarn, their breath is something to watch out for, as it can strip the flesh and the life from someone in just one exhalation.

Quiver and Quill Tavern – The tavern run by the Altoriae's parents.

R

Rassu – People who claim to be Innarnian, but who use trap doors, sleight of hand, and tricks to reproduce the effects of what a real Innarnian can do.

Rasshday – Fifth day of the week on the Realm of Lissae. The other days are **Adonday**, **Inthday**, **Kerday**, **Narday**, **Vebaday**, and **Zoeday**.

Rataeo – A virtually uninhabited Dark ice Realm, with a time speed double Lissae's. It is home to the **U'tan.**

Realms – Planets which inhabit various parts of the multiverse on three main levels: Dark, Grey, and Light. Although there can be many sub-levels and a mix of Dark and Grey or Grey and Light within the same level. Dark Realms are places with little to no natural sunlight. Most lights in these Realms are made by Innarn. Grey Realms are places with a similar amount of light to Lissae and Earth's equator. Light Realms are places where there is an abundance of natural light.

Returned – The name given to those from Ronah who survived being eaten by Anriluka.

Ridden Hall – The school on Ronah.

Roefill – A Dark Realm.

Rutenberry – The frosted, dark-purple skin of the rutenberry hides the chocolate-like fruit inside. It can be eaten raw, although the skin can be bitter. Skinned, mashed, and cooked, it can be added into cakes, biscuits, and other sweets, including drinks.

S

Saundun – A Dark Realm. Home to the famous crystal forest.

Sedolic – Green, scaly, dog-like animals with two large pincers at their front that are a favoured food of the U'tan.

Sephina silk – Collected from silkworms that feast on the Darfionious Oak tree, which is only found in the Sephina Ranges. It is the warmest, softest, strongest fabric on Lissae, and there's just something about it that makes it immune to Fire and Water Innarn.

Send/Sent – The word used for telepathic communication.

Sentient – Able to perceive or feel things, capable of thought and communication.

Sentinel, The Shifting Island – The major source of news for the Shifting Islands of Lissae. Available on your crystal slab with the low-cost subscription of 3 ziom beads a day!

Shem'ar – Shem'ar are small dragon-like creatures, no bigger than a large dog and about as intelligent as canines as well. Kept most often as familiars, guard creatures, messengers, and family pets. They have soft, furry hides that come in almost any colour. Although incapable of Innarn or talking, owners of the shem'ar can communicate telepathically with the creatures, some of whom understand more than others.

Shemmegote Stinger – A smoking, green alcohol that Sanithane is partial to.

Shifting – The Innarn art of mental teleportation from one space to another.

Shifting Islands – The name of the group of islands that travel around Lissae's seas, seemingly on a whim. They are sentient beings who care for the residents who make them their home. See: **Akoren, Cantash, Ginorti, Rakemyst, Ronah, Talhan,** and **Vannali.**

Shunar – A Grey Realm home to blue-skinned cyclopes.

Sivote – Refugees from the Grey Realm of Riomache, now living on Lissae.

Spirit Realm – A Realm that is found alongside Lissae, where the spirit or souls of the deceased go when their physical bodies are no longer needed.

Startide – Capital city of Tocithas, home to the Aestques.

Strilite – A race from the Grey Realm of Rilite.

Sulanta – A fixed island on Lissae.

Suncrest – The final month of summer on the Realm of Lissae.

Sunfall – The first month of autumn on the Realm of Lissae.

Sylpan – A double-headed being native to Bazaven, who hunts and imprisons those they consider have 'done them wrong'. What is wrong to a Sylpan depends on the day and hour, but if they feel slighted at all, they will hunt you to the end of the Realm to bring you to justice.

T

Talhan – One of the sentient Shifting Islands on Lissae, and the only one to start with an all-human population. He now accepts immigrants from all races on Lissae.

Techno Centre – Located on Talhan, it is the hub for all of Lissae's crystal and technological advances. The dual heads of the Techno Centre have been given the nickname of the technomancers, due to the number of times their advances have brought the seemingly deceased back to life. The building also holds the Healing Centre, and the labs of the technomancers and Talhan's Linked.

Teeldrit – A small, friendly population of Teeldrit refugees live in the desert region of the continent set aside on Lissae for refugees.

Teroupi – Dark Realm

Tevon – A fixed island on Lissae.

Tocithas – Water Realm

U

U'tan – A race of extraordinarily powerful strategists who live on Rataeo.

Uleulan – A race of four-armed humanoids from Lissae. Usually found on Sulanta, they have distinct features: a single, large eye and translucent skin. Amongst them are some of the Realm's high-level Water and Spirit Innarnians.

Ulnan – Temira's home Realm. It was destroyed, and all that remains is a burnt door in the Ducibus' Hall.

Ulnanian – A race from Ulnan. The only known surviving member is Temira.

V

Vebaday – Sixth day of the week on the Realm of Lissae. The other days are **Adonday, Inthday, Kerday, Narday, Rasshday,** and **Zoeday.**

Vladine – Refugees from the Grey Realm of Vinneča, now living on Lissae.

Vastilda – A Dark Realm with an ice door. Its inhospitable cold weather made it the perfect place to hide the *Hekkor Mafae*. Home to the four-armed Vastildian cyclops.

Vendalbara – A continent on Lissae.

Vutolea – A Grey Realm. Home to the Joratre.

W

Wards – Innarn shields designed to protect specific areas.

Wiaxatale – A Light Realm whose gateway into Lissae is currently under external attack.

Widdershins – To turn in an anti-clockwise direction.

Wirri Leaf – A herb hung in the entranceways of Daen homes to keep the bad luck out.

Wisara – Primarily ocean-dwelling beings whose bodies, although humanoid, look like the tangled roots of lotus flowers. Their 'hair' is the leaves of the lotus, and the flowers act as adornments. Wisara can change form to a more traditional humanoid shape and inhabit land areas in either form. They move around as gypsies and trade between the continents and islands of Lissae by walking the ocean beds. They are the perfect oversea (or in this case, undersea) merchants, as storms have little to no effect on them. Custom dictates that the Wisara are offered fish and bread and other items to restock their larder by the towns they visit. As payment, the Wisara would tell the Tales of Lore. Only the eldest of the Wisara is given the title of **Lore Keeper**, although anyone could tell the tales.

X

Xanderri – A cloud-like race relying on the bodies of their hosts to move around.

Xanterians – A race from the Dark Realms.

Y

Yrusri – A race from the Dark Realms.

Yaqueona – An oblong-shaped red, gourd, best served stuffed or roasted. Native to Cantash.

Z

Zarsuth – Ancient aquatic fish native to Tocithas

Ze/Zir – A gender-neutral pronoun.

Zhahyeem – Be calm.

Ziom – The hardest metal in the Realms, found on Lissae. Used for the creation of housing frames, precious jewellery, and weapons.

Ziom beads – A form of currency on Lissae.

Zoeday – Seventh day of the week on the Realm of Lissae. The other days are **Adonday**, **Inthday**, **Kerday**, **Narday**, **Rasshday**, and **Vebaday**.

Zooghe – A Dark Realm.

BEINGS AND CREATURES

Annotated by the Guardian's Apprentice, Samuel.

Adeon – The God of the Element Fire and husband of Ke'ra.

Aharny – An Ilutri Travel Innarnian, formerly working out of Dento.

Akoren – One of the sentient Shifting Islands on Lissae. Originally home to Lissae's deities, now ze is inhabited by a few, select representatives of the races that came from the other Shifting Islands.

Amara – currently of Ronah. Formerly of Cantash. Former candidate for the Guardian's Apprentice. New member of the Altoriae's Guild. *How does she manage to constantly trip over air?*

Amauran – of Ronah. One of the Returned, and a member of the Altoriae's Guild.

Anika Thorne – of Ronah. Student at Ridden Hall. Blank. Stylist to the thirteenth Altoriae. *And the Guardian. And me. I feel like I've been branded.*

Anriluka – of Rataeo. This U'tan is older than Lissae's calendar. She almost devoured Ronah's entire population before Muran Curtis's Guardian banished her back to her home Realm. Anriluka was finally defeated by Shari Dawn, the thirteenth Altoriae, in the spring of 4059.

Anthea – of Vutolea. The Joratre giant has midnight-dark skin and a blinding white smile. An ally of the 13th Altoriae.

Antya – of Talhan. One of the patrol leaders.

Arilla Dawn – of Ronah. Mother of Shari Dawn, wife of Calem Dawn. Owner of the Quiver and Quill Tavern.

Ashbek – Elder of Roefill.

Ashlen – One of the Returned, and a member of the Altoriae's Guild

Still not sure what to make to the minotaur.

Asterion – formerly of Atlantis. A former professor who donated his mind to become myth embodied. Currently residing on Ronah.

Belfar – of Rakemyst. Mate of Wolf Dawn. Second in command of Elder SilverCloud's guards.

Ben – of Kenorvia. Elder.

Berrimon – of Talhan. One of the patrol leaders.

Calem Dawn – of Ronah. Father of Shari Dawn, husband of Arilla Dawn, son of SilverCloud, and brother of Wolf Dawn. Owner of the Quiver and Quill Tavern. *Highly suspicious of me. Don't know why...*

Cantash – One of the sentient Shifting Islands on Lissae. He is home to the Daens.

Captain Rappen – of Jinkor. Under Elder Chamele's command.

Chamele – of Jinkor. Elder.

Charin – of Rakemyst. One of the patrol members in Wolf's group. Spouse of Varlee.

Ciaran – of Talhan. A Blank with a scarred face.

Collis – of Ronah. Unofficial leader of the Returned. Sworn guardian of Ronah's Linked. Member of the Altoriae's Guild. *Should say – of trouble and mayhem. Never trust a talking crystal.*

Crystal Intelligence – of Lissae and Atlantis. Defeated by the 13th Altoriae and her guild.

Her bells are both a blessing and a curse.

Cylanthar – The Q'Aralide deity of destiny. She makes her presence known by the ringing of bells when events which have the potential to change her disciples' lives occur.

Should know better than to play with talking crystal. Do these mortals ever learn?

Cyrus Petram – of Talhan. Talhan's Linked.

Datzal – A Grey shapeshifting race conquered by the Q'Aralide and used as spies by the Queen.

Dealon – currently of Ronah. Formerly of the Wisara. Former candidate for the Guardian's Apprentice. New member of the Altoriae's Guild.

Edward Thorne – of Ronah. Husband of Harmony. Elder of Ronah. Grandfather of Anika Thorne.

Elani – currently of Ronah. Formerly of Ginorti. Member of the Altoriae's Guild.

Elder Shansky – of Ronah. Elder of Ronah.

Elder Silverstone – of Ronah. Elder of Ronah.

Esse – Tania's escape-artist chicken. *Snack with blue feathers*

Eva – of Talhan. Orphaned. Femto crystal tester.

Fenix – of Cantash. Cantash's Linked.

Fortesque – Travel Innarnian. Formerly of Lawrgaea. Currently residing on Talhan.

Gazn – Deceased Q'Aralide. *I deeply regret your passing, my friend*

Ginorti – One of the sentient Shifting Islands on Lissae. He is home to the Satyrs.

Grace – of Jinkor. Former slave of Chamele.

Gwyn – of Vendalbara. Elder.

Healer Edwards – of Ronah. Healer.
Their job would be easier if Jonathan and Shari would stop dying all the time.

Healer Holli Doonavan – of Ronah. Head Healer.

Healer Ribeck – of Ronah. Healer.

Helk – Master Warrior of the Q'Aralide. *Giant pain in my tail.*

Istaniern – Sanithane's replacement as Head Priest.

Where did you go?

Izarrk – Sanithane's Q'Aralide mentor. Now deceased.

Jaileth – Bronze Q'Aralide. Sanithane's mate.

Jetonyx – Whereabouts unknown. Kin to Samuel.

If you see my hatchling, send to me immediately! Your reward is not getting eaten next time I'm hungry

Jillon – of Talhan. Elder.

Jonathan Buan – of Ronah. The Guardian to the thirteenth Altoriae. Owner of Books 'n' More. *This fool is mad enough to want me around, and they leave him in charge of an entire Realm?*

Jordan Hollingsworth – of Ronah. Husband of Liza, father of Caleb, Christopher, Alistair, Tania, and Jessica. Deputy headmaster of Ridden Hall.

Joshua Izzaya Clemise – of the Spirit Realm. Formerly of Ronah. Former Guardian.

Kay'imi – The first Altoriae. She lived until she was 1217 years old when a lone Ahana archer killed her.

Ke'ra – God of the Element Plasma and husband of Adeon.

Kieran – One of the Returned, and a member of the Altoriae's Guild.

Lakin, Prime – Prime Lakin is second in line to the Throne of Startide and the people of Tocithas.

Larn – of Talhan. One of the patrol leaders.

Lerryn – Travel Innarnian.

Lira – currently of Ronah. Formerly of Tevon. Member of the Altoriae's Guild.

Lissa – Sarina's daughter.

Liza Hollingsworth – of Ronah. Daughter of General Morrow. Wife of Jordan, mother of Caleb, Christopher, Alistair, Tania, and Jessica. Headmaster of Ridden Hall.

Lizbeth Ribeck – of Ronah. *My friend Hurt her, and I will rip you into tiny pieces, bathe you in acid, and blend what's left into a drink. Go on, try it. I'm thirsty*

Mayor of Ronah – See **Alan Pratt**.

Mick – of Cantash.

Milo – of Cantash. Self-appointed secretary to Cantash's Linked.

Mu – currently of Ronah. Formerly of Nindonia. Member of the Altoriae's Guild.

Muran Curtis – formerly of Ronah. The sixth Altoriae. Died after being eaten by Anriluka and returning to Ronah. *In my defence, I was saving Jonathan. He's surprisingly unaware of his surroundings.*

Na'reh – Goddess of the Element Spirit and wife of Vebnah.

Neeth – of Talhan. One of the patrol leaders.

~~Oalark~~ – Queen of the Q'Aralide.

Pala – Leader of the Ducibus and sentinel of Lissae's gateway.

RainbowMist – Deceased wife of SilverCloud, mother of Calem and Wolf Dawn.

Rakemyst – One of the sentient Shifting Islands on Lissae. He is home to the Ilutri.

Rasshnae – Goddess of the Element Water and wife of Zoemer.

Raven – currently of Ronah. Formerly of Freeson. Former candidate for the Guardian's Apprentice. New member of the Altoriae's Guild. Excellent tracker.

Reah – of Talhan. Recently lost her sight.

Remmy – of Ronah. One of the Returned.

Ronah – One of the sentient Shifting Islands on Lissae. She is home to a variety of races and the traditional home of the Altoriae. Ronah's current Linked is Tania Hollingsworth. Ronah is one of the six gateways to the Realms.

Ruker – Deceased Q'Aralide.

Samuel Caragnton – currently of Ronah. Formerly of Altum. Golden Priest of the Q'Aralide. The Lissaen Guardian's Apprentice.

Sanithane – See **Samuel Caragnton**. *Last of my kind… is there anyone else left?*

Sarina – Mother of Lissa.

Shadow – of Ronah. The only creature to be one of the Returned. See **Zoomer**. *My first pet, and a reason to come home.*

Shari Dawn – of Ronah. The thirteenth Altoriae of Lissae and creator of the Altoriae's Guild. *Quite possibly the toughest being in all the Realms.*

SilverCloud – of Talhan. Father of Calem and Wolf Dawn. Grandfather to the thirteenth Altoriae. Head Elder of Rakemyst.

Skye – Aide to Elder Suni.

Sneeze – One of Cantash's draci.

Suni – of Lawrgaea. Elder.

Talhan – One of the sentient Shifting Islands on Lissae, and the only one to start with an all-human population. He now accepts immigrants from all races on Lissae.

Talofa – currently of Ronah. Formerly of Sulanta. Member of the Altoriae's Guild.

Tania Hollingsworth – of Ronah. Ronah's Linked. Daughter of Liza, stepdaughter of Jordan. Sister to Caleb, Christopher, Alistair, and Jessica. *I still can't figure out why all these mortals want me as their friend. I used to be the most feared being in all the Realms.*

Temira – of Talhan. Formerly of **Ulnan.** Also called the technomancer, Temira is Head Healer and head of the Techno Centre.

My apologies for the destruction of your Realm. My race is... horrid. And possibly no more, if that's any comfort.

Terrance Thorne – of Ronah. Saved by disembowelment by the Guardian.

Titch – of Cantash. Draci keeper who works in the Gardens.

Torden – of Ronah. One of the Returned, and a member of the Altoriae's Guild.

Tormorylth – of Altum. Tiny Q'Aralide.

Another hatchling under my protection. Find them both and I'll double the reward I won't eat your family either.

Vannali – One of the sentient Shifting Islands on Lissae. He is home to the Weavers.

Varlee – of Rakemyst. Third in command of Elder SilverCloud's guards. of. One of the patrol members in Wolf's group. Spouse of Charin.

Vebnah – Goddess of the Element Air and wife of Na'reh.

Vice – Deceased Q'Aralide.

Voxis – of Rakemyst. Silver-winged Ilutri youth. Nephew of Zana, Linked of Rakemyst.

May he rot in the bowels of the Altum beast for all eternity

War'Jan – Former leader of the Q'Aralide. Now deceased.

Wolf Dawn – of Rakemyst. Mate of Belfar. Brother of Calem Dawn, and uncle to the thirteenth Altoriae. Commander of SilverCloud's guards. Previously known as LoneWolf Dawn.

Xani – of Talhan. Also called the technomancer, Xani was Head Healer and head of the Techno Centre. Deceased. *Braver than most mortals*

Zac Husdon – currently of Talhan. Formerly of Ronah. Techno apprentice.

Zana – of Talhan. Talhan's Linked. Eldest of the Linked, and an accomplished diplomat.

Zirgha – Ambassador of Otike. *Now comes in corpse form.*

Zoemer – God of the Element Earth and husband of Rasshnae.

Zoomer – Shari's palon. The only creature to be one of the Returned. See **Shadow**.

MAP OF GANTASH

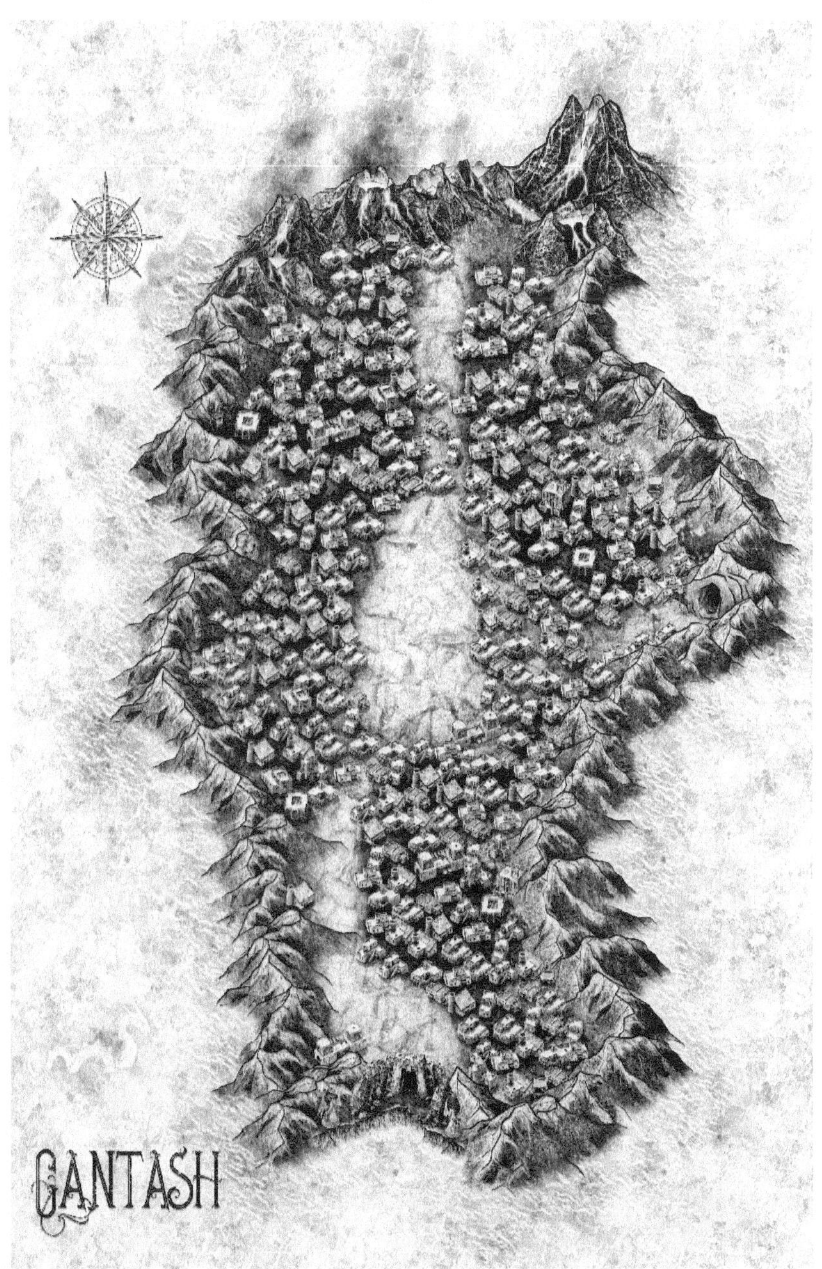

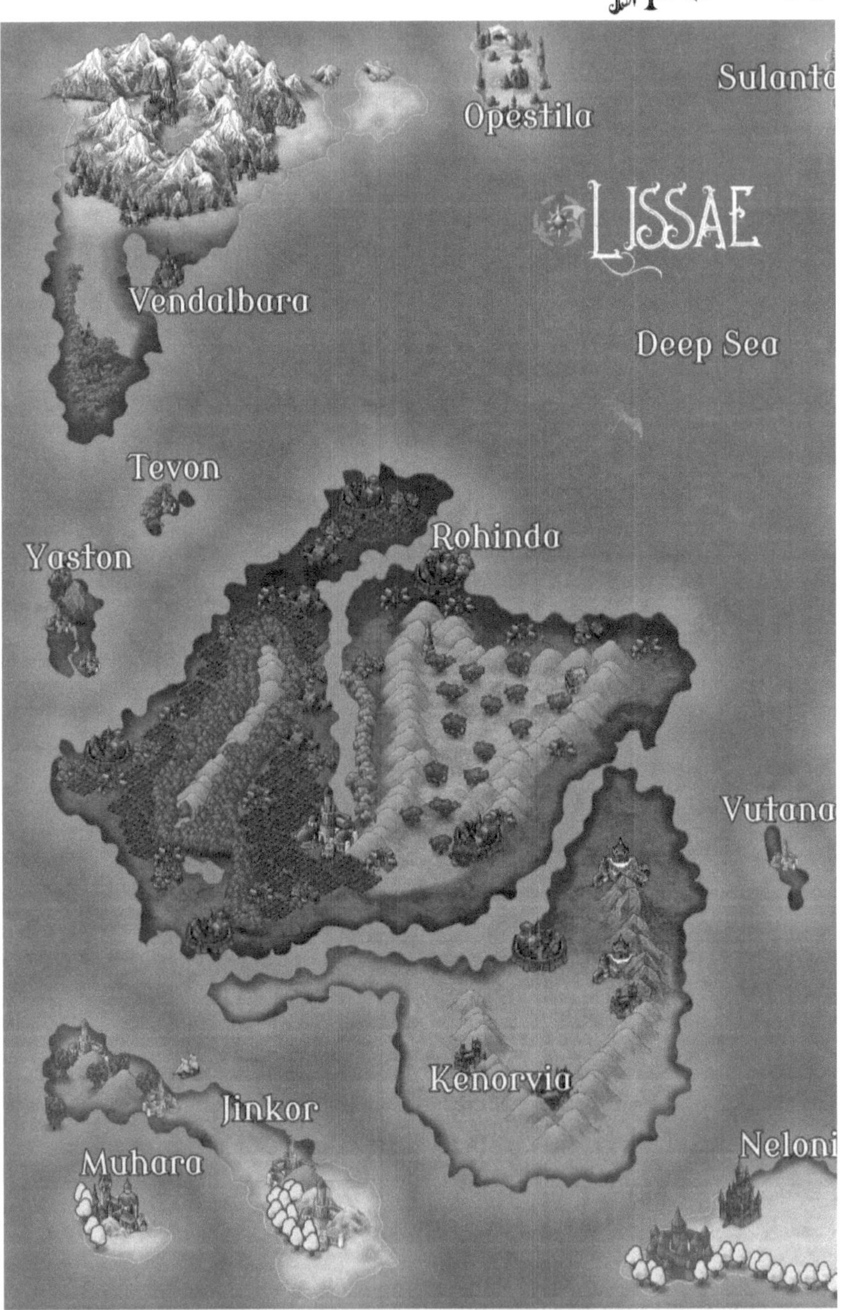
Sulanta
Opestila
LISSAE
Deep Sea
Vendalbara
Tevon
Rohinda
Yaston
Vutana
Kenorvia
Jinkor
Neloni
Muhara

LISSAE

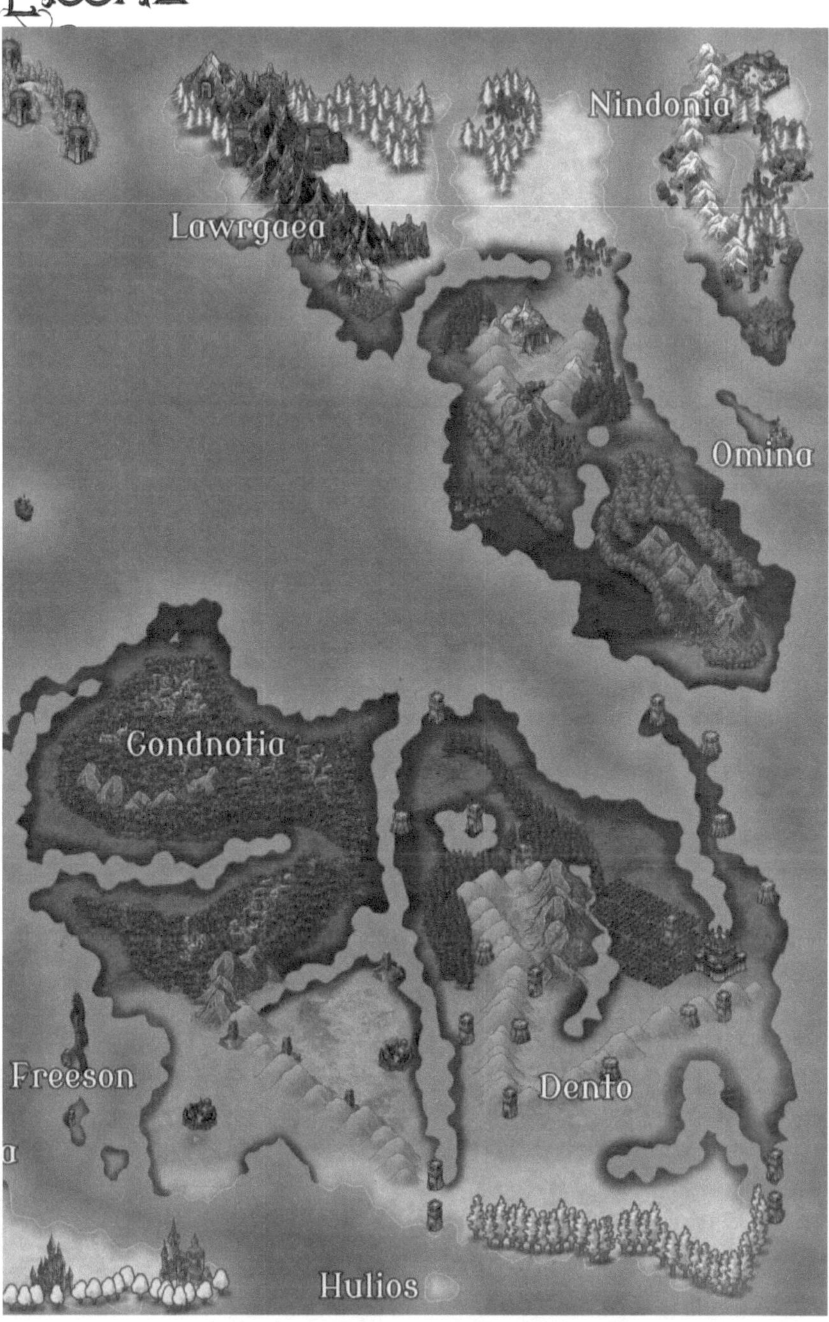

Map of Altum

ENJOY THIS BOOK?

You can make a big difference

Reviews are the most powerful tools in my arsenal when it comes to getting attention for my books. They help me gain visibility, and they can bring the Realm of Lissae to other readers who may appreciate the journey.

If you have enjoyed this book, I would be incredibly grateful if you could spend just a few minutes leaving a review (it can be as short as you like) at your favourite bookstore, or on the Goodreads page. You can jump right to the page by clicking below.

Find it in your preferred bookstore - books2read.com/cantash

Goodreads - goodreads.com/book/show/62601739-cantash

Thank you very much.

ACKNOWLEDGEMENTS

A book is never a solo effort. So many talented people have come together to make this fantastical world alive on the pages. I owe you all my eternal gratitude.

Jodie, Cyrus, Ruth, Kathy—my beta readers extraordinaire! Thank you for prodding at things to make Cantash a better book. Sorry about the cliff-hangers.

My beautiful editing team—thank you Anna from CREATING ink for fine-tuning the manuscript and Lauren for putting up with endless questions. Desanka, your lessons from Rakemyst stayed with me.

I can't thank Vanesa enough for the stunning covers she continues to create—the Q'Aralide is perfect! Lissae wouldn't look the same without you.

Special thanks to Cyrus, Lisa, Kathy, Michelle, and Ruth for some of the new character names.

Of course, I can't forget my family and friends—thank you for your endless support, probing questions, and giving me time to write.

Husband of mine, the original technomancer. You are the best sounding board I could ask for. I love you. Here's to another 20 years (with fewer electrocutions, I hope).

Cyrus, the DnD campaign you ran in the caldera helped to shape Cantash. Thanks to you and the gang for the inspiration!

Corin, as always, thank you for the concept of the technomancer. You continue to enrich my world just by being you. Never stop.

Savannah, your eternal enthusiasm keeps me going. Watching you devour the books means worlds to me.

Ruth (aka Mum), your nit-picking is what this book needed. Thank you for being so thorough.

Danielle, your encouragement has shaped the worlds both in the book and the one outside it.

To the amazing team at Sunshine Coast Libraries who always seem so excited to hear about what I've been up to in the writing world–endless gratitude for all your encouragement, particularly Tom, Christine, Rohin, Karen, Patricia, Amanda, and Jo.

To the developers who created and maintain 4theWords. Your amazing website helped to get this book, and so many others, finished.

I cannot forget you, the reader! Thank you for exploring the Realms within these pages. I bid thee well.

ABOUT THE AUTHOR

R. Lennard is the Australian author of the young adult fantasy series *Lissae*. She is an avid fantasy and sci-fi reader, and in her spare time, she works as a librarian. She enjoys learning about ancient civilisations, cosplaying, and drinking endless cups of tea.

Residing on the beautiful Sunshine Coast in Queensland, Australia, Rebecca enjoys the natural beauty of both the beach and the bush. She lives with her family and is ruled over by her cat.

Rebecca is a fan of many things, and has spent far too many hours playing *The Sims* in all its varying iterations.

To find out more about Rebecca, head to rlennard.com

After More to Read?

The *Eni Inside* is a short story prelude to the Lissae series included in the 3rd Australian Pen anthology, *The Evil Inside Us*.

The headmaster of Ridden Hall, Lawrence Anderson, went out on patrol, but never returned. Instead, a being bent on taking over Lissae came back in his place.

Full of stories about dark secrets, you'll want to join the masses and buy your copy of *The Evil Inside Us* now!

Available at: lissae.com/short-stories

When a sentient Realm asks you to be her protector, how can you say no?

Shari Dawn appears to be just another teen, until a band of wandering Wisara visit her home—Ronah—a sentient, Shifting Island of Lissae.

Now her secret identity has been uncovered, Shari must learn how to control her powers, preparing to be tested in a prophecy passed down from the ancients, which will determine her role in the future of the Realm.

But sinister forces infect the dreams of Ronah's people. With a team she didn't want by her side, Shari must decide who lives and who dies.

The fate of the Realm is in her hands...

Buy *Ronah* and step into Lissae today!

Available at: lissae.com/ronah

How do you live after being eaten by a monster?

After he died, Collis found himself in a nightmarish Realm full of creatures who wanted to eat him. Waking up after the fiftieth time he'd died wasn't any easier than the first.

Stuck in a pocket Realm, Collis and the residents from Ronah must defend themselves against the deadliest creatures from across the Realms. But survival comes at a cost.

And if they die? They reform. Over and over. Just how are they going to escape?

Find out in *Returned*.

Available at: lissae.com/short-stories

His choice could change the very fabric of the Realms...

The most feared being to walk the Dark Realms was once a mere hatchling. Scrawny, weak, and half-mortal, Sanithane strives to gain enough power to ensure his tormentors never bother him again.

But when his Queen sets an impossible task, Sanithane has to choose—his kin, or his life?

Find out the story behind the Golden Priest in *Shadows*.

Available at: lissae.com/short-stories

Something is watching them from the shadows...

After a devastating betrayal, Shari longs for life to return to the way things were.

But she has little time to dwell on normality. A disturbing new foe rises, and former enemies become allies in the fight to save Lissae.

Juggling school by day and patrolling by night, it will only take one slip up to bring everything crashing down. Shari must battle her way to the heart of her problems... or die trying.

Buy *Talhan* and discover the heart of Lissae today!

Available at: lissae.com/talhan

Keep up to date with the Lissae series and receive exclusive extras by signing up for the newsletter at:

lissae.com/welcome

www.ingramcontent.com/pod-product-compliance
Lightning Source LLC
Chambersburg PA
CBHW051312190726
48290CB00001B/112